CADET GRAY

BOOKS BY THE AUTHOR

Seasons of Harvest
The Awakening Land
Shadows on the Land
(A three-volume trilogy of the Corrales Valley)

Unlike Any Land You Know
The 490th Bomb Squadron in China-Burma-India

Coon Creek
A Novel of the Mississippi River Bottoms

Lonesome Whistle Blow
A Novel of Hard Times

Journey
A Novel of America

Cadet Gray
Stories of Morgan Park Military Academy

CADET GRAY

Stories of Morgan Park Military Academy

A Collection of Short Stories

James M. Vesely

iUniverse, Inc.

New York Lincoln Shanghai

CADET GRAY

Stories of Morgan Park Military Academy

Copyright © 2006 by James M. Vesely

iUniverse books may be ordered through booksellers or by contacting:

iUniverse
2021 Pine Lake Road, Suite 100
Lincoln, NE 68512
www.iuniverse.com
1-800-Authors (1-800-288-4677)

This is a work of fiction. All of the characters, names, incidents, organizations and dialogue in this novel are either the products of the author's imagination or are used fictitiously.

ISBN-13: 978-0-595-41680-6 (pbk)
ISBN-13: 978-0-595-86023-4 (ebk)
ISBN-10: 0-595-41680-2 (pbk)
ISBN-10: 0-595-86023-0 (ebk)

Printed in the United States of America

CADET GRAY
is dedicated to the Corps and Faculty
of Morgan Park Military Academy,
where the youthful bond of friendships
made remain intact—after more than
half a century.

Acknowledgements

I am indebted to Barry Kritzberg, Instructor of English & History, Archives & MPA Historian, for making the MPMA Archives available to a creaky old alum.

My thanks to Sara White Grassi ('71), Director of Alumni Affairs, for all her help and hospitality.

I'm also grateful to the following alumni for sharing their memories. Their contributions were a great help in writing this book: Jim McClure ('35) Spence Johnson ('37), Phillip C. Freund ('42), C.W. "Bill" Getz ('42), Henry E. Doney ('44), Don Soldan ('49), Paul W. Berezny, Jr. ('52), Phil Rosi ('55), Henry Lang ('55), John Frank ('56), Ed Jerabek ('56), Art Canfield ('56), Jack Dietz ('56), Jim Paloucek ('56), Bob Kiefer ('56), Rich Vitkus ('57), Andy Selva ('57), John Inman ('57), Brian Donnelly ('57), and Frank Fonsino ('58).

My gratitude finally, to Mr. Lee Pederson, Ph.D., Charles Howard Candler Professor of English at Emory University, who taught English Literature and coached football at MPMA so many years ago—for introducing us to the great adventure of books and letters.

Preface

CADET GRAY is first and foremost a novel.

In attempting to dramatize forty years at Morgan Park Military Academy, I have tried to present the stories with individuals and events that either did exist, or reasonably might have. Much of the book is fiction and some is fact. Occasionally, it was necessary to invent fictional characters, historical detail, or whole occurrences, to further the narrative. All instructors are either actual people, or in some cases, their names and characters have been altered.

Borrowing liberally from the Academy's website, the present Morgan Park Academy was originally called Mt. Vernon Military and Classical Academy, and founded on a high ridge above "Horse Thief Hollow" during the second term of Ulysses S. Grant.

The school was started just in time for the "Panic of 1873." It survived that economic upheaval, as well as a number of others in its history, yet it has endured and grown as an independent school for well over a century.

It became Morgan Park Academy in 1874, with the Civil War still a recent, painful wound in the nation's memory and while U.S. military operations were concerned primarily with the Indian Wars in the West.

Tuition in the 1870s was $400 per year and included twelve pieces of "Board Washing" each week, along with "Mending of Under Garments." Modeled after those of West Point, traditional cadet gray uniforms added another $64.50 to the bill.

When William Rainey Harper became the founding president of the University of Chicago in 1892, MPA became the coed (quite unusual for that time, although the experiment did not survive the decade) preparatory school for the university. Harper's teachers at the Academy held university rank and one of them, Amos Alonzo Stagg, coached football at both institutions.

Two of MPA's alumni—Jesse Harper ('02) at Notre Dame, and Wallace Wade ('13) at Alabama and Duke—became coaches who were later elected to the College Football Hall of Fame.

In 1893, MPA participated in the first high school basketball game played in Illinois, just a single season after James Naismith invented the game in far-off Massachusetts.

After William Rainey Harper's death in 1907, the University of Chicago discontinued its relationship with the Academy, and the school once again became a boy's military boarding school.

Part of Harper's legacy, which continues to the present day, is a tradition of high standards, exemplary teaching, and a remarkable loyalty to the school on the part of its faculty, administration, staff, students, and alumni. Consider the long tenures of MPMA's and MPA's leaders: Harry D. Abells (1898–1945), Haydn Jones (1899–1946), Francis S. Gray (1917–1960), and David A. Jones (1957–1998).

Perhaps the most dynamic decade in the school's long history was from 1958–1967 following the decision to demilitarize. Young women were admitted in 1959 for the first time in the 20th century, *Military* disappeared from the school's name, boarding was phased out, and the Academy became integrated.

Morgan Park Academy not only survived these many changes, any one of which might have driven lesser schools to close their doors, but it endured and prospered.

Under different names and different academic configurations, Morgan Park Academy has stood fast with a long, solid tradition of educational excellence.

In closing, I have chosen to portray the Academy as it was from the 1920s through the 1950s. From that point forward, there is surely another book still to be written, but I'll leave that effort to someone in a later generation of alumni.

James M. Vesely
Corrales, New Mexico
September 2006

Prologue

Captain Francis S.Gray, L.L.B.

As he finished buttoning his worn and wrinkled khaki shirt, the old man adjusted his round, wire spectacles, gently drew aside the lace curtain and peered past the row of increasingly bare oaks and elms toward 111th Street. Rows of automobiles had been stopping at the curb all morning, discharging anxious parents and nervous sons. Just a short walk from the elderly gentleman's modest frame home, Morgan Park Military Academy's newest freshmen class was gathering on the concrete steps of Alumni Hall.

The September day was crisp and clear, with the hint of a cold Chicago winter coming—registration day at the Academy—with the yellowing leaves beginning to fall, and a brisk easterly breeze to pick them up and send them bouncing and skittering across Post Walk and over the school's long, rectangular parade ground.

"Look at them," the old man muttered, shaking his head as his wife snugged the knot in his tie. "They're frightened little boys out there, stepping all over their own feet."

"How many of those frightened little boys have you helped get through this school?" She asked, taking a step back to examine his tie. "Right now, every one of them is filled with doubt and self-consciousness—that's inside every boy trying to grow up. Don't be so critical, Frank. Remember, you were young once, too—about a hundred years ago."

Noticing the laugh lines around her eyes, the old man grunted. He'd long ago lost count of how long they'd been married or for how many years he'd been in love with his wife. Anna Gray was as much a part of his life as drawing breath.

As was usually the case, the old man thought, Anna was right. Four years from now, with the patience and blessing of whatever gods were smiling down, most of those peach-fuzzed knuckleheads lining up to register would emerge as proud young men standing at the starting point of their lives. He wondered for a brief moment if he'd still be in the game to see them receive their diplomas.

Well, no matter. I've had a good run, he told himself, thinking of cadets he'd taught who by all rights should have outlived him by many years—but hadn't.

In 1918, just a year after he'd started teaching at the Academy, six boys were taken out of school. A week later, four of them were dead—victims of the strange, deadly influenza epidemic that was sweeping the country.

George Kanin, who ranked second in the Class of 1930, joined the Abraham Lincoln Brigade, sailed for Spain on Christmas Day of 1936 and was killed fighting Franco's Nationalists a year later at Jarama. Somewhere in the archives, the old man knew, The school still had the letter it received from George three months before his death...*there are things that one must do in this life that are a little more than just living. In Spain there are thousands of people who never got a fair shake...don't let anyone mislead you by telling you that all this had something to do with Communism. The Hitlers and Mussolinis of this world are killing Spanish people who don't know the difference between Communism and rheumatism, so if anybody asks, that's why I went to Spain, to help these poor people win this battle...*

George Kanin was a fine young man, Frank Gray thought, but wars have robbed us of so many of our fine young men.

Lou Hembrough, Cadet Captain, Class of 1935—who'd taken a platoon of infantry ashore at Omaha Beach and within minutes, was dead on the beachhead, his blood mixed with Normandy soil.

Severyn Hildner, Senior Class President, Class of 1936. Lost when his B-25 Mitchell medium bomber went down on a mission out of Warazup, Burma in 1945. The wreckage of the aircraft and the bodies of the crew weren't found until eight years after the war was ended. Severyn's remains still wore his senior ring.

Yes, the school had given up its own—leaving them to rest on the volcanic sands of Tarawa and Iwo Jima, and beneath the torn and shredded coconut palms of Saipan. In the bloodstained snow of Longvilly on the road to Bastogne, and in the cold, black depths of the rolling North Atlantic.

Like Severyn Hildner, others had fallen from the skies as well—fallen over Cologne and the Ploesti oilfields, over Hamburg and Friedrichshafen.

The old man sighed and shook his head. Some of his boys had survived that long war only to be pulled back five years later when North Korean troops swarmed over the 38th Parallel in June of 1950. Then, the Academy would once again leave more of its sons in strange places—Pusan, Inchon, and the Chosin Reservoir.

Closing his eyes, he could see their faces still. They were faces no different than those registering today.

This new bunch will be the Class of '57, he reflected, thinking back to when he was their age. In those distant days, a soft drink called Coca Cola was something brand new, and the newspapers were carrying stories of the Apache chief Geronimo finally being captured in the Arizona Territory.

Feeling every arthritic ache of his eighty-three years, the old man crossed the small bedroom and checked his appearance in the dresser mirror.

We're both of us bent and old now, Anna Gray thought as she watched him, but there's still a twinkle in his eyes.

"I've no use for faculty meetings," her husband grumbled. "A goddamned waste of time as far as I can tell."

"Wear your overcoat, Frank," Anna urged. "It's chilly out."

Captain Francis S. Gray—Instructor of Mathematics, and a legend on the Academy campus. Slow of step now, and spare with praise, the old man prized effort and academic excellence above all else, offering limited attention and even less comfort to any cadet satisfied with doing less than his best.

Inside the Academy's old Blake Hall, where radiators hissed, the stairs creaked, and the Gothic red brick façade was as timeless as the Pantheon in Rome, Frank Gray pursued the exact disciplines of mathematics as if it were the only academic field of endeavor worth learning. The years had been long and the changes many—years that had left him stoop-shouldered, white-haired, and already annoyed by the prospect of three hours of polite conversation and tedious discussions involving lesson plans and revisions to the new semester's curriculum.

The deep lines and creases in the old man's face resembled the rough bark of some immovable, ancient tree, but as he'd dutifully done each autumn for nearly forty years, Captain Gray made his way through the uneasy freshmen and the overly anxious parents who'd brought their sons to military school and were now hesitant to leave—suddenly unsure of their decision and reluctant to let the youngsters fully abandon the nest.

Freshmen day students, those who lived within easy traveling distance of the school were able to register and then go back home to their familiar lives. But the freshmen boarding students, those whose homes were too far away, or out of town, would be assigned a sparsely furnished room in Hansen Hall.

Passing, the old man heard snatches of hushed conversation.

"Oh, man," a new boy complained, staring at the ivy-covered dormitory. "That's where we gotta live? That place looks like it's a hundred years old."

"It'll be fine," his mother told him. "You'll get a roommate."

"You going to be all right?" A man asked another boy under his breath. "Your mother's a little worried."

"I'll be okay, Dad—why don't you and mom go home now?"

"You need any money?" Another father asked his son. The man was stout and red-faced. He wore a light gray homburg and smoked a thick Cuban cigar.

"No Pa, I don't think so."

"Hell, take a twenty anyhow," the man said, pressing a folded bill into the boy's hand. "Just in case."

Cadet 1st Lt. Iver Sinclair, his summer vacation cut short by a Saturday on which he was Officer of the Day, saluted smartly as he left Alumni Hall and came upon Captain Gray approaching. Cadet Sinclair had been one of the cadet officers given the responsibility of making sure this new class of freshmen, along with any of their apprehensive parents, managed to get through the registration process with a minimum of worry and confusion.

The old man returned Cadet Sinclair's salute with a slight nod and a salute of his own—a slack return, timeworn and sloppy—just a brief touch of fingers to the cracked visor of his battered army service cap, a salute with no snap to it at all.

Mr. Sinclair, Captain Gray reflected critically, a senior now, an officer and a fine footballer—but the boy struggles with math, and this year he's got college algebra to get through.

I've got him again this term, Sinclair told himself, convinced the old man thought him a dunce. If the old bastard flunks me, I won't graduate.

"Prepared for my class, Sinclair?" Captain Gray grunted.

"Yes sir," Iver said, certain the old man knew he was lying. "I studied a little over the summer."

"Good, good. Your older brother was a first-rate math student. I hope you'll follow in his steps—do better than last term."

"Yes sir, I hope so, too."

"Where will you attend college?" Gray asked.

"The University of Illinois, sir. Where my brother's at—he's a junior now."

"Good. Be on time to class next week. Try to learn—an A or a B in my class will bring your average up."

"Yes sir," Cadet Sinclair said, saluting again.

Among those students attending his classes, Captain Gray had his favorites, although he would never let those feelings show. The old man knew and accepted the fact that many of the Academy students were privileged boys—boys whose parents had the means to afford the school's yearly tuition. But he also knew that other cadets came from less fortunate means, boys whose parents had to do without to send them there. For a few others, rumors had it that it was a choice of military school or a reformatory.

Most of these troubled boys dropped out quickly, unwilling to endure the military discipline, and often intellectually unequipped to compete in a preparatory school environment.

But although Captain Gray treated everyone fairly, his wife knew that it had always been that middle group of students—those with limited wealth and abilities who worked hard and succeeded, that her husband quietly, secretly favored.

The captain was well aware of the system—a system ingrained in Academy tradition even before he'd begun his own teaching career there. Opportunity was given to each and every boy and the result was hardly different than life's own struggle—some boys succeeded, and others failed in varying degrees. But the cream rose to the top, and those cadets with the ability and determination were rewarded.

As was the case in most high schools, athletes were the most popular boys on campus, and those exceptional cadets who kept their grades high and *also* excelled in sports—were usually assured of cadet commissions and class leadership positions in their senior year.

But what satisfied Frank Gray's sense of proper academic direction was the fact that good grades *always* trumped athletics in a cadet's four-year pursuit of class honors and an officer's rank. The bright, hardworking boys would make it, the old man knew, while those who excelled *only* in throwing a football or pinning an opponent to the mat would fall behind—no matter how athletically gifted and popular they might be.

This autumn, like every other in the school's long history, the Academy's start-up procedure was routine. The varsity and frosh-soph football teams and coaches had been coming to the gym each day for the past three weeks, working their way through pre-season tryouts, learning new plays and building up endurance after a summer of leisure.

In the afternoon on this Registration Saturday, the sophomore, junior, and senior cadets would begin arriving on campus to be assigned their rooms in Hansen Hall barracks, the dorm for upper-school boarding students.

Cadet 1st Lieutenant Sinclair, himself a boarding student, cast an upperclassmen's eye on the new group of freshmen. Aside from the trials of Cap Gray's trigonometry class, Iver Sinclair's senior year would be predictable and relatively easy—the exact opposite of what these freshmen could expect.

They were about to enter high school and leave their boyhoods behind, Iver thought.

Secondly, many of them would be away from home for the first time in their lives.

And finally, for the next ten months they'd be *plebes.*

Curious about the origin of the word, Iver had once looked it up in the school library, learning that in Ancient Rome the *plebs* represented the general body of Roman citizens, distinct from the privileged class, or *patricians.* An individual member of the *plebs* was known as a *plebeian.* Later, plebeian came to mean the poorer members of society in general. During the Roman Empire. the term was often used of anyone not in the senatorial or equestrian orders, and the word lived on in *plebe,* the term for a freshman at West Point, Annapolis, and The Citadel—as well as at Morgan Park.

Sinclair remembered his own plebe year four years earlier. His older brother had dropped hints about it, but even those hadn't prepared him for what was to come.

At Morgan Park, his class was told, military life was the norm of conduct. Every cadet was governed by well-defined regulations. Whatever was not specifically covered by official regulations was encompassed by the customs and traditions of the Academy.

Over the years, these had grown out of the experiences of past classes of cadets. The plebe traditions that had become fixed Corps customs were enforced by the upperclassmen, who made sure that freshmen observed them carefully during their first year in school.

Plebe traditions, they were told, were meant to imbed in them rigid disciplines that could never be learned from reading books or memorizing definitions. Iver and the other first-year men, fresh from the ease and comfort of civilian life, had to be hardened to the rigors and hardships of regimented life at the Academy.

"During your first semester, you will be required to learn all the customs, traditions and regulations of Morgan Park Military Academy," they were told by a cadet officer.

"You will memorize the United States Army General Orders, and be tested on them.

"By mid-term, you will know all upperclassmen by name and rank, as well as the names of all members of your company.

"You will familiarize yourselves with all military customs and courtesies, as well as the United States Army General Orders and be able to recite them when ordered to do so," the lecture went on.

"You will know all songs and cheers of the Academy by the first scheduled football game."

Cadet 1st Lieutenant Sinclair remembered listening silently as the next ten months of his life, and the lives of his classmates, were harshly revealed.

They would be required to ask upperclassmen anything they could not inform themselves about. Unless on sick call, they would not be allowed to sleep anytime between reveille and taps.

Unless accompanying parents or guests, they were required to use only the north or south entrances of Hansen Hall barracks.

They were to be in uniform whenever they left their rooms for any purpose between reveille and taps.

"You will be required to attend all Academy social functions, including athletic events and dances.

"You will come to attention when any upperclassman enters your room, and you will address all upperclassmen, no matter what their rank, as *sir*.

"At all battalion formations, you will be present at the place of assembly before first call.

"At every mess in Alumni Hall, you may not use the backs of the chairs. You may use only the forward portion of your seat."

The joys of being a plebe went on an on, Sinclair recalled, but never mentioned and traditionally ignored by the school's staff and faculty, was the fact that ten months of being a plebe equaled ten months of virtual servitude.

Almost every evening of his freshman year, Iver stayed awake long after taps had been sounded, until both his shoes *and* those of Cadet Capt. Herb Yeager had been polished to a glossy black—spit shined to a mirror finish.

And a few days before every Sunday parade, Yeager would call Iver to his room, handing him his black leather garrison belt and brass buckle, his full dress blouse with its three rows of brass buttons, and his brass crossbelt buckle—expecting all of it to be cleaned and brightly polished before Saturday evening.

At the beginning of every year, a senior cadet would pick two or three plebes to do his personal work and bidding. This would include shining shoes and polishing brass, cleaning rooms, making beds, and running errands. If the freshman was fortunate, he was chosen by a senior grounded in good judgment and possessing a sense of fairness and decency.

But some plebes weren't so lucky. They were hazed, screamed at, and often struck by seniors overly impressed by their own lofty status as upperclassmen and prone to show it through brutality. Looking back, Iver Sinclair realized that most of those seniors who indulged in harsh treatment had often been victims themselves—during their own unhappy plebe year.

Looking at the new boys, Iver could only wish them well.

"**H**ow was your summer, Frank?" Asked Maj. George Mahon. The major was an instructor in physics and the school's principal. His own son, George Jr., was a graduating senior and cadet captain this year. The two men shook hands.

"And how is Anna?" Mahon enquired.

"Passable," the old man grunted. "Feeling her age, just as I am."

"How long is it now, Frank? Thirty-four—thirty-five years?"

"This semester will be my thirty-seventh year."

"Remarkable," Mahon said. "A splendid achievement."

Gathered in the large room of upper Alumni Hall were both old and new faces. Coffee and tea was being served along with a tray of bakery. Captain Gray shook hands with Maj. Bert Grove, who was Dean of Cadets and taught biology. Also there to greet him were Maj. John Chesebro, Professor of Military Science and Tactics, Capt. Leland Dickenson, Assistant to the Commandant, and Maj. Arthur Gumbrell, who was Commandant of Cadets, and whose army service had left the major with a long, crescent-shaped scar across his left temple and what was rumored by the cadets to be a metal plate in his head.

A few of the Academy's staff and instructors were retired military officers who'd served on active duty, while most of the others had been commissioned by the Illinois National Guard only as long as they taught at the school.

Captain Gray enjoyed a donut and a cup of black coffee as he watched three or four new instructors getting acquainted. Most of them appeared uncomfortable and somewhat ill at ease in their unfamiliar army uniforms. It was this way every year, the old man thought. A solid core of teachers, those who felt comfortable at the school, renewed their contracts and stuck with the Academy, while each year a few new ones were recruited to replace those who'd tried MPMA on for size and then decided to leave.

Frank Gray glanced out the window and noticed the growing numbers of upperclassmen now beginning to arrive on campus—shouting greetings, laughing and shaking hands as they mingled on the long walkway between Alumni and Hansen Hall.

School was starting again. My thirty-seventh year here, the old man thought. Can that really be possible? He studied the faces of the upperclassmen below— boyish faces four years ago, and now the faces of young men.

In his time he'd seen so many pass through this place. He thought of students, of parades, and of memorable football games—his memories touched triumphs and failures, good times and bad, the pleasures of teaching, and during war- time—the sadness and wrenching pain of loss.

Captain Francis S. Gray slowly sipped his coffee, watching the gathering Corps of Cadets and the beginning of another semester unfold, and like the faded and yellowing leaves of the crisp Illinois autumn; the years began to fall away.

1920–1929

CHAPTER 1

▼

THE COUNTRY BOY

Fall Term, 1920

Looking around him, Henry Seybold stepped off the Rock Island coach at the 111th Street Morgan Park Station, walking a few steps through a cloud of warm steam. It was the farthest Henry had ever been from home—his parents' farm on the outskirts of Ottumwa, Iowa. Setting down his father's valise, he watched the locomotive make steam and continue its run south.

Even though his apparel was a few years out of fashion, Henry looked as if he were dressed for church. He wore a straw boater, a high starched collar and striped shirt. His three-year old suit was from the Sears Roebuck catalog—a gray, three-button worsted that fit him just a little too snug, and a pair of brown brogans, scuffed from years of wear.

Henry stood for a moment, looking around him—admiring the station's handsome arched windows. Across the street to the west, he could see the Morgan Park United Methodist Church.

As the train left the station, he noticed a scruffy young fellow standing on the planked platform hawking copies of the *Chicago Tribune.* The boy smoked a cigarette and stood next to a low stack of newspapers, waving a copy high above his head. Even through the clouds of steam, Henry could easily read the tall, bold type of the paper's front-page headline: *"Shoeless" Joe Jackson to Testify Before Cook County Grand Jury!*

The Black Sox Scandal, Henry thought, staring at the paper. It was big news even back in Ottumwa. The 1919 World Series a year before had given the country the most famous scandal in baseball history. Henry's father had told him all about it.

Eight players from the Chicago White Sox had been accused of throwing the series against the Cincinnati Reds. It was front-page news across the country.

With the War in Europe over, and the threat of the influenza epidemic hopefully behind them, most folks in America had once again become mad about professional baseball, but the Black Sox Scandal threatened to damage people's interest in the game.

His thoughts were interrupted by the honk of a horn. Glancing to his left, Henry spotted a Ford Model T jitney that had *Morgan Park Military Academy* painted on its side. Behind the wheel sat a young fellow wearing what looked like a gray military uniform.

"Are you the farm kid?" The driver called out.

"I guess so," Henry answered. "My old man's got a farm."

"Well, if you're here to register, they sent me to pick you up."

Henry climbed into the front seat and sat with his suitcase in his lap. He stuck out a big hand and the other fellow took it.

"Henry Seybold—from Ottumwa. That's in Iowa."

"Wally Valentine," the driver said. "I'm a senior this year."

"It's fine to meet you, Wally."

"Listen, once you're registered," Valentine said. "You better forget the Wally business—you'll have to call me *sir.*"

"That a fact?" Henry asked, slightly amused. "Why, you don't look much older'n me."

"That might be, Bub," Valentine said, grinding the jitney into a lower gear as it labored up the long hill from the railroad station. "But I'm an upperclassman and you're a plebe. This is a military school and that's how things are done."

As they drove, Henry had been marveling at the great number of large, two-story brick homes on each side of the street. "What's a plebe?" He asked, trying the word out. "I don't think I ever heard that word before."

"Plebes are first-year men—the lowest form of life there is."

"Shoot," Henry mumbled. "That don't sound good."

"That *don't* sound good?" Wally Valentine repeated, shaking his head. "Damn, Captain Bouma will have his hands full with a hayseed like you."

"Who's Captain Bouma?"

"He teaches Freshman English," Valentine answered.

"It's somewhat unusual when the Academy gets a boy from so far away," Col. Harry D. Abells stated, as Henry stood in front of the superintendent's massive oak desk. In all respects, Abells was an impressive looking individual, very distinguished in his tailored army uniform. Henry suspected that the silver-haired colonel was the finest-looking, most dashing gentleman he'd ever seen.

"How was your trip, son?" The colonel asked.

"Well, I never been on a train before, sir," Henry said. "But it seemed long to me. Took the Chicago, Rock Island and Pacific to a big place the conductor told me was the LaSalle Street Station and then come south on another train out of there—and here I am."

There was a knock at the door.

"Come in, Mr. Clopp," Colonel Abells called. Willard Clopp was the school's Business Manager. Mr. Clopp nodded at Henry as he briskly walked past, then whispered something to the colonel and handed him a piece of paper.

"It seems that we've received a wire from your father, young man," Colonel Abells said. "Advising us that you are carrying your entire semester's tuition as well as an additional amount of cash for personal expenses on your person. Is that the case?"

"Yessir," Henry said. "I got it tucked away in my valise."

"I see," the colonel said, shaking his head. "Highly unusual, I must say. I would think your father could have just as easily wired us the funds through his bank."

"Oh no, sir. Pa don't trust banks very much—don't want them holding on to none of his money—my Uncle Clete says Pa's damn near as tight as a pig's ass at fly time."

Willard Clopp stood with his mouth agape as Colonel Abells cleared his throat. "Yes well, a colorful expression, young fellow. Mr. Clopp will see to it that your financial obligations to the school are expedited, and once you've finished matriculation, the officer of the day will assign you to your room." The colonel offered his hand. "We're happy to have you with us, Cadet Seybold."

Henry had never seen anything like it. He wasn't really in the army, but he might just as well have been. In a letter to his folks a few weeks after he'd been at the Academy, he told them that he was what the school called a *cadet*. He wrote how they blew bugle calls all day long, about the scratchy wool uniform he wore every day, how he and the other boys stood in formation morning, noon and night, and how he'd had to memorize all sorts of rules, and march up and down Post Walk toting a Springfield rifle.

Henry still wasn't certain why his parents had sent him off to Morgan Park Military Academy in far-off Chicago, but suspected it was his mother's doing.

Cora Mae Seybold placed great store in education. She herself had attended the Albia Normal School, west of Ottumwa, and was active in the Ottumwa Chautauqua Society. She'd taught for a few years and then met Everett Seybold, who'd just inherited seventy acres of prime Iowa farmland from his dead father—a man who went too hard for his age and collapsed in his own soybean field two days before his eighty-third birthday.

Henry's parents courted for a year before marrying, and once their vows were made, Cora sacrificed her love of teaching to settle in as a farmer's wife—far from town and removed from the world of chalkboards and books.

But she read the *Des Moines Register* faithfully and knew how young people were beginning to act these days—the end of the war had brought an end to the earlier ragtime music rage, which Cora was happy to see. But now, the country's young people had their heads full of what was being called Negro jazz.

These things always started in the big cities, Cora knew, but it was only a matter of time before they began to seep into smaller and quieter communities like Ottumwa where the young ones were vulnerable. First came the outrageous music and dancing, then the smart-alecky slang, and finally the hip flasks of whiskey, drinking, and petting.

Others might commit wrongdoings, Cora decided, but she was determined not to let her Henry be exposed to such things in what she called his formative years.

"A military school?" Everett Seybold had said when his wife first brought up the matter. "Cora Mae, brother Cletus was a sojer. Clete was over there in the Philippines with Black Jack Pershing in nineteen ought two, fightin' them durned fuzzy-wuzzy Hindus or whatever they was called—he didn't care much for it, neither."

"Everett, those people were Muslims, not Hindus," Cora told her husband, waving a small advertisement she'd clipped out of the back pages of *Good House-keeping.* "And I want you to take a look at this—Morgan Park Military Academy—it's on the outskirts of Chicago. According to the advertisement, the school stresses habits of orderliness, cleanliness, and promptitude—a preparatory school for boys."

Ev Seybold grunted. "Preparatory school? Godamighty, will it prepare the boy to run this farm after I'm dead and buried?"

"It will prepare him for college," Cora pointed out. "And keep him out of trouble."

Her husband shook his head. "I'd say that's faulty thinking. Henry don't need college to run the farm, and the boy won't get in no trouble if he stays right here on this land—growin' Iowa corn for his living."

As usual, his mother got her way, Henry thought as he stood in morning school formation—what everybody called AMSF. And now he was all trussed up in a uniform and high, black boots, just to go to this fancy military school where you were inspected every morning and played soldier every day. As the two companies that comprised the Academy's Corps of Cadets stood at attention, a few of the upperclassmen holding officer's rank shouted out orders and gave reports. Henry was a plebe in the 1st Squad of B Company's 3rd Platoon.

On his head was a gray service cap with a shiny, black visor. Beneath his cadet overcoat, he wore a tailored gray jacket that had a high collar and a black stripe running down the front. Completing Henry's everyday uniform were gray jodhpurs tucked neatly into high, black boots.

His first year curriculum of Algebra, English, Ancient History and Latin kept Henry occupied for most of each day. In addition, he and the other freshmen were expected to learn close-order drill, extended order drill, the nomenclature of weapons, military tactics, and bayonet training.

The first-year cadets were highly impressed by their instructor, professor of military science and tactics Maj. Edward Dwan, United States Cavalry, who'd recently commanded troops chasing Mexican bandits down near the border at San Ygnacio, in Zapata County, Texas.

The day Henry stepped off the train at the 111th Street station; Wally Valentine predicted he'd have trouble with Captain Bouma who taught Freshman English. Yet Bouma proved a patient teacher who made a determined effort to improve Henry's manner of rural speech.

Instead, it was algebra that caused him problems—taught by a gangly, young teacher who peered at his students through round, wire-rimmed spectacles. Captain Francis S. Gray was in his third year of teaching mathematics at the Academy. He'd already earned his reputation as an instructor who tolerated no nonsense in his classes, unforgiving of any student who gave less than his best.

"Seybold," Captain Gray announced one afternoon, as he held Henry after class. "I know you're a farm boy, but so am I, and as I see it, that fact doesn't give you leave to be a dunce."

"No sir," Henry said. "I try awful hard, sir. I know how to add and subtract, multiply and divide—but I guess algebra don't make much sense to me—all them Xs and Ys and equals. How's that stuff gonna help me run Pa's farm—which I'll probably have to do some day."

Captain Gray shook his head and tossed a small piece of chalk in the air, deftly catching it behind his back. "Does your pa raise chickens, Mr. Seybold?"

"Yes sir. Leghorns and Plymouth Rocks."

"Look here," Captain Gray grunted, scrawling *Chickens* on the blackboard. "How many birds does he keep?"

"Oh, fifty or sixty, I guess."

"All right, let's say sixty," Gray said, writing that number after the words *Population size*. Then he wrote *Rate of reproduction* on a second line. "How many chicks are born each year?"

Unsure, Henry guessed at a number and Captain Gray wrote it down. "And how many does your pa lose each year?"

Taking into account starvation, disease, exposure, foxes and coyotes, Henry guessed at a number again. This time it was written in after *Rate of attrition*. On the last line, Captain Gray wrote *Time = 1 year*.

"All those numbers are different," Captain Gray pointed out as he stepped back from the blackboard. "But what do they have in common, Mr. Seybold?"

Blinking at the board, Henry shook his head dumbly, feeling like an imbecile.

"C'mon, young fellow," Gray said impatiently. "Use that lump of jelly the Deity saw fit to wedge between your ears."

"Well sir," Henry said nervously. "I just guessed at some of them numbers I wasn't sure about."

"So they could be different? They could change?"

"Yes sir, I guess they could."

"Very good, Mr. Seybold," Captain Gray said. "And those are what algebra calls *variables.*" He wrote that word down, too, with a line slashed under it. "Now to simplify an equation, we express our variables with single letters...P is the Population size, C is the number of chicks that are born and survive, or what we called the Rate of reproduction, and D is the number that die each year—or the Rate of attrition. See how it works?"

"Yes sir, I think maybe I do."

Captain Gray grunted. "Good, good. Now to go further and to express the equation in these terms we say if P is the population at the start of the year, and C is the number of chicks that are born and survive, and D is the number of chicks that die in a year, then the population of your pa's hen yard on New Year's Eve is stated as: P plus Y equal D...get it?"

Henry nodded. He thought he understood.

With that, Captain Gray spent the next ten minutes explaining expressions and equations, patterns, relations and functions, and finally linear equations. "You won't have it down pat right away," his instructor assured him. "But now you know the terms we use in algebra are nothing to be afraid of."

"Yes sir, thank you, sir—I'm sure obliged."

Captain Gray shook his head and tossed the chalk across the room where it landed squarely on the eraser rail. "No need to thank me, Mr. Seybold. I could see you were trying hard and that's the only reason I invested twenty extra minutes in your education. If you stop trying in my class, though, I'll flunk you so fast it will make your head swim."

Henry quickly learned that days and evenings at the Academy seldom varied in their routine. Boarding cadets were awakened by reveille at six, then allowed a hurried half hour to wash, shave, and dress before daily room inspection and breakfast assembly on Post Walk.

At breakfast, the cadets stood at attention as grace was said. At the order "Seats," they seated themselves and sat at attention until given "Rest." Breakfast, or Mess I, usually consisted of cold or hot cereal, milk, and fruit juice. Depending on which day of the week it was, pancakes with butter and syrup alternated with platters of rubbery scrambled eggs, greasy strips of bacon and slices of limp toast, with coffee served only to faculty officers and senior cadets.

Breakfast lasted exactly an hour. At its end, the cadets stood at attention and were dismissed—filing back to their dorm rooms to prepare for AMSF—the morning school formation consisting of roll call, company reports, and uniform inspection.

Once AMSF was over, Henry and the others attended classes from eight in the morning until noon, when the cadets once again assembled on Post Walk for Mess II—usually a meal of soup, cold or hot sandwiches, and a desert of either pastry, ice cream or fruit flavored Jell-O.

After the lunch hour, the remainder of the day was again filled with classes until four in the afternoon, when time was given over to recreational activities or athletics.

Mess III was the most elaborate meal of the day, served only to the boarding students. It usually featured beef, pork, or chicken, mashed potatoes and vegetables, followed by desert. After supper, the cadets were allowed fifteen minutes to be back in their rooms for study hour, homework, or writing letters, then another hour to shine their boots and brass for the next morning's inspection. Then it was tattoo, taps, and lights out.

At the beginning of the school year, Henry had been assigned to a small second-floor room in West Barracks, along with another freshman cadet named Dutton Harkey from Chicago's fashionable Lincoln Park area on the city's north side.

Dutton was two years younger than Henry, and seemed to be interested in only two things—jazz music and girls.

Dutton Harkey's father drove a black Packard Twin Six sedan, favored satin lined derby hats and held a prestigious seat on the Chicago Stock Exchange.

"What's that mean?" Henry asked his roommate. Most of the grown men he'd known in and around Ottumwa made their living growing corn and soybeans, fixing things, running stores, or selling farm equipment, and he had no idea of what a seat on the Chicago Stock Exchange might be. "Are you tellin' me your pa just sits?"

"Henry, you sure are a hayseed," Dutton laughed, shaking his head. "He's a broker. He trades equities."

"What's equities?"

"Stocks," Dutton answered patiently.

"Well, shoot, now you're talkin'," Henry said. He'd watched his own father buy and sell stock a few times, and thought he knew a thing or two about it. "Cows or hogs?"

On a visit one afternoon after the Sunday parade, Mrs. Harkey enquired of her son's roommate, "Will you be traveling home for the Easter holiday, Henry?"

"No ma'am, I expect not," Henry answered. He was sitting on his bed and the room's radiator was banging and clanking. It was a little over a week until Easter vacation and as of yet he'd received no funds for a train ticket to Ottumwa. "I went home for Christmas but I guess I'll be stayin' here for Easter."

"Perhaps you'd enjoy spending the holiday with us," Marilyn Harkey suggested. She was a gracious, openhearted woman having sympathy for those Academy boys who, for one reason or another, had to spend holidays alone.

"Well, I don't know, Mrs. Harkey," Henry said, surprised by the offer. "Maybe Dutton don't want—"

"Heck," Dutton Harkey said. "It'd be okay—I can show you some of the sights."

The Harkeys lived in a large three-story brownstone on West Altgeld Street, close to Chicago's downtown and just three blocks from DePaul University. It was a manicured neighborhood of quiet tree-lined residential streets that held some of the city's finest and most expensive homes.

Mr. and Mrs. Harkey employed a maid, a housekeeper, and a cook. Their housekeeper was Yugoslavian—an immigrant woman who spoke only a few words of English. She arrived by streetcar once a week to clean the big house, and rarely talked to anyone.

The live-in cook was an enormous black woman named Asia. She stood no criticism nor brooked any suggestion on how to run her kitchen. Quick-tempered and sharp-tongued, Asia's domain was not limited to the kitchen. It extended to the drawing room, as well, and there were times when even Mr. Harkey was intimidated by her.

"Asia's got a behind that's half the size of this house," Dutton told Henry, laughing behind her back. "But she's a great cook, and you can joke with her if she likes you."

The energetic little maid was a bird-like Irish woman named Binne. "It means sweet or melodious in the Irish, Mum," she'd told Mrs. Harkey when she'd applied for the position. "It was the name of several fairy women in Irish legend."

Henry had some idea of how wealthy people lived, but he had never been in a house that had servants, and he wondered what his mother might think of such a thing. He decided to write and tell her about it as soon as he was back at school.

Asia and her late husband had immigrated to Chicago from the South Carolina low country, and on Easter Sunday she went all out to prepare a traditional Southern feast for the Harkey's and their young guest. Henry's eyes were wide as Asia and the maid brought out what seemed to be limitless servings of succulent roast turkey, cornbread, Brussels sprouts with orange chestnut butter, steaming fluffy high rise biscuits, oyster dressing, candied yams sprinkled with walnuts and bourbon, toasted pecan wild rice, soft, buttery mashed potatoes, and fragrant spiced peaches.

Before beginning the meal, Mr. Harkey's blessing consisted of a business-like thank-you for the family's health and wealth, and a brief prayer that the country's president-elect, Warren G. Harding, might infuse even more vigor and vitality into an already booming stock market. "...and may God bless the Republican Party," Tyler Harkey concluded, helping himself to a thick slice of turkey breast and allowing the maid to pass the platter to his wife.

"How does the Academy suit you, Henry?" Mr. Harkey asked. It was the first time Dutton's father had spoken to him since he'd been in the house.

"I expect I like it well enough, sir," Henry answered as Binne the maid held a platter of dressing in front of him.

Mr. Harkey nodded approvingly. "Well, that's splendid, young man," he said. "Unfortunately, our son doesn't care for it at all—isn't that correct, Dutton?"

"Not very much, Father," Dutton agreed.

Tyler Harkey grunted. His wife sat silent. "Our Dutton doesn't like it much at all. You see, Dutton fancies himself somewhat of a sheik these days. He'd much rather spend time with the girls than tend to his studies and learn some discipline."

"Me'n Dut study together sometimes," Henry said, hoping to put forward a small case for his roommate.

"Not enough, it seems," Mr. Harkey pressed. "His grades have been deplorable."

"Must we talk about this now, dear?" Mrs. Harkey interjected. "Why not just enjoy this lovely meal Asia prepared?"

Mr. Harkey just grunted and fell to eating his dinner. A few minutes of awkward silence around the big table felt like hours to Henry. His parents rarely carried on conversations at mealtime, but only because they were busy eating. The Harkey's sudden lack of discourse was fraught with tension, and Henry was relieved when Mr. Harkey finally spoke again, asking him about his own family.

"We're just farmers, sir. My folks own seventy acres outside Ottumwa—that's in Iowa. We grow mostly corn and soybeans. Ma was a teacher once, but she gave it up when she married Pa."

"Farmers are the backbone of civilization," Mr. Harkey stated firmly, thinking back to his younger days when he'd first made the beginnings of his fortune trading farm futures at the Chicago Board of Trade. "Don't ever say you're *just* a farmer, my boy. Without your father and thousands of others like him, dinner tables all over this country would be empty today."

"Yessir," Henry said, glancing at Asia who was bringing out a dish of lemon-garlic steamed broccoli. "I suppose you're right."

"Of course I am," Mr. Harkey grunted, addressing the remains of his dinner once again.

"What sort of teaching did your mother do, Henry?" Marilyn Harkey asked, smiling, as Binne carefully refilled her glass with an amber splash of cream sherry.

"She taught grade school, ma'am," Henry said, putting down his knife and fork. "In a little town called Pleasant Corner—mostly reading, writing, and arithmetic."

"*Hmpff*—farmers and teachers," Mr. Harkey grunted, wiping his mouth with a napkin. "This old world would be in a sad state of affairs without them."

"Yessir, I expect it would." Henry agreed again. Mr. Harkey seemed to have firm ideas about these things, and wasted little time in voicing his opinion.

Although his mother was an exceptional cook, Easter dinner at the Harkey's was the finest meal that Henry could ever remember having. When it was over, Mr. Harkey lit a long cigar and excused himself, retiring to his book-filled study, while Mrs. Harkey went off into the kitchen to supervise Asia and Binne.

Dutton Harkey had been fidgeting in his chair as he waited for both his parents to leave the room. When they finally did, he poked Henry in the arm and nodded toward the front hallway. "Let's get out of here," he whispered.

Henry was surprised. "Where to?"

"A place I know about," Dutton said. "I hope you like jazz."

With their coat collars turned up against a biting March wind coming off Lake Michigan, the boys walked east on Altgeld a few blocks until they reached Halsted Street. So far, March had been cold and wet in Chicago, and Easter Sunday proved no different. Henry felt a shiver go up his back. "Ain't your folks gonna miss us?" He asked Dutton. "Why, we just up and left."

"They won't care," Dutton said, reaching into his coat pocket for a crumpled package of Chesterfields. "You want one?"

Henry shook his head. "Where're we goin' anyway?"

"Slumming," Dutton said, lighting his cigarette. "We'll catch the streetcar here and take it all the way south to 35th, and transfer to one going east to State Street—then we're in Bronzeville."

"What's Bronzeville?"

"Jigtown," Dutton said cheerfully. "You don't have anything against coloreds, do you?"

"I guess not," Henry answered. "We don't have many colored folks in Ottumwa."

Dutton nodded as a red and yellow streetcar approached and slowed to a stop. "Well, there's plenty of them in Bronzeville," he said. "They run the gin mills and the jazz joints down there—black and tan clubs where being colored or white doesn't make much difference."

"I never heard jazz music," Henry admitted.

"Say, you aren't a bluenose, are you?" Dutton asked.

"No, I don't guess so," Henry said.

"Well, you'll hear some tonight," Dutton told him. "And when those spades play, brother, they hit on all six."

Although he was older than his roommate, Henry felt Dutton Harkey was far beyond him in experience. Dut had grown up in the city and acted like he knew everything there was to know about it. Henry's mother had sent him to Morgan

Park Military Academy to shelter him from what she considered the immoral temptations of modern life. Yet, now Dut was taking him someplace to hear what his mother often disparaged as race music, and without saying it, he wondered what she might think about all this.

Settling in on the streetcar's wicker seat, Henry stared out the window as the trolley made its way down Halsted Street. On both sides of the avenue were countless storefronts, small neighborhood restaurants, churches, modest two-story homes, and saloon after saloon—all of them closed now by Prohibition.

Halsted Street changed as the neighborhoods changed. Passing the Maxwell Street Market, Dutton pointed out all the ramshackle, empty merchandise stands waiting the next day's hectic commerce. "Everybody calls this place Jewtown," he stated.

As the streetcar traveled further south, the store signs began to change—with words and characters Henry had never seen before. "Greektown," Dutton explained.

Henry had always assumed that Chicago was just one big city, but the way Dutton described it, the whole thing seemed made up of little connecting towns—they'd just passed through Jewtown and Greektown, and now they were on their way to Jigtown.

"I swear, Dut," Henry pointed out. "These places don't look nothing like where you live."

Dutton chuckled. "I told you we were going slumming."

When they finally reached 35th and State, Henry could barely believe his eyes. Most of what he was seeing was so far beyond his frame of reference that he could just as well have been looking at the moon. The entire area was a congestion of sawdust-floored gin mills pulsating with jazz music. Almost everywhere he looked, he saw cabarets, nightclubs, and the black and tan clubs Dutton had told him about—jazz clubs that provided locations for the intimate association of blacks and whites.

"Well Bub," Dutton grinned. "How do you like Bronzeville?"

"Shoot," Henry gulped. "If my ma could see me now, I expect she'd fall over in a dead fit."

"My folks, too," Dutton admitted, grinning. "They don't know I come down here. Asia the cook told me about it."

With Henry in tow, Dutton hurried down 35th Street until they reached a small joint that had recently been a corner garage. It was now called the Sunset

Café and a poster in the window read: *Direct from New Orleans—King Oliver's Creole Jazz Band!*

"This is the place," Dutton said.

As they paid the cover charge and walked in the door, Henry began to blink. His eyes stung from the smoke-filled air. On the podium, an all-Negro orchestra was playing a tune called "Dipper Mouth Blues." Henry saw a few well-dressed black men drinking and dancing with young and attractive white women sporting short, bobbed hair and flapper outfits, while at tables in the far corner of the room, a small scattering of white men were busy entertaining eight or ten equally stylish black women.

"I God," Henry whispered to his friend. "I never seen nothing like this in Ottumwa."

As the small orchestra worked their way into another number, the boys found an empty table and sat down. "Is there really a King Oliver?" Henry questioned. "That's sure a queer name."

Dutton nodded enthusiastically. "That's him up there," he told his roommate. "That fellow in the derby playing cornet."

Dutton explained that when Oliver was a boy in New Orleans he'd been blinded in one eye, and now often played while sitting in a chair or leaning against the wall. "See how he tilts that derby hat of his?" Dutton went on. "It hides his bad eye."

"You sure know your onions, Dut," Henry offered. He'd heard of New Orleans, but wasn't even sure of where it was.

A Negro waitress approached their table. "You gen'lemens got your hips?" She asked.

"Just one," Dutton said. He reached into his coat and took out a thin metal flask, handing it to her.

"This sport ain't drinkin'?" The waitress asked, looking over at Henry as he shook his head, averting her gaze. "He some kinda Holy Roller or what?"

"He's from Iowa," Dutton offered.

"Well, Lordamighty," the waitress chuckled, showing a bright gold tooth. "Don' nobody drink bootleg in Iowa?"

Dutton shrugged. "He lives on a farm. He's sort of a hayseed."

"I ain't either," Henry mumbled, embarrassed. Dutton and the waitress were talking as if he wasn't there. "Just don't have a flask is all."

"It's okay," Dutton said, giving the black woman three dollars. "We'll share mine."

One sip of the Sunset Café's bootleg hooch was enough to put Henry off for the rest of the evening. He'd tasted what they called white mule a few times, compliments of a visiting cousin of his pa. Everett Seybold's cousin, Emmett Colby, had a house and a still in the Appalachian foothills near Roan Mountain, Tennessee. Every few years Emmett would drift on through on his way to someplace or another, leaving a Mason jar or two of mule as a gift for Henry's father.

Unlike most of his neighbors, Emmett Colby took particular pride in his product and let it age slowly—usually for two or three years. When Henry reached an age to become curious and worked up enough gumption to sneak into the pantry and steal a sip of that Tennessee mash, he recalled that it had gone down a lot easier than whatever the waitress with the gold tooth was serving Dutton.

As Dut finished his flask and called for a refill, King Oliver's Creole Jazz Band launched into one popular number after another—"Canal Street Blues," "Alligator Hop," "Workingman's Blues,"—and it seemed as if Dut was able to identify each tune after only the first two or three bars. Just as he'd told Henry earlier, King Oliver played his cornet leaning against the wall or sitting in a chair most of the time. Throughout each different number, the stout musician used mutes, bottles and cups, and even his own derby hat, to affect a wide variety of sounds from his brightly polished horn.

But most of this was lost on Henry. In the next two hours, as the urgent beat went on, as Negroes and whites swayed and danced to the moan of the music, he watched his roommate slowly slide into a state of intoxication.

"Dut, you gonna be okay?" Henry kept asking.

"Sure—be okay," Dutton slurred. His eyes were glazed and he had a stupid grin on his face. "Just a little fried, tha's all."

When Dut tried to stand and make his way to the men's room, he wobbled on his feet and fell back onto his chair, still grinning. "Can' walk so good," he giggled, shaking his head.

"Dut, we better go home."

"Home?" Dutton slurred. "Sure—le's go home."

Henry realized that Dut couldn't go anywhere on his own, and that it would be up to him to get them back to Altgeld Street. He wasn't at all familiar with the city and as the driving music of King Oliver's band swelled in his ears, he shut his eyes tight and tried to make his brain backtrack the way they'd come. Suddenly, the quiet and familiarity of the MPMA campus would have been welcome, the safe and cloistered quarters of his small room in West Barracks was where he wanted to be.

"Your fren' ready for another hip?" The black waitress asked. "Maybe you sports be lookin' for some reefer or a little poon?"

Henry shook his head. He had no idea what she meant. "No ma'am, I got to get him home."

"*Wooeey,*" she whistled, looking at Dutton as he grinned up at her foolishly. "This boy lit up like a store window, ain't he?"

"Yes ma'am, we got to go."

"We don' discourage tips, honey," the waitress said.

"Oh, sure," Henry said, slightly embarrassed. As he lifted Dut to his feet and helped him into his coat, he reached into his own pocket and placed four dollars on the table. "Is that okay?"

"Tha's jus' fine," she said, scooping up the money. "You boys don' be gettin' in no trouble, now."

"No ma'am, we won't."

Once outside and back on the street, Dutton managed to throw up on himself. Henry braced him up against a lamppost and tried to clean him off as best he could—using a few crumpled pages of the Negro weekly *Defender* someone read, and then tossed into a trash can in an alleyway.

"Dut, listen," Henry said. "Do we take the trolley on this street back west to Halsted Street?"

Dutton groaned and wiped his mouth. "Halsted Street—tha's right. Where're we goin' now?"

"Home," Henry told him. "Get you to bed."

"Home—tha's good—wanna go home."

When they boarded a 35th Street streetcar, the conductor made it a point to comment on Dutton's condition. "Jesus, the kid smells like a goddamned billygoat—looks like he pissed his pants, too. He ain't gonna puke again in my car, is he?"

"No sir," Henry said. "I'll watch that he don't."

When they reached Halsted Street, Dutton was sleeping with his head against the window. Henry had to wake him and struggle to get Dut to the open door so they could get off and transfer to the northbound Halsted trolley.

"Is Algeld Street to the north or south?" Henry asked.

"It's north," the conductor grumbled, relieved to be rid of the two of them. "Just a block past Fullerton."

It was past midnight when Henry reached into his roommate's coat pocket for the keys to the front door. When he got Dut into the hall, Henry looked up to see Mr. Harkey, wearing slippers and a silk bathrobe, standing at the bottom of the stairs. "Henry, I would consider it a great favor if you'd help my son upstairs and put him to bed—and then join me in the library."

"Join you, Mr. Harkey?"

"Yes, my boy, if you would."

Once Dutton was passed out on his bed fully clothed, Henry removed his roommate's shoes and drew the covers over him, then he slowly went downstairs, fearful of what Mr. Harkey was about to say to him.

Tyler Harkey's study smelled of good cigars. It was paneled in oak and equipped with a massive antique Victorian twin pedestal mahogany desk and matching leather chair. Around the room were a sofa and four upholstered club chairs, with an equal number of fine oriental rugs gracing the floor. A portion of each paneled wall supported floor to ceiling bookcases. The dark, rich paneling was broken only by a set of double doors, a stone fireplace, and a large picture window that looked out onto Altgeld Street. Each bookcase was stacked full with bound volumes and periodicals. Aside from the Academy library, Henry had never seen so many books.

"Sit down, Henry," Mr. Tyler said. "Do you care to join me in a glass of sherry?"

"No sir, thank you, sir."

"I take it you don't drink, young fellow?"

"No sir, not very often—my ma don't like it much."

Tyler Harkey nodded. "That's good, son. However, I find that spirits can be a comfort, used judiciously of course."

"Oh, yes sir."

"Henry, I'll not beat around the bush," Mr. Tyler said with a heavy sigh. "I'm not pleased with the direction Dutton seems to be taking in life. He aspires to nothing beyond self-gratification. He is spoiled, indolent and lax in his studies. He's discovered bootleg liquor at much too early an age, and abuses it whenever he can."

Henry sat silent, uncertain of what to say. Ever since the day he and Dutton had been paired as roommates, he realized Dut was disinterested in schoolwork and much preferred to spend his free time in pursuit of girls or lounging in the basement weeder, trading dirty jokes and smoking cigarettes.

"I have a proposition for you, Henry," Mr. Harkey went on. "I would like to place Dutton in a totally different environment for a few months and would be prepared to pay your family the sum of a thousand dollars for Dutton's room and board this summer."

Henry shook his head. "I ain't sure of what you mean, sir."

"Take him home with you when school is out in June," Tyler Harkey suggested. "Let your father put him to work on your farm—show the boy what it's like to labor for a living."

Henry could barely believe what Mr. Harkey was proposing. It was a suggestion he knew his father would accept immediately—a thousand dollars for three months of bed and board that would also give the farm an unpaid hand for the summer. Everett Seybold was a practical man with an eye for profit, and Henry was certain his pa would jump on this opportunity like a dog on a bone.

"I can write my pa and ask him," Henry told Mr. Harkey. "Just as soon as me'n Dut get back to school."

"I can't believe my old man's doing this," Dutton groaned two weeks after Easter. Henry had just received a letter from his father: *You can bring the boy home with you,* Everett Seybold had written in answer. *Plenty of work to keep him busy. Bring the money, too.*

"It won't be so bad, Dut," Henry said. "Summers are fun."

"Oh yeah? What sort of fun?"

Henry shrugged. "Well, we can swim and fish, I guess—and usually there's a carnival or two, and a Fourth of July parade and a picnic for sure." Then he added, "And the Saturday night dances in Ottumwa."

Dutton Harkey just rolled his eyes and groaned again.

Early in June, once the school year ended, Tyler Harkey and his wife took Henry and Dutton to the LaSalle Street Station where they were to board the Chicago, Rock Island and Pacific coach that would take them as far as Grinnell, Iowa, where Henry's father had made arrangements to meet them at the station.

Dutton was glum, saying little—just staring out the Packard's window as they neared the station.

"Do you have the money for your father, Henry?" Mr. Harkey asked as he drove the big car east on Harrison Street.

"Yes sir," Henry answered from the back seat. "I got it packed away nice and snug in my valise."

"Did you count it?"

"No sir."

Tyler Harkey chuckled. "You should always count your funds in any financial transaction, young fellow."

Henry shrugged. He was anxious to see the farm again. "Well, the way I see it, Mr. Harkey, you're a real honest man. Besides, it's not my money, and my pa'll damn well—excuse me, Mrs. Harkey—my pa will *durn* well count it when I give it to him. You can bet on that."

Suddenly Dutton spoke up as they got closer and closer to the LaSalle Street Station. "Pa, do I really have to do this?"

"Yes, my boy, you do. A summer on Henry's farm will do you a great deal of good."

"It will be an adventure, dear," his mother assured him. "Look at it that way."

Early that afternoon, as their train left Rock Island station and rattled across the long steel bridge spanning the Mississippi River, Henry pressed his face against the coach's window. "We're back in Iowa, Dut."

"You mean *you're* back in Iowa," Dutton muttered bleakly. "I haven't ever been here before."

"Cheer up," Henry cajoled. "You'll like it fine."

The train pulled into Grinnell just after suppertime, and Henry spotted his father's Dodge half-ton parked off to one side of the station. The truck had been built for the army during the Great War and Everett Seybold managed to buy it at a government auction for two hundred dollars.

Stepping down from the coach, Henry saw his father waiting for them. "Hello, Pa," Henry said, offering his hand.

Everett greeted his son and then looked at Dutton. "Welcome home, boy—this your friend?"

"Yes sir, this is Dutton Harkey—we just call him Dut."

Henry's father nodded. "Well, glad to have you," he said, and then motioned toward the truck. "Guess we better get a move on—it's near forty mile to the house. Your ma made sandwiches for the trip home."

As they neared the truck, Everett took Henry by the sleeve and whispered in a low voice. "His pa send the money?"

"Yes sir, it's in my valise."

"You count it?"

"No sir, I figured you'd want to do that."

Ev Seybold grunted. "I do, but you best take it out of your grip and give it over before we start—sure wouldn't want that money to bounce out somewheres along the road."

The drive back to the farm was mostly quiet—but punctuated by questions about Morgan Park whenever Everett Seybold felt the quiet become awkward.

He'd never talked much to his son, usually limiting their conversations to weather, stock, and work around the farm. Rather, it was Henry's mother, much more educated than her husband, who took pleasure in casual discourse.

"That school teachin' you to be a good soldier?" Everett asked as they bounced along the rutted county road.

"I guess so, Pa," Henry answered. "Last semester they taught us infantry drill, bayonet drill, map reading, signaling, first aid, and marksmanship—I got a sharpshooter's medal."

"Well, I'da guessed as much," his father asserted. "Many's the time I seen you tumble runnin' cottontails with that little old .22 of yours."

"How about Dut?" Everett asked. "He a sharpshooter, too?"

"No sir," Dutton admitted, still sounding glum. "I can hit the target okay, but nobody's as good a shot as Henry."

The Dodge truck rattled south toward the Seybold farm.

After breakfast early the next morning, once Cora Seybold had satisfied herself by hearing a little about every course Henry and Dutton were assigned during the past semester—Algebra, English and Literature, Latin, and Ancient History—Ev Seybold lost little time in bringing the gab to a close and putting the boys to work.

It was a day-to-day life Dutton Harkey never knew existed. He was soon to learn what Henry already knew—the summer months were a time of hard labor and long hours on the farm. Sunrise came early, and the whole family, including Dutton, awoke before dawn to deal with the early morning chores first, before settling down to bacon, eggs, and coffee.

They made allowances for Dutton's inexperience, putting him to tasks requiring little skill or knowledge—feeding the chickens and hogs, gathering eggs, helping cut hay and store it in the barn.

With the help of Everett's brother, Cletus, and two other hired men, Ev had started plowing fields and planting crops back in May when the weather turned fair. But there was still the rest of June to plant. By July, crews of men and teams of horses would be moving from farm to farm with big threshers for the wheat and oats, crops that had been planted the previous fall.

Neighbors gathered together to help with the threshing and to cook huge meals for the hungry field workers. In July and August, once the corn and soybeans were in, Cora Seybold spent most of her time canning and putting up vegetables from their own garden, as well as appraising the latest fads, fashions and fancies that were appearing in *McLures, Vogue,* and the *Ladies' Home Journal,* all popular magazines to which she subscribed.

Just as his father had hoped, the summer spent on the Seybold farm was transforming Dutton Harkey. The long days and grueling work did most to change him, but the rural lifestyle he was living did its share as well.

Dutton hadn't seen a telephone since he'd left Chicago. On the farm there was neither indoor plumbing nor electricity to power a radio—to bring him the drums, bass, and horns of the jazz music to which he'd once been so partial. And he hadn't had an opportunity to mess with whiskey since he'd been there.

Instead, if the day's work was finished, he and Henry might go swimming bare-assed in Hookert's Creek, or take the cane poles to fish for bluegill and catfish in a half-dozen small farm ponds.

On the Fourth of July they piled into the truck and drove into Ottumwa for the fireworks and parade, and the closest Dutton was able to get to a night on the town were the Saturday evening young people's socials at the Ash Grove United Methodist Church where there wasn't a flapper or a hip flask to be seen.

And as the summer wore on, he didn't miss them anymore.

On a Friday morning in August, two weeks before they were scheduled to go back to the Academy, Henry and Dutton hooked the spreader to a hitch on the rear of the Dodge half-ton. Cora had instructed them to clean out the henhouse.

"What's in there?" Dutton asked, crushing out his smoke and nodding toward the long, paint-peeling wooden shed.

"Whadd'ya think's in there?" Henry said, as he pulled on his worn leather gloves. "A big pile of chicken shit is what."

Dutton groaned, rolling his eyes. But it was an act, just to get a laugh from Henry. The few months he'd been with the Seybolds had hardened Dutton's muscles and strengthened his self-reliance to a point where there wasn't much he wouldn't do.

They tied bandannas over their noses and mouths, then picked up their shovels and entered the henhouse, scattering protesting Leghorns and Plymouth Rocks out into the large chickenwire pen.

"Jeez, it stinks in here," Dutton complained.

"It's chicken shit, Dut," Henry pointed out. "Not roses."

"Well, it sure does stink."

Henry couldn't help but laugh, looking at his friend ankle deep in the grayish mess of chicken droppings. "I, God—look at you, Dut, who's a hayseed now?"

Two hours later, once the henhouse had been shoveled out and the manure loaded into the spreader, they got into the truck, with Dutton at the wheel, and hauled the load to one of the unplowed fields Everett Seybold was planning to put into winter wheat.

The spreader was heavy with its mass of nitrogen-rich chicken muck, but before getting started, Henry went around to the back of the spreader, unbuttoning the fly of his worn bib overalls. "Hold on a minute, Dut, I gotta take a leak." Leaning against the sharp metal tines that shredded the manure, he began to urinate.

Already weary and sore from the long morning's work, Dutton was anxious to finish the job, but he welcomed the short break. He leaned back and fumbled in his pocket for a stick match to light a cigarette, and for some reason they were never able to determine, the Dodge slipped into gear.

For a moment, Henry almost became the manure. His left arm was grabbed by the tines and wrenched so far in that it locked the spreader's wheels. After slamming on the truck's brakes, Dutton jumped to the ground and raced around back to where Henry was caught. His roommate was hurt and groaning—with the spreader's tines digging into the bloody muscle and bone of his arm.

"Jesus, Dut, my arm's stuck and I think it's all busted up. Run for the house and get my pa. And hurry!"

"Oh Christ," Dut gasped, feeling helpless. "I don't know what happened, Henry, I—"

"Just run, Dut," Henry screamed. "And bring pa back here!"

Cora Seybold almost fainted as her husband worked to release Henry's arm from the machinery that had crushed it. Once freed, the arm was lifeless and already swollen dark yellow, patched with purple bruises, and showing pieces of splintered bone protruding through the flesh. Seeing her son's shattered limb, Cora had to turn away, feeling sick to her stomach.

At Everett's instruction, Dutton had set himself to the task of unhitching the spreader from the truck. Groaning, Henry seemed to be in and out of consciousness as they held him on his feet and put him in the Dodge.

"She won't fit four," Everett told Cora as he climbed in behind the wheel. Henry was between his father and Dutton, with his chin resting heavily on his chest. Cora Seybold clutched her apron and wept, reluctant to stay behind.

"I'll get the boy to the hospital," Everett assured his wife as he crunched the truck into gear. "Them doctors in Ottumwa will know what to do for him—try not to worry, Cora Mae."

Speeding north, the Dodge swerved in the ruts and was raising a long, low cloud of grayish dust as it bounced along the unpaved county road. Dutton sat silently, staring straight ahead. Every now and then, Henry would shift in the seat, slowly lift his head to look around and then fall back to what almost looked like sleep.

"Was you boys payin' attention to what you was doin'?" Ev Seybold finally asked, breaking the silence in the truck.

"Yes sir," Dutton mumbled. "We weren't doing anything that would've caused this to happen—the truck just slipped into gear is all, and I don't know how."

Everett shook his head. "Seems queer," he said. "Nothing like that ever happened to me with this truck."

"It was an accident, Mr. Seybold, but I was behind the wheel so I guess it was my fault." Dutton said, almost sobbing.

Everett Seybold only grunted. His knuckles were white on the steering wheel as they raced toward Ottumwa.

Four hours after arriving at the Ottumwa Hospital emergency room, Dr. Nolan Hurley came out to see them. Hurley had done his internship and residency at Cook County Hospital in Chicago, and later spent nine months as a field surgeon in France during the late war. He was not a man to sugarcoat bad news.

"He came through the surgery fine, Mr. Seybold," Dr. Hurley offered. "These farm accidents are usually grim, but your son was lucky—it could have been much worse. As it was, the boy's arm was too badly damaged to save. I had to take it."

Ev Seybold blinked. "I ain't with you, Doc—"

Nolan Hurley sighed. These things never got any easier. "I had to amputate your son's arm, sir, just below the elbow."

Hearing this, Dutton felt sick to his stomach. The morning had started like any other, but now Henry had lost an arm. How could such a thing have happened?

Dr. Hurley sighed. "I'm afraid manure spreaders harbor a rich stew of infectious bacteria. I was careful to remove any suspicious tissue from the site, but until we're certain the boy is free of sepsis and healing properly, we'll need to keep him here—that could be two to three weeks."

Before leaving, Everett Seybold looked in on his son, who was still too groggy from the morphine, nitrous oxide and diethyl ether anesthetic to understand anything that was happening around him.

The long trip back to the farm was made in total silence. What had happened to his son, Everett thought, and the hospital bills that would result were sure to hurt them badly. Their profit margins just weren't high enough to absorb such unexpected misfortune.

It was late when they finally pulled into the yard between the house and barn. Ev Seybold killed the engine, and never looking at Dutton, just stared straight ahead. "You best pack your things, son. My wife will drive you to the train in the morning. I don't believe I got it in me to do it myself."

Dutton's shoulders shook as he began to sob. "Mr. Seybold, I didn't mean for Henry to get hurt...I don't know what happened. It was an accident, I swear."

"What's done is done," Ev Seybold said quietly. "I just want you off this place, boy—just go on back home."

Tyler Harkey lit a cigar and blew out the match. He and his son were seated in the study. "Of course it was an accident, son," Mr. Harkey said. He could see the pain and sorrow still visible in Dutton's eyes and it was a side of his son he'd never seen before—a maturing of sorts. He felt something had changed in the boy, and that whatever it was, was for the better. "But you were behind the wheel of that truck, Dutton, and I expect that makes you somewhat responsible for what happened."

"I got a letter from Henry last week," Dutton said with a heavy sigh. "He says he probably won't be back to school because with the hospital bills and all, his folks can't afford the tuition. He told me that what happened wasn't anybody's fault and that I shouldn't blame myself." Dutton sniffed and went on. "Henry said he should have never been leaning against those tines."

Tyler Harkey nodded. "That may be so, my boy. Nevertheless, I'm in a position to help Henry and his family, and I fully intend to do so."

"Mr. Seybold wouldn't even look at me," Dutton said, feeling as if he were about to break into tears again.

"No," Mr. Harkey offered quietly. "And I can understand that. You will too, someday, when you have children of your own. He's a father grieving over his son's hurt and suffering—"

Tyler Harkey turned his head and wiped a tear from his own eye, then added in a choked voice. "—just as I am over yours."

By the middle of that week, an accounts receivable clerk in the Ottumwa Hospital billing department was in receipt of a telegram instructing their office to forward any and all charges having to do with Henry Seybold to Mr. Tyler Harkey at his West Altgeld Street address in Chicago.

The same day, Col. Harry D. Abells opened a letter in which was a personal check from Tyler F. Harkey to cover the next three years of young Henry Seybold's education—should the boy decide to return to the Academy.

On a warm June afternoon three years later, a day before the Class of 1924 was to graduate, Tyler Harkey, Everett Seybold, and their wives sat on newly painted bleacher seats and watched with pride as Morgan Park Military Academy's Corps of Cadets passed in review at the final full dress parade of the year. Cora Seybold wept and dried her eyes with a damp cotton handkerchief.

The sun shone brightly, and robins sang their song of spring in the stately oaks and elms surrounding the green grass of the parade ground. Carried by the color guard, the unfurled flags of country, state and school waved as company guidons snapped in the breeze. Captain Hirschy's band was in fine form as well, playing rousing renditions of "The Washington Post" and "The Thunderer."

"We have you to thank for this day," Cora whispered to Tyler Harkey through her tears. "Without your generosity I don't know what Everett and I would have done."

"That's just nonsense," Tyler told her gently. "It was Henry's strength that brought him to this day. Whatever help I was able to offer was the least of it."

It had been an eventful three years. With Henry's tuition paid, he'd been anxious to return to school and insisted on Dutton as his roommate. It had been difficult at first. With only one arm, most of the school's athletic activities weren't possible. It took nearly a full year of trial and error and constant practice for Henry to develop his own techniques of handling a rifle in close order drill. He never asked for special consideration, nor did he receive it. With athletics closed to him, Henry threw himself into his studies—finishing his senior year as president of the prestigious Philomathean Literary Society, captain of the debating team, and to his mother's pride he was to graduate with an impressive 3.9 grade average.

But it wasn't until two years after the accident that Ev Seybold let loose of his sorrow and anger. That July, Dutton and his folks drove the black Packard more than three hundred miles from their home in Chicago to visit the Seybold farm.

Cora Seybold was thrilled to have the Harkeys as guests, while her husband remained aloof and distant. One evening, just before bedtime, Tyler Harkey stepped out onto the front porch as Everett was lighting his pipe.

"Thought I might join you for awhile, Mr. Seybold."

"No law against it, I suppose," Everett replied coolly.

"It seems our women get along just fine," Tyler observed.

Everett nodded. "I reckon."

"And our sons are the best of friends."

"Yessir—seems that way."

"Everett," Tyler started hesitantly. He was not a man to mince words. "Both our boys lost a great deal from that accident."

Ev drew on his pipe, saying nothing and staring into the dark.

"But they gained a great deal, too," Tyler went on. "Henry is one of the finest cadets in that school, and our Dutton has put away his toys and follows your son a close second."

Ev Seybold nodded. "Mr. Harkey, my wife and me are obliged to you for Henry's tuition," he replied sadly. "But money can't buy that boy his arm back."

"No," Tyler agreed, shaking his head. "Nor will it buy away the sorrow Dutton will feel for the remainder of his life. But those boys have put it behind them—I wish you and I could, as well."

He put out his hand and Everett hesitated for a moment before taking it. "I don't warm to people easy."

Tyler nodded. "Take all the time you need, Ev."

"Oh, look at them," Cora sighed. "Just look at them."

"Yes, look at them," Marilyn Harkey repeated.

Seated off to one side with other faculty officers, Capt. Francis S. Gray reviewed the Corps as well, and was greatly impressed by that year's battalion commander—Cadet Lt. Col. Henry Seybold, whose father raised Leghorns and Plymouth Rocks, and whose left sleeve hung half-empty at his side.

Holding his wife's hand, Ev Seybold, who'd been a farmer all his life, was for this brief time unconcerned with the daily price of corn and soybeans, or the vagaries of livestock, crops and weather. This day, Everett wiped tears from his own eyes and listened to the stirring music as he watched in wonder the briskly marching lines of cadets who filed past—saluting his only son.

Henry stood tall in his summer full dress uniform—flanked by his adjutant staff and facing the passing ranks. As each company commander brought his unit past, the order of "Eyes—*Right*" was barked. Officer's sabers were raised, hilts to the chinstrap of their shakos, then snapped down and to the right—held there in salute, heads turned toward the staff and the bunting-draped review stand.

As C Company passed in review; Cadet Capt. Dutton Harkey grinned briefly as he raised his saber in salute. He and Henry had remained close friends and roommates for their entire four years at the Academy. Their eyes met for a moment—in silent recognition of a bond and a friendship that had endured, despite the horror and tragedy that had fallen over both of them in an Iowa wheat field three years before.

CHAPTER 2

▼

CAMP REVERSE

Summer, 1924

Cadet Willis St. John sat bolt upright in bed, his eyes wide open as he stared at the other boys in the cabin. "What the hell was that?" Willis asked with a distinct note of apprehension, recalling a book he'd once read titled *Wild Animals I Have Known,* by the Canadian author and naturalist, Ernest Thompson Seton. "Was that a wolf?"

"No Willy, just a loon," someone said sleepily.

"What's a loon?"

"It's a bird—swims in the water like a duck."

"Well, it gives me the creeps," Willis said. He'd never learned about loons—or about poison ivy, how to swim, paddle a canoe, or build a fire without matches.

Willis St. John had been raised in a twelfth-floor apartment on North Michigan Avenue and his outdoor experiences were limited more to concrete and steel than forests and lakes. At the end of his second year at Morgan Park Military Academy, his father decided it might be a first-rate idea to send young Willis off to the school's Camp Traverse for eight weeks during that hot summer of 1924.

"I don't wanna go," Willis had protested.

"Nonsense, my boy," his father retorted. "You'll have a first-rate time and it will do you a world of good."

"But Dad, I'd rather spend the summer in the city."

"Don't argue, Willis," his father had said. "Your mother and I are going to France and Italy for the summer and we can't merely leave you here all alone. Have your bag packed in time to catch the train."

Camp Traverse, on Michigan's heavily forested Spider Lake, was the result of prosperous times at the Academy. Just five years earlier, student enrollment began to grow, successful alumni were generous in their donations for new school buildings, and a sense of affluence was being felt at board meetings and on campus.

Camp Traverse was all about the outdoor life—initiated by the Academy's Capt. Herman Mayhew who shortly after coming to the school, became acquainted with Lord Baden Powell, veteran of the Boer War and founder of the Boy Scouts of America.

Captain Mayhew's camp assistant was Capt. Floyd Fleming who, during the school year, was MPMA's athletic director as well as instructor of history and commercial arithmetic.

Camp Traverse consisted of a two-story lodge, with facilities for cooking, sleeping, and a large, screened in porch that was the mess hall. It was perched on a hill overlooking Spider Lake, almost four hundred miles from Chicago and thirteen miles southeast of Traverse City, Michigan.

Captain Mayhew was partial to saying that the outdoors "was the only place for boys to grow into real men," and his basic rule for running the camp was "Safety first, and then a good time."

It hadn't taken irreverent cadets long to find things to poke fun at about Camp Traverse—soon described as Camp Reverse, on the shores of beautiful Bacteria Bay, in far off Afghanistein.

Willis St. John sat glumly, staring out the window, as the Pere Marquette Railway coach swayed and rattled around the bottom of Lake Michigan and up through Benton Harbor and Muskegon. The round trip coach fare set the cadet's parents back $11.60 and would take the boys as far as Traverse City by train, while a jitney would carry them the rest of the way to Spider Lake.

As the train passed through Muskegon, Willis caught his first glimpse of the lower peninsula Michigan forests, thick with birch, maple and jack pine. "You think those woods have grizzly bears in them?" He asked the boy sitting next to him, a cadet named Hobart Platt. Hobart Platt would be a junior next semester, too—but unlike Willis, Hobart was looking forward to the next eight weeks.

"Not grizzlies," Hobart said. "But black bears, maybe."

"I'd rather be home," Willis said, dejected.

"They let us swim in the lake, I hear," Hobart said happily.

"Who wants to swim in a lake?" Willis grumbled. "If there's fish in it, they crap in that water."

"Jeez Willy, you better not let Mayhew or Fleming hear you."

"So what if they do? I don't want to go swimming anyhow."

Hobart shrugged. "Well, you got to. That's part of camp."

"They can't make me if I don't know how," Willis argued.

"They teach you," Hobart said. "That's part of it, too."

"Aw, crap," Willis mumbled, turning back to the window.

A week after camp started, Willis studied the weekly schedule and his jaw dropped. His name was on a list of cadets who were to be taught how to swim. That summer, Capt. Francis S. Gray was spending a few weeks at camp, and the notice went on to announce that Captain Gray would be in charge of swimming instruction.

"Jeez, I'm scared," Willis said after breakfast.

"Scared of learning how to swim?" An older boy asked. He was a senior named Chum McNab.

"Yeah," Willis admitted. "But I'm scared of Cap Gray, too—I heard he's pretty tough."

Chum nodded sympathetically, patting Willis on the shoulder. "You can overcome that fear, Willy—that's what summer camp is all about."

"Oh sure," Willis said. "That's easy for you to say."

Chum McNab had been coming to Camp Traverse ever since the end of his plebe year. The Academy had even approached him about being a camp counselor after he graduated.

"Willy, did you ever hear of Eagle Claw?"

"Who?"

"Eagle Claw," Chum said, nodding toward the shore of Spider Lake. "He was a young Chippewa brave, and his tribe lived on a lake that was five times the size of this one."

"Oh yeah," another senior cadet named Ed Noonan exclaimed. "That's a great story."

"What about him?" Willis asked hesitantly. Chum McNab was a senior next year, a veteran of summer camp, and a big favorite of Captain Mayhew, but Willis was still unsure of how a story about some Chippewa Indian had anything to do with him learning how to swim under the tutelage of Captain Gray.

"Well, Eagle Claw fell in love with Bright Feather, the chief's daughter," Chum said, as five or six other boys edged in closer to listen to him spin the tale. Chum lit a cigarette as he settled into the story. "It seems the old chief didn't approve of Eagle Claw and when the young warrior worked up enough nerve to ask for Bright Feather's hand in marriage, the chief became furious and sent his daughter to live alone on a large island in the middle of the lake."

"An island?" Willis asked, glancing out toward what they all called Fifth Island—one of five that dotted Spider Lake.

"Yep, all alone," Chum added dramatically. "So that her and Eagle Claw could never see each other."

"How'd she get food?" Willis wondered aloud.

"Well, she probably caught fish," Chum suggested, sounding annoyed. "Anyway, Willy, what difference does it make? Do you wanna hear the story or not?"

"Sure, I guess so." Willis didn't want to make Chum angry.

"Okay," Chum continued. "Every evening, Eagle Claw would stand on shore and call out to her across the water—telling her how much he loved her. And each night Bright Feather would weep and answer, telling Eagle Claw of her feelings for him.

"Then, after many weeks, with his heart breaking, Eagle Claw couldn't take any more," Chum went on. "And he decided to swim across the big lake to be with his love.

"'No, you must not,' the tribe's medicine man told him. 'The island is far and the lake is deep. It is much too dangerous.'"

"'I don't care,' Eagle Claw argued stubbornly. 'I must be with Bright Feather.'"

"So what happened then?" Willis asked.

Chum leaned back and took a long drag on his smoke. "Well, with the whole tribe looking on, Eagle Claw stripped down to his breechcloth and dove into the dark, cold lake.

"He began to swim," Chum told Willis, as the rest of the boys nodded. "Trying not to think about how far he had to go. He swam and swam, but felt his arms getting heavy as he began to grow tired. But the people on shore cheered his courage, and after he caught a glimpse of Bright Feather waving to him from the far-off island, Eagle Claw vowed to press on."

"Hold on a minute," Willis interjected. "Where'd you hear this story, anyway?"

Chum McNab sighed. "There's some Chippewas that live near Mayfield, okay? They told it to us my first summer up here."

"That's right, Willy," Ed Noonan agreed. "I was here, too, and they told us all about it."

"Okay," Willis said, satisfied. "So what happened?"

Chum lit another cigarette, deliberately building the suspense. "Eagle Claw was more than half way to the island," he finally said. "When a storm came up."

"A storm?"

"Yeah, a bad storm, too—lightning and thunder and wind. The sky got dark and the lake took on five—six foot waves."

"Jeez," Willis whistled.

"As Bright Feather stood on shore and urged him on," Chum said. "Eagle Claw kept swimming toward her. Closer and closer he got—but he was exhausted. Finally, just fifty yards from where she stood, a giant wave crashed down on Eagle Claw and sent him to the bottom—and nobody ever saw him again."

"Aw crap," Willis said. "That's a crummy story."

"Maybe so," Chum McNab allowed. "But the old chief was so astonished at the young warrior's bravery that he proclaimed the lake would be forever named in Eagle Claw's honor."

"Eagle Claw Lake?"

"Naw, Willy," Chum laughed, as Ed Noonan and the rest of them began to hoot in delight. "He just called it Lake Stupid."

As a small boy, one of Frank Gray's older cousins had taught him to swim in the Sangamon River. The experience had consisted of no more than being tossed in from the riverbank, and then being urged to paddle and kick his way back to shore—as Cousin Claude stood by, ready to pull him out if little Frank looked like he was about to go under and drown.

It wasn't the best way to learn, Captain Gray suspected, but it had served him well all the years since. He hadn't seen the ocean, but throughout his life he'd never encountered a body of water that worried him, not the Sangamon River or even Lake Michigan, and certainly not Spider Lake.

"Come on boys," he called to Willis and four other cadets who stood on shore watching him wade out to waist-deep water. "You can't go canoeing until you learn to swim. Just step in and walk out to me—nothing to be afraid of."

Willis stuck his toe into the cold water and shivered. He didn't much care to go canoeing either, so what difference did it make if he learned to swim or not? It was a hot July afternoon, and by the time he'd waded out far enough to reach Captain Gray, the water felt refreshing and the fine sand beneath his feet was smooth and soft. But if being waist-deep in Spider Lake wasn't as bad as Willis thought, he still wasn't interested in learning to swim.

"You boys may think you can't swim," Captain Gray began. "But you're wrong. Although I may have my doubts at times, all of you are human beings, and human beings are mammals.

"All mammals can swim," Frank Gray went on. "Even cats. In fact, there are very few creatures that can't swim in one form or another. Many don't, or at least not often, but they are able should the need arise. Elephants, cows, squirrels, snakes, rabbits, mice—even tiny insects. So none of you have an acceptable excuse for not acquiring aquatic skills."

He first had the boys take a breath and hold it, close their eyes and put their heads under water—an exercise designed to get them past the fear of being submerged.

Reasonably satisfied with their efforts, Captain Gray looked at the five boys around him before fixing his eyes on Willis. "Mr. St. John, you'll be the first to learn. I'm going to put one hand on your chest and the other on your back. When I do, just let yourself fall forward and let your legs float out behind you—don't worry, you won't sink."

Willis balked. "Sir, I don't think—"

"Rubbish," Captain Gray stated firmly. "You don't want to be a quitter before you start, son."

"I'm not a quitter, sir," Willis said nervously. Not many cadets balked at a request from Frank Gray. "But I'd feel better watching the others do it first."

Captain Gray grunted. The day was growing hot and he was in no mood to argue or cajole. "Very well, Mr. St. John, then you can stand in the water and shiver while I teach Cadet Dabkunas how to avoid drowning."

Nicholas Dabkunas was a second-year cadet, a husky, amiable Lithuanian boy from the old Marquette Park area of Chicago. Nick was a talented lineman on the frosh-soph football team and an all-around good athlete, but Nick's father never swam a stroke in his life and saw no reason why his son would ever need such a skill.

Nick Dabkunas let his chest and legs stretch out in the water as he felt Captain Gray's hand under his chest. "Good, now start kicking your feet," Gray instructed.

Soon, with little influence by his instructor, Nick was kicking and moving through the water in a circle as Cap Gray pivoted with him. From this point on, without being held up and careful to stay in shallow water, Nick was taught a more controlled kick, the dog-paddle, breaststroke and freestyle—all in less than thirty minutes.

Captain Gray watched satisfied. "Kicking will keep you afloat and moving your arms will pull you forward," he shouted to Nick, who was now happily thrashing about in Spider Lake. "In shallow water or fathomless depths, Mr. Dabkunas, those are the rudiments of swimming. Practice them whenever you can and you'll become skilled at it—who's next?"

One by one, the others stepped forward and placed themselves in Captain Gray's hands. Within another hour, everyone but Willis was paddling about, splashing each other, laughing, and whooping like wild Indians.

"Had enough of being a spectator, Mr. St. John?" Frank Gray asked, turning toward Willis again. "Ready to join the fun?"

"I—I guess so, sir," Willis mumbled, reluctantly accepting the fact that he could stall no longer.

"Let yourself fall forward," Cap Gray instructed, extending a hand under Willis. "And just let your legs trail out behind. I won't let you sink."

Willis sighed, took a deep breath, shut his eyes tightly and did what he was told, but as soon as he felt his feet no longer touching bottom a cold wave of panic engulfed him. Fearing he was about to drown he began to splutter and shout for help. Kicking and flailing his arms, Willis managed to inadvertently strike Captain Gray in the face as the officer was trying to calm him.

"*Agh*, goddamnit," Willis heard the captain swear.

Almost immediately the other four boys rushed in to help and quickly had Willis on his feet again. Blowing water from under his nose, he was shivering and embarrassed. "I'm awfully sorry, sir. I didn't mean to hit you."

Captain Gray shook his head. He too, was flailing around in the water now, seemingly searching for something. When the boys glanced in his direction, Cap Gray's face looked somewhat odd—as if the skin around his mouth had begun to sag.

"Are you okay, sir?" One of them asked.

"My teeth," the captain mumbled, still groping underwater. "I lost my goddamned teeth, you brainless young fools."

Oh God, I'm sunk, Willis thought as he watched the four other cadets repeatedly dive beneath the surface, feeling around on the lake bottom for Cap Gray's dentures—but to no avail.

I'm through at this school, Willis told himself, suspecting that no MPMA cadet had ever even talked back to Captain Gray, much less knocked the man's teeth out of his head.

For almost a week afterward, Jim Green, the camp's Pullman-trained cook prepared special soft meals for Captain Gray—now as toothless as one of Spider Lake's catfish, but nevertheless doing his best to carry on.

Each day Willis avoided the captain, who everyone knew was scheduled to leave Camp Traverse the following Sunday. He didn't know what the irascible mathematics instructor might say if they happened upon each other, and he wasn't eager to find out.

Finally, five days after the unfortunate mishap, a second-year cadet named Harvey Prentice stepped on something hard and sharp while wading out toward the dive platform. At first Harvey thought it was a rock or maybe even a clamshell, but as he reached down and retrieved the object from the muddy bottom, he was surprised to find himself holding a set of fine white dentures, intact and none the worse for wear.

"Let Willy return them," Chum McNab suggested. "He needs to smooth things over with the captain."

Early that same evening, with a tightening knot growing in his stomach, Willis intercepted Captain Gray, who was on his way to another soft supper that Jim Green concocted. "Excuse me, sir, but I think these might be yours." Willis held out the lost dentures and watched as Cap Gray took them from his hand, briefly looked them over, and then put them into place.

"*Hmmpf,* just in time," Captain Gray grunted. "Haven't seen you around here lately, Mr. St. John," the captain observed. "Been avoiding me?"

Willis nodded. "I suppose so, sir. I was afraid you were mad at me for what happened."

"You mean my lost choppers?"

"Yes sir."

Captain Gray shook his head. "Hell, son, I was angry with you all right, but not because of that. Knocking my teeth into the drink was an accident, but what gets my dander up is a young fellow like you being too afraid to learn to swim."

"I'm sorry, sir."

Cap Gray snorted. "Mr. St. John, *I'm sorry* is the most useless, most overused phrase in the English language. Especially if that's all you've got to offer."

"Yes sir."

"I'm cross with you, son," Captain Gray went on. "And I plan to stay cross all summer long, and for your next two years at the Academy if need be—unless somebody comes and tells me you've finally learned to swim."

That evening after supper, Willis sought out Chum McNab. "I need a favor, Chum. Can you swim pretty good?"

"Sure, Willy," Chum laughed. "Who can't—besides you?"

Captain Gray left camp early that Sunday, boarding the jitney for the short, dusty ride to Traverse City where the Pere Marquette Railroad would take him back to Chicago.

For the remainder of the summer the campers kept busy with a daily round of outdoor activities—baseball, hiking, fishing and the like. They gorged themselves on cherry pie at the annual Traverse City Cherry Festival, went fishing in Lake Michigan where a cadet named Donald Fry managed to land a twelve-pound lake trout—a new camp record. They made an overnight hike to nearby Rennie Lake, and told ghost stories around the campfire, took a mud bath at the spring on the Bordman River, and earned free tickets to the circus—*Robinson's Famous Shows*—by watering the animals and helping set up tents in Traverse City.

But every evening for two weeks, Chum McNab and Willis St. John could be seen in the shallows of Spider Lake. Under Chum's tutelage, Willis progressed from an awkward, clumsy dog-paddle to a just-passable breaststroke and finally, to an almost-acceptable freestyle. When Chum was reasonably certain that Willis wouldn't drown himself, they swam out to the diving dock together.

"Well, pal—you can manage to stay afloat," Chum said. "Now comes step two—learning to dive."

"Aw jeez, Chum," Willis protested weakly. "Isn't learning to swim good enough?"

Chum shook his head. "Nope, I don't want ol' Cap Gray sore at me because I didn't teach you everything he would have. Hold your nose, Willy, and just start by jumpin' in—"

The last weekend of the season, those boys still left in camp at the end of summer washed their necks and slicked down their hair to attend a chuckwagon supper and a square dance at Miss Steer's Camp for Girls on nearby Lake Arbutus.

Boarding the train the next day, Willis was suddenly surprised when he tried to recall the last time he'd thought of his parents and their trip to Europe, or of life on Chicago's Gold Coast. He'd been living in the woods of Michigan for eight weeks and in that time he'd learned to swim, how to make a campfire, how to paddle a canoe and how to catch a fish. He'd done some hiking and played baseball. He was stung on the forehead by an angry yellowjacket, but also managed to avoid poison ivy and sunburn, unlike a goodly number of his less fortunate fellow campers. He'd learned how to shoot a bow and arrow, gotten to see the circus, eaten barbequed spareribs and munched corn on the cob, and even danced with two or three pretty girls the night before.

As he found a seat on the coach and looked out the window, Captain Mayhew and Captain Fleming were checking off the role, marking off names in a notebook. Not all the boys had stayed in camp the full eight weeks. Some were only there for two, or four, or six. Those who'd stayed the entire season numbered only ten or twelve.

Well, it'd been a fine summer, Willis thought as the day coach chuffed out of Traverse City's small railroad station, and in just another week he'd be starting his junior year at the Academy.

Erasing the morning's algebra problems from the blackboard, Captain Gray heard a light knock on his classroom door. "Excuse me, sir—"

"Who's that?"

"It's me sir, Cadet St. John."

"*Hmpff*—Mr. St. John," Cap Gray grunted, tossing the eraser in the air and catching it behind his back. "Do I need to hide my teeth in the desk?"

"No sir," Willis said, somewhat embarrassed that the captain remembered the unfortunate occurrence of a month before. "What you told me before you left summer camp, sir—well, I didn't want you sore at me. So I brought this to show you."

Willis unrolled a piece of paper, made to look like parchment by being soaked in black coffee. The document had a hand-drawn border much like an official certificate. Within the border, Chum McNab had printed in an amateurish Old English style:

To whom it may concern:
Be it known that Cadet Willis St. John
has successfully completed the
Camp Traverse swimming course
and is now a proficient nătātor.

Certified by:
Cadet Charles "Chum" McNab
August 20th, 1924

Captain Gray adjusted his glasses to study the poorly rendered certificate. "Am I to surmise from this document that you learned to swim, Mr. St. John?"

"Yes sir," Willis said proudly. "How to dive, too."

"That a fact," Cap Gray grunted. "McNab taught you?"

"Yes sir."

"What's the meaning of *nătātor,* Mr. St. John?" Captain Gray asked as he glanced at the certificate a second time.

"It's Latin, sir. It means *swimmer.* Chum—I mean Mr. McNab thought it sounded pretty good."

"*Hhmmpf*—do you have any classes with me this year?"

"Yes sir, advanced algebra, sir—next semester."

"Good, do you know what *măthēmătci* means?"

"No sir."

Cap Gray nodded, holding back a grin. "It's Latin, too, Mr. St. John—it means *mathematician.* And that damn well better be what you are in my class next term. Otherwise you'll wish you'd made things a lot easier this summer and just drowned yourself in Spider Lake when you had the chance."

CHAPTER 3

▼

A GIFT OF THE LONE
EAGLE

Cadet Private Nathan Caulder was hopelessly enamored of aircraft. Although still only a plebe, young Nathan's fervor for anything with wings assured his membership in both Morgan Park Military Academy's small but enthusiastic Model Airplane Club, as well as the school's equally popular Aviation Club.

At 7:52 in the morning, on May 20th, 1927, less than a month before MPMA's senior class was to graduate, a young flyer named Charles Lindbergh throttled up the 220-horsepower Wright "Whirlwind" engine of the specially built Ryan monoplane he'd christened "Spirit of St. Louis" and ran it down the dirt runway of Roosevelt Field on Long Island. Heavily laden with fuel, the plane bounced along the muddy field, gradually becoming airborne, and barely cleared the telephone wires at the field's edge. The crowd of over five hundred onlookers was convinced they'd just witnessed a miracle. Thirty-three and a half hours and 3,500 miles later Charles Lindbergh landed in Paris, the first to fly across the Atlantic Ocean alone.

Nathan read about it in the *Chicago Tribune* the Monday after. He'd been in the school's library, studying for his course in ancient history, when he spotted the newspaper lying on a table. *Lindbergh Lands In Paris!* The headline shouted. Excited, Nathan brought the paper with him to Captain Gray's freshman algebra class the next day, and it was all the boys could talk about.

"Quiet down, quiet down," the captain barked as the bell rang. "Sounds like a herd of braying jackasses in here—bring that paper up here, Mr. Caulder."

For Captain Gray, this particular freshman class had been a difficult one, slow to understand and worse, reluctant to study.

Each morning, as they came into his class, he saw their spirits sink. On the chalkboard they could only see a mysterious language of polynomials and slope intercepts that looked no more familiar or understandable than Egyptian hiero-glyphics.

Captain Gray was disheartened. For the first time in his career, he had no promising mathematicians in his class—not a single one. Each of these boys, he knew, would face another day of confusion, another day of pretending to follow along, and all of them would be taking the course again next year.

Frank Gray studied the headline and read the first paragraph of the article before glancing up at his class. "You fancy aviation, is that it, Mr. Caulder?"

"Yes sir," Nathan exclaimed. "Most of us do."

"That a fact?" Gray said, interested. He was always alert to the opportunity of rendering the mysteries of mathematics practical and relevant to the boys. He tossed a small bit of chalk in the air as he talked. "Want to be an aviator someday, do you?"

"Yes sir."

"What if I told you that algebra plays a big part in aviation?"

The class squirmed in their seats, looking skeptical as Captain Gray nodded and went on. "I was still a young fellow when Wilbur and Orville Wright flew at Kitty Hawk in North Carolina. All the newspapers made a big hullabaloo about it then, too—just like they are about this young flyer, Lindbergh."

One of the boys, a cadet named Roger Blount, was bolder than the other stu-dents. He raised his hand and asked, "What's all that got to do with algebra, sir?"

"Algebra's a pretty versatile character," Cap Gray said. "It'll be useful in a lot of things you do."

"Flying, too?" Nathan asked, unconvinced.

Gray nodded again. "An aviator needs to know how far he can fly on a gallon of fuel. He needs to determine barometric pressure and changeable tempera-tures—algebraic expressions will let him do that.

"Equations," the captain went on. "Can determine a loci when the aircraft flies a certain number of miles in different directions.

"And percentages," Gray concluded. "Percentages can help an aviator figure how much added fuel he'll use when his miles per gallon are reduced by increased payload weight—or by changing velocities of head winds and tail winds."

The captain flipped his chalk again, then tossed it across the room where it landed on the eraser rail. "Yessir, algebra will do it for you every time—if you learn it, and then use it—which most of you jugheads don't seem inclined to do."

"I'd like to offer it to my first-year algebra class, sir," Captain Gray explained to Superintendent Abells a few days later. "Most of those boys will fail my course if they don't buckle down."

"An airplane ride, Frank?" Col. Harry Abells asked in some befuddlement. "At the Academy's expense?"

"Yes sir," Gray explained. "A reward for the student who does best on my final exam. It would be a prize, colonel—an incentive to study. They're all crazy about airplanes and flying these days. This Lindbergh fellow is their latest hero. What do you think?"

"Whichever boy should win," Colonel Abells cautioned. "Will need permission from his parents, Captain Gray—and he'll need it in writing, stamped and signed by a notary."

"I understand, colonel."

Harry Abells shrugged. "An unusual idea to be sure, but why not give it a try?"

The next morning, before putting problems on the board, Cap Gray sat on the edge of his desk, holding a pointer, and addressed his freshman algebra class.

"This year's coming to an end, boys," the captain told them bluntly. "And Colonel Abells and myself are concerned about this class. All of you are doing poorly and I'll have to fail you if you don't apply yourselves on the final examination."

The young cadets sat silently, most of them disliking algebra, fearing that it was now too late in the semester to buckle down, and dreading the thought of repeating the course next year.

"So we're going to have a little contest," Cap Gray went on as he fiddled with his pointer, twirling it like a baton. "After our talk the other morning, it seems that most of you admire Mr. Lindbergh and would like to fly." He turned the pointer toward the class. "Is that correct, Mr. Auden?"

"Yes sir," Cadet George Auden responded.

"Is that correct, Mr. Caulder?"

"Yes sir," Nathan shot back with enthusiasm.

Captain Gray grunted. "I assume the rest of you feel the same, so here's what we're going to do…"

Nathan and the rest of the class were dumbfounded to hear the captain's proposal. The cadet receiving the highest passing grade on the final algebra exam, he told them, would qualify for a thirty minute airplane ride—with their parents' permission of course, and at the Academy's expense.

Cadet Mike Worden raised his hand. "Sir, what if two or more of us get the same high grade?"

"Colonel Abells has agreed that in the case of a tie, each cadet who tied will get to fly."

Hot damn, that'd be nifty, Nathan thought. He'd never been so excited. He'd study twenty-four hours a day for the chance to fly in an airplane—but he wasn't all that sure that his parents would give the school their permission. His bedroom at home was filled with scale model airplanes. They sat on every shelf and hung from the ceiling, but letting him climb into the cockpit of the real thing was something he doubted his parents would allow him to do.

"Let our fourteen-year old boy go up in an airplane?" Eleanor Caulder questioned her husband. "Oh, daddy, I just don't know."

"Most people say it's safe, dear," Robert Caulder countered. "And getting safer by the day. These are modern times, Eleanor."

"I know, I know—but it still makes me nervous."

"Well, if it'll help the boy get a better grade, I'm for it."

Nathan was stunned.

Suddenly, Captain Gray was amazed to find himself lecturing a first year algebra class of excited students. Each day, boys were asking questions, pestering him for special study sessions in the afternoon. He was putting problems on the board and seeing his class attack them with logical thought and infectious enthusiasm.

Nathan in particular was pushing himself as hard as he could. No other cadet in freshman algebra was going to beat him out of an airplane ride, he vowed to himself, convinced that although each of his classmates hoped to win, none wanted to fly as badly as he did.

On the last Friday in May, the boys filed into class with their pencils sharpened. Cap Gray could see all of them were as nervous as long tailed cats in a room full of rocking chairs—as his father used to say. Moving down the aisles, he passed out the exam and tried to encourage them.

"This class has studied diligently over the past few weeks," he said. "And I'll take this into account when I'm grading your tests. There aren't any surprises on this exam. None of the problems I've given you are problems you haven't dealt with before. Use what you've learned, boys, think about what you're doing, and you'll do just fine."

Nathan let his eyes wander quickly over each problem. He saw the captain was telling the truth. It was basic, designed to measure their ability to perform basic algebraic operations and deal with problems that involved elementary algebraic concepts.

He ticked them off in his head; operations with real numbers, polynomials, expressions including factoring; solving first-degree equations and inequalities; graphing and solving linear equations; solving quadratic equations; solving equations with exponential functions; determination of areas inside polygons; and finally, solving word problems.

Nathan took a deep breath and went to work.

On a bright June Saturday morning, just a week before school was out for the summer, Nathan Caulder, along with his parents, Capt. Francis Gray, and at least fifty other cadets, were assembled in front of a tall wooden hangar at Maywood Airport.

As the crowd watched, young Nathan celebrated his B+ score on Captain Gray's freshman algebra final by strapping himself into the narrow front cockpit of a bright yellow, surplus Curtiss JN-4 "Jenny" biplane.

"Will we do any loops or rolls, mister?" Nathan asked.

"No stunts, son," the pilot said. "I ain't no barnstormer. We'll just fly straight and level."

As the boy waved to his parents, the cough and roar of its 90-horsepower, Curtiss OX5 inline engine sent the swift little aircraft trundling down one of the asphalt runways.

Quickly lifting its tail, the roaring, bouncing Jenny built up speed and as its wheels lifted from the ground, Nathan's eyes were as wide as sugar cookies inside his goggles.

At the controls in the rear seat was an experienced mail pilot named Charlie White. White had flown Nieuports and Spads over France during the war, as a member of Capt. Eddie Rickenbacker's 94th Pursuit Squadron.

He took the Jenny up in a fast, steep climb and banked toward downtown Chicago and the lake, leveled off, and flew east above empty lots and cornfields. As they neared the outskirts of the city's growing west side, White dropped low over tenement houses and stores. Nathan peered over the cockpit padding, and could easily see people waving up to him and excited dogs barking in the street. Then White brought up the Jenny's nose and they climbed again.

Reaching a cruising altitude of nine thousand feet, it wasn't long before they were high over the bright, blue expanse of Lake Michigan. White tapped Nathan on the shoulder and passed him a note instructing the boy to take over the controls.

Nathan was at first amazed at how simple flying seemed to be. Back on the ground, before they'd even started the engine, Charlie White had explained the controls. A touch on the throttle to raise or lower engine speed, pressure back or forward on the stick would raise or lower the nose, and the foot pedals controlled the rudder.

By the simple method of passing notes forward, Charlie White instructed Nathan to climb, lose altitude, bank left or right, hold a certain air speed, keep the aircraft straight and level—and finally, to fly in this or that direction. At five thousand feet, they passed lazily over Oak Street Beach and the boy was amazed at the size of the city seen from the air. It was so big and spread out—strangely distant and removed from his more common perspective of riding down its streets in a trolley or in his father's Chevrolet.

Flying west again, toward the rural farms that ringed the city, Nathan felt the wind rushing past his face and heard the whistle of it through the guy wires. In front and below them he could see tall factory chimneys and church steeples, and passing beneath their wings was the Chicago River—curved and shining—like a copper penny in the morning sun.

Taking his instructions from Charlie White's notes, Nathan banked southwest over the city and brought the Jenny down to a thousand feet. Through the grayish blur of the propeller, he could see houses and neighborhoods begin to grow thin as they flew west again toward open farmland.

Tapping him and pointing down, White shouted over the noise of the wind. "That's Ogden Avenue down there and there's where it crosses Harlem. Bank to the right now, and take us north. It's time to head back to the airport."

Nathan nodded and did what he was told. Flying north again, he looked down and saw only wide fields of green beans and corn, along with smaller gardens near scattered farm houses, and small, grazing groups of cows.

Flying low, he was able to tell the difference between Fords and Chevrolets traveling the roads. He could see workmen building a new barn and children waving at him from their porch. As they flew north, White took back the stick and brought the Jenny back to altitude, banking northwest toward Maywood Airport where the boy's friends and family were waiting.

Approaching the field, Nathan studied the movements of the dual controls as Charlie White brought the Jenny in. Watching the stick and rudder move he could plainly see how an airplane was landed. As the wheels touched ground, the aircraft bounced once, then settled in, and as they throttled up and taxied back to the hangar, Nathan Caulder had the feeling that his young life had just been changed forever.

The boy's final exam grade had been a high B, bringing his semester average to a C. Most of the other students had passed the course as well, and Captain Gray was pleased.

Watching the yellow Jenny taxi back toward them, Frank Gray thought about Charles Lindbergh's lofty accomplishment—flying across the Atlantic alone.

And studying on it for a moment, he couldn't help but wonder which might be considered the greater triumph—the solo flight itself, or its motivation of a bored and faltering class of high school students to take their study of algebra a bit more seriously.

CHAPTER 4

▼

NO EXCEPTION WILL BE MADE

Fall Term, 1928

Captain Gray had endured the irritating sounds of hammers, saws, and the loud; often profane shouts of the builders all summer. They had started in the early spring, long before the Class of 1927 had received their diplomas, and they were still at it in on Labor Day—just finishing the framing and roofing. He hoped the stonemasons would begin before long. The men who laid brick were deliberate and quiet—much less annoying.

The Academy was growing, Frank Gray reflected, seemingly right beneath his bedroom window.

Alumni Hall, a magnificent new memorial building was going up, and a new dormitory, too. It was to be called Hansen Hall and would be the latest technology in dorm construction—completely fireproof, with terrazzo floors in all corridors and student rooms, and an efficient heating system to be fed by a central steam heating plant in the basement of old Blake Hall.

By mid-October, both buildings were nearly finished, bringing peace and quiet back to campus, but Captain Gray suspected that with the completion of these two new school buildings, the cadets, alumni, and faculty were fated to soon endure a lengthy afternoon of tedious speeches and dedication addresses.

Passing in front of Blake Hall, the walkway leading to Alumni Hall's impressive entrance was still unpaved, and the steps that led to the building's massive oaken doors were temporary—just planks of wood hastily nailed together. In both Alumni and Hansen Halls, there was still work to be done—final coats of paint on the plaster walls, a few more toilets to be installed, last minute wiring to be completed. But these still unfinished tasks did little to discourage the afternoon ceremonies held on that third Sunday of October.

Harvey Small, class of 1908, watched proudly as his son Neil, a freshman this year, marched across the long, broad meadow with the Corps, halting and marching in place as single columns broke from the battalion and filed into Alumni Hall. It was a far different school now, Harvey thought, than it had been when he'd graduated tenth in his class.

Harvey Small's first three years at the Academy were the final years of William Harper Rainey's period of influence as president of the University of Chicago. Harper had chosen the Academy as the non-sectarian preparatory school for the university in 1892, and changed its name from the Illinois Military Academy to Morgan Park Academy of the University of Chicago.

In 1906, at the age of forty-nine, Harper succumbed to cancer—two years before Harvey was to graduate. Morgan Park Academy added *Military* to its name and again became a military boarding school. Harvey could still remember how dumbfounded he and his classmates had been when unexpectedly faced with the unfamiliar discipline and regulations of a military institution.

"None of us knew anything about drill, saluting, or marching," he told young Neil before sending him off to MPMA in 1928. "It was like being a youngster again—and playing soldier."

But that was more than twenty years ago, Harvey thought, and the cadets had come a long way since then. In their gray tunics and high black boots, the battalion marched to a crisp, uniform cadence—accompanied by the school band playing the "Thunderer" and "Washington Post March." As Harvey watched, he spotted young Neil marching in the Second Platoon of B Company, and his chest swelled with pride.

"There he is," Harvey exclaimed, pointing their son out to his wife. "Our boy looks swell, doesn't he?"

"He looks wonderful," Lois Small agreed. "I'll bet he makes captain someday."

"Maybe even battalion commander," Harvey speculated.

After graduation, Harvey Small had prospered in his father's real estate firm. He'd married young and started his family early. Neil was their firstborn son, and Ted came along three years later. It was assumed by Harvey and Lois that as long as the business was doing well, both boys would follow in their father's footsteps and attend MPMA.

Harvey was exactly the type of alumni the Academy courted—wealthy and successful, proud of their time spent at the school, and extremly generous in their financial support.

The speeches were deadly dull. Regarding Alumni Hall, Army Col. Horace J. Mellum droned on, exhorting each cadet present to take his place in the making of the country's common history.

Then, Mr. Enoch J. Price, a respected member of the board of trustees, stepped to the podium and praised the virtues of the late Mr. Jens Carl Hansen, president of the Security Bank of Chicago, a highly-regarded MPMA trustee—and the man whose name would be honored in bronze above the main entrance to Hansen Hall.

When the parade and dedications were over, the battalion was dismissed and Harvey and Lois Small took Neil and his younger brother out for banana splits at the Modernistic Ice Cream Shoppe at 128th and Western.

"How are your studies going, son?" Harvey asked. The family was squeezed into a booth by the window.

"Pretty good, I guess," Neil answered, spooning a large dollop of whipped cream from his sundae.

"You guess?" Lois Small said. "Don't you know?"

"Well, I'm not doing so good in algebra."

"That's absurd," Lois countered. "You're as bright as any boy in that school. If you're doing poorly, it must be the teacher's fault. Who's your instructor?"

"Captain Gray," Neil said. "He's pretty tough."

Harvey Small nodded and scribbled *Capt. Gray* on his napkin. "Perhaps the man's incompetent. I'll speak to Colonel Abells about it one day next week."

"Captain Gray has been on staff since 1917," Colonel Abells told Harvey in his office the following Tuesday. "He's an excellent mathematics instructor and highly regarded by our upperclassmen. In fact, he's usually selected as senior class advisor each year."

"That may be the case, Colonel Abells," Harvey said. "But my son doesn't seem to be profiting from the man's tutelage."

The superintendent shook his head. "We're doing everything we can to help the boy, Mr. Small—Captain Gray tutors Neil and a few other cadets having trouble in a special study hall after regular classes are over—on the captain's own time, I might add."

"Commendable," Harvey Small sniffed. "But perhaps a better solution might be to just excuse Neil from algebra—why allow one course to bring down the boy's grade average?"

Colonel Abells sighed and leaned forward in his leather chair. "I'm afraid what you suggest is impossible, Mr. Small. Freshman algebra is an established part of the school curriculum—structured by the State of Illinois."

Harvey lit a cigarette and crossed his legs. "My wife and I are very proud of the boy, Colonel."

"As well you should be," Abells said. "Neil will overcome this difficulty. It's part of his education—learning to meet challenges and to triumph over obstacles."

Harvey Small nodded, choosing to ignore the superintendent's words of encouragement. "Perhaps I haven't made myself quite clear, sir," he pressed. "We're also proud of...our relationship with the Academy...our financial largesse, you might say."

"No alumnus has been more generous," Abells agreed.

Reasonably certain that Superintendent Abells understood his meaning, Harvey stubbed his cigarette in an ashtray and stood, his coat and homburg in hand. "Because of this, Colonel, I would hope the school might do everything in its power to ensure that Neil will warrant a proportionately generous grade in algebra."

Colonel Abells also stood and offered his hand. "I understand your concern, Mr. Small," the colonel said, noncommittally. "And rest assured that both Captain Gray and myself shall do everything we can to achieve that result."

Harry Abells was outraged and amused in equal parts. "It was out-and-out extortion, Frank," the superintendent insisted, shaking his head. "Mr. Small offered a clumsy, heavy-handed warning that as an alumnus, he might withhold future financial assistance if his son should receive a poor grade. Why, I could have been talking to Al Capone."

Captain Gray shook his head. "The boy has poor aptitude for mathematics, Colonel—but neither does he try very hard."

"What can we do to help him?"

Frank Gray shook his head and shrugged. "Only more of what we're already doing, I expect. Maybe increase his study halls from three afternoons to four."

A realistic, practical administrator as well as a straightforward man, Abells nodded and looked Captain Gray in the eye. "Harvey Small and his wife are extremely generous givers, Frank," he said honestly. "And I don't need to tell you how important people like the Smalls are to a private school like ours. I can't overly stress the critical need to bring their son up to speed."

Grunting, Captain Gray stood to go. "I'll do the best I can with the boy, sir."

Cadet Neil Small couldn't stand his algebra class and had an even lower regard of Capt. Francis Gray. The man was unarguably a curmudgeon, and the veteran mathematics instructor's reputation had already neared legendary proportions on campus—liked and admired by some, feared and disliked by others in equal measure—a demanding teacher who at one time or another caused trepidation in nearly every cadet who sat in his class—especially those who were lazy or unprepared.

"He's gonna flunk me," Neil told his parents one Sunday two weeks before the Christmas holiday. "Captain Gray's algebra final is next week and I don't know enough to pass it."

"Don't be silly," Lois Small told her son. "Your father talked to Colonel Abells—everything will be fine."

Harvey Small glanced up from reading the *Sunday Tribune.* "I explained to the colonel that a failing grade just wouldn't do. Not for a boy whose parents have contributed as much as we have to that school—and who'll undoubtedly contribute a great deal more in the future."

"You mean you bribed him?" Neil asked, astonished.

Harvey chuckled, shaking his head. "I wouldn't call it a bribe, son. I merely made the superintendent aware of the practicalities of the situation."

"And Captain Gray is going along with it?"

"Just like the colonel," Harvey Small reassured his son. "I'm sure Captain Gray understands who butters his bread."

The following Tuesday, feeling buoyed by his father's actions, Cadet Neil Small was unusually chipper in Cap Gray's after-class study hall. He hadn't even bothered to look over the four problems Gray had assigned for over the weekend. What was the point?

Looking to his notes, Captain Gray duplicated one of them on the blackboard and then turned toward Neil. "Can you enlighten us with the answer, Mr. Small?"

"No sir, I guess not."

"You guess not," the captain repeated. "Why not?"

Neil shrugged. "I just don't know the answer, sir."

"Did you study the assignment problems, Mr. Small?"

"No sir."

"I see," Frank Gray said, holding back his anger as he recalled Colonel Abells' appeal to do everything possible to help this cadet earn a passing grade. "Well then, close your book and sit there like a goddamned dummy, Mr. Small—you and I will have a chat when this study session is over."

"I do this tutoring on my own time, Mr. Small," Captain Gray told Neil after the other boys left the room. "Without extra pay. Do you want to enlighten me as to why I should put myself out like this for a bonehead like you who doesn't bother to study?"

"I—I didn't think I had to, sir."

Frank Gray was astonished. "And why is that?"

"Well sir, my father had a talk with Colonel Abells," Neil said hesitantly. "And he said the colonel probably talked to you, too."

"About what?"

"Well, I guess—I guess about giving me a passing grade, sir. On account of my folks give so much money to the Academy."

Frank Gray blinked, not believing what he'd just heard. "Good galloping Christ, son—you mean to tell me your pa thinks I'll pass you just because he's got deep pockets?"

"Yes sir, I guess he does."

Captain Gray was incensed. "Let me tell you something, Mr. Small. Your algebra final is Friday and if you don't make a passing grade, I'm going to fail you in this course—and I don't give a good goddamn how much money your father showers on this place."

Cadet Small swallowed hard, suddenly nervous and unsure of himself. Whatever his father had told him the day before—Captain Gray sounded very much like a man who buttered his own bread.

"Do you understand?" The captain pressed.

"Yes sir."

"That's good," Gray grunted. "Now let me ask you this, son—how much do you want to pass my course?"

Neil shook his head and stared at the floor. "I've gotta pass it, sir. I'm getting As or Bs in everything else—but if I flunk algebra, my pa'll kill me."

Frank Gray nodded. "I'll have a talk with Colonel Abells after supper," he said. "If he tells me what I want to hear, we will study each day from after regular classes until ten o'clock at night. We'll start tomorrow and go until Thursday night. I'm going to start from the beginning and try and give you a semester's worth of algebra in three nights—in an environment where you've got nothing else to do but learn. Do you want to pass bad enough to do that?"

"Colonel, even being tutored, it looks as if Cadet Small may not pass his algebra final. If that happens, I've no choice but to fail him. Do you have a problem with that, sir?"

They were in Colonel Abells' office, and although it was long after administrative hours, Captain Gray had taken the precaution of closing the superintendent's door.

Abells shook his head sadly. "That's a shame, Frank. The boy is doing well in everything else."

"So he tells me."

"Is there nothing more we can do?" Abells asked.

"There might be," Captain Gray said. "But before I'd commit myself to the task, I need to be assured that you'll allow the boy to receive a failing grade."

"If he earns one?"

"Yes sir."

"Why, of course," Colonel Abells said. "Why wouldn't I?"

Frank Gray had given himself little choice but to just come out with it, even though he detested suggesting such a thing. "For fear the boy's father might draw the purse strings tight."

Colonel Abells had been sitting on the edge of his desk. Now he stood up and moved behind it. Sitting down in the worn leather chair, he looked at Captain Gray and smiled. "I'm a bit surprised you'd find it necessary to ask me a question like that, Frank—how long have we known each other."

"More than ten years, sir."

Abells nodded. "Then you ought to know by now that no cadet at this school gets a pass unless he earns it. If Cadet Small receives a failing grade, then fail him—no exception will be made."

Captain Gray forced a thin, taught smile, one of the few times the superintendent had seen him do so. "That being said, Colonel, here's what I propose to do for the boy—"

They started immediately after the regular tutoring study hall and continued until almost 10:30 that first night. Earlier in the day, Colonel Abells had briefed the faculty officer in charge and the cadet officer of the day as to the fact that Cadet Small would be missing from Mess III formation, normal evening study hour, and possibly taps as well—for the next three evenings.

Neil's only break in the schedule would be a ten-minute pause to go to the bathroom or to eat supper—delivered by a cadet waiter wearing a reefer over his white jacket. Even as Neil wolfed down his meal, Captain Gray remained animated—lecturing, explaining, and scribbling examples on the dusty blackboard. Every half hour or so, he would pause. "Are you getting all this, Mr. Small?"

Neil would nod. "Yes sir, I think so."

And it was true. Neil was astounded by the fact that, putting aside his preconceived distaste for algebra and his doubts that he could actually do it, the fog was beginning to lift. Concentrating as he was, what had seemed incomprehensible gibberish at the start of the term was now, in fact, beginning to actually make sense.

Captain Gray had started their first session with variables, then advanced to expressions, equations, and by the end of that evening, Neil was struggling to solve basic equations—and to the captain's satisfaction—getting more of them right than wrong.

Over the next two grueling afternoons and evenings, Neil was totally immersed in simplifying equations, combining like terms, simplifying with addition, subtraction, multiplication, and division—and finally, word problems and sequences.

Finally, exhausted, he heard Captain Gray say, "That's it, Mr. Small—we're out of time and I've run out of steam. Think you've learned anything?"

"Yes sir, I think I have."

Gray sighed and nodded. "I hope you're right, son. You've put in a tough three days and tomorrow's the final—you ready for it?"

"I guess so, Captain Gray."

The captain nodded again. "But you need to know something, Mr. Small. *Everything rests on this exam.* Squeak by and I'll pass you—fall short and you'll fail the course—understood?"

"Yes sir."

Frank Gray sat on the edge of his desk and lit a cigarette. He was tired, too, and hoped what they'd done over the past three days would be of help to the boy. "Check in with the officer in charge and get a good night's sleep, son. We've done all we can do."

"Yes sir," Neil groaned, barely remembering to salute. "Thank you very much, sir."

Trudging back to Hansen Hall with his reefer collar turned up against the biting cold of the December night, Neil could see only one light on—in the first-floor office where the officer in charge was posted. For just a moment, before checking in with the O.C., Neil Small wondered to himself why he'd ever been one of those cadets who disliked Captain Gray so much.

Seated at their kitchen table, the captain spent all Saturday and Sunday grading his various classes' final exams. Monday morning, at the end of freshman algebra, Captain Gray posted the test grades for that class on his bulletin board—with a grunt to Cadet Small to stay after the others had left.

Neil sat at his desk, watching his classmates check their grades and then file out of the room. He could have stood up and looked at his own grade, but a strong force, a stomach-churning fear, kept him rooted in his seat.

After the last cadet had left, Captain Gray stood in the empty classroom and looked straight at him. "No interest in how you did, Mr. Small?"

Neil swallowed hard, feeling drained. "Yes sir—just afraid to find out, I guess."

"You scored a low C, son. You managed to squeeze through."

"I—I passed it?"

"Yes, you did—just barely, but you passed."

Neil slumped in his desk. He felt weak with relief and thought he might be on the verge of tears—*a low C*—he'd passed!

Captain Gray casually tossed a piece of chalk across the room, grunting as it landed squarely on an eraser rail. "I don't put much stock in Cs," he muttered. "But it's grade enough to put you in my plane geometry class next year. Think you'll do better?"

"Yes sir," Neil said. "I'll do a lot better."

"That's good, Mr. Small," Captain Gray said as he turned off the lights. "And there's one other thing. If he asks, you tell your pa that this school appreciates his support, but that you passed algebra on your own nickel, and that I'd have flunked you quicker'n spit if you'd failed this test."

"Yes sir."

I damn well would have, too, Cap Gray told himself as he left the room. *No exceptions could be made.*

1930–1939

CHAPTER 5

▼

A MAN AND HIS BOYS

In late August of 1932, as the country was struggling through the early years of what the politicians and newspapers were calling the Great Depression, Capt. Francis S. Gray cleaned his wire-rimmed spectacles with a fresh, white handkerchief and eyed a few of the year's new instructors with satisfaction.

"I would suspect it's a credit to the school, Colonel," he told Superintendent Abells, "that you're able to attract gifted teachers such as these young fellows seem to be."

"You might be right, Frank," the colonel said, nodding. "But I expect these hard times have a good deal to do with it as well. A lot of very high caliber men are migrating into teaching these days and when they can secure a position offering free room and board I suspect they feel themselves fortunate, indeed."

Gray grunted. Having been a member of the faculty for fifteen years, he understood that a teaching post at Morgan Park was far from financially lucrative, and that during the '20s, when earning a first-rate salary was relatively easy, few young teachers were able or willing to endure the particular hardships that teaching in such an environment as the Academy imposed on a man and his family.

Gray knew that an MPMA teacher never completely got away from the job. An instructor dined at the head of a table populated with teenage boys each night of the school year, more often than not acting as a surrogate parent.

And teaching jobs usually came with more responsibility than just teaching. Instructors who came across as athletically inclined might be asked to coach one or more of the Academy teams. Many were asked to serve as faculty advisors to the school newspaper, a whole host of student clubs and organizations, or the yearly Junior Class yearbook effort—the *Skirmisher*. All at no extra pay.

Academy teachers usually lived in a nearby house that was old and far beneath the expectation of their wives, and those that were bachelors fared even worse—expected to live in, and supervise the cadet barracks in Hansen Hall.

If his own Anna had been a different sort of woman, Captain Gray often thought, he himself might not have stayed. But his wife knew how much he loved teaching mathematics and how much he enjoyed the structure and rigid discipline of the school—and that the Academy valued him in return.

Unknown to Frank Gray, resting in his personnel file was a carbon copy of a letter written by Harry Abells to the downtown store of Carson Pirie Scott & Company. The credit manager of the upscale Chicago mercantile had written an inquiry to the Academy, asking if Mr. Francis S. Gray could be considered a reliable risk if he were allowed to open an account at the prestigious store.

Colonel Abells lost little time in sending back a reply. *"He is absolutely all right in every particular. Frank Gray comes of that old Scotch-Irish stock that is single-track in its honesty."*

Over the past fifteen years, Captain Gray's repute had become clearly defined, a part of every new freshman's introduction to the Academy.

"Your first year, he'll scare the crap out of you," the new boys were advised by those upperclassmen who took it upon themselves to impart worldly advice. They called him Cap Gray, and above all else, he was to be feared.

The second-year men, feeling more confident in their abilities, merely looked upon him with a certain amount of caution.

By their junior year, the cadets were beginning to recognize and appreciate the man's singular talent in teaching his much loved mathematics.

And by their fourth year, Cap Gray was invariably nominated as senior class advisor—a gruff, no-nonsense teacher who could always be depended upon to offer wise counsel, and one who was genuinely interested in any Cadet who tried his best to succeed.

Teaching advanced algebra to a class of that year's juniors, Captain Gray found himself both pleased and annoyed with Cadet Sergeant Grice. Steve Grice was a student with a razor-sharp mind and a talent for math, and he usually took whatever problems were thrown at him in stride.

Grice was so smart, Frank Gray suspected, that he was bored—so bored that he occasionally dozed in class.

One spring afternoon, with the windows thrown open and the birds singing happily, Grice's head nodded, rolled, and fell back as a horrendous snore engulfed the classroom.

Annoyed, the captain hurled a blackboard eraser the length of the room, bouncing it squarely off Grice's forehead. The offending cadet sat up with a start.

"If you're so bound and determined to sleep in my class, Mr. Grice," Captain Gray said. "Have the decency to be quiet about it. You're making noises like a goddamned feedlot hog."

"Sorry sir," Grice apologized.

"Why don't you just bring in a damned pillow?" Gray asked sarcastically, as the entire class held back a collective guffaw.

Cadet Grice said nothing, but later in the week fell victim to the dares and urging of his friends.

"Cap Gray likes you, Steve," they pointed out. "You're a whiz in math and you can get away with anything in his class."

"I'm not so sure," Grice protested.

"*Aw* c'mon, we dare you to do it."

Finally folding to the pressure, Steve Grice arrived early at his next scheduled advanced algebra class and took his seat with a pillow stuffed in his briefcase.

Halfway through class, as Captain Gray faced the blackboard performing his singular feat of deftly scribbling equations with his right hand while at the same time erasing others with his left, Grice withdrew the smuggled pillow, plopped it on his desk, and nestled his head down into it.

The class could not hold back their laughter.

At the sound of eighteen cadets snorting and hooting, Captain Gray turned to observe his finest student acting like a fool.

"Grice!" He shouted, pointing to the door. "You'll find that life is hard, and even harder when you're stupid. Oooouuuuttt! You get an F—I'll see you in this class again next year if you manage to become a senior—sleep on that, you damned dummy."

"Frank," Colonel Abells said the next day. "You can't fail the boy over a bit of horseplay."

Gray nodded sheepishly. "Yes sir, I know. Young Grice is one of my best students. The lad has a splendid grasp of mathematics."

Abells grunted. "We have a demerit system to handle behavior of that sort. We'll lay a Springfield on his shoulder, and a pack of rocks on his back—and march him around for a day or so."

Captain Gray agreed. Cadet Grice had shown a sense of pluck and spirit, and he admired spirit in a boy.

Thinking about it later, the incident brought to mind a similar occurrence in his solid geometry class two years earlier. He'd been unhappy with a student's answer to his question and told the boy, "Mr. Inman—why not just take your textbook out and show it to a jackass, it would have more sense than you."

To the utter astonishment of the class, Cadet Inman promptly and recklessly got up from his desk and brought the book up to his instructor. The class broke into laughter, and even Captain Gray managed a chuckle, but Inman was still sent to the commandant's office and spent the following Saturday morning with a heavy pack on his back and over eight pounds of rifle balanced on his shoulder—marching up and down the length of Post Walk.

But, in bringing it to mind, Captain Gray recalled that Cadet Inman had received a B+ in solid geometry that semester.

Cadet Paul Berezny, a freshman boarding student, had been assigned to Captain Francis Gray's dinner table in the Alumni Hall dining room. Berezny was one of three plebes at the long table, the other diners being Captain Gray's wife, Anna, along with third and fourth-year upperclassmen.

"It's a crappy table," Paul was warned. "Outside of class, Cap Gray doesn't talk to cadets very much—he mostly just mutters and grunts, and he doesn't like a lot of gab going on during dinner."

The Gray table was in a far corner of the great room and one dark November evening, in the midst of Mess III's chatter and with silverware and glassware clinking, Beresny glanced up to see the captain pointing a finger at him.

"*Ugh,*" Frank Gray grunted.

Paul picked up a dish of mashed potatoes and passed it in Cap Gray's direction.

Another impatient *ugh* made him do the same with the near-empty platter of pork chops.

A third grunt, sounding annoyed now, was accompanied by an increased wagging of the captain's finger. Nervous, Paul grabbed the vegetable platter and passed it forward.

Finally, seeing Cap Gray glaring at him and shaking his head, Paul passed the salt and pepper, too, then heard a raspy, irritated voice call out, "You goddamned fool, turn on the lights!"

Cadet Cpl. Henry Doney was a second-year man when he found himself in Captain Gray's plane geometry class. Doney had had a different algebra instructor throughout his freshman year, but now, in the first month of the new semester, he sat nervously in the third row, observing this man he'd heard so much about.

Look at him, Doney told himself, thin and scholarly, wearing round wire rimmed glasses. He sure doesn't look all that scary.

Captain Gray relaxed in front of the class on a raised platform behind his desk, with his hands laced behind his head, his chair tipped back and his feet crossed and resting on the desk. He'd been teaching in the same room for so many years that when he cared to demonstrate the skill, he could casually toss a piece of chalk to any blackboard in his class room, making it land in the chalk tray either directly or by bouncing it off the blackboard—he rarely missed.

Captain Gray had lectured for about ten minutes on a problem concerning parallel lines cut by a transversal when he pointed at Doney and motioned him to come up to the front of the room.

"What's your solution to the problem?" Gray asked.

"Sir, I—I'm not sure, sir," Doney stammered.

"Not sure—or you don't know?"

"I'm not sure, sir," Doney said, stumbling over his own words. "I mean—I'm not sure if I don't know, or if I'm just not sure."

Captain Gray cocked his head and narrowed his eyes. "What the hell does that mean?"

By this time, the class was attempting not to laugh. They knew that, for whatever reason, Henry had been singled out and now was in for it. They were relieved as well, for there were only five or ten minutes left to class, and as long as Henry Doney was on the spot, none of them would be.

"Come on, Mr. Donkey," Gray said. "I want an answer."

"It's Doney, sir," Henry said.

"*Hhmmppf,*" Cap Gray snorted. "Seems more like a donkey to me. What's your answer, Mr. Doney?"

"I—I'm sorry, sir. I'm not prepared."

As quick as lightning, Captain Gray's hands came out from behind his head and slammed the top of the desk while both feet came down and smashed onto the wooden platform—both actions producing a sudden, frightful noise.

"Not prepared?" Captain Gray barked, pointing a finger at the door. "Doney, you don't know, you don't care, and you don't give a good goddamn. All you want to do is sit in the PX and drink soda poppy—get ooouuuttt!"

Henry was embarrassed and mortified. Throughout the rest of the semester, he never came to class without an accurate answer to any problem Captain Gray proposed, and he managed to earn an A+ in Plane Geometry.

But it wouldn't be until his junior year that Henry learned the true nature of the man. The 1933 football season was already well underway with three wins and no losses as Henry labored hard in scrimmage, playing the position of left guard. He barely noticed when the cadet officer of the day appeared on the practice field that afternoon and approached Coach Woodworth.

A few moments later, Woodworth blew his whistle and pulled Henry out of the line. "Doney, you need to see Colonel Abells."

"When?" Henry asked.

"Right now," the coach told him. "He's waiting for you."

"What's it about, sir?"

"I dunno," Woodworth said. "But you best get over there."

Henry had a quick shower, donned his uniform and ran from the gym to the superintendent's office. "Sir," Henry said, saluting at the colonel's door. "Cadet Doney reporting as ordered."

"Come in, Mr. Doney. Close the door and sit down. I'm afraid I have some unpleasant news for you."

"What is it, sir?" Henry was almost afraid to ask. He'd worked hard all last semester and this year, too. His grades were just below an A average.

"We received a telephone call from your folks, son. It seems they're unable to maintain your tuition payments. These are hard times, you know. I'm afraid you'll to have to leave the Academy."

Henry was stunned. "Leave, sir? When?"

"As soon as possible would be best," Colonel Abells told him sadly. "They're coming to pick you up this evening, after mess. These are not easy times, Mr. Doney—and your parents have done the best they could. I'm very sorry."

Henry skipped supper and spent the time packing. If he had to leave the school, he hoped to leave without embarrassment or a lot of sad farewells to his roommate and his friends. It would be much easier that way.

Less than a week later, as Henry was preparing to register in a neighborhood high school, his parents got a telephone call from Colonel Abells. "Mr. and Mrs. Doney, can you come to my office this afternoon—and bring Henry with you?"

"Is something wrong?" His mother asked.

"Quite the contrary," the Superintendent told her. "I think the three of you will be pleasantly surprised by this turn of events."

Later that day, Colonel Abells ushered them into his office and began to explain the reason he'd called them back. "When word of Henry's dismissal reached his instructors and classmates, many of them talked with their parents and since then we've had many calls offering donations to keep Henry in school.

"That's very kind," Henry's father said frankly. "But we won't accept charity, sir."

Abells nodded and smiled. "I assumed as much, Mr. Doney, and you're to be admired for your sand. But in addition, every one of Henry's instructors, with Captain Gray leading the charge, have petitioned me, asking to find a way to reinstate your son. Captain Gray and the others feel that a boy of his spirit and ability should not be denied a first-rate education merely because of money.

"Such consideration by his classmates and teachers has to be recognized and appreciated as a great compliment to your boy.

"Consequently, the administration has decided that Henry is to receive two scholarships—one for scholarship and the other for athletics. And if he's willing to serve as a waiter for the remainder of his time in school, we'd be pleased to welcome him back."

"How about it, son?" Mr. Doney asked. "Are you willing to wait on tables in the mess hall?"

"You bet, Pop," Henry answered. "The waiters get all the food they want—three times a day."

"Well, I guess that's it, then," Henry's father said, offering his hand to Colonel Abells.

"Have him back tomorrow," Abells told Mr. and Mrs. Doney. "You both can be very proud of your son."

As they left the Superintendent's office, Henry hesitated for a moment and then stepped back inside. "Sir, may I ask a question?"

"Of course."

"Did Captain Gray really speak up for me?"

"The loudest and the longest," Abells assured the boy.

Henry grinned, saluted and did a crisp about face, then walked out the door. "I'll be damned," he said to himself.

Frank Gray smoked a cigarette and watched through his living room window as Henry Doney and his parents got into their aging Ford and drove away.

Brushing cigarette ashes from the front of his khaki shirt, Cap Gray gave a satisfied grunt. The boy and his parents had looked to be grinning, he thought, and Doney would no doubt be back in his classroom tomorrow—Great Depression or not. Satisfied that the promise and future of a bright, hardworking young man like Henry Doney wouldn't be compromised by lack of funds, Captain Gray stubbed out his smoke, walked out the door of his house and made his way back onto campus, heading for Blake Hall and his one o'clock Trigonometry class.

"Cap Gray's amazing," Cadet Sgt. Oliver Nagle said as he and his roommate exited the aging teacher's solid geometry classroom on a cold Monday morning in January.

"Oh yeah," Ollie's roommate responded sarcastically, "the old man's a real peach."

"No, I mean it," Ollie countered. "You know how he's always flipping his chalk across the room—or over his shoulder?"

"Yeah, what about it?"

"He either makes that little piece of chalk land on the eraser rail," Ollie pointed out. "Or he catches it behind his back. And I've been keeping score—he makes it about nine times out of ten."

"So what's that prove?"

"Not sure," Ollie Nagle mused. "It's almost like the old man's got some kind of spatial measuring device inside his head."

"Oh sure, just like Flash Gordon."

Ollie laughed. "More like Ming the Merciless."

A month later, sitting with other faculty members who took an interest in the school's athletic program, Captain Gray squirmed in the stands as he observed a frustrated MPMA basketball team on their way to ignoble defeat at the hands of a marginally talented squad from Pullman Tech.

When the game ended, with cadets, faculty and parents filing glumly toward the doors, Frank Gray excused himself from a group of his fellow instructors and sought out Ollie Nagle, who'd been playing first-string end in that evening's game.

"Nagle, I watched you for four quarters," Captain Gray said. "You seem to exhibit the same flair for free throws that you do for solid geometry. I think my Great-Aunt Minnie has a better free throw game than you do—and she's ninety four."

"Yes sir, I'm sorry sir."

Frank Gray grunted. "Don't just be sorry, young fellow—try to improve. Sorry's less profit than a puddle of spit—being sorry won't earn you a passing grade or win you any ball games."

Embarrassed, Ollie said nothing. He was having trouble with solid geometry, and knew more than anyone else how poor he was at free throws. He also knew how hard he'd tried to develop the skill—with little result.

"I do try, sir. But it doesn't seem to help."

"Hmmppff," Cap Gray grumbled. "Tomorrow's Sunday, do you go to the chapel service at eight?"

"Yes sir."

"Be at the gym early, Mr. Nagle—5 a.m. tomorrow."

Ollie was up and dressed before reveille. It was bitter cold and windy. With his reefer collar turned up around his ears and his stomach growling for breakfast, he made his way along Post Walk in the dark. When he reached the gymnasium, the front doors were unlocked and stepping inside, he heard the unmistakable sound of a basketball on the gym floor.

"You're late, Mr. Nagle," Captain Gray grumbled, glancing at his wristwatch. "It's three minutes past five." Wearing his uniform and in stocking feet, the old man had been shooting underhand free throws. "Take off your boots and come out here on the floor—I'll try and teach you a few things."

With Cap Gray coaching him, less than two hours later Ollie was consistently making eight out of ten shots he tried. With each successful free throw, Captain Gray would nod his head and utter satisfied grunts. "It's a combination of eye, mind, and body," Gray said. "Some people are capable of learning it, and some never do. Truth be told, Mr. Nagle, I wasn't certain if you were one of those that could, but that soft glob of fat between your ears seems to be working all right— at least as far as basketball goes."

"Yes sir, thank you, sir."

"Think you can hang onto this newly developed skill for the Onarga game next weekend?"

"I hope so, sir."

"Well, see that you do, Mr. Nagle," Captain Gray said. "And I won't have squandered a Sunday morning in vain."

"Sir—excuse me, sir—but what you said about the eye, mind, and body, is that how you hardly ever miss when you toss chalk in class?"

Cap Gray grunted again as he tied his shoes and stood up, and just for an instant, Ollie thought he saw a twinkle in the old man's eye. "I was forced to develop that talent, Mr. Nagle—as a remedy against the tedium that results from year upon year of attempting to drum the beauty and balance of higher mathematics into classes of melon heads like yourself."

"Yes sir," Ollie said, holding back a grin as Frank Gray turned on his heel and made his way toward the gymnasium doors and out into the chill morning air.

CHAPTER 6

▼

SATURDAY NIGHT WITH SALLY RAND

Spring Term, 1933

Cadet Sgt. Tommy Lentz wiped sweat from his forehead as he put the final touches on his spit shined full dress black brogans. It was the last Friday in May, classes were over for the week, and by late afternoon the day was still sweltering hot.

Half the corps was marching tomorrow morning. As a member of Morgan Park Military Academy's color guard, Tommy would carry the Stars and Stripes—not in just another of the Academy's routine weekend parades, but as escort to the Queen of the Century of Progress and her court, at the opening of the 1933 Century of Progress Exposition.

Three military high schools had been chosen to take part in the opening day parade and ceremonies—Morgan Park, St. John's Military Academy from Delafield, Wisconsin, and Culver Military Academy from Culver, Indiana.

"Looks like Culver gets the cream again," went the grumbling on both the MPMA and St. John's campuses as the announcements had been posted. "They get to march with the army and navy while the rest of us bring up the rear."

"I don't know about that," Tommy Lentz maintained. "Escort duty for the queen is okay by me. I saw her picture in last Sunday's *Trib*. Her name's Lillian Anderson and she's a real hot patootie. I won't mind bringing up a rear like that."

"Speakin' of rears," Sol Schwartz suggested. "Maybe we get a bunch of the guys and go to the Exposition some Saturday. I heard they got a hootchy-kootchy show. Some dame named Sally Rand."

"C'mon Solly," someone kidded. "Good little Jewish boy like you? What's the rabbi gonna say?"

"He can't say much," Sol laughed. "You oughta see the *tuchis* on *his* wife."

Sol Schwartz became popular early in his MPMA career. At the start of his freshman year, he'd come upon an old shoebox in his father's closet. It held more than twenty of the most popular eight-pagers in circulation at the time—*Maggie & Jiggs, Tillie the Toiler, Popeye,* and all the rest. He smuggled the box to school and the dirty little comic books, eventually becoming dog-eared and torn, were passed around Hansen Hall barracks for more than a decade afterward. Sol never bothered to return them to his father's closet, and although Mr. Schwartz suspected his son to be the thief, he'd been far too mortified to grill him about their whereabouts.

Held to commemorate the one-hundredth anniversary of the city's incorporation and the fortieth anniversary of Chicago's first world's fair, the Century of Progress Exposition was scheduled to run from May through November of 1933.

The exposition was officially billed as a celebratory tribute to the growth of science and industry during the previous hundred years. The sprawling Hall of Science dominated the central section of the fairgrounds. Inside the hall, exhibits paid homage to recent breakthroughs in science and technology.

One explained the process by which petroleum was refined into gasoline. Another delved into the realm of atomic physics by examining the behavior of cathode rays in vacuum tubes.

The Electrical Building dazzled visitors with demonstrations of neon gas lighting, while the Travel and Transport Building explained recent innovations in automobiles and aircraft. The main purpose behind these exhibits was to educate the public as to the benefits of scientific research and technological discovery.

But for most visitors the Century of Progress Exposition was not so much about the past achievements of science as it was about rekindling hope for a more pleasurable, more prosperous future.

Designed as a sprawling wonderland of leisure attractions, the Exposition amused fairgoers by partially gratifying their dreams for a more carefree way of life.

The colorful, fun-filled Midway, the double-decked Dance Ship, the risqué Streets of Paris peep show, the lakeside bathing beach, the lively Pabst Blue Ribbon Casino, and the popular, twin-towered Sky Ride gave cash-strapped Chicagoans and thousands of out-of-town visitors the opportunity to indulge in a broad variety of urban pleasures even though most were suffering from almost four years of grim, unrelenting Depression.

Chartered buses carrying two companies of MPMA cadets left the campus at six o'clock on Saturday morning. By the time they arrived at the staging area, the cadets were already hot and itching in their wool full dress blouses.

As Tommy Lentz carefully adjusted his double-strap leather carrier, making sure the flag mount was secure, he took position in front of a series of red floats that held Queen Lillian Anderson and her court—fifty pretty girls costumed in white and cream dresses, with broad-brimmed hats of red. Queen Lillian sat in a red throne under a feathery red canopy and Tommy would later swear that he saw her smile and wave at him.

Tommy looked up to see sausage-shaped, fat blimps from the Great Lakes Naval Aviation Base floating overhead. Soft, white puffs of smoke and parachutes of bursting bombs filled the sky.

The scheduled line of march was along Michigan Avenue and down a ramp into the vast bowl of Soldier Field Stadium, where Morgan Park's varsity football team had won tickets to watch the Chicago Bears play the Chicago Cardinals earlier that year.

Starting the parade was the band from the Board of Trade Post of the American Legion, with its blue and white uniforms, massed banners and two drum majors. They arrived on the field as they played "America." The crowd stood and remained standing as the postmaster-general; James A. Farley, Governor Horner, Mayor Edward J. Kelly and other officials rode into the stadium in black Packard touring cars.

Then a squadron of thirty-six Boeing F4Bs, soaring wing to wing, roared over—so low they seemed scarcely likely to clear the tower of the Sky Ride—and following them was another group of eighteen aircraft. This was the signal for the arrival of the regular army and navy contingents along with the troop of Culver cadets.

A band playing the caisson song preceded a rolling exhibit of nickel-plated cannon—one gun from each battery of the 122nd Field Artillery and behind them rode the famed Black Horse troop of Culver Military academy—horses glistening ebony and their riders uniformed in gray and white.

Color and shadow were constantly flowing as other marching groups completed their entrance and circuit of the field. Fife and drum corps in maroon and scarlet, mauve, red, and purple. Bands in kilts skirling bagpipes. Bands in khaki and red streaming with ribbons and twirling long white sticks on deep red drums. Colored legionnaires with silver trumpets and royal blue coats. Blue jackets in serge and white. Polish veterans in horizon blue and Boy Scout troops in olive drab and brilliant green.

Then national groups followed the military and semi military organizations to add further detail to the scene. Irish and Greek and Armenian, Swiss and Italian and German. To Tommy Lentz, it looked like something out of the newsreels.

The parade ended at just past noon. Then came the speeches of the dignitaries, followed by the singing of the National Anthem by Cyrena Van Gordon, the popular mezzo-contralto of the Chicago Opera Company, and the ceremonial introduction of Postmaster-General Farley to Queen Lillian. Flags of all nations were released on small parachutes from more aerial bombs over Soldier Field, a document was signed with an official pen and the 1933 Century of Progress Exposition was formally opened.

Early next Saturday morning, Tommy Lentz, Ed Volpe, and Sol Schwartz checked out of Hansen Hall barracks on an overnight pass. They hurriedly changed into civilian clothes and boarded the Western Ave. streetcar—the first of a series of transfers that would deposit them at the south exposition entrance off 34th Street.

"Hot damn," Ed Volpe exclaimed as they put down their fifty cents for admission at the gate. "It sure looks like there's a helluva lot to see."

"Where do you guys wanna start?" Tommy asked.

"Where's the hootchy-kootz?" Sol Schwartz said with a laugh. "Just point me in that direction."

"Dunno," Ed said, scratching his head. "Maybe we better ask somebody—this place is so big."

They walked north until they met a pimply, redheaded boy not much older than themselves. On his shirt, the fellow was wearing an official Century of Progress employee badge. He was sweeping the walkway and picking up trash.

"Say," Sol said, approaching the street sweeper. "Where's the hootchy-kootchy dancer at—that Sally Rand?"

The boy stopped for a moment and looked up from his work. To Sol, the sweeper's eyes looked tired and rheumy. "Miss Rand? Well, I guess I can tell you—but I gotta get a tip out of it—gimme a nickel."

"Sure," Sol said, digging into his pocket for a coin. He flipped the five-cent piece in the air and the sweeper caught it.

The red-haired boy pointed past them, to the north. "Miss Rand's up that way, in the *Streets of Paris* village. You fellas got a long walk to get there."

"Thanks pal," Sol said, eagerly turning toward his friends. "So what are we waitin' for? Let's go."

"Wait a minute," Tommy offered. "If we go see her first off, then we'll be bored the rest of the day. Maybe we ought to save the kootch dancer for last and look at some of the other stuff first."

Ed Volpe agreed. "Let's go on some of the coasters."

"Aww, okay," Sol agreed unenthusiastically, relenting to the majority vote. Then, with the wicked promise of Miss Sally Rand and her infamous fan dance to cap off the day, the three MPMA cadets were off to see the fair.

Along the way, they ignored such attractions as the Ukrainian Pavilion and the Poultry Show, the Pageant of Transportation and the Gas Industry Hall—heading instead for the roller coaster rides and the soaring span of the Sky Ride, near the North Lagoon.

"Hey, how about the Sky Ride?" Ed Volpe suggested, pointing toward the two imposing towers. "The newspapers say you can see four states from the top—they're sixty-four stories high."

The climb to the top of the towers took less than one minute in Otis Automatic High-Speed Elevators. When they stepped out onto the steel observation deck, Tommy felt his knees go rubbery and his stomach turn. He'd never been up so high in his life.

"Jeez, will'ya take a look at that," he said, forcing himself to edge closer to the railing. Chicago's buildings, factories and homes sprawled away as far as they could see, and on the opposite side of the platform, the bright and sparkling blue of the big lake stretched eastward to the faint shoreline of New Buffalo, in Michigan.

Ed shook his head and whistled through his teeth. "Everything sure looks different from this high up."

"How can I tell I'm lookin' at four states, though?" Sol asked, craning his neck.

"Well, you just are," Ed told him. "It ain't all marked, like it is on a Chicago Motor Club map."

Skeptical, Sol shook his head. "Four states—that's probably just bullshit they tell you."

The three boys stood on the observation deck for ten minutes or so, trying to locate their neighborhoods. Ed Volpe even thought he could see his house, but he wasn't sure. Finally, growing bored, they took the elevator back down to the lower level and got aboard one of the "Rocket" cars for the tram ride over the Science Bridge that separated the north and south lagoons.

Steel cable overhead tracks connected the towers and gave an unmatched observation ride from the double-decked rocket shaped cars suspended beneath the rails. The cars had been built to give an unobstructed view in all directions, and as the boys peered out the windows, a traction cable took four minutes to draw them across the span. There were ten cars that made the trip, each one in charge of a certified aerial pilot.

Back down on the ground, they sought out a few of the rides they'd heard about—the Flying Turns and the Cyclone, along with the much tamer Whirl-O-Plane—all three of which turned out to be disappointing.

"Hell, that Sky Ride was okay," Sol said. "But they got better coasters at Riverview."

Tommy and Ed agreed, "You can't beat the Bobs."

When lunchtime came, they stopped at one of the refreshment stands that were scattered all over the grounds, wolfing down hot dogs, mealy tamales and bags of greasy French fries, washed down with Dixie cups full of Coca-Cola. When their stomachs were full, they strolled aimlessly around the fair, taking in certain attractions and ignoring others.

They were fascinated by a gadget called television, on display at the Electrical Building. For one of the demonstrations, Sol was called out from the audience and brought on stage to stand in front of a camera and appear on the flickering screen. Self-conscious and trying to be funny, the best Sol Schwartz could think to do was make faces and thumb his nose at his friends.

"You're a real comedian," Tommy told him.

"Yeah," Ed added as they walked back out onto the Midway. "A regular Buster Keaton."

Just as they passed the Midget Village, Ed heard a man's deep voice shouting out to him: "Hey kid, how 'bout you try your luck? Dunk the jigaboo and win a prize!"

The concession was called the "African Dip," and consisted of a colored man who sat inside a large cage, perched on a delicately balanced platform over a tank of water. Promoters had proudly declared the World's Fair open to Negroes as well as whites. But most of the colored people who managed to land jobs there wound up shining shoes or tending washrooms. A few, like the fellow in the cage, worked as targets in the African Dip—a Midway frolic in which a customer's well-thrown baseball would plunge the caged black man into a pool of water.

The concession owner took money and handed out baseballs while the Negro's job was to hurl insults at white male passers-by, attempting to goad them into spending money to throw balls at the round dunk tank lever—three pitches for a quarter.

"That don't look like such a bad job on a hot day," Ed pointed out. "Why don'cha give it a try, Sol?"

"I've seen that guy before," Sol said. "He works the jig tank at Riverview, too."

"Hey c'mon, white boy," the Negro called out, pointing at Sol. "Win them two girlfren's of yours a cupie doll."

"Girlfriends?" Tommy said, annoyed. "I got a quarter. I guess I'll show the burr head who he's callin' a girl."

"Dunk him," Sol laughed as Tommy took three balls from the man running the show. "Get Sambo wet!"

"Onliest thing wet is maybe yo' pants," the Negro taunted.

"Sonofabitch," Tommy grunted as he fired the first ball high and to the left. It smashed harmlessly into the cage.

The black man was laughing and bounced up and down on his platform. "C'mon—try it again, you peckerwood ofay!"

"In you go, coon," Tommy growled, throwing low and inside, and bouncing it off the wooden tank.

"Oh my, you jumpin' salty, now," jeered the dip in the cage.

"Is you Amos or is you Andy?" Tommy shouted back, laughing at his own wit. But he had only one ball left.

"Ah's yo' momma's sugah daddy," the black man shot back with a wide grin. "That's who I is."

Tommy stopped suddenly, glancing over at the man who was selling tickets. "Hey mister, that spade's talkin' about my mother—you gonna let him get away with that?"

The ticket man lit a cigarette, "Just shut up and throw the ball, kid. He don' mean nothin'—he gets paid for talkin' that way."

Tommy's third pitch was right on the money. It hit the release mechanism and the black man was unceremoniously dumped into water up to his chest. He made a big show of coughing and spitting water as he quickly jumped back up to his perch.

"How about my prize?" Tommy asked.

"You only dunked him once, kid," the shil said. "Three out of three gets you a prize."

"Man, what a gyp."

The ticket man shrugged. "Tough luck, kid—try it again."

"Dat all you got, white boy?" The dip shouted out, looking for another quarter. "You throw like yo' momma."

"I might be dumb," Tommy said as they walked away. "But I ain't stupid."

They went on to watch a man wearing a pith helmet and boots wrestle with an alligator, they stared at the oddities inside Ripley's Believe It-Or-Not attraction—a fellow who could completely turn his head around on his shoulders, a married couple who were able to lift heavy weights with only their eyelids, and a man named Leo Kongee, who called himself "The Human Pincushion."

By early evening, Sol Schwartz was getting impatient. "Okay, ain't we seen enough? It's gettin' dark—time for the main event. Let's go see Sally Rand."

All the Chicago newspapers were in a tizzy about Sally Rand and her fan dance at the fair. Both editorials and the Letters to the Editor sections had been debating both sides of the dancer's risqué performance all week long, and Sol was fearful of the show being shut down by the city before he had a chance to see it.

They made their way to an attraction whose entrance had been constructed to resemble a renowned steamship of the French Line—the famous *Ile de France*. Inside the entrance was to be found the "Streets of Paris," where a sign read: *"Here's where you'll get your real French atmosphere. Cafés and bars, artist quarters, shows, dancing, shops, street scenes, and free continuous entertainment—with no cover charge."*

"Hot damn," was all Sol could say as they bought tickets and stepped into a long line of men waiting in front of a fake cabaret to see Miss Rand's fan dance.

Once inside, the house lights dimmed, the music began, and an announcer's voice intoned: "Ladies and gentlemen, I give you the one and only Miss Sally Rand." Then, a single spotlight came up, illuminating Miss Rand in all her glory as she descended a set of red velvet steps, shielded only by her flowing blonde hair and two large, pink ostrich-feather fans.

"Jeez, will you get a load of that," Sol whispered to Tommy as Sally Rand began her graceful dance. "She's butt naked."

"I ain't so sure," Tommy said, squinting through the smoky air of the cabaret.

"Whaddaya mean?" Sol questioned. "Just look at her."

Unknown to the audience, Sally Rand's nudity was actually a flesh-colored body stocking. But whatever the reality, the illusion was sensational. As the diminutive blonde dancer manipulated the two ostrich fans that concealed and revealed both everything and nothing at all, most of the men in the room were fooled.

"Jeez, I think I saw it," Sol exclaimed excitedly.

"Saw what?" Ed Volpe asked. He didn't think he'd seen much of anything yet.

"Y'know—her coozie. I think I saw it."

"Aw, you're seein' things," Ed said, annoyed that he couldn't say the same, and straining to get a better look.

Suddenly, Tommy hushed them both. "Holy crap," he said in a low voice. "I don't believe it."

Sol and Ed looked in the direction Tommy was staring and for a moment, they couldn't believe it either. Across the room, directly to their left and dressed in civilian clothes sat Capt. Francis S. Gray—and to their horror, he seemed to be staring back at them through his familiar round spectacles.

"What the hell is Captain Gray doin' here?" Sol asked in some befuddlement.

"It's a free country," Tommy muttered. "I guess he can come to a World's Fair if he wants to."

"What do we do now?" Ed Volpe asked, unbelieving.

"Just watch the rest of the show, I guess," Tommy offered. "I don't know what else to do."

Five minutes before Miss Rand finished her performance, Cap Gray stood up and left the room. The boys saw him go, but none of them knew what his leaving might mean.

When the show was ended and the whistles and applause died down, the boys got in line to exit, hoping they'd somehow be hard to spot in the crowd.

When they were back on the Midway, Tommy was thankful it was dark—but only for a moment. He stiffened when he heard Cap Gray call out their names.

"Mr. Lentz, Mr. Volpe, Mr. Schwartz."

Frank Gray was standing outside the entrance, eating a vanilla ice cream cone. The boys had no other option but to approach him.

"Captain Gray, good evening sir," Sol said lamely.

"Good evening, boys—here to brush up on your French?"

"Well sir, no sir—uh, we were just, I mean we—"

"I know, I know," Cap Gray said, nodding. "I've been reading the papers and I was somewhat curious, myself."

"Yes sir," the boys said as one.

"Mrs. Gray is off inspecting the House of Tomorrow," Captain Gray explained sheepishly. "So I decided to wander over here to see what this fan dance fuss was all about."

"Same here, sir," Ed Volpe interjected.

Captain Gray looked at him. "And what conclusions have you come to, Mr. Volpe?"

"Well, sir, I—I mean we—well, I guess I don't know."

"How about you, Mr. Schwartz?"

"Same here, sir," Sol mumbled.

"What did *you* think of it, sir?" Tommy asked boldly.

Captain Gray grunted, finishing his ice cream. "I've come to the conclusion that people are funny, Mr. Lentz. Some object to the fan dancer and others object to the fans."

"Yes sir, I think you're right about that."

"Monday's my college algebra examination," Gray reminded them. "Are you fellows ready for it?"

"Yes sir," they replied in unison.

"Good, good," the captain said. "And I see no reason why any reference to this evening's scholarly diversion should be discussed any further on or about the campus—do you?"

"Oh, no sir," Tommy volunteered. "None at all."

"Splendid," Cap Gray said with a nod. "I wish you the best of luck in your examinations, gentlemen—good evening."

"Good evening, sir."

As their mathematics instructor strolled off toward the House of Tomorrow, Sol Schwartz giggled in glee. "How about that," he chuckled. "We got the old bastard right where we want him."

"How's that?" Ed asked.

"Right in our pockets, you dummy. Cap Gray can't ever give us an F anymore. We got too much on him now."

Tommy shook his head. "I wouldn't bet on that, Solly. If I was you, I wouldn't bet on that at all."

Sol Schwartz nodded. "Yeah, maybe you're right."

They walked for a while without talking. Finally Sol broke the silence. "Say, did you fellas see it?"

"See what?"

"Her coozie—Sally Rand's cooz. Did you see it?"

"Nope," Tommy replied.

"Me neither," Ed said.

"Well I sure did," Sol gloated happily.

"I wouldn't bet on that, either," Ed Volpe muttered.

CHAPTER 7

▼

A MATTER OF HONOR

It was an unusually mild evening for October in Chicago. Almost seven o'clock at night, Frank Gray noted as he glanced at the small thermometer on the porch, and the temperature was still holding at nearly sixty-eight degrees.

He lit a Chesterfield cigarette and slowly settled into the worn wicker chair they usually kept out on the porch until the first snow. He and Anna had just returned from dinner at Mess III, and as he drew on the cigarette, he heard her call from inside the house. "Are you wearing your overcoat, Frank?"

"I am," he called back, amused that even after all their years together she still tended to fuss and treat him like a child.

"Why not come inside?" His wife asked, opening the screen door and looking at him. "You act like it's the Fourth of July."

"Wanted to sit by myself and think for a while," Captain Gray said, adding, "Without having to listen to all your chatter."

"Is something wrong, Frank?" Anna asked, stepping out of the doorway a little further.

Frank Gray sighed. "It's the matter of the Stolley boy."

Anna shook her head sadly. "Such a shame about that boy, and he was such a fine student, too. Will he be expelled?"

"Of course," Gray snorted, "as he deserves to be. The boy's a thief—he stole from his teammates and his friends."

Anna Gray was puzzled by both the story and her husband's sudden preoccupation with it. Cadet Edwin Stolley, a junior on the varsity team, asked to be excused from afternoon football practice four days earlier, saying that his stomach hurt. Coach Woodworth had promptly agreed, telling the boy to shower and report to Nurse Blachly at the infirmary.

Finding himself alone in the locker room, Ed Stolley had gone through every locker he found unlocked and took all the money he could find from the unguarded wallets of his classmates. Not only was it a violation of the Academy's rigid honor code, it was in fact the *worst* violation of the code anyone could remember.

Questioned by Coach Woodworth the next day, the boy at first refused to admit guilt. Questioned further, Stolley finally confessed that he'd stolen the cash and had planned the theft for weeks.

The Guardians Disciplinary Committee had promptly met to consider the case. The Guardians were an elected group of cadets who acted as a link between the administration and the Corps—and Captain Gray was their faculty advisor this year.

"The boy will be expelled," he told his wife. "That's beyond question. But a number of cadets feel strongly that stealing money from friends and teammates goes far beyond merely just expulsion. The Disciplinary Committee wants to make an example of Stolley by publicly drumming him out of the Corps, and I'm not sure that I approve."

"Can you stop it?" Anna Gray asked.

Frank Gray sighed and shook his head. "The Guardians belong to the cadets," he told her. "I may be their faculty advisor, but my interference with any decision they make would invite resentment and weaken their purpose.

"We meet tomorrow to discuss it," he went on. "So I'll listen as they make their case. But in the end, the decision is theirs. I can only advise."

"Come inside the house, Frank," Anna said. "Before the night turns cold."

After classes the next day, the Disciplinary Committee met in the cadet lounge, on the second floor of Alumni Hall. It consisted of five senior cadets and Captain Gray.

"The theft was premeditated," argued Cadet Capt. Bob Faulk who was the primary spokesman for the group. "And Stolley stole from fellas he's known and played football with since plebe year."

Frank Gray grunted. "Why not just expel the boy, Mr. Faulk? One day Cadet Stolley is here, the next day he's gone—clean as a whistle. Why do you think such a public ceremony is necessary?"

"I think just sweeping it under the rug is a mistake, sir," Bob Faulk said. "Because he not only stole their money, but betrayed the trust of his teammates and friends, I'm convinced that a harsh example should be made."

"But drumming out?"

"Yes sir," Faulk answered. "A drumming out ceremony would have two positive effects: it would deter anyone else from stealing again, and it will make other cadets think long and hard about their actions before disobeying the school's honor code."

"Has it ever been done before?" Cap Gray asked.

"I don't think so, sir—at least not at MPMA. But it *is* a routine punishment at the Virginia Military Institute."

Captain Gray looked at the others. "Do all of you agree on this matter?"

"Yes sir," answered Cadet Capt. Rudy Stiles. "We've talked it over and we're all in agreement, sir."

"What are *your* reasons, Mr. Stiles?"

"Sir, I believe this will be beneficial to Stolley later in life. It will teach him a valuable lesson that perhaps would not be taught if he receives a lighter punishment."

Captain Gray grunted. "When I was just a small boy, I stole a fancy pearl-handled pocketknife from our town's hardware store—have you ever done anything like that, Mr. Stiles?"

"Yes sir," Stiles said. "But I never stole from my friends."

Nodding, Frank Gray leaned back in his leather chair, looking at each cadet in turn. Their sentiments were unanimous and as grim as the procedure might prove to be, he felt it was their duty to carry out the honor code, not his.

"You're all of the same mind?" He asked again, as each of the five senior cadets nodded in agreement.

"Very well then," Captain Gray assented. "But being that I'm your faculty advisor—let me advise you of something.

"This will be a very degrading thing for young Stolley to go through," Gray went on. "It will be a hard thing for the Corps to be a part of, and I suspect that, as those making the decision to press on with this punishment, each of you may find it weighing heavily on your minds for some time to come."

At the close of AMSF two days later, a long snare drum roll was heard, then followed by a single repeated bass drum beat. At the order of the battalion commander, company commanders and platoon leaders brought their units into line formation, forming two long ranks on either side of Post Walk—a silent gauntlet stretching from the front doors of Hansen Hall barracks to 112th Street where it was being whispered that Ed Stolley's grandparents were parked and waiting for him in their car.

The entire Corps of Cadets stood facing each other as Stolley appeared at the barracks door, escorted by two cadets. He carried a suitcase and was dressed in civilian clothes. As the grim beat of the drum continued, Stolley began his hundred-yard walk toward the street and off the campus. As he passed them, each cadet did an about face, turning their back to him. Stolley's chin trembled and there were tearful streaks on his face. A few cadets were hesitant to turn their backs as squad leaders broke ranks and physically forced them to do so.

Stolley's long, painful march through the two gray lines of his fellow cadets and toward the green sedan waiting on 112th Street was a study in humiliation. His shoulders shaking, the boy trudged slowly forward between his silent escorts. It seemed as if he forced himself on only through sheer power of will, until he stumbled the last twenty yards and began to run, following his suitcase into the back seat of the Buick, which hurriedly pulled away.

It was over. The order rang out and was echoed throughout the quiet, subdued ranks. "Battalion—*dismissed.*"

Three weeks later, Cadet Faulk lingered after Captain Gray's college algebra class. "Sir," Faulk said, once the room was empty. "Can I speak to you for a minute."

Cap Gray had already started erasing notes and equations from the board. He stopped and looked over his glasses. "What's on your mind, Mr. Faulk?"

"It's about Ed Stolley, sir," Faulk said hesitantly. "How he left the Academy."

"What about it?"

"Well, sir—the thing is, I guess I'm not feeling too good about it. I was for the drumming out, but now I'm not so sure we should have gone that far."

Gray nodded and put down the eraser. "The other boys feel the same way? Mr. Stiles and the rest of them?"

"All of them, yes sir."

"What's changed your feelings?"

Bob Faulk shook his head. "The five of us talked to Stolley the night before he left. He told us he'd hoped for a second chance, but he wasn't surprised when he learned he was getting kicked out."

Faulk hesitated a moment, then went on. "But he was shocked when we told him how he'd be leaving. Stolley said he didn't know what drumming out was. He started to cry when we told him what it meant and that it was the first time anyone had been drummed out of the Academy. I guess all of us are wondering if we went too far, sir. After it was over, we never thought it would be that hard to do."

Captain Gray nodded. His khaki shirt was smudged with white chalk. "Well, maybe you fellows learned something. Humiliating a person is different from punishing them, and degradation is much different from disgrace. I could have stopped you, but the cadets created the honor code and elected you five boys to enforce it.

"Cadet Stolley was the worst sort of thief," Cap Gray went on. "The boy chose to put personal gain before personal honor, and did it by betraying his comrades. With this in mind, his dismissal was justified."

"But not the drumming out?" Faulk asked.

Frank Gray shook his head. "I wouldn't have done it that way, Mr. Faulk. On the other hand, the boy wasn't forced. Stolley could have left the Academy anytime he wished without marching down that sidewalk. Instead, he took his punishment like a man."

"That might be part of what's bothering us," Faulk said.

"Wouldn't surprise me," Cap Gray told him. "It's learning that nothing is black and white—especially people. None of us are all bad or all good, Mr. Faulk—we all have feet of clay."

"Maybe you should have stopped us, sir."

"Maybe," the captain shrugged. "But instead I chose to forfeit a boy who'd already disgraced himself, hoping you and the others might learn that authority comes with a responsibility to do things right. If you fellows are suffering mixed feelings about what was done, then learn from those feelings.

"You've been sent here to receive an education, Mr. Faulk," Captain Gray went on. "And sometimes you just don't get it out of books."

CHAPTER 8

▼

SOMEBODY'S FATHER,
SOMEBODY'S SON

Fall Term, 1938

Cadet Alfie Potter first saw the one-armed tramp early in the fall semester, on his way to catch the streetcar home from school.

Beginning his junior year at MPMA, Alfie was a day student and each afternoon after classes were over, he'd board the streetcar on 111th and Western and take it to 67th Street, then walk seven blocks west to the small brick bungalow on Fairfield Avenue that his folks had mortgaged in 1926 when times were better.

These dark days, with the Depression stubbornly hanging on, Alfie's father was grateful to still have his shift supervisor's job at Commonwealth Edison. Depression or no, the city still needed its electricity, and as long as it did, Herb Potter suspected his job was fairly secure—but he never knew for sure.

The tramp with one arm looked to be a sad case. Sitting on the sidewalk next to a barbershop, he was getting all he could out of a cigarette butt no more than half an inch long. His hair was gray and scraggly and fell down around his ears. His right eye seemed permanently shut, and his clothing was dirty and ragged. What few things he owned—a quilted furniture pad that once belonged to the Bekins Moving Company and now served as his blanket, a pair of black rubber galoshes, a muffler and a right-handed glove, a few dog-eared books and tattered magazines, and a cardboard sign that said *On the skids—spare change?* were carried along with him in a rusting old Radio Flyer wagon.

The first time Alfie walked past, he'd avoided looking at the fellow, but the next afternoon their eyes met for a moment and the man nodded at him, tapping a finger on his cardboard sign. Alfie stopped, dug into his pocket and brought out a nickel.

"That's all I got," Alfie said. "The rest is car fare."

The beggar nodded again and Alfie briefly wondered if other people ever gave the fellow money, or if he was just letting himself be played for a sucker. "How much you made today, mister?" He asked, curious.

"A buck, maybe," the beggar said. "Not countin' your nickel."

Alfie laughed. "Heck, that's more'n I got in *my* pocket."

"You got a home, ain'tcha?"

"Sure," Alfie answered.

"Well kid, that's more'n what's in my pockets, too."

By nature and temperament Alfie Potter was a curious boy, ill suited to rules and regulations. His was a freer spirit, his eye on the horizon, his youthful imagination fired by what wonders might lay beyond it.

His parents were exactly the opposite. Theirs was the need for comfort and security. They'd rarely traveled far from home, were prudent with their money, and these days his father seemed always tense and nervous, obsessed with keeping his job at Edison.

The next day, the beggar wasn't there and Alfie didn't see him again for nearly a week. The boy wondered if anything happened to him. Maybe the coppers picked him up, Alfie thought, they were always putting the collar on bums and hobos these days.

But the following Monday the man was back on the sidewalk, sitting in exactly the same place. "Whaddya know, kid?" He called out as Alfie was walking toward the streetcar stop. "Can you spare another dime?"

"I gave you a nickel last time," Alfie told him.

The one-armed beggar shrugged. "No harm in tryin' kid." he grinned, nodding at the gray cadet uniform Alfie wore. "You some kinda sojer boy, or what?"

"Military school," Alfie said, pointing over his shoulder. "Just down the street."

"Yeah," the man laughed. "I was a sojer, once. In the war."

"That how you lost your arm?"

The beggar laughed and shook his head. "Hell, I come through that war without a scratch. Had me the shits a few times, but that's all. *Naw,* I lost it tryin' to nail a fast freight out of Indianapolis and bound for Terre Haute. That was five years ago."

"Did it hurt? Losing your arm, I mean."

The man gave a snort. "Damned right it hurt. The stiff with me tied his belt around what was left. It was a tourniquet, I guess, and it saved my bacon for sure."

"My name's Alfie Potter," Alfie said, putting out his hand.

The man shook it. "You can call me Fly."

"Fly?" Alfie asked. "What kind of name is that?"

"It's my stiff name," Fly said. "My moniker. But, I guess Fly ain't such a good one anymore—with one wing gone, and all."

"What's a stiff?"

"A tramp, a hobo—like me," Fly told him. "Don't they teach you kids nothin' in that school?"

Alfie reached into his coat pocket, dug another nickel out, and placed it in Fly's hand. "Well, I gotta go, Mr. Fly. That streetcar's about due. Maybe I'll see you tomorrow."

"Sure kid, see you tomorrow."

All the way home and later that night, Alfie thought about the tramp who called himself Fly. What was his life like? Did he have family somewhere? How would it be to travel around the country as free as the wind? He couldn't imagine. All of his life, Alfie had been in school—first at St. Margaret's Grammar School, where the nuns were so strict, then at Morgan Park Military Academy where regulations and rules dominated everything. To have the freedom Fly enjoyed was beyond Alfie Potter's ability to imagine.

In Captain Gray's solid geometry class the next day, Alfie was standing at his desk, having a great deal of difficulty explaining the isometries of an irregular tetrahedron.

"Did you study the lesson last night, Mr. Potter?" Gray asked.

"Sir, I—yes sir, I studied, but I—couldn't—"

"Sit down then," Cap Gray barked impatiently. "Don't inflict your ignorance on the rest of the class."

Alfie was embarrassed and angry at himself for having let his concentration wander the night before when he should have been studying. He hadn't been able to get Fly off his mind—or the siren song of absolute freedom and the open road.

He often spent time in the Academy library, just turning pages of a Chicago Motor Club road atlas, studying the names of cities and towns all over the country, playing the sound of them over his tongue—Kalamazoo, Albuquerque, Broken Bow, Oshkosh. Thief River Falls, Winnemucca, San Francisco, Duluth.

Alfie knew all the cities and all the roads that led to them—if you were going east to west there would be Route 66 from Chicago to California, the Pike's Peak Ocean-to-Ocean, the National White Way, National Roosevelt Midland Trail and the Victory Highway, National Old Trails and New Santa Fe Trail, the Kansas Colorado Boulevard, the Atlantic Pacific Highway, and the Union Pacific Highway. The main north-south road was the Meridian Highway, sometimes shown as the Pan American Highway; others were the Capitol Route in the east and the Red Star Highway in the west.

The boy knew each of them in his imagination and had vowed to someday see them all.

"Hold on, Mr. Potter," Cap Gray grunted as the cadets left his room at the end of class. The instructor sat on the edge of his desk, tapping the floor with his pointer. "You're usually not a dunce, Mr. Potter—care to tell me where your mind was today?"

"I was—I guess I was daydreaming, sir."

"Daydreaming?" Cap Gray questioned. "I'd expect springtime to be the time for daydreams, not the first cold days of winter."

"I daydream all the time, sir," Alfie admitted.

"That so? What about?"

"Traveling mostly—bumming around the country."

Cap Gray nodded. "Bumming, huh? Well, lots of young fellas doing it these days, I suppose. But as far as I can tell, all you learn from bumming is how to be a better bum."

"Yes sir."

"You're a third-year man, now, Mr. Potter," Gray pointed out. "And the rest of your time in this school will go by pretty fast. You giving any thought to what you'll do after graduation?"

"College, I guess," Alfie mumbled.

"You guess? Don't you know, son?"

"My folks want me to, sir, so I probably will."

Cap Gray grunted again. "But you'd rather go on the bum?"

Alfie shrugged. He'd grown tired of the conversation. Captain Gray had rooted himself at MPMA back in 1917—that was more than twenty years ago. The old man might know his algebra, Alfie thought, but what could he know about being young and restless, about lying in bed at night, listening to the mournful whistle of the GM&O or the Wabash, and wondering where they were bound and what the rest of the country was like?

"I don't know, sir—I think about it sometimes."

Gray nodded. "You've got a bad case of wanderlust, son. I had it myself when I was a pup. All I can tell you is it isn't fatal."

The next day the city had snow flurries, the first of the season, and Alfie stopped in to talk to Al Jasinski and John Halper, the two men who ran the MPMA tailor shop.

"What happens to old uniforms?" Alfie asked.

"We send them back to the Charlottesville Woolen Mills," Al told him. "We get a small credit on the fabric."

"Any chance I could have an old reefer, Mr. Jasinski?"

"I suppose we got a few. What do you need it for?"

Alfie shrugged, nervous about asking. "Well, this fella I know—he's got no home and it looks like winter's coming."

"Charity case, huh?" John Halper said.

"Sort of," Alfie told him.

"Sure, I guess we can spare an old one for a good cause," John said. "The elbows will be worn out though."

"I brought you a warm coat, Mr. Fly," Alfie said, handing him the heavy wool reefer he'd gotten from the tailor shop. "It's got a nice high collar. You don't want to be out here this winter with just that skimpy jacket."

Fly was in his usual place, sitting on the sidewalk and reading a torn, tattered copy of *Ace High Magazine.* His cap was lying on the concrete and Alfie noticed two dimes and a quarter in it.

"Well, lookit that," Fly chuckled. The gray cadet coat still had staff sergeant's chevrons sewn on its sleeves. "Looks like I'm back in uniform, don't it, kid?"

"It's pretty worn out," Alfie said. "But it should be okay."

"Much obliged, kid. I owe ya."

"What's it like, being a hobo, Mr. Fly?"

The one-armed man looked up at him. "Why? You thinkin' of takin' up the trade?"

"I was just wondering."

Fly shook his head, pulling the reefer on right over his lighter windbreaker. "Well, I ain't a hobo no more, kid, just a tramp and a beggar. Nobody can nail a drag with only one arm, so I don' travel too far anymore, and I get where I'm goin' on foot."

"But what *was* it like?" Alfie pestered. "When you could still do it, I mean."

Fly reached into the windbreaker's pocket and took out a half-smoked cigarette. He lit it with a wooden match and leaned back against a wall. "Not too bad," Fly said, exhaling smoke. "I came and went whenever I wanted—heard me some big talk and saw me some big towns—just like the song says."

"Did you ever go to California?" Alfie asked. From everything he'd ever heard or read about California, it sounded like as fine a place as anyone could want to be—warm, sun-splashed weather, coconut palms and beaches, and fresh oranges to be plucked right off the trees.

"Oh sure," Fly said, spitting on the sidewalk. "Been there lots of times—Frisco and Los Angeles. Spent a few days in Hollywood and even saw Bette Davis and Merle Oberon once or twice."

Alfie whistled through his teeth. He'd have given anything to go to California and see all the famous movie stars.

"The bulls was rough in California, though," Fly added. "Hell, they'd bust a stiff's head wide open if they caught him anywheres near the drags."

"Someday, maybe I'll hit the road, too," Alfie boasted, picking up his book bag. It was getting time to meet the streetcar.

Fly nodded, taking a pint of cheap tokay out of the wagon. As he took a long pull on the bottle, Alfie could smell the sweet aroma of the wine. "Say kid," Fly asked, wiping his mouth. "Maybe you got another nickel to go with my new winter coat?"

Finishing his homework early, Alfie joined his parents in their modest living room, where they were enjoying the *Burns and Allen* show on the Philco radio. "Say Pa," Alfie interrupted. "You think we could take a vacation this summer?"

Herb Potter looked up from the radio. "A vacation? You mean leave the house? Go somewhere?"

"Sure," Alfie said. "Drive up to Wisconsin, or maybe even out to California."

"Listen to him," Herb said, turning to his wife.

"Alfie," Loretta Potter explained. "They've canceled vacations at Edison. They had to lay so many off in the last few years that they can't afford to give your father and the other supervisors any time off. Nobody gets vacations anymore."

"Except the big shots, maybe," Herb Potter grumbled.

"I thought you were a big shot, Pa."

"Not hardly, son," Herb said. "Not these days, anyway. Maybe someday we can all take a real trip. Your mother's always wanted to see the Grand Canyon."

Alfie's brain went into overdrive and the Chicago Motor Club road atlas in his head began to work. *The Grand Canyon*—that meant taking Route 66 southwest out of Illinois, down through St. Louis and Joplin, Tulsa and Oklahoma City, on through Amarillo, Texas, to a town in New Mexico named Tucumcari. After that it would be Albuquerque. Once they crossed the Arizona line, they'd pass through Holbrook and Winslow—then north from Flagstaff to the canyon itself. The enchanting place names tumbled through his mind like hard, sweet candies.

"When do you think that'll be, Pa?" Alfie persisted.

Herb Potter shook his head. "Maybe when President Roosevelt gets this damned country back on its feet again."

The Chicago winter came in full force in early December with heavy snow and bitter winds blowing off the big lake. Alfie tried to stop and talk to Fly whenever the tramp was there, giving him a nickel or a dime whenever he could.

As the days grew colder, Fly seemed to get smaller—an effect Alfie suspected, caused by the vagrant trying to bury himself more and more deeply into his layers of clothing.

"Your old man got any whiskey at home?" Fly asked one day. His cheeks and the tip of his nose looked cherry red. "Maybe you could swipe some?"

"Naw," Alfie said. "He doesn't drink. All he does is eat, sleep, listen to the radio, and go to work."

"Sounds like a wage slave to me," Fly suggested, lighting up a cigarette butt he'd found by the curb.

Alfie nodded. "Yeah, my pa works awfully hard."

Fly took a long drag and exhaled the smoke. "My old man was a hard-workin' sonofabitch, too—he was a bargeman on the New York State Canal System, haulin' everything from lumber to table lamps. That old bastard was hardly ever home."

"Is that where you're from, Mr. Fly—New York?"

"Yessir, small town called Palmyra."

Alfie was pretty sure he remembered Palmyra being just south of Lake Ontario. "Have you got family back there?"

Fly nodded, staring off into space. "The old man's still there, I think. He ain't kicked the bucket yet, as far as I know. I got a wife and a little girl back in Palmyra, too. That is if she ain't remarried by now and moved someplace else. I think she might've divorced me after I went on the bum."

Alfie blinked and didn't say anything. He just couldn't picture Fly being a husband and a father, much less somebody's son.

"Workin's for chumps," Fly added. "I picked lettuce once, and even tried sellin' apples and pencils, but it's a helluva lot easier to just panhandle."

Then, Alfie heard a familiar voice. "Hello, Mr. Potter. On your way home?"

The boy turned to see Captain Gray standing behind them. His algebra instructor was bundled up in a woolen army overcoat with the collar turned up against the wind.

"Yes sir," Alfie said. "Sir, this is Mr. Fly."

Looking over the rim of his glasses, Frank Gray peered down at the one-armed vagrant. "How do you do, sir?"

"Nice to meet'cha, General," Fly said, coughing.

"I was on my way to the drugstore to get a few things for Mrs. Gray," the captain said. "Care to walk along with me, Mr. Potter?"

Alfie picked up his briefcase. "Maybe I'll see you tomorrow, Mr. Fly."

"Sure kid," the beggar said, still coughing. "See ya around."

"That a friend of yours, son?" Cap Gray asked as they walked.

"Just a guy I met, sir. I talk to him on my way home."

"That so? What about?"

"Before he lost his arm, sir, he traveled all over the country," Alfie explained earnestly. "I'm hoping he'll tell me about it."

Gray nodded. "I wouldn't put too much into what that fellow tells you, Mr. Potter. He's just a poor soul—he'll be lucky to make it through the winter."

"I brought him a warm coat, sir," Alfie said. "I got it from Mr. Jasinski and Mr. Halper in the tailor shop."

Cap Gray grunted. "I wondered about that reefer—a Christian deed, son, but don't get too friendly with him—and whatever you do, don't give him any money."

Too late for that, Alfie thought. Fly always asked for money and Alfie usually gave it to him—not much, but whatever he could afford. I'd just buy soda pop or a candy bar with those nickels and dimes, the boy reasoned, so he needs them more than me. Besides, he hoped that sooner or later Fly would get around to describing all his travels and adventures on the bum.

"Your pa work pretty hard?" Cap Gray asked as they parted at the corner.

"Yes sir," Alfie told him. "Seems like that's all he does."

"Well then, that's the man to admire," Frank Gray suggested. "Not that unfortunate derelict on the sidewalk who'll fill your head all full of notions. The school you're attending is first-rate, Mr. Potter, but it isn't cheap, and any man who can afford to give his son the fine education you're getting, especially during these tough times, is a man that has to be looked up to—you remember that."

"Yes sir," the boy promised. "I will."

Fly and Alfie rarely talked in the morning. Fly always looked to be asleep and Alfie was usually hurrying to class, with little time to spare. But the first school day after the Thanksgiving holiday, he brought the homeless beggar cornbread stuffing and three pieces of turkey from the family's Frigidaire.

"You gotta eat it cold, I guess," Alfie said.

"That don't make no difference," Fly grunted, wolfing down the food and wiping his mouth on his sleeve when he was done.

"That's the first time I ever saw you eat anything," Alfie said.

"I don' eat much," Fly admitted. "A bag of potato chips from the drugstore, maybe—or some Ritz crackers."

"I'll give you a nickel on my way home," Alfie told him. "But you gotta tell me—I don't know—maybe what Florida's like."

"Florida," Fly repeated, shivering a little. "Sure kid, I'll tell ya all about Florida—I wish to Christ I was there now."

By now, their meetings were predictably routine. Knowing the boy was always good for some spare change, Fly made it a point to be at the same spot each afternoon, and Alfie, knowing Fly would always tell him about some new and exciting place, one adventure or another, was sure to be there at least fifteen minutes before the streetcar arrived.

Whether true, or just figments of Fly's imagination, the stories and descriptions fascinated Alfie. The one-armed man spun tales of riding the rails all over the country—through the cool, blue mist of Washington State's Cascades to warm, lazy nights in hobo jungles along the Mississippi River bottoms. From panhandling on the old streets of New Orleans' French Quarter to picking lettuce with the Mexicans and Filipinos for a penny a head in the Salinas Valley.

Through Fly's stories, Alfie was able to see the snow-covered peaks of the Rockies, the parched deserts of the southwest, and the green-blue spruce forests of Michigan and Minnesota. After his classes in English, advanced algebra, physics and Latin, the fifteen minutes he spent with Fly each afternoon became the high point of the boy's day.

And every day, their parting was similar. "Throw a nickel or a dime in the cap, will ya, kid?"

Sure I will, Alfie would say, thinking *someday*—someday I'll see everything he's seen.

Alfie brought Fly more leftover food when Christmas vacation was over—a thick slice of ham and some sweet potatoes. But this time he looked away while the vagrant ate. It looked as if Fly had tears in his eyes and Alfie was confused. He didn't know why Fly would suddenly begin to weep, and he didn't want to see it.

"Nobody's been as good to me as you have, kid," Fly sniffed, blowing his nose in an old rag. "Not in a long time, anyways."

"Heck, it's only some leftovers," Alfie told him.

"Kid, listen to me," the tramp said, wiping his nose. "All them stories I been tellin' you—about the mountains and them forests—that ain't the whole picture."

"What's that mean, Mr. Fly?" Alfie asked.

"Bein' on the bum ain't just seein' pretty places."

Alfie just nodded, saying nothing, not altogether sure what Fly was trying to tell him now.

"What I mean to say," the tramp went on. "Is that I ain't some big bug you oughta always be listenin' to."

"But you've been all over," Alfie objected, remembering what Captain Gray had tried to tell him weeks before.

"Maybe so—but I ain't told you all of it. I ain't told you how it feels to be so goddamned hungry that you'd kill a man for a hunk of bread and a plate of bacon grease, or what it's like to be sick in your chest and alone at night in some strange town, knowin' that nobody else gives a shit if you live or die—"

Alfie tried to interrupt. "But, Mr. Fly—"

"Shut up, kid—just listen. You been good to me, and now I'm tryin' to do you a favor back. Bein' on the bum ain't worth a damn unless you got a home somewheres to go back to. I lost an arm on the road, I been sick and hungry, I been robbed and beat up, tricked and cheated, cold, wet, and miserable, and sometimes so damned scared, I shit my pants."

Fly reached into the pocket of the reefer and brought out a pair of sealed envelopes. His hand was trembling as he handed them to Alfie. "Kid, if anything ever happens to me, will'ya see these get mailed? One's to my wife and one's to my old man."

Alfie looked at the two envelopes. They were addressed with a shaky hand and written in pencil. There was no return address and neither envelope bore a stamp.

"What's gonna happen to you?" Alfie asked hesitantly.

"Who knows?" Fly told him. "And that's another part of bein' on the bum."

The second week in January brought a blizzard and bitter cold. Post Walk was slick and slippery with ice and packed snow and the cadets made their way to classes with their reefer collars turned up, most of them wearing gloves, earmuffs, and mufflers.

Walking from the streetcar to campus, Alfie hadn't noticed Fly that morning, but thought little of it as the tramp usually found a nearby gangway in which to sleep at night, out of the wind and out of sight of passersby.

But later that day, on his way home, Alfie was surprised to see a small crowd gathered around the space between two buildings, close by the spot Fly usually sat. There was a cop car parked there, too—and a white ambulance with a Red Cross and *Little Company of Mary Hospital* painted on the side.

As he approached, Alfie saw the cop and the ambulance driver talking. The ambulance man was writing something in a notebook. Out of the corner of his eye, Alfie noticed the rusty old Radio Flyer wagon. There was nothing in it anymore.

Certain the policeman would ignore any questions, Alfie went up to a portly man in the crowd. "What's goin' on, mister?"

The man looked at him and chewed on his cigar. "They found a dead bum in the gangway, kid—poor sonofabitch froze to death last night. That's what the copper says, anyways. They already put him in the meatwagon."

Alfie watched as the ambulance pulled away. He realized that Fly was inside, but that in itself seemed unreal. They'd had their last chat yesterday afternoon, before it started to snow. "Maybe old Santa'll make a second trip this winter," Fly had joked, coughing again. "Bring this old stiff a bottle of Thunderbird."

When the ambulance turned on Western, Alfie began walking toward the streetcar stop. He could feel the snowflakes melting on his cheeks. *Don't forget my nickel, kid.* Those were the last words Fly had said to him.

The boy recalled Captain Gray's words, too: *He'll be lucky to make it through the winter.*

Alfie rode the streetcar home staring out the window—lost in thoughts of death and memories of Fly. When the trolley let him off on 67th Street, he trudged seven blocks through the snow, went into the house through the back porch, and made for his bedroom dresser where he took out the two letters Fly had given him.

He must have known, Alfie told himself, looking again at the envelopes. *He knew two weeks ago that this might happen.*

He rummaged through his drawers until he found two three-cent stamps among the pencils, erasers, and notebooks that he used for school. Fly said he had a daughter, Alfie thought, wondering if she'd be sad to learn of her pa's death. Would she even remember who he was? He'd traveled all over the country, Alfie told himself, but a wife and a daughter and an aging father—that was all Fly had in the world and all that he'd ever leave behind.

After supper that evening, Herb and Loretta Potter finished the dishes and relaxed in the living room, tuning in *The Shadow* on the radio. Halfway through the broadcast, Alfie came into the room in his pajamas and sat on the sofa next to his father.

"Finished your homework?" Herb Potter asked.

"All done," the boy said. "Pa, can I tell you something?"

"What's that?"

"Thanks for what you do," Alfie said. "You know, working so hard and everything—I mean—just for us."

Herb Potter turned to look at his wife. "Well, listen to him," he said, with a grin on his face.

1940–1949

CHAPTER 9

▼

"WE'LL BID FAREWELL TO KAYDET GRAY..."

Fall and Spring Term, 1941

Cadet Sgt. Roger Buczkowski enjoyed winter Sundays on campus. Almost half the cadet corps was made up of day students, and on weekends, the Academy grounds were relatively empty and quiet.

Even though football season was over, Christmas vacation was just around the corner and because of Chicago's chancy weather there were no Sunday parades during the winter, therefore no need to spend all morning shining shoes and polishing brass. Roger was a perfectionist as far as his uniform was concerned, preferring to do those chores himself, even though as a senior he had his pick of plebes to do that work.

Roger, with his roommate Harry Takahashi, and a few other Hansen Hall upperclassmen, had wolfed down a Sunday lunch of hamburgers and French fries and were settled in Upper Alumni, playing gin rummy and listening to the Chicago Bears game being broadcast on the radio. The Bears were playing the Cardinals at Comiskey Park—the last regularly scheduled game of the season.

Suddenly, the game was interrupted and an announcement was crackling over the air. *"We interrupt this broadcast to bring you an important bulletin from the United Press. Flash! Washington—the White House announces a Japanese attack on Pearl Harbor. Stay tuned for further developments as they are received—"*

"Wait a minute—what the hell was that?" Bill Toomey said, glancing toward the big Zenith Console radio.

Roger leaned over to turn up the volume. "Something about an attack—on Pearl Harbor."

"Where's Pearl Harbor?" Toomey asked.

"Hawaii," Harry Takahashi said, concern and worry showing in his face. "It's on the island of Oahu—where my folks live."

"Jeez, Taki," Roger said. "You think they're okay?"

"I don't know, I sure hope so."

It wouldn't be until much later that the cadets at Morgan Park Military Academy and the rest of America learned the true scope of the carnage that had occurred on Oahu. The early morning air attack had crippled the entire United States Pacific fleet. Five battleships, the *Arizona, Nevada, Oklahoma, West Virginia,* and *California* were resting on the shallow bottom of Pearl Harbor, while three others were badly damaged. Two hundred American aircraft were destroyed as they sat on the ground, and twenty-four hundred American sailors and soldiers had been killed.

"Goddamned Japs," Bill Toomey muttered, just as the Bears and Cardinals came back on the air.

"Shut up, Bill," Roger said. "Taki's Japanese."

"Oh yeah, I forgot," Toomey said sheepishly. "Sorry Taki, but how'd we let something like this happen, anyway?"

"I don't know," Harry Takahashi said quietly.

Monday morning, all was confusion. None of the cadets were sure of what was happening. Finally, classes were canceled and the entire Corps of Cadets was instructed to assemble on Post Walk, then brought into the chapel in Blake Hall as President Roosevelt made an address to a joint session of congress.

Every member of the faculty and staff was already there. As Superintendent Abells glanced at his wristwatch and switched on the radio, there was a strange, heavy silence that hung like a shroud over the gathered cadets, and Roger Buczkowski noticed the usual muffled din of conversation was missing that morning.

The moment President Roosevelt began to speak, everyone's eyes were fixed on the radio. Roger had the feeling that something was about to happen that would change his life forever.

"*Yesterday,*" the president began, "*December 7, 1941—a date which will live in infamy—the United States of America was suddenly and deliberately attacked by naval and air forces of the Empire of Japan...*"

Harry Takahashi fought to keep from standing up and fleeing out of Blake. His chest ached, his heart was pounding, and his legs felt weak.

"...The United States was at peace with that nation, Roosevelt went on in a tone somber and indignant, *"and, at the solicitation of Japan, was still in conversation with its government and its Emperor looking toward the maintenance of peace in the Pacific..."*

A sneak attack. Harry was too ashamed to look around him at the faces of his friends and classmates. He took his eyes from the radio and stared at the floor, only half-hearing what the President was saying.

"...The attack yesterday on the Hawaiian Islands has caused severe damage to American naval and military forces. Very many American lives have been lost. In addition American ships have been reported torpedoed on the high seas between San Francisco and Honolulu..."

Roger suddenly realized their days of worrying about girls and football games were ending. In Europe, the Nazis were making life a living hell for Poland, most likely including many of Roger's own relatives, and he had no doubt that the country was about to go to war with Japan—and maybe Germany, too. Glancing briefly at his roommate, Roger saw that Harry's lower lip was trembling and there were tears in his dark Oriental eyes.

"...Yesterday the Japanese Government also launched an attack against Malaya. Last night Japanese forces attacked Hong Kong. Last night Japanese forces attacked Guam. Last night Japanese forces attacked the Philippine Islands. Last night the Japanese attacked Wake Island. This morning the Japanese attacked Midway Island..."

Should I quit school? Harry wondered. Go back to Oahu and be with the folks? His father was a successful merchant with two profitable hardware stores and an upscale restaurant on Kalakaua Avenue, just off Waikiki Beach. They owned a luxurious home in the finest part of the city and employed a Filipino cook, gardener, and houseboy. But now, Harry wondered if Japanese people would even still be welcome in Hawaii.

"...As commander-in-chief of the army and navy, I have directed that all measures be taken for our defense..."

As Roosevelt talked, Harry thought about how long his family had been living in the islands. His grandfather, Takai Takahashi, was one of the *Gannen Mono,* the "first year men," who'd arrived in Hawaii from Yokohama in 1868. They numbered approximately one hundred fifty men and women, mostly city dwellers, displaced samurai and an assortment of rogues.

In February of 1885, seventeen years later, the steamer *City of Tokio* brought nearly nine hundred Japanese immigrants to Hawaii. Mostly single men, working under three-year binding contracts to the big plantation owners, they came with the intention of making their fortunes in Golden Hawaii and returning to Japan with status and wealth.

These immigrants were the first of what would become wave after wave of *Issei*—the first generation. Each Issei group was as anxious as the next to find wealth in Hawaii. By 1924, so many Japanese had come to the islands that they constituted over forty percent of the population.

Working for poor wages in the huge cane and pineapple fields, day-after-day, year-after-year—hauling, cutting, and burning cane, the Issei gave their muscles, blood and sweat to buttress the great plantation fortunes.

"...With confidence in our armed forces—with the unbounded determination of our people—we will gain the inevitable triumph, so help us God..."

Harry remembered his father telling him that in the early days, the lives of Hawaii's Japanese immigrants were contained within the narrow confines of their plantation camps. Yet even in poverty, his father said, a sense of community, pride and permanency began to take hold.

Eventually, picture bride marriages were arranged so as to perpetuate the traditional Japanese family. It was in this way that Grandfather Takai had married. Young Japanese women, crossing an ocean to meet husbands they'd never known, began not only to serve the home and give birth to the *Nisei*—the second generation, but to work alongside their men in the fields.

Those early years, young Harry had been told, were a time of learning. At home, his father's generation was taught the duties of a child to its parents, respect for family, and the simple virtues of Japanese behavior. When he was a small boy at Japanese language school, Harry learned the language of his parents. But in public school, from listening to the radio and going to the movies, from friends who were non-Japanese, he learned English and how to be an American.

"...I ask that the Congress declare that since the unprovoked and dastardly attack by Japan on Sunday, December seventh, a state of war has existed between the United States and the Japanese Empire."

Well, there it is, Roger told himself—*War*. He looked around the chapel, wondering how many of the others in that old building realized their futures had suddenly, abruptly changed.

When the president completed his address, the radio began to play "The Star-Spangled Banner." On the first note of the National Anthem, the Cadet Corps stood and snapped to attention with their hands over their hearts until the last note trailed off.

Colonel Abells stepped to the speaker's stand and tapped the microphone. "Gentlemen, you have just heard our president speak. These words will prove fateful to most of you.

"The country is now at war against a ruthless, cunning enemy—and upon graduation, you will undoubtedly be asked to serve. Now you'll learn the true meaning of those words the Academy long ago adopted as its credo—*Duty, Honor, Country.*

"In the meantime, as long as you are in school, you will serve your country best by studying as hard as you can so that when you graduate—you will be well prepared to take your places both as members of our armed forces, and later, when victory is assured, as leaders of our nation's destiny."

The superintendent paused for a brief moment. "Gentlemen, that is all. Regular classes will resume after Mess II—I wish you all good luck and Godspeed in the future."

All day, talk of war filled the campus, and that evening after study hour, Harry Takahashi was quiet. He closed his physics book and turned his chair, staring through the window into the darkness of the December night. He recalled stories that Grandfather Takai had often told about their ancestor's fighting ability. The Japanese opinion of battle was one of finality, Grandfather Takai had stated. A Japanese soldier would never allow himself to be taken prisoner by the enemy. You willingly died for the emperor and lived forever in glory. Feeling sick at heart, Harry suspected that any American soldiers captured in this war would be thought of as despicable and deserving of death.

"Let's hit the weeder, Taki," Roger suggested, closing his own textbook. "I could use a smoke before tattoo."

Harry shook his head. "You go ahead, Ski. I'm tired. I think I'll just hit the sack."

"You sure?"

"Yeah, I'm sure. But you go ahead."

Downstairs, on the first floor of Hansen, the senior weeder was crowded. Just as it had been earlier in the day, talk of war was the single topic of conversation.

"Those dirty Japs," a cadet named Bob Fahey growled. "Man, I can hardly wait to get into the army, get a rifle, and start shooting those slant-eyed, little yellow bastards."

Roger was suddenly relieved that Taki had stayed upstairs. He lit a Chesterfield and asked if there was any fresh news.

"Not much," Dex Statler said. Dex was the basketball team's star center. He didn't smoke, but the weeder was the only place for a senior to socialize between study hour and tattoo. "The radio said the Japs bombed our planes at Clark Field in the Philippines, too. Twenty-five B-17 bombers blown to bits."

"Jesus," Roger whistled, shaking his head.

"Just lemme at those Japs," Bob Fahey stated again.

"I guess we'll all get our chance," Dex offered. "I'll be headed for the air corps."

"To do what?" Jack Boyer asked.

"Be a fighter pilot—what else?"

Boyer laughed. "Hell, you're too tall, Dex. They'd have to cut off your legs at the knees to stuff your ass in the cockpit."

"Up yours, Boyer—you'll see."

"You could be a control tower, Dex," another cadet said. "The air corps needs control towers."

"Or maybe join the navy," somebody else suggested. "And be a lighthouse."

"Fuck you guys," Dex Statler muttered. "You'll see."

"*Fuck* you guys?" Jack Boyer repeated. "What do you fellas make of that from brother Dexter?"

"Shocking," someone laughed.

"Language unbecoming an MPMA cadet," another added.

The room soon filled with smoke and talk of war. They were young men staring into the dark face of an uncertain future. If the war dragged on for any length of time, most suspected, there was a good chance that some of them sitting in this room might be dead before it was over.

"Say Ski," Bob Fahey asked. "What's Taki got to say about all this—the war and all?"

"What do you mean—what's Taki got to say?"

"Well hell, he's a Jap, isn't he?"

"Taki's Hawaiian," Roger said. "His family's been in Hawaii for almost seventy-five years—and the last I heard, Hawaii was a U.S. Territory."

"He's still a Jap."

"Shut up, Bob," Jack Boyer said. "Taki's okay."

Fahey shrugged and stubbed out his cigarette. "Well, you guys can argue about it—I'm going to bed."

All week, they were glued to the radio. News of the war was glum, and getting worse. On Wednesday, Japanese forces invaded the Philippines and captured the American protectorate of Guam, and the following day they invaded Burma.

After a few days, the importance of the war seemed to fade as far as the first and second-year boys were concerned. For them, the prospect of graduation was still too far away, and the prospect of going to war even more distant.

But for the juniors and seniors it was different. Their futures were already determined, and in military class that day, the cadets were surprised and angry by what seemed Japan's quick, effortless march across the vast expanse of the Pacific. Lt. Colonel Howland, the school's professor of military science and tactics, was asked if Japan could actually win a war with America.

Howland lit his pipe. "The Japs have a tough army," he told the boys. "They're disciplined soldiers and they follow a military code that's as fanatic as it gets. But they lack two important things needed to win a war—oil and industry.

"They sucker punched us at Pearl Harbor," Howland went on. "And they'll make some headway until this country builds its army and gets its factories cranked up for war production. Then we'll overwhelm them, gentlemen—it's just a matter of time."

The colonel's assessment of the war in the Pacific made them feel better, but they became nervous again every time they listened to the news. It was like watching an opposing football team pile up the score early in the game.

Now they were at war with Germany and Italy, too, and the following week, Japanese armies invaded Borneo, Hong Kong, and Luzon in the Philippines—and it was announced that Gen. Douglas MacArthur had been ordered to withdraw his staff, himself and his family, from Manila to Bataan.

Unlike Messes I and III which fed only boarders, Mess II was accompanied by the usual clatter of dishes and low-key hubbub of the entire Corps of Cadets at lunch. Each table had a faculty officer at its head, and the meal was served by white-coated members of the cadet wait staff.

Roger and Harry shared a table with four other seniors, three junior cadets, and two plebes who were required to sit at brace. At the head of the table was Lt. Jerome Kloucek, who taught English and social studies. It was Kloucek's first year at Morgan Park. He had a master's degree and was easygoing and well liked by his students.

Halfway through the meal, the lieutenant excused himself to answer a telephone call and a senior named Barry Stearns turned to one of the plebes, whispering something.

"Sir?" The plebe asked, unsure of what he'd been told to do.

"You heard me, Mister," Stearns said under his breath. "Just do it."

"But sir—"

"Do it!"

The plebe was sweating and his eyes were wide. "Yes sir," he stammered. "Uh—Sergeant Takahashi, sir, would you rather have the waiter bring you a big plate of egg foo yung?"

"Oh Jesus," Stearns guffawed, slapping the table with the flat of his hand. "That's rich." Some of the other boys laughed as well.

Harry Takahashi ignored the terrified plebe, staring instead at Stearns. "Egg foo yung's Chinese," Harry said coldly. "And that's a rotten thing to do to a plebe."

"Okay," Stearns said. "Then how about a large bowl of chop suey, Taki?"

"Why don't you shut your mouth, Stearns," Roger said, just as Lieutenant Kloucek came back to the table. A few of the boys were still poking each other and laughing.

"What did I miss, fellas?" The lieutenant asked amiably.

"Not much, sir," Roger said, glancing at Barry Stearns. "Just an asshole shooting off his mouth."

"Mr. Buczkowski, that is inappropriate table talk."

"Yes sir, I'm sorry, sir."

"Don't let it happen again, or I'll have to put you on report."

"Yes sir."

After taps that evening, Harry told his roommate that he was thinking of leaving school and going back to Hawaii.

Roger was stunned. Harry had always been popular. He was a member of the HiY Council, and a star on the debating team. In addition, Harry Takahashi carried a B average in his grades.

"That's nuts, Taki," Roger argued. "Hell, it's only six months until graduation—why would you do a stupid thing like that?"

"You heard Stearns today, didn't you?"

"Stearns is a jerk."

"Maybe so, but it's already starting."

"What's starting?"

Harry took a deep breath and Roger could hear him sigh in the dark. When he spoke again, there was a slight quiver in his voice. "Ski, I'm the school Jap, and we're at war with Japan. Things are gonna get a lot worse."

"Jeez, Taki—don't worry about it."

Harry raised himself up on an elbow and looked across at his friend and room-mate. "I got a letter from my parents yesterday and it was pretty bad, Ski. My lit-tle sister's only seven years old, but in school some of the other kids spat on her and called her names.

"My mother says all through the islands, the war department is closing Japa-nese language schools, Shinto shrines and Buddhist temples. She says that other oriental kids are wearing nametags to distance them from the Japanese—nametags that say *I am Chinese,* or *I am Korean."*

"Well, that stinks," Roger admitted. "But it's still no reason for you to leave the Academy."

But Harry wasn't certain. He could see what was happening. He'd heard on the radio that in California, with a population that included almost a hundred thousand Japanese Americans, rumors were already circulating of Japanese treachery and sabotage. The announcer had said a growing number of politicians and journalists were condemning the Japanese as a risk to the nation's security.

"Some—perhaps many—are good Americans," exclaimed the *Los Angeles Times* the day after Pearl Harbor. "What the rest may be we do not know, nor can we take a chance in light of yesterday's demonstration that treachery and double-dealing are two weapons of the Japanese."

A Los Angeles radio announcer had put it even more bluntly, warning listen-ers that, "Ninety percent or more of American-born Japanese are disloyal to this country."

The United States military was voicing suspicions, too. Gen. John DeWitt, who was in charge of security along the West Coast, said of the nation's Japa-nese-Americans, "I have no confidence in their loyalty whatsoever."

And finally, the radio reported, one congressman stated, "I'm for catching every Japanese in America, Alaska, and Hawaii now, and putting them in concen-tration camps. Damn them! Let's get rid of them."

Less than a week later, Harry received another letter—written by his father—urging him to stay in school. *We are Hawaiians and good Americans,* his father told him. *But we are Japanese as well. Because of what has happened at Pearl Har-bor, our country has dishonored us, but to run away from your heritage would bring even greater dishonor upon both you and our entire family.*

So that was that, Harry told himself, folding his father's letter and placing it in his desk drawer. Whatever happens, I must endure it without shame.

But just two days before Christmas leave began, the *Chicago Tribune's* front page reported that a Japanese submarine had fired on the tanker *S.S. Agwiworld* off Monterey Bay in California.

And the next morning, painted in red on the door of Roger and Harry's room, were the words TOJO and DIRTY JAP.

"Those bastards," Roger said. "We'll scrub it off tonight."

"Sure," Harry sighed. "We'll just scrub it off."

Captain Gray had become concerned with Harry Takahashi as well. For almost four years, the cadet had been a fine student in his math classes—always prompt with the answers, and never lazy or lackadaisical as were many of the knotheads who took up space in his classes, but it suddenly seemed as if Cadet Takahashi's interest had waned—almost as if he'd become reluctant to speak.

As the bell rang on Monday morning, ending solid geometry class until the start of the New Year, Captain Gray wished the boys a Merry Christmas, and took hold of Harry's sleeve as he was on his way out the door. "Hold up a moment, Takahashi—I'd like to have a word with you."

Harry was surprised. Other than lecturing his students in class, Captain Gray rarely spoke to most of them. In fact, Harry couldn't recall himself or another cadet having a personal conversation with Captain Gray in the four years he'd been at the Academy.

"Have I done something wrong, sir?"

Captain Gray said nothing for a minute—instead, he sat on the edge of his old desk, tossing a piece of yellow chalk up and down. After the last of the cadets had filed out, he looked at Harry. "What seems to be the trouble, Mr. Takahashi?"

"I'm not sure I understand, sir."

"It appears you've become somewhat dull-witted of late."

"Sir?"

"Have you lost your interest in mathematics?"

Cap Gray was looking straight at him, tossing the chalk up and down, and waiting for an answer. Harry swallowed hard. "No sir, I guess I just have some problems on my mind."

"What problems?"

"Well sir, I'm Japanese—"

"Is that a fact, Mr. Takahashi? I hadn't noticed."

Harry smiled. "Some of the other boys have, sir."

Captain Gray grunted. "So, that's what it's about?" He said in what seemed to Harry a slightly dismissive tone. "They're making things tough on you because you're Japanese?"

"Yes sir, I guess that's it."

Frank Gray was aware of his reputation for being distant, not a friend to the boys, but instead a strict, authoritarian instructor who scorned inattention or laziness, and who paid little attention to the cadets except when they were in his class. He didn't do very much to discourage this impression, feeling the boys were there to learn from him and nothing more. He'd concluded that his students had friends among each other and didn't need him to assume that role as well.

But every now and then, he took an interest in a fine student, and if the student faltered for any reason, it set off an alarm he was unable to ignore. Harry Takahashi was such a case.

"They think you're a traitor? Maybe a spy? Is that it?"

"I don't know, sir," Harry admitted. "I guess so. There's a lot of strong feelings against Japanese now—both in this country and in Hawaii where my family lives."

Captain Gray grunted. "It's to be expected. Pearl Harbor was a dastardly deed."

"Yes sir, I feel the same way about it."

"Then ignore the taunts, Mr. Takahashi, and set your mind on the task for which your parents sent you here. Study hard and make good grades. No one knows you as well as you know yourself, so be proud of who you are, and make your family proud as well. I'll do my best to help you all I can."

"Yes sir, thank you, sir."

"If you have the answer to a problem," Captain Gray went on. "Don't be afraid to speak up in my class. You've always been one of my best students—and I don't want you just sitting there like a bump on a log. I won't have it."

"Yes sir."

"How will you spend the holidays, Mr. Takahashi?"

"I've been invited to spend them with my roommate and his family, sir," Harry said. "We don't get enough leave time for me to go home to Hawaii and even if we did, with the war on, travel for a civilian is probably pretty tough."

Captain Gray grunted and stood up. His khaki tie and the front of his uniform shirt carried chalk dust. "Well, have a fine vacation, Mr. Takahashi. Remember what I told you and come back ready to do some first-rate work."

"Yes sir," Harry said. "And Merry Christmas to you and your family, sir."

A light, dry snow began to fall the night before Christmas, but on Chicago's Southwest Side, and across the rest of America, the first Christmas of the war proved bleak and gloomy. The conflict hadn't totally dampened the Christmas spirit, but blackouts and the prohibition of outdoor lights made the usual glow of Christmas in the city much dimmer than usual.

A holiday editorial in the December 23rd issue of the *Chicago Tribune* said, "Just as there will always be Santa Claus, there will always be Christmas Trees."

"Sure, I agree with that," Roger's father said. "We managed to find a real nice one this year—a Scotch pine." Roman Buczkowski was second-generation Polish. In 1897, his parents had immigrated to Chicago from the small Polish town of Kamieńsk, just south of Warsaw. When he was sixteen years old, Roman was offered the job of press operator's helper at a mid-sized printing company on Archer Avenue. He worked hard and saved his money, learned all facets of the business, and eventually arranged a business loan to help buy the company when its aging owner decided to sell.

Now, through long hours and hard work, Roman Buczkowski and his wife, Teresa, had made a fine life for themselves. They had a large, two-story brick bungalow on west 59th Street, drove a new Buick Deluxe Sedan, and had enough in the bank to send their son to a private military school.

"Do they decorate Christmas trees in Hawaii, Harry?" Roger's mother asked, as she fussed with a few strips of tinsel on theirs. On the radio, Bing Crosby was singing "I'll Be Home For Christmas."

"Yes ma'am," Harry told her, suddenly feeling homesick for the soft, warm sea breezes of the islands. "We have Norfolk Island pines, but they look more like a tall fern than a pine tree."

Harry and the Buczkowskis enjoyed a traditional Polish dinner early on Christmas Eve, and as much as they tried to avoid it the conversation drifted to talk of war.

After a prolonged siege and frequent Japanese air attacks, the embattled American garrison on Wake Island had fallen that same day, and in Eastern Europe, the Warsaw Ghetto was now a prison to more than three hundred and fifty thousand Polish Jews.

"First they will take the Jews," Roman Buczkowski predicted, enjoying his plate of kielbasa and boiled potatoes. "The Poles will come next—and then the Catholics. We have many relatives over there, Harry. This war is a terrible thing."

"Yes sir," Harry answered, unsure of what else to say.

"Pop, is it okay if Taki and me take the Buick tonight?" Roger asked, hoping to change the subject.

"Sure, I guess so—where are you going?"

Roger shrugged. "I don't know—just driving around I guess, maybe to the movies."

"You be back in time for midnight mass," Teresa Buczkowski told her son. "Harry, are you Roman Catholic? You're welcome to join us."

"No, Mrs. Buczkowski—I was raised a Shin Buddhist, but I'm not very religious anymore. Thanks anyway, but I'll just stay home and hit the sack."

After the boys left, Roman watched them pull away and then turned away from the window with a deep sigh. He shook his head, nervous about having Harry Takahashi staying with them over the holidays, but the invitation had been extended a month before the attack on Pearl Harbor.

Roman glanced at his wife and shook his head again. "What were you thinking, Teresa? How would it look to our neighbors if we brought a Japanese boy to church with us?"

His wife nodded, embarrassed. "You're right Roman, I guess I was only trying to be polite."

"Being *that* polite could get our windows busted."

Out of sight of the house, Roger offered Harry a cigarette and lit one for himself, then turned the Buick north on Cicero Avenue.

The streets were empty and traffic was light on Christmas Eve. Roger switched on the Buick's radio and tuned it to a station that was playing Duke Ellington's "Take The A Train."

They took Cicero north to Cermak, then made their way east toward Michigan Avenue—just past Chinatown. Michigan Avenue would take them north to the Loop and State Street.

"You want to see a movie?" Roger asked.

"Sure Ski," Harry said. "What's showing?"

They drove around the Loop, checking the marquees of the big downtown movie houses. Most of the department stores were still open and people were doing last minute shopping. The boys settled on the State-Lake Theater. It was advertising *The Sea Hawk,* with Errol Flynn.

They parked the car a few blocks south, pulled up their collars against the cold, falling snow and walked back to the theater. After paying for their tickets, they bought popcorn, two Baby Ruth bars, and Coca Colas from a vending machine in the lobby that served soda in cone-shaped paper cups.

The boys slid into a row of seats behind two young ladies who were sitting together. There weren't many others in the theater and the girls seemed to have their eyes glued to the screen. Each time Errol Flynn appeared in a scene, they would squeal in delight, poke each other in the ribs and giggle.

Roger nudged Harry with his elbow. "What do you think?" He whispered, nodding toward the girls.

"About what?" Harry asked.

"These two skirts."

"Aw, I don't think so, Ski—forget it."

"Forget it? The hell I will," Roger chuckled, bouncing a kernel of popcorn off the head of the girl sitting in front of him.

The girl brushed her hair and turned around in her seat. She was cute, with short bangs and a button nose. "Say, cut it out—you some kind of wise guy, or what?"

"You girls here all by yourselves?"

"What's it to you?"

"Nuthin'," Roger grinned, leaning forward. "We just thought you might like some company, that's all."

"Who's *we?* The girl said, turning in the opposite direction to get a look at Harry. "Say, what is this? Is he a Jap or something?"

"He's Hawaiian," Roger said quickly.

"No, you're right, miss," Harry told her. "I'm Japanese."

The other girl stood up, clutching her purse. "These two guys are creeps, Doreen—let's find some other seats."

"Yeah," Doreen said, looking at Roger. "Tell your slant-eyed friend that we'd rather kiss a nigger than a lousy Jap."

After the girls took new seats in the balcony, Roger and Harry watched what was left of the Errol Flynn swashbuckler without talking to each other.

In the car and on the way home, it was Roger that broke the silence. "Jeez, Taki—why'd you tell them you were Japanese?"

"That's what I am, Ski."

"Sure, maybe so—but hell, it queered the whole deal."

Harry turned and looked out the Buick's window. The streets and sidewalks were covered in snow, and now it was falling in wet, heavy flakes. Although he'd seen calendar pictures of Mount Fuji covered with snow, never having been to Japan he found it difficult to picture snow in that far-off land his grandfather had left so many years before.

In fact, the frigid winter of his freshman year at the Academy was the first time he'd ever seen snow or felt cold weather. He'd been somewhat of a novelty, a boy who'd come all the way from Hawaii to attend the school. They all called him Honolulu Harry in those days, and they made him feel welcome.

Now he was—what did that girl call him? *A lousy Jap.* As the Buick took them back south toward Roger's house, Harry closed his eyes and let his head lay back against the seat.

"Sorry, Ski," he sighed. "I didn't mean to screw things up."

"Yeah, sure," Roger said. "Forget about it."

On Christmas morning, after a big breakfast of ham and eggs, the Buczkowskis gathered in the living to open presents and Harry was surprised to receive a gift. It was a soft black leather shaving kit embossed with his initials. It was a fine present and he thanked them for it more than once.

Soon after the holidays ended, the Corps returned to campus with a month left before the second semester would start. Usually, the second term was a heady time for the seniors. With the bulk of their graduation requirements behind them, most hoped to breeze through the rest of the school year, take nine days off for spring furlough, get through the annual tribulation of GI Inspection in May, and then just coast the rest of the way to the senior prom and graduation.

But with the war, and discouraging news seemingly every day, there was an ominous cloud of gloom and uncertainty hanging over the closing months of this school year.

When he and Roger got back to Hansen Hall, a Christmas card from Harry's parents lay on his bed. It had a bit of money and a letter tucked inside. The letter described an unusual incident that had occurred on December 7th. His mother wrote that a damaged Japanese torpedo bomber had crash-landed on the island of Niihau, southwest of Kauai.

A young Japanese flyer, an Airman 1st Class named Shigenori Nishikaichi, survived the landing and was at first treated as a guest by the people of the island. The pilot was able to enlist the support of a local Japanese-American family to obtain weapons.

To make a long story short, Harry's mother wrote, *the native Hawaiians of Niihau found out about it and quickly overcame and killed the Japanese pilot. The collaborating Japanese-American committed suicide and his wife was imprisoned.*

Harry tore the letter up and threw it away. Just the suggestion that Hawaiian Japanese would help an invading enemy pilot might make things doubly hard on him at the Academy. He didn't want anyone to see what his mother had written—not even Roger.

Three days later, with their reefer collars turned up against the raw, wet cold of early February; the cadet battalion was assembled for morning formation on Post Walk.

Before the report, one of Company B's platoon leaders, Cadet Lt. Phil Busse left his position on the grass and approached Harry, who was Busse's platoon sergeant. "Did you shine those boots this morning, Takahashi?"

Harry glanced down at his gleaming black boots. "Yes sir."

"Well, they look like crap, Mister Jap—five demerits."

The three squads of freshmen, sophomores, and juniors in the platoon looked at each other astonished. It was almost unheard of for a senior to rebuke a fellow senior in front of anyone.

In his position as platoon sergeant in Company C, Roger heard the exchange and lost his temper, leaving his position and storming over to help his roommate.

"Buczkowski," his own platoon leader was shouting. "Where the hell are you going? Get back in ranks."

"Up your ass," Roger mumbled, setting his course straight for Phil Busse.

By this time, the entire battalion knew something was amiss. The ranks were starting to wobble and go soft as the curious cadets strained to see what was happening. "Dress right, dress," platoon leaders and company commanders ordered. "Dress it up!"

Out in the middle of the meadow, Battalion Commander Cadet Col. Davis Blake and his adjutant watched the unfolding spectacle in horror.

Roger stopped and spun Busse around to face him. "Did you call Taki a Jap, you jerk?"

"Five demerits for you, too, Buczkowski," Busse hissed.

"Listen, dope," Roger said. "Taki might be a Jap, but he's *our* Jap—and I watched him shine those boots last night—you're not gonna stick him five of anything."

"Now he gets ten, and you do, too. You wanna keep shooting your mouth off? You goddamned Jap lover."

"Nope, not anymore," Roger said, as he stepped back, planted his right foot, and hit Cadet Lieutenant Busse with a right hand that smashed his nose and knocked him down.

At the suggestion of a fight, discipline in the ranks crumbled. The orderly platoons and squads wavered and started to come apart as each cadet was eager to catch a glimpse of what was happening.

"Get back in ranks!" Cadet Colonel Blake bellowed, his face flushing red. "Baaattalion—ten-shhuuuttt! Company commanders—dress your companies."

Capt. George Mahon and Lt. Colonel Howland happened to be walking past when the mayhem began. Howland stepped in front of Roger and held him, while Captain Mahon helped Phil Busse get back on his feet. "Do you want to settle this in the boxing ring after classes, Mr. Busse?" Mahon asked.

Busse had tears in his eyes. "I think my nose is broken, sir."

Mahon looked him over and nodded. He was the Academy's football coach and had seen his share of broken noses. "I believe you're right, son, and it's busted up pretty good, too. Best you get over to the infirmary. The nurse can have a look at it and then send you to see Dr. Woods."

"What about you, Buczkowski?" Howland asked Roger.

"I'm okay, sir."

"He smacked me when I wasn't looking," Cadet Busse said as he pressed a white handkerchief over his nose. There was blood on his reefer collar.

"Sir," Harry Takahashi interrupted. "This whole thing was my fault."

Howland nodded. "Looks to me like all three of you boys have got yourselves a date to see the commandant."

Commandant of Cadets, Maj. Campbell Jackson, interviewed each of them separately—Cadet Lieutenant Busse first.

"How's your nose, Mr. Busse?" Jackson asked. He could see the boy's nose was covered with a protective splint and bandaged, undoubtedly still swollen and sore.

"The doctor says it'll be okay, sir."

"Do you care to tell me what occurred at AMSF yesterday?"

"Yes sir—my platoon sergeant, Cadet Takahashi, was present at morning formation with unpolished boots. I called him on it and stuck him five demerits."

"And then?"

"And then Cadet Buczkowski punched me, sir."

"Anything else?"

"No sir, that's it—it was a sucker punch, sir."

When Roger reported to the Commandant's office ten minutes later, the major got right to the point. "Mr. Buczkowski, did you strike Cadet Busse at formation yesterday?"

"Yes sir."

"Without provocation?"

"I'm not sure what that means, sir."

"Did he threaten or provoke you?"

"Sir, he called my roommate a Jap, sir."

Major Jackson stood and came around to the front of his desk, tapping his leg with a brown leather riding crop. "I take it that you are referring to Cadet Takahashi."

"Yes sir."

The major grunted, sitting on the edge of his desk. "Have you any proof of Cadet Busse's alleged slur, Mr. Buczkowski?"

"Sir, there were other cadets who heard him say it."

"If that proves true," the commandant said. "Cadet Busse will be disciplined accordingly."

"Yes sir."

"In the meantime, Mr. Buczkowski, may I remind you that this is a military institution, not a schoolyard playground—fistfights in ranks cannot be tolerated under any circumstance.

"In the army," Major Jackson went on. "The punishment for a noncom striking a commissioned officer in wartime could be death by firing squad. In peacetime it would be a dishonorable discharge, forfeiture of all pay and allowances, and a damned long stretch in a military prison—I wish to impress this upon you, mister, because I assume your immediate prospects include enlistment in the armed services of your country."

"Yes sir."

Jackson nodded. "Well then, Cadet Buczkowski, for assaulting a cadet commissioned officer, I'm restricting you to campus for a period of six weeks, assigning you twenty hours of extra duty, and demoting you to the rank of private. Have you anything to say?"

"No sir." Roger said, swallowing hard.

"That will be all, mister—you're dismissed."

"It stinks, Ski," Harry Takahashi said. "You getting busted for sticking up for me." He was almost in tears.

Roger shook his head as he sat on his bed and pulled off his slippers. Taps was about to sound. Aside from the embarrassment of being one of only three seniors graduating with the rank of private, demotion didn't bother him all that much. "Don't worry about it Taki, being platoon sergeant is no big deal. We both know that."

"That's not the point," Harry argued. "I told Jackson the same thing you did, and Busse only got a slap on the wrist."

Roger shrugged. "That's because nobody else who heard what he said out there would back us up."

"Yeah sure, because I'm just a slant-eyed Jap."

"Aw jeez, Taki," Roger groaned. "It's not that important."

"I don't want you going out on a limb for me anymore, Ski."

"That's bullshit," Roger told him. "We've been roommates for almost four years—you'd do the same for me."

"Well you won't have to much longer," Harry said.

"What's that mean?"

"Nothing, turn out the light."

Each morning of the week, before donning his uniform, it was Captain Gray's habit to stroll down to the Academy Drugstore on 111th and Western to buy a package of Chesterfields and a copy of the *Chicago Herald-American.*

After making small talk with the store's owner and paying for his paper and cigarettes, he stepped back outside, surprised to see Cadet Takahashi in civilian clothes, gripping a small suitcase and pacing nervously in front of the trolley stop. Frank Gray glanced at his wristwatch and noted that Harry Takahashi was scheduled to be in his college algebra class in less than two hours.

"Going somewhere, Mr. Takahashi?"

"Uh, Captain Gray—I didn't expect to see you here, sir."

Harry was embarrassed. He'd packed his valise the day before and hid it beneath his bed, then quietly snuck out of Hansen Hall before reveille, hoping to slip away unnoticed. Now he was caught.

"No," said Cap Gray, sitting down on the trolley stop bench. "I don't suppose you did. Maybe you'd care to tell me what you're up to?"

Harry took a deep breath and looked his instructor straight in the eye. "Yes sir, I—I've decided to run away. I like the Academy, but I don't want to stay someplace I'm not wanted."

"Not wanted?"

"Yes sir," Harry said. "Like I told you once before, some of the guys figure that because I'm Japanese, I'm against this country—a traitor or something."

"Do all the boys feel this way?" Gray asked.

"Not all of them, I guess," Harry said. "My roommate, Roger Buczkowski, tried to stick up for me, and got busted for doing it. I don't want to make any more trouble, sir."

Captain Gray grunted, seeing something in Cadet Takahashi's eyes and hearing something in his voice that said the runaway boy didn't really have his heart in this enterprise.

But he also sensed that any forcible action to stop him might just strengthen Harry's resolve.

Frank Gray remembered Cadet Alfie Potter three years before—the boy had been enamored by stories of a hobo's life until the hobo turned up dead, frozen solid in a gangway. So much for the romance of the road. Alfie Potter was in his second year at DePaul University now, Cap Gray knew, and was doing fine.

The old man recalled running away himself when he'd been a small boy on his father's Illinois farm. He'd gotten as far as the Sangamon River when night fell and the owls began to hoot. It hadn't taken him long to make his way back home.

The April morning had turned windy and Cap Gray was glad he'd worn his heavy overcoat. "Well, if you're running away," he told Harry. "You'll need to have a good plan. Got any idea where you're headed?"

Harry shrugged and sat down as well. As of yet there were no streetcars in sight. "I'm not sure yet, sir. Maybe California. There's a lot of Japanese in California."

"Not so many as you might think," the captain said, tapping the newspaper with his finger. "Government's been rounding most of 'em up—sticking them in internment camps all over the west—Idaho, Utah, Montana."

"Maybe that's where I'll head then," Harry replied stubbornly. "Montana."

Gray nodded. "Montana, huh? Well, remember there's Indians in Montana, too. And they're the ones that wiped out Custer, if my memory serves. You certain you want to give up all the comforts of Morgan Park to go off and live someplace that's surrounded by hostile savages?"

Harry looked over at his teacher, wondering if Captain Gray was trying to pull his leg. "Sir, if I'm not mistaken, I think all those Indians are on reservations now."

"Maybe so, maybe so," Cap Gray said, lighting a smoke. "But it still won't be easy. You'll need to watch out for rattlesnakes, hungry wolves, and the stray mountain lion now and then."

"Excuse me sir, are you trying to discourage me?"

Captain Gray shook his head. "No, Mr. Takahashi, I just wish you'd reconsider, give some of those boys who've been making it tough a chance to mend their ways—maybe keep you with us until you graduate in June."

Harry spotted a northbound trolley coming toward them. "I'm sorry, sir, but I'd better be going now."

"Well, goodbye then, and good luck," Cap Gray said, offering his hand. "Do you mind shaking hands, Mr. Takahashi? It sounds like you might be bound for some wild country and I'm not getting any younger. We may never meet again in this life."

"Yes sir, thank you sir," Harry stammered, shaking hands with his instructor as the trolley came to a screeching stop. "I hope we'll see each other again, some-day."

Captain Gray nodded, turned, and walked away. As Harry got aboard the streetcar, the heavyset conductor looked him over. "Say kid, are you a Jap?" The conductor asked.

"Chinese," Harry mumbled, handing the man his fare.

"A Chinaman, huh? Well, I guess that's okay then."

Harry Takahashi made his way toward the back of the car. He avoided look-ing at other passengers, and thinking of his father he slumped down in an empty wicker seat and stared out the window—at that moment feeling more ashamed of himself than he ever had in his life.

When reveille sounded at six that morning, Roger opened his sleep-filled eyes, sat up and glanced around the room, surprised to see his roommate's bed already empty.

An hour later, as the barracks emptied and the boarding cadets assembled for breakfast, Roger was beginning to worry—Taki was still nowhere to be seen. He asked a few of the others, but nobody else remembered seeing his roommate that morning either.

"Maybe he's in the infirmary," someone suggested.

"He wasn't sick last night," Roger said, discounting it.

"Probably went back home to say hello to Tojo," another boy laughed, impressed by his own wit. Some of the others laughed as well, but Roger ignored the comment.

By the time the boarders were done with breakfast, the word had already spread throughout the mess hall—*Takahashi's AWOL!* And, at AMSF, as the company commanders formed their units for morning inspection, Cadet Capt. Donald Hollings, commanding B Company, had to report one of his platoon ser-geants, Sgt. Harry Takahashi, indeed absent and unaccounted for.

At that same hour, Captain Gray was seated in the office of the school's com-mandant, Maj. Campbell Jackson, reporting his early morning encounter with Cadet Takahashi. "I think you should have stopped the boy, Frank," Major Jack-son said. "I'm not comfortable with the idea of one of our cadets wandering the streets alone."

Frank Gray nodded and sighed. "You may be right, Major, but this school is not the army, and it's not a prison. I'm not altogether sure that we have the power to keep a boy here against his will."

"We have a responsibility, though," the major argued. "To the cadet's parents, and for each boy's safety."

"We give them leave each weekend," Gray pointed out. "With no concern for their safety, no restrictions on where they can go."

Commandant Jackson stood and stared out his window just as the Corps of Cadets was being dismissed. He watched them make their way toward their various eight o'clock classes, then turned back to look at Captain Gray, who'd been teaching mathematics at the Academy for almost twenty-five years. "Nevertheless Frank," he stated nervously. "I'm concerned about Cadet Takahashi—and I think your judgment may have been poor."

"I'm of the opinion the boy will be back, Major," Gray said.

"When?"

"I'd guess today."

"How sure are you, Frank?"

Captain Gray shrugged. "I'm confident of it."

Jackson nodded. "That's good, because your position at this school could very well be in jeopardy. Should anything happen to the boy, I'm afraid Colonel Abells would have no choice but to ask for your resignation."

"I understand, Major Jackson."

Halfway through his morning college algebra class, Captain Gray looked up to see Harry Takahashi enter the classroom. The boy was back in uniform and carrying his briefcase. Captain Gray held back a deep sigh of relief and casually tossed his small nubbin of yellow chalk across the room where it unerringly landed on the eraser rail.

"Nice to have you join us, Mr. Takahashi."

"I'm sorry I'm late, sir," Harry apologized.

"Take your seat."

"Yes sir."

"Anybody else would get chewed out good," a senior named Bob Tidwell grumbled as Harry sat down.

Cap Gray turned toward him. "What was that, Mr. Tidwell?"

"Aw, nothing."

"Speak up, Mr. Tidwell."

"Sir, I said anybody else would probably get chewed out good if they walked in a half hour late."

Captain Gray crossed the room to retrieve his chalk. "Tidwell, you'd be far better off worrying about the problem that I've put on the board—it sounds to me as if you've got diarrhea of the mouth and constipation of the brain."

The class laughed and Tidwell turned bright red. "Just because Takahashi's a Jap," the embarrassed cadet protested. "The teachers treat him with kid gloves."

"That's enough, Mr. Tidwell," Captain Gray barked. "You'll apologize to both Mr. Takahashi and the class for your remark."

Bob Tidwell shook his head. "Uh-uh, I won't apologize to any damned Jap."

"Apologize, Mr. Tidwell—now!"

"Sir, it's okay," Harry said, looking at Captain Gray and trying to calm the situation. "It really is."

"Shut up, Taki," Tidwell said. "I don't need help from a slant-eyed monkey like you."

Captain Gray stepped up, grabbed Tidwell by the necktie and pulled him from his seat, slamming him against the wall. "Nobody pops off like that in my class, you dunce," Gray said, pointing to the door. "Now get the hell out of here."

"Frank, I appreciate the need for discipline in the classroom," the superintendent said, looking across his desk at the most senior instructor Morgan Park Military Academy had. "However, when the parents of a cadet complain to me about a teacher manhandling their boy, I'm obligated to look into it."

"I understand, Colonel," Frank Gray said.

"What's this business with Cadet Tidwell all about?"

Captain Gray explained that Tidwell's behavior had gone from disturbing the class, to which he responded with a sharp reprimand, to a racial insult against another cadet and then outright defiance of an instructor's authority.

"I see," Colonel Abells said. "And this racial slur was against Cadet Takahashi?"

"It was."

"And you *did* slam Cadet Tidwell against the wall?"

"I did."

Colonel Abells chuckled, shuffled some papers and shook his head. "Frank, you're not a strapping young fellow fresh out of the Clark Teacher's Agency any more."

Gray smiled. "You're right about that, Colonel."

"Tidwell's a footballer—he might have thrown *you* against the wall."

"I'm afraid I lost my temper with the boy, sir," Gray admitted. "Nevertheless, I felt justified in doing what I did to maintain order in my class."

Abells nodded. "Yes, yes, I agree. So I'll mollify Mr. and Mrs. Tidwell with an apology and my assurance that such an occurrence will not happen again. In the meantime, you will reinstate the boy in your class, carry him through graduation, and give him whatever final grade you feel he's earned."

"Yes sir."

"But this matter begs my attention to another problem," Abells said. "I've heard rumors and had disturbing reports concerning the feelings of a number of our cadets toward Mr. Takahashi. This school has never condoned bigotry of any sort, Frank, and I'll not allow it to get a foothold now."

"We're all aware of the problem, sir," Captain Gray said.

"Yes," Superintendent Abells muttered. "The question is what am I to do about it?"

Captain Gray shifted in his chair. He'd known Harry Delmont Abells for almost twenty-five years. No man was more receptive to the advice and opinions of his subordinates.

"Colonel, I suggest you do nothing."

"Do nothing? That's an unusual recommendation, Frank."

Captain Gray shook his head. "The boy is Japanese, living in a country that's now at war with Japan. As long it continues, there's not much we can do that will make a difference in how people feel. This is something young Takahashi will have to learn to deal with, and protecting him from the worst of human nature will not help him become a man."

Colonel Abells said nothing, just stared over his glasses at this revered instructor whom old alumni always came back to see.

"That's the reason I didn't stop Cadet Takahashi from running away when I found him at the bus stop," Captain Gray went on. "It was something the boy had to learn on his own—that you can't run away from the injustices in life, that you're better off facing them foursquare and dealing with them on your own terms.

"I'm of the opinion, sir, that this school has a responsibility to teach its students not only history, science, and mathematics, but the fundamentals of dealing with life as well."

Colonel Abells nodded. "Quite a speech, Frank—perhaps the most I've ever heard you say at one time. All right, we'll try it your way. For the boy's sake, I hope you're right."

Cadet Harry Takahashi struggled through his last semester at the Academy— except for his loyal roommate, Roger, and a small handful of others, the Japanese attack on Pearl Harbor had cost him most of the friends he'd made in school.

The first warm days of June, 1942, witnessed both graduation at Morgan Park Military Academy, and the chilling specter of war raging throughout much of the world. In the Ukraine, the Germans had the port city of Sevastopol under siege, and in North Africa, German General Erwin Rommel was poised to capture the seaport of Tobruk—while in Asia, battle-hardened Japanese troops overran Burma and were relentlessly moving westward toward the sub-continent of India.

The graduating class of 1942 was the first in years to be off to the crucible of war. In their honor, a traditional tune was borrowed from the United States Military Academy at West Point. Performed by the cadet chorus, "Army Blue" had been sung in one version or another since 1848:

> *We've not much longer here to stay,*
> *For in a month or two*
> *We'll bid farewell to Kaydet Gray,*
> *And don the Army Blue.*

Each graduating senior knew that all men eligible for military duty were being called upon to fight, and that their own turn would come very shortly.

All except for Harry Takahashi. After Pearl Harbor, Japanese-American men had been given the category of 4C—non-draftable. Moreover, they and their families were being uprooted from their homes and placed into concentration camps by the government.

In Hawaii, things were much different, Harry learned in letters from his family. The government just couldn't incarcerate Hawaii's vast population of Japanese-Americans.

The vital economy of the islands had always been based on the labor of Japanese farmers, fishermen, everyday workers and shop owners. Government curfew laws had been put into effect, Harry's mother wrote, but all-in-all, she assured him, the overall treatment of Japanese-Americans in Honolulu was far better than the insults and humiliation being endured by the mainland Japanese.

"That's where I'm headed, Ski," he told Roger a week before graduation. "Back to Oahu, to be with my family."

"Good deal," Roger had grinned. "But I'll miss you, you damn pineapple head."

Harry didn't go to the senior prom, or to any of the graduation parties afterward. He didn't know any Japanese-American girls in Chicago, and there weren't many non-oriental girls who'd be seen with him these days. It was a bad time to be far away from home and family, he thought, but that would soon be remedied.

After the last diploma was presented, the band played Morgan Park's Alma Mater, and then "Auld Lang Syne."

When the music ended, Colonel Abells stepped to the podium, gazed out over the eager faces of his Corps for a moment, and then wished them farewell. "Commencement ceremonies for the Class of 1942 are closed."

A great *whoop* went up as sixty-two senior's caps were thrown high into the air. Kodaks clicked and cadets embraced—many with tears in their eyes, wishing each other luck in the uncertain months to come.

Harry just let his garrison cap drop to the grassy meadow, and without looking right or left, made his way through the crowd of faculty, parents, and cadets—toward his room in Hansen Hall.

He changed into a civilian shirt and slacks and carefully hung his summer full-dress uniform in the tall wardrobe closet. Looking around his small room for the last time, he lifted his suitcase and made his way down the stairs and out the side door of the barracks.

As he walked west on 111th Street, once again headed toward the trolley stop, Harry Takahashi wondered what would become of Duty, Honor, Country, now? What would his duty be, when his own country doubted his honor?

Staring out the streetcar's window, the question nagged him all the way to Union station, and afterward, as he boarded the first of a series of trains that would carry him across the country to San Francisco. On the west coast, almost three days later, Harry joined other transpacific passengers bound for the Hawaiian Islands and beyond, and boarded the late-afternoon TWA China Clipper at the Port of the Trade Winds—the bustling Art Deco seaplane terminal at Treasure Island in San Francisco Bay.

As the huge Boeing B-314 traveled westward, eight-thousand feet above the sea, Harry looked at the new MPMA senior ring that was on his left hand. Already it seemed, memories of his four years at the Academy were fading, as if were another lifetime ago.

Eight months later, the United States Government reversed its decision on not allowing Japanese-Americans to serve in the armed forces. In February of 1943, it announced the formation of the all-Japanese 442nd Infantry Regimental Combat Team.

Harry enlisted in April 1943, was sent back to Camp Shelby in Mississippi, serving as a platoon sergeant in E Company of the 2nd Battalion, where he saw heavy fighting in France.

After the war, the 442nd was recognized as the most decorated unit in United States military history. Eighteen thousand awards were bestowed upon Harry and his Japanese-American comrades—over nine thousand Purple Hearts, fifty-two Distinguished Service Crosses, Seven Distinguished Unit Citations, and a Congressional Medal of Honor.

Harry Takahashi, Class of 1942, thought of the Academy often for the rest of his life, but never returned to visit.

CHAPTER 10

▼

A LOVE STORY

Fall Term, 1942

Toward the end of scrimmage on a windy afternoon in October of 1942, Fred Stapp threw a block that effectively took out both the opposing right guard and right tackle, leaving one of them nearly unconscious, and opening a hole for his fullback to make a twenty-yard gain.

"Good job, Stapp," Coach Mahon shouted. "That's the way to open a hole."

"You okay, Norman?" Stapp asked, helping the one boy up.

"Yeah, I guess so," Norm Kopecky said, blinking and shaking his head. "Jeez, Fred—scrimmaging against you is like getting run over by a train."

"Didn't mean to hurt you," Stapp grunted, patting Kopecky on the shoulder pads. Fred Stapp was the only freshman playing first-string varsity football. Once Coach Mahon had seen him at frosh-soph practice, he tapped Fred to try out for the varsity.

"The boy's just too big to be playing against the lightweights," Mahon told Coach Marberry, who'd been given the thankless task of building 1942's sluggish frosh-soph squad.

"You might as well take him," Marberry agreed. "Most of my boys are afraid of him and I'm getting an awfully lot of complaints from their parents about his size."

Stapp was a big boy, at six foot one and two hundred pounds. His face was heavily pockmarked and he often gave the impression of being somewhat slow-witted.

The seniors had been reading Steinbeck's *Of Mice and Men* in Lieutenant Shaver's fourth year English class, and one commented that if they had to pick someone to play Lennie Small—it would be Fred Stapp.

Like Steinbeck's fictional lummox, there was no sign of the bully in Stapp, but rather a plodding, clumsy gentleness—he liked buying peanuts in the PX and feeding them to the chattering gray squirrels that had long ago claimed the campus as their own.

As a plebe, he was obedient to the upperclassmen and friendly with everyone else, but on the football field and in the boxing ring, Stapp became a hulking brute—seemingly ignorant of his own size and strength.

When the boy signed up for the intramural boxing tournament, Coach Harry Mahoney watched incredulous as Stapp stepped into the ring for a practice bout with a husky senior heavyweight named Harvey Cobb.

Cobb had walked away with the heavyweight championship in his junior year and held it ever since. Stapp had been the first to go up against him, and as Coach Mahoney laced his gloves, Fred was hesitant. "Maybe I shouldn't be boxing an upperclassman, Coach," he whispered. "I'm only a plebe."

"That doesn't matter in intramural sports," Mahoney told him. "You just defend yourself the best you can—Cadet Cobb's a first-rate boxer."

"Yes sir, I'll try my best," Stapp said.

Each bout was made up of three three-minute rounds, giving Harvey Cobb plenty of time to show his stuff. Cobb wasted little time, bouncing and weaving, jabbing his left hand into Stapp's face at will, and then following with powerful right hooks that smashed into the plodding freshman's chest, shoulders and head.

"Jesus Christ, Stapp," Coach Mahoney shouted. "Put up your hands and defend yourself!"

But for two and a half rounds, Fred Stapp only shuffled about in a small circle, keeping himself face to face with his opponent as Harvey Cobb pummeled him with rights and lefts—blows the big plebe merely ignored, almost as if he were shrugging off the buzz of an annoying mosquito.

At the break between the second and third rounds, Cobb was breathing hard and his arms felt as heavy as lead. The heavyweight looked up at Cadet Assistant Coach Jack Gans as Gans wiped the sweat from his eyes. "It's like hitting a side of beef that doesn't hit back," Cobb complained, breathing hard. "He doesn't even try to block a punch, Jack, but nothing I got seems to hurt him."

Jack Gans shook his head. "He's a palooka, Harv—just keep smacking him and the fight goes to you on points."

Cobb nodded, stood at the timekeeper's call, and went back in for the third round. He and Stapp touched gloves and then Harvey Cobb continued to pound Stapp again—with the same heavy flurry of blows that produced the same frustrating result—nothing.

Then, with no warning, as if he'd unexpectedly become bored with the game, Stapp brought his right hand around and smashed it into the side of Harvey Cobb's head. A single right hook, the only punch Stapp threw in over two minutes and thirty seconds of the contest put the school's undefeated heavyweight champion flat on his back—feebly struggling to get up.

"Are you okay, sir?" Fred Stapp said, bending over to help his opponent, worried that he might have gotten himself into trouble.

"Don't touch him!" Coach Mahoney shouted. "The round isn't over yet."

When time was called with Harvey Cobb still on the canvas, Mahoney came through the ropes and hustled Fred Stapp out of the ring. "What the hell kind of exhibition was that, son?" The coach asked, unlacing Fred's gloves. "You let him beat you silly for more than two rounds."

"Aw, it didn't bother me much," Fred said.

"Stapp, you only threw one damned punch in the whole fight—I'd like to know why."

Fred shrugged. "Well, I didn't want to hurt him, sir."

They had to give Fred Stapp the heavyweight championship. Harvey Cobb turned down a re-match, and no other cadet in school was big enough to fight him.

That was when Fred turned his attention to football.

Scrimmage finally ended. Coach Mahon told the team to run a lap and then hit the showers. Holding his helmet in his hand, Fred had just about circled the field, jogging the final stretch along Bell Avenue when he heard a girl's voice call out, "Hey you—number twenty!"

"That's Erna Mae," a junior named Ollie Reiger said. "I think she's calling you, Stapp."

Fred slowed. "Who's Erna Mae?" He asked, turning to see the girl waving at him.

"Go over and see her," Ollie urged. "You'll find out."

Fred wasn't sure of what to do. As best he could remember, no girl had ever talked to him before, even growing up in the old 18th Street neighborhood—but now this one, dressed in a blue coat with white piping, was calling out and waving to him.

"Maybe she needs help," he wondered out loud.

"She needs help all right," Ollie said. "Go help her, Stapp."

"She said number twenty, didn't she?" He looked down at the large, white numerals on his uniform jersey.

"She sure did," Ollie grinned. "Must be your lucky day."

Fred nodded and walked across the brownish October grass to where the girl was standing. Approaching, he was surprised to see her smile and wave to him again. He hadn't noticed her earlier and wondered how long she'd been standing there.

"Hi," the girl said pleasantly, holding out her hand. "I'm Erna Mae Keller. I've been watching you play—you're pretty good."

"Uh, I'm Fred," he told her, shaking hands.

"Fred what?"

"Fred Stapp."

She smiled again. "Fred Stapp," she repeated. "Well, that's a real nice name. I wonder why boys never have two first names like some girls do?"

"What?" He asked, unsure of what she was talking about.

The girl shrugged and brushed her hair back. "Oh, you know—I'm Erna Mae. I know one girl named Mary Ann and one named Rose Ellen. But I never heard of any boy named Ed Pete or Johnny Mike—have you?"

Fred thought about it a moment. "Well, no—I guess not."

Erna Mae Keller was not a pretty girl, even by Fred's limited experience—which was basically none at all. One of her teeth was crooked and another was chipped. Both showed when she smiled. Her face was broad, but her brown hair was long and smooth, and her eyes seemed to follow his. The winter coat she wore covered her figure, but Fred managed to notice that she had trim ankles and was wearing white socks and saddle shoes.

"I got my big brother's car," Erna Mae said, nodding toward an old 1934 Ford sedan that was parked on the street. "How about me and you going down to the Hale Pharmacy for a soda—after you take your shower?"

"I—I can't," Fred stammered. "I gotta be at Mess III by six o'clock—that's when we eat supper."

Erna Mae nodded. "Well, you're kind of cute and you're a real good player." She took a piece of paper out of her purse and wrote something on it. "Here's my phone number. Call me sometime and maybe we can go out."

Fred was nearly speechless. He stared at the phone number on the piece of paper she'd given him and nodded. "I—I will."

"Okay, see you around, then."

"Okay, sure," Fred said. He gave her an awkward wave as she walked across the street to the car.

That night, as the last long note of taps drifted away, he lay in bed thinking about the events of that afternoon. After supper, he'd purposely kept himself busy shining his boots and those of Cadet Captain Forrest, a senior who'd taken Fred as his personal plebe at the start of the semester. After finishing these tasks, he'd tried to study, but his mind kept wandering off—with thoughts of the girl in the blue coat.

Why had she even bothered to talk to him? Fred wondered.

As far back as he could remember, ever since he'd been a boy, girls never bothered with him. "You're too big and ugly for girls," a pinch-faced nun had told him once in school. "You're a big ox, and they're afraid of you—they run away. Maybe God wants you to be a priest, Frederick."

But Erna Mae Keller hadn't seemed scared, and she didn't try to run away, even though she could have. He thought of the folded piece of paper in his desk drawer. She'd even given him her phone number, asking him to call her, and suggesting they might go out sometime. Did that mean she wanted to have a date with him? Fred wondered. He'd never had a date with a girl and was sure he would be ignorant of what to do on a date, and probably end up making a fool of himself.

In the darkness, Fred touched the side of his cheek and felt the extreme acne scarring that covered his face. But she'd seen his face too, he thought, and she'd asked him to call her anyway.

Taking all week to build his courage, on Saturday morning he went downstairs and used one of the pay phones in the dorm lobby. As he was dialing the number, he started to sweat and he could feel his stomach churn.

On the third ring, a man's voice answered.

"Uh—is Erna Mae there?" Fred asked.

"Yeah sure, hold on a minute."

Fred's forehead was wet. He could feel his heart pounding as he held the phone. After a moment, he decided to hang up, and was about to when he heard a noise on the line and then a girl's voice saying, "Hello—this is Erna Mae."

"Hello—this is Fred."

"Fred? Fred who?"

His heart seemed to flop in his chest. Oh jeez, he thought. She doesn't even remember. "Uh—Fred Stapp. You talked to me after football practice the other day."

"Number twenty? Oh sure, I was afraid you'd never call."

She was afraid he wouldn't call? Fred could barely believe his ears. "Yeah—uh—well, I'm sorry but they've been keeping us awful busy."

"What are you doing, Fred?" Erna Mae asked.

"Well, we got a football game today—against Lemont."

"Are you playing?"

"Sure—right guard."

"That's terrific," Erna Mae said. "Maybe I'll come watch."

Fred swallowed hard. "Well, I got a Saturday night pass, and I—uh—I was wondering if—if maybe after the game, uh, maybe we could go out together. Go see a movie or something?"

"That'd be super," Erna Mae said excitedly. "They're showing *King's Row* at the Capitol and I got my brother's car."

"Okay then," Fred said, incredulous. "I guess I'll see you after the game."

"Okay—it's a date. I'll be parked on 112th Street."

"It's a date?" He asked her, hesitantly. "A real date?"

"Sure it is," Erna Mae laughed. "See you after the game."

Bounding up the stairs two at a time, Fred nearly collided with a slight little freshman named Al Pape on the second floor landing. He grabbed the diminutive plebe by the shoulders and lifted him in the air. "I got a date tonight, Little Al—with a girl!"

That afternoon, the Academy Warriors trounced Lemont High School by the lopsided score of thirty-nine to nothing. Not a single Lemont running back gained more than a yard running the football over MPMA's right guard position. Fred even recovered a fumble and ran it back for a touchdown in the third quarter.

He showered quickly after the game. The locker room was full of rough horseplay and the boisterous celebrations of the winning team. If it was just a normal football Saturday, Fred Stapp would have joined in, but this Saturday was something special. After he'd showered, he hurriedly dressed and checked his appearance in the locker room's full-length mirror. Disconcerted by a deep cut across the bridge of his nose, Fred turned up the collar of his reefer and quietly snuck out the side entrance of the gymnasium.

As soon as he stepped outside, he spotted Erna Mae waiting in her brother's Ford. She was filing her nails and had a copy of *True Confessions* propped against the steering wheel. Fred knocked on the passenger side window and she slid over on the seat. "You can drive," Erna Mae told him, rolling down the window.

"You made a touchdown," she said, as he adjusted the seat and slipped behind the wheel. "I was rooting for you."

"Aw—I was just lucky."

"What happened to your nose?"

"I think I got kicked."

"Well, the movie starts at seven," she told him. "We'd better step on it if we want to see the coming attractions."

They bought popcorn and soda and settled into balcony seats just as the theater lights dimmed. Even though it had started to rain and the temperature was unusually chilly for October, the Capitol was crowded on Saturday night—filled with both old and young moviegoers.

Fred had never sat next to a girl at the movies before, in fact he'd never sat this close to a girl before—and he was as jumpy as a bug, terrified that he might do or say something stupid.

After the coming attractions, *Fox Movietone News* flashed on the screen—showing grim newsreel footage of Marines in combat with the Japanese on Guadalcanal, in the South Pacific.

"My brother's over there somewhere," Erna Mae whispered.

"I hope he's okay," Fred said, knowing nothing more helpful to offer. Then he added, "I just hope the war lasts long enough for me to go, too."

King's Row was about a budding doctor and his hometown. It starred Ann Sheridan, Robert Cummings, and Ronald Reagan, and it seemed to Fred that every single character in the movie had to overcome at least two deaths, some sort of painful experience and a tortured lost-love. Erna Mae had tears in her eyes when it was over, but Fred hadn't cared for it very much, although he wouldn't tell her that.

The double feature included an old western called *West of the Divide* with John Wayne. Neither one of them wanted to see it, and Fred was feeling hungry. "Maybe you want to get a hamburger or something?" He asked. He still hadn't mustered up the courage to use her name.

"Sure, I'd love a hamburger—where do you want to go?"

Fred was stumped. Up to now, he'd rarely left Hansen Hall to go anyplace, and he didn't know the neighborhood at all. "Let's go to your favorite place," he suggested, pleased with what he felt was quick thinking.

Erna Mae considered it. "Well, there's a pretty good little grill on 110th and Vincennes, near school. It's called Shorty's. They've got good hamburgers, and they've got a fountain, too."

Following her directions, Fred found Shorty's Grill and parked the Ford on the street directly in front of it. When they walked in the door he noticed a group of boys lounging in one of the booths. Looking up, one of them grinned. "Hey, Erna Mae, how's it goin', kiddo?"

"I'm doing just fine, Eddie," she said.

"Who's the apple boy?"

"This is Fred Stapp," she told the boys. "He plays football and he took me to the movies tonight."

"Hey, nice to meet'cha, Freddy boy," Eddie said as one of the others, a boy called Derby, pushed himself up in the booth and saluted. "How you doin', General?"

"Hello, fellas," Fred said, affably.

"Let's go sit down, honey," Erna Mae said.

"Honey!" Eddie laughed. "Whooo—ain't love grand?"

As she and Fred took a booth, Erna Mae put her hand behind her back and gave Eddie and his pals the finger.

"Jeez, the guy looks like Frankenstein," Derby said.

They picked a far booth next to a window and after settling in, Erna Mae took a crumpled pack of Lucky Strikes out of her purse. "You want a smoke, Fred?"

Fred shook his head. "No, I can't. Coach Mahon won't let any of us smoke during football season."

"That's mean," she said, pushing a book of matches across the table. "Will you light it for me?"

A chubby, curly-haired blonde waitress brought them menus and glasses of water. "What's an apple boy?" Fred asked under his breath.

"Aw, that's just what the boys at my school call you Academy fellas," Erna Mae told him as he lit her cigarette.

"What's it mean?"

"Oh, you know—they say you guys are polishing the apple all the time—but don't pay any attention to them. They're just creeps and they're jealous."

"Of what?"

She shrugged. "Who knows? You ready to order, honey?"

Fred nodded dumbly. That was the second time she called him honey, and he didn't know what to make of it. He remembered his mother calling his father that many years ago, when he was just a little boy—but that was before they began to fight all the time.

Erna Mae liked to talk, and Fred was thankful for that because he found it hard to think of anything interesting to say. She talked about her parents, and about her brother Tommy, who'd enlisted in the Marines when he'd turned eighteen. She told him about school and how she planned to go to California someday. Hollywood, she said—maybe become an actress. "The movie magazines say you gotta be real pretty, but those starlets use lots of makeup, I hear."

"My ma's someplace in California," Fred said. "A town called Long Beach—she helps build airplanes for the war. She says it's real pretty out there."

"If I ever get there, I'll send you a post card," Erna Mae told him. "Maybe I'll even be in the movies."

"I could never do anything like that," Fred said, lamely. "Not with my looks, that's for sure."

"What's wrong with how you look?"

He shrugged. "You know, all these scars and stuff—I had acne real bad when I was younger."

"Is that why you've never had much to do with girls?"

Fred could feel his face turn red. "How'd you know that?"

Erna Mae laughed lightly. "I can just tell—you're real shy and you don't talk much. Most of the fellas I know jabber all the time, mostly about themselves—like that Eddie over there."

"Is he a friend of yours?"

"Eddie? Oh, he calls me for a date every now and then—when he feels like it, I guess."

"This is the first time I been on a date," Fred admitted. He was starting to relax a little, although learning that Erna Mae had dated someone else sitting only a few booths away had him feeling some vague measure of jealousy. "Do you go out a lot?"

"Oh, sure," she said, dragging on her cigarette. "I've dated a lot of boys at the Academy. Most of them were day students—they don't have to be back in the barracks so early."

The blonde waitress brought them their hamburgers and asked if they wanted to hear the jukebox. "It's three songs for a dime."

"Yeah, sure," Erna Mae said, stubbing her cigarette out in the table's glass ashtray. "Give her a dime, Fred."

The waitress went over and fed the Wurlitzer. The first song to come out of it was, "Shoo-Shoo Baby," by the Andrews Sisters.

A few minutes later, the other boys got up to leave. "Hey Erna Mae, I'll give you a call, okay?" Eddie called out.

"Sure, sure," she said, without even bothering to look at him. "I'll believe it when I see it, big shot."

"Good luck, General," the one called Derby said, laughing and saluting again.

"Okay, thanks," Fred answered, not quite sure of what the boy thought he needed luck for. "Good luck to you, too."

"Jeez, he's a real dunce," Eddie whispered, whistling as they went out the door. "You could chop wood with a face like that."

"Which face you talkin' about?" One of the others whispered. "Erna Mae's, or the General's?"

The door closed on their laughter.

Fred's Saturday pass was good until 11:30. He and Erna Mae took their time at Shorty's, sipping Cokes and listening to music on the jukebox. Finally, he glanced at the wall clock hanging over the counter and sighed. "Well, I guess I gotta get back."

"Hon," Erna Mae whispered, as she had him help her with her coat. "Don'tcha want to leave something for the waitress?"

"What?" Fred asked.

"Y'know—fifteen cents maybe, for a tip?"

"Oh," he said dumbly, fumbling in his pocket. "Oh, sure."

When they neared the Academy, she suggested that he pull the car around to the parking lot in back of Hansen Hall. "It's real dark back there," she said, lighting another cigarette.

Erna Mae was right, and for a minute he wondered how she'd known the parking area was so dark. There were no lights on in the barracks. Taps had been sounded an hour ago and the only one still up would be the officer of the day, anxiously awaiting those with passes to check back in so he could finally go off duty and turn all responsibility over to the faculty officer in charge.

Fred turned off the headlights, but left the engine running so the car would be warm while the radio played. They were listening to Les Brown's "Sentimental Journey" as Erna Mae slid over next to him. "Do you boarders always have to be in by 11:30?"

"No," he said, wondering what she was doing pressing against him so close, even closer now than she'd been at the movies. "We can get overnight passes, too, and if there's no Sunday parade, we don't have to be back until Sunday night."

"Well, get one of those next time, honey," she said, laying her head on his shoulder.

Listening to the music, Fred sat straight up behind the steering wheel, staring out the windshield with his arms at his sides, as Erna Mae began to wiggle around, making odd little noises and pressing herself against him. He wasn't altogether sure what she was doing, but he knew he only had about fifteen minutes before he had to be checked in and back in bed.

"Honey," she said softly. "Don't you want to kiss me?"

The question caught Fred off guard. She not only wanted to go out on a date with him, now she wanted him to kiss her, too—right out here in back of the barracks. Suddenly he felt like a fool, a big, stupid oaf. He'd never even come close to kissing a girl before, and had no idea of how it was done.

"Yeah sure, I guess so," he said, feeling as dim-witted as he'd ever felt in his life. "I'm not sure—"

"Here honey, let me show you how," she said, moving her lips to his. He felt his body flush with warmth as she kissed him, then was surprised to feel the curious, but pleasurable sensation, of her tongue pushing his mouth apart. She tasted of cigarettes and Juicy-Fruit gum. Fred was astounded by what was occurring. He'd never felt anything like a girl's tongue in his mouth before—never even knew such things were done, and for an instant he was worried that he might be doing something wrong.

"That's what's called French kissing, honey," Erna Mae said in a low voice. "Now put your arms around me and do it back."

He did as he was told, suddenly feeling like he did whenever a pin-up magazine of girls with hardly any clothes on made its way around Hansen Hall and finally came to him.

As they kissed, Erna Mae started to groan. She unbuttoned her coat and pulled it open, taking Fred's hand and guiding it up under her soft wool sweater. "You can feel me up if you want," she said.

Fred lost all track of time. Suddenly it didn't matter much if he was late or not. He suspected that what Erna Mae was letting him do was exactly what the priests and nuns had warned the boys and girls about when he was at Blessed Sacrament Catholic School, but he didn't care—all that mattered now was the music on the radio, the warmth and darkness of the car, and this knowing girl who was taking him to places he'd never been before.

Suddenly she stopped, gently pushing his hand away. "I've got my period, honey," she said. "Otherwise we could do it." Her hand fumbled for his belt in the dark. "But you can just lay back and I'll make you feel real good."

As her fingers found the zipper of his trousers, Fred closed his eyes and started to say a silent Hail Mary—interrupting it halfway through when he was suddenly ashamed of himself for making the Holy Mother any part of what was happening in that car.

By the time he reported in, it was past midnight. "You're late, plebe," the OD said, looking Fred over and writing something on a clipboard. "Where the hell you been—in a fight?"

"No sir," Fred said. He felt like the whole world knew what he and Erna Mae had just done.

"Then straighten your tie and tuck in your shirt. You look like a bum." The OD sat behind a desk with his pencil poised. "Where you been? I got to make out a report."

"I went to the movies, sir," Fred explained. "And then for a hamburger with my girlfriend."

"And you were necking and forgot about the time?"

"Uh—yes sir, I guess so."

"Buy a watch, mister," the OD said, scribbling something on the clipboard. "Okay, you're checked in but you're on report. Get upstairs and go to bed."

Fred saluted. "Yes sir. Thank you, sir."

His roommate, another freshman named Jerry Hoke, was fast asleep and snoring loudly. Leaving the lights off, Fred undressed quietly and slipped into bed. He pulled the covers over him and lay on his back in the dark, thinking of Erna Mae Keller and staring up at the ceiling. It took him three hours to fall asleep.

Restricted to barracks the following weekend, Fred rushed to the telephone every night after study hour. Each time he talked to Erna Mae, it was easier, and he couldn't get her off his mind.

"We could maybe go out again if I wasn't restricted," he said gloomily.

"That's okay," she told him. "Maybe the weekend after."

Then Fred's eye caught an announcement someone had put up on the bulletin board. The Emblem Club Dance was scheduled for the Saturday after next. Coach Mahon had already told him that he was to get his varsity football letter. That made him the only plebe eligible to attend.

"Would you like to go to a dance?" He asked her.

"A dance? Where?"

"Here, at the Academy."

There was a long silence on the phone, and he wondered if he had said something wrong. "Erna Mae?" Fred said, using her name easily now. "Are you still there?"

"I'm here," she sniffed, almost sounding as if she were crying. "But it ain't nice to tease a girl about something like that."

"Something like what?"

"Taking me to a dance."

"I wasn't teasing," he protested. "Would you go with me?"

"Oh, my gosh," she said suddenly. "You're serious—I never been to a dance there."

"I thought you told me you've been out with a lot of the fellas at the Academy."

"I have—but they never asked me to none of the dances."

"Well, would you go with me?"

"Oh honey," she squealed. "I'd love to."

At first Erna Mae wanted to get a proper dress for the dance at the fancy Beverly Vogue Dress Shop, but her parents quickly put a stop to whatever thoughts she had in that direction. "We ain't the Rockerfellers, Erna Mae," her mother told her. "Just get your dress at Kaden's."

For his part, Fred had to ask an upperclassman what he needed to do in preparation for the formal event.

"Just make sure your brass is polished, plebe," Cadet Captain Charlie Forrest told him. "And call Evergreen Florists—put in your order for the girl's corsage right away."

"What's a corsage, sir?" Fred asked lamely.

"Flowers, Mr. Dumbjohn," Forrest told him. "They're usually roses or orchids. What's your date wearing?"

"I dunno, sir—a dress, I guess."

Forrest shook his head, astounded at how clueless these plebes could be. "Is it a strapless dress, plebe?"

"Sir, I dunno, sir," Fred repeated, feeling stupid. How was he to know what kind of dress Erna Mae might wear?

"Call her and ask," Forrest advised him patiently "Find out the color of her dress, and whether it's strapless or not. Then come and let me know, and I'll tell you what kind of corsage to get her."

"Yes sir, thank you, sir."

With its football-themed decorations, the Emblem Club Dance was held on the basketball court in the gymnasium, with goal posts erected at each end, and play diagrams painted on the floor.

Fred was nervously waiting for Erna Mae as she pulled the old Ford up to the curb on Hoyne Avenue. When she got out of the car she was wearing her winter coat over a pale pink chiffon cocktail gown, and to Fred, she looked stunning.

They made their way to the gym, and once she'd hung up her coat he handed her a box he'd been carrying. A delivery truck from Evergreen Florists had delivered it and a few dozen others an hour or so earlier. The box was still cool from being in the florist's cold storage "It's an orchid," Fred stated proudly. "They call it a wrist corsage."

"Honey, it's beautiful." She slipped it on her wrist. "Nobody's ever bought me a corsage before."

The Emblem Club had hired the Johnny Rankis Orchestra for the dance and the music was mellow. Clumsy on his feet, Fred was embarrassed by his lack of skill on the dance floor. Instead, he and Erna Mae spent most of the evening sitting off to the side, drinking punch and watching the other couples dance.

"I never learned how," Fred explained, feeling mortified.

"Oh, it's okay," Erna Mae told him. "It's a lot of fun just bein' here." She was enjoying herself more than she ever had in her life, feeling feminine and pretty in her new pink dress. On her wrist was both the orchid Fred had given her, and the dance favor—a small booklet with the date of the affair, the name *Football Frolics,* and a miniature plastic football attached.

As she hummed along with the orchestra, watching the other cadets in their full dress grays, and dancing with their dates. Erna Mae realized that she knew so many of their names and faces from other urgent, heated nights, in the dark backseats of other cars, but that was something Fred didn't need to know.

Near the punch bowl, Ollie Reiger nudged another cadet, a left end named Toby Short. "Jeez, look at that," Ollie said. "Fred Stapp actually brought Erna Mae to the dance—that takes guts."

"Or no brains," Toby Short muttered, holding two paper cups of fruit punch. "I'll bet that dog biscuit has screwed half the guys in this gym. Why would he bring *her* to a dance?"

Cadet Short felt someone tap him on the shoulder. He turned to see Captain Mahon looking at him. "Pardon me, Mr. Short," the football coach said. "But I couldn't help overhear your opinion of Cadet Stapp's date."

"Yes sir," Short said. "I meant no offense, sir."

"That's not how it sounded, Short. Have you ever seen Cadet Stapp in the boxing ring?"

"No sir, I have not, sir."

Mahon grunted and smiled. "Stapp's only a freshman, son, but I'd wager he could whip your ass until your gonads popped out of your ears."

"Yes sir."

"Then let's have no more talk like that, Mr. Short."

"Yes sir, sorry sir."

The last tune of the evening was "Moonlight in Vermont," and when it was ended, Fred and Erna Mae hurried out the door. The November night was bitter cold after spending hours in the heated gym and by the time they reached her car, Erna Mae was shivering.

"You sure look pretty," Fred said as they got in the Ford.

"Thanks, honey," Erna Mae said, kissing him lightly on the cheek. "Have you got an overnight pass?"

"Uh-huh, I was able to get one."

"Good," she said. "I know a place where we can go."

"Uh, excuse me, sir, can I talk to you?"

Cadet Captain Charles Forrest carefully marked his spot with a finger and looked up from his chemistry textbook to see who was disturbing his study. With the volume on his Philco portable radio turned down, Jo Stafford was singing "Long Ago and Far Away," and Forrest's roommate, Cadet 1st Lieutenant Bob Lutz was curled up on his bed, already fast asleep and snoring.

It had been a quiet Sunday, with no disturbances or horseplay in Hansen Hall barracks this snowy November night. Up until now, Charlie Forrest had been able to study for his next day's chemistry test virtually undisturbed.

The cadet who stood nervously in Forrest's doorway was Fred Stapp, who Forrest had tapped as his own personal plebe at the beginning of the year. The principle concerning plebes was that in addition to hazing them and using them to perform chores, seniors were responsible for their development and guidance throughout the plebe's first year. Charlie Forrest took this duty seriously. By Academy standards, he'd practically held Stapp's hand through the entire last semester.

Charlie studied Stapp quietly for a moment. It was nearly taps and the barracks was settling down to sleep. What was Stapp doing wandering around at this hour? Forrest shook his head. Poor guy, he thought, it wasn't that Fred Stapp was stupid; he was just slow, good-natured, and sort of innocent—almost too innocent for dorm life and the rigidity of Plebe Year at the Academy.

Forrest sighed and smiled inwardly. He'd always liked Fred and the sight of the hulking freshman standing awkwardly in the doorway wearing a too-small bathrobe was almost comical.

"You interrupted my studies, plebe. Is that your best imitation of a brace?"

"No sir, sorry sir," Fred responded, snapping to attention.

"Stow it, Stapp," Forrest barked, trying to sound harsh enough to camouflage affection for his oversized young charge. "You need to get squared away and make your request properly this time, Mr. Dumbjohn."

"Sir, yes, sir." Fred did his best to stand ramrod straight, suck his gut in further, and jam his chin into his neck. "Sir, Cadet Stapp requests permission to speak to Cadet Captain Forrest, sir."

Forrest stood up and walked around his plebe, examining him as though looking at a specimen under a microscope. He could see that Stapp was nervous, although not as nervous as he'd been at the start of the year, before Forrest had taken him under his wing and started whipping him into some kind of shape.

Fred Stapp might have been uneasy, but he wasn't frightened. He'd come to Morgan Park Military Academy from a poor, tough part of town—his tuition paid by his local parish.

Stapp never seemed to be afraid of anything. Forrest had seen proof of that on the football field and in the intramural boxing ring. But tough or not, Fred Stapp was the sort of freshman that tried to please. He could often be seen cheerfully lugging three or four book briefcases between Blake Hall and West Hall—one of his own, and the others belonging to seniors.

"At ease, Mr. Stapp," Forrest said finally, watching as Stapp eased out of his brace. But not too far. Plebes learned quickly that upperclassmen drew a line between being at ease and being a slob. Stapp took a deep breath, and for a minute, Forrest thought the kid might have changed his mind about talking, but finally the words came, in an unsure, halting tone.

"Sir, I want to—report an—honor code violation."

Forrest suddenly stopped in his tracks. Rarely discussed, the honor code was serious business at the Academy. As a member of the Guardians, Charlie Forrest had the distasteful duty earlier in the semester to recommend to Maj. J. Ray Cygon, the commandant, that a second-year cadet be expelled for stealing.

He crossed the room and sat back down, pointing toward his roommate's empty chair. "Why don't you close the door and sit down, Mr. Stapp."

"Yes, sir," Fred said, doing as instructed. He sat upright in the chair, unable to relax in an upperclassman's presence.

Forrest looked thoughtfully at the plebe, wondering for a brief moment how he himself had looked to the upperclassmen when he was a plebe at the Academy three and a half years earlier. Had he looked then, as Stapp looked now—like a deer in the headlights?

"Against whom do you make this charge, Mr. Stapp?"

Unlike West Point, Morgan Park cadets weren't duty bound to report transgressions by their fellow cadets. There wasn't any *'nor tolerate those who do'* attached to the code, which simply said that "MPMA Cadets do not lie, cheat, or steal."

Forrest had a hunch the offense must be extremely serious to have brought Stapp to this point—especially if the offending cadet were an upperclassman.

"Sir," Fred stammered, trying to be courageous, but looking every bit the oversized seventeen-year-old boy that he was. "It's against myself, sir."

"Against yourself?" Charlie Forrest asked, not sure he'd heard correctly.

"Yes, sir."

"Cadet Stapp, do you realize the ramifications of what you've just told me?"

"What's *ramifications* mean, sir?"

"Consequences—seriousness."

"Oh—yes sir."

Why did it have to be my plebe? Forrest wondered. He leveled his gaze at the nervous freshman.

"Have you stolen something, Mr. Stapp?"

"No sir, nothing like that."

Forrest relaxed a bit. Thank God, he thought. He didn't think the disciplinary committee was ready for another thief.

"Have you cheated in your studies?"

"No sir, not that either."

"Then I take it, Mr. Stapp, that you have told a lie."

"Yes, sir," Fred said with a gulp. "I think so, sir."

Forrest cocked his head and furrowed his brow. "You *think* you've told a lie, Mr. Stapp?"

"Yes sir."

"You think, but you don't know. Maybe you want to explain that to me?"

"It was last night, sir," the plebe began haltingly. "My girl and me were at the dance. Maybe you know her—Erna Mae Keller. She's a sophomore at Morgan Park High School."

Charlie Forrest knew Erna Mae Keller, as did nearly half the senior class and most of the football team. Erna Mae was a girl the boys described as a dog biscuit or a charity case—unattractive, and willing to sleep with just about anybody. She'd been the talk of the school for a long while, but she seemed to drop out of sight earlier this year.

"I don't know her," Charlie lied. "Get on with it."

"Yes sir." Fred took a deep breath and went on. "Well, I had an overnight pass last night and all day today, sir, and we—*uh*—we—"

"C'mon, Mr. Stapp, spit it out," Forrest barked, growing tired of the plebe's timidity.

Taps began to sound.

"Sir, I better go," Fred said.

"Stay put," Charlie ordered. "Tell me what you came in here to say. I won't let bed check report you."

"Yes sir. Erna Mae's brother is in the marines so she had his car and we—we stayed overnight at a motor court. That little one on 95th Street. We—*uh*—we did it last night, sir."

"Did what?"

"You know, sir—we—we screwed and stuff."

"It's not an honor code violation to screw a girl, Mr. Stapp," Forrest said sternly. "Get to the point."

"Yes sir," Fred gulped again, and then blurted out, "Sir, I told Erna Mae—she's my girl—I told Erna Mae that I loved her—"

Forrest waited, wondering what would come next.

"—and I don't know if I really do," Fred said.

It wasn't easy but Forrest kept from grinning. Obviously Stapp took this seriously so Forrest knew he had to take it seriously too. Or, at least appear to. He knew that laughing at one's subordinates was not the way to gain or keep respect. He was just thankful that his roommate, Bob Lutz, was still fast sleep. Bob was a lady's man and Fred Stapp's concerns would have put Lutz into stitches.

"I see," Forrest said softly, trying to figure out what to tell his plebe. "And you believe this violates the honor code?"

"Yes sir, that is—" Fred slumped for a moment, his anxiety and uncertainty finally overpowering his plebe discipline. "I don't know, sir—but I've been worried about it all night."

"What worries you more, Mr. Stapp? Forrest asked. "Having misled your girl-friend, or having violated the honor code?"

"The honor code, sir," Fred said quickly—a little too quickly in Forrest's mind. He'd never cared for the 'I love you' ploy to *bag the dolls,* as he'd heard other fellows call it. But, at the same time, he couldn't fault the freshman for tak-ing the honor code to heart.

"When did you make the statement, Mr. Stapp?"

"Sir?"

"When, Stapp? Before you two screwed? As bait to lure her to the trap? While you were doing it? Or maybe afterwards, to thank the young lady for her favors—when did you utter the lie?"

Fred's face turned a beet red. Forrest had never seen anyone blush such a vivid red. Again, he suppressed laughter and waited patiently for the plebe to overcome his embarrassment.

"Sir, during—during—you know, sir. During—"

"Yeah," Forrest said, cutting Stapp off. "I get the picture."

He turned to his bookshelf where a dozen or more textbooks were lined up. He reached for the thickest one and pulled it off the shelf, making sure that Stapp couldn't see the title. He then began to page through it deliberately, as though searching for something specific. After a moment, he slammed the book closed, laying it on his desk, with the cover down and the spine title against the wall. Once more, he turned his attention to Stapp.

"What book was that, sir?" Fred asked.

"The Manual of Cadet Behavior," Forrest said. "Given only to senior commissioned officers here at the Academy."

"Oh, yes sir."

"After consulting it and considering your case, I believe I can save the Disciplinary Committee some trouble, Mr. Stapp," Forrest stated firmly. "*The Manual of Cadet Behavior* says that statements made to a young lady while in the heat of passion are not subject to the honor code unless made with the express intent to deceive, and from what you've told me, Miss Keller had already succumbed to your charms. Hence the statement could not have been deceitful."

"Do you really think so, sir?"

"That's what the manual says," Forrest said. "Besides, Stapp, I'm not even sure it was a lie. Do you love the girl or not?"

"Sir—I don't know, sir."

"Well, did you love her when you told her?"

"Oh, yes sir—you bet," Fred insisted. "But now, I'm not sure if it was true."

Charlie Forrest nodded gravely. "The important thing is that it was true when you said it. If you told me today that your favorite food was roast beef and then you had fried chicken tomorrow and changed your mind, would you report an honor code violation the next day?"

"No sir, I guess I wouldn't," Fred said, suddenly relieved of his burden. He recognized the path Forrest was clearing for him to overcome his moral dilemma.

"Then why worry, Mr. Stapp? You didn't tell a falsehood and so there has been no honor code violation."

Fred was grinning from ear to ear. "Are you sure, sir?"

"I'm sure,"

"Thank you, sir."

"But," Forrest went on, raising his finger. "You need to reflect on your responsibility to be honest and truthful with young ladies. They're not just trophies to be put behind glass in Alumni Hall."

"Yes sir," the plebe said cautiously. "It's just that—"

Forrest waited. "It's just what?" He asked, when Stapp failed to finish his sentence.

Fred looked embarrassed again. "To be real honest sir, it's the other fellas. They've all done it, and I never—"

"You mean *they all say they've done it,* Mr. Stapp."

"They're always talking about it, sir. And they make fun of me because I never—well, you know." Fred blushed again. "I'm kind of clumsy, and with my face like it is, I guess I never had too much luck with girls."

Forrest nodded, still able to remember how it was to be a plebe and away from home, surrounded by other fellows trying to prove their manhood. Talk was cheap in Hansen Hall.

"There's nothing wrong with being inexperienced, Mr. Stapp," Forrest said. "And there's nothing wrong with your face."

Charlie Forrest suddenly wondered how he'd gone from being a high school senior to being a father figure to an oversized kid just three years younger than himself. "In fact, I didn't enjoy the favors of a girl until my junior year—so you're almost three years ahead of me."

"Is that right, sir?" Fred said, his eyes wide with wonder that his upperclass mentor had been so slow.

Forrest stood up sharply. "I think that will be all for now, Mr. Stapp. If bed check gives you a hard time, tell them to come and see me."

"Yes sir!" The plebe snapped to attention. He turned smartly and walked to the door. As he reached for the knob, Forrest called his name. Stapp turned to face him again.

"Relax, Fred," the senior said. "You'll be all right."

A grin washed across Fred's face. "Yes sir!" He said, making his way to his room with a spring to his step.

After Stapp was gone, Charlie Forrest glanced at his sleeping roommate and shook his head. Jesus Christ, he thought, as he got out of his pants. I should've been a priest.

If Cadet Captain Forrest thought he'd solved Fred's problems with Erna Mae Keller, he was wrong. Late in January, three weeks after the Corps had returned from Christmas leave, Fred was at his door again. The hulking, broad-shouldered freshman seemed glum and forlorn. "Sir, I've got some bad news," Stapp mumbled. "And a favor to ask you."

"What's wrong now, Mr. Stapp?" Forrest asked. "You having trouble with your studies?"

"No sir, but I've got to leave the Academy, sir."

"Leave the Academy?"

"Yes sir, I've got to drop out."

"Why?"

Fred took a deep breath. "It's Erna Mae, sir. She's gonna have a baby."

At first, Charlie Forrest was angry. Erna Mae Keller had been with so many cadets over the past two years, and who knew how many other guys from Morgan Park High School? Now she was in trouble and she was blaming it on this poor, slow, outsized kid.

"Are you sure the baby's yours, Mr. Stapp?"

"Yes sir, I'm sure."

"How do you know that?"

"Why, she told me it was, sir. Erna Mae wouldn't lie."

Forrest nodded. The hell she wouldn't, he thought. He'd heard rumors about a place in Calumet City where a girl could go to get rid of a baby, but he had no idea of where it was and realized that anything like that would be her decision anyway. But it sure wasn't fair to pin it on his big, slow-witted plebe.

"So, you're going to quit school?"

"Yes sir. Me'n Erna Mae plan to get married."

The upperclassmen nodded again. "I see," he said. "And what was the favor you wanted from me."

"Well sir," Fred Stapp said slowly. "Erna Mae's brother is in the Marine Corps, and I don't have many real close friends here at the school—I was hoping—uh, I was hoping you might be my best man, sir."

"Your best man? Stapp, I'm not sure—"

"I'd be real proud if you would, sir."

Suddenly an idea came to Charlie Forrest. He couldn't turn the plebe down, but he could try and head this thing off before Stapp did something he might regret.

"Sure, Fred," Forrest said. "I'll be your best man, but I'll need to talk to Erna Mae first."

Fred was confused. "About what, sir?"

"Why, to make sure she approves. Every girl likes to approve of her groom's best man."

"I didn't know that," Fred said, confused.

Forrest patted Cadet Stapp on the arm. "Trust me, Mr. Stapp—it's traditional."

The next afternoon after class, Charlie Forrest was waiting at a long, wooden table at the old Walker Branch Library on 111th and Hoyne. When Erna Mae came through the door and looked around the room, he stood up and motioned her over.

"Fred called last night and said to come here," Erna Mae said, looking around at all the shelves full of books. "I never been inside such a big library. I'm supposed to meet somebody, Fred said."

"I guess that's me," Forrest told her, putting out his hand. "I'm Charlie Forrest. Fred's my plebe—I mean I've sort of looked after him this year."

They shook hands and she sat down. "What's this all about?"

"Fred asked me to be his best man," Charlie said.

"Gee—that's real nice." Erna Mae smiled at him.

"He wants to quit school."

Erna Mae nodded, looking sad. "Well, he has to, Charlie," she whispered under her breath, glancing around to make sure no one could hear. "He got me in trouble—we're gonna have a kid."

Charlie sighed and leaned back in his chair. Erna Mae looked a little frightened, and he wasn't looking forward to this, but it was something he had to do.

"Erna Mae, we don't know each other, but a lot of the fellows at school *know* you, don't they?"

"Maybe," she said, defensively. "So what?"

"How does Fred know one of them didn't get you in trouble?"

"Because he's the father, that's how," she said, on the verge of tears. "If it was anybody else, I'd just kill myself."

Charlie nodded and leaned forward, resting his elbows on the table. "But it *could* be somebody else, right?"

"No!" She exclaimed loudly, then lowered her voice. "Fred'n me have been seein' each other ever since October. I ain't gone out with nobody else since I met him."

"You've got him believing he's the father," Charlie pressed.

Now she began to cry, tears running down her face. "He *is* the father, Charlie—I swear to God he is. I couldn't lie to Fred—"

"—I love him so much," she added, blowing her nose into a handkerchief. "I love him more than anything."

"What's so lovable about Fred Stapp?" Charlie asked her. He had to push. "Tell me why you love him so much."

Still weeping, she stared at the tabletop for a long while before she started talking again. "I got a mirror in my room, Charlie," she said, looking up. "And I know what I look like. But that doesn't matter to Fred. He thinks I'm pretty—or at least he says he does.

"Every other fella I ever knew," Erna Mae went on, "Just took me out to get whatever they could get. And I let them do whatever they wanted because I knew I was homely, and I knew that was the only way boys would have anything to do with me.

"But Fred took me to a dance." She began to cry again. "Fred bought me an orchid and took me to a real dance—nobody ever did that before. Fred let me bring him home to meet my folks. Before that, no boy even cared where I lived.

"He's awful sweet to me, Charlie. Whenever we're together, he treats me like I was something   like a real lady. Why wouldn't I be crazy about somebody like that?"

"Do you think he loves you?" Charlie asked her.

She nodded and wiped her eyes. "He told me he does."

Then Charlie recalled the time the plebe had come to his room just before taps—Fred Stapp had been ready to turn himself in for telling a lie—telling this girl he loved her, when he wasn't really sure. That was when? Back in November?

"When did he tell you that, Erna Mae?" Charlie asked. "When did Fred say he loved you?"

She straightened up and looked at him. "He tells me that every time we're together—every time we talk on the phone. I believe him, too. Fred wouldn't lie to me."

Charlie Forrest nodded and sighed again. He knew Fred Stapp, too. "No, Erna Mae, he wouldn't. Fred doesn't lie."

"He doesn't have nobody," Erna Mae went on. It seemed as if once she started talking about Fred, she couldn't stop. "His ma got divorced after his pa ran off, and his parish priest put him in the Academy after his ma left him behind and went to California to work in a defense plant.

"My folks invited him to spend Christmas with us, otherwise he would have spent the holidays at the Blessed Sacrament rectory with Father Druska. My parents like him an awful lot, too."

"Fred's pretty likeable alright," Charlie agreed, wondering for a moment why he was even sitting here. It was pretty obvious that Fred and Erna Mae were in love with each other. The matter of the baby was a complication to be sure, and yet Morgan Park Military Academy wasn't the whole world to most people, and Fred Stapp wouldn't be the first guy that quit school to support a family.

"I'd be awfully good for him, Charlie," Erna Mae said, almost pleading. "I'll be a real good wife to Fred."

Yes, I'll bet you will, Charlie Forrest thought. He didn't think Erna Mae Keller lied, either.

"Well, I better tell Fred you approve, then," he said, taking her hand and winking. "Do you want me at the ceremony in a tuxedo or in my dress grays?"

The wedding of Fred Luther Stapp and Erna Mae Keller took place at Blessed Sacrament Catholic Church three weeks later. The bride wore a cream-colored taffeta V-necked dress which had been made by her mother from a popular Sears-Roebuck pattern—with four taffeta rosettes across the shoulders, each with center petals of real wax, long sleeves, puffed shoulders, and a formal-length train.

Fred had left the Academy a week earlier, staying with Father Druska. He changed into his rented tuxedo in the rectory.

Charlie Forest borrowed the family Plymouth and drove to the church in his full-dress winter uniform, including maroon sash and officer's saber.

It was a small wedding. Fred had no one there but Charlie, and Erna Mae's family numbered only twenty people.

After the ceremony, the wedding party had a simple reception at Mickleberry's Log Cabin Restaurant on 95th Street. There were no funds for even a brief honeymoon, and the newlyweds planned to live with Erna Mae's folks until they could afford to rent a place of their own.

The Monday morning that followed the wedding, Fred and his father-in-law took the Pulaski streetcar north to 42nd Street, then walked three blocks west to Stone Container Corporation, where Matt Keller, who'd been a factory worker with the company for ten years, had secured a job on the shipping docks for his new son-in-law.

Cadet Captain Charlie Forrest graduated that June, enlisted in the army, took basic training at the newly constructed Fort Leonard Wood in Missouri, and applied for officer candidate school. As a 2nd lieutenant in the 6th Infantry Division, he was sent overseas and awarded a Purple Heart after losing a leg to a Japanese grenade at the Battle of Lone Tree Hill on New Guinea.

Charlie Forrest came back from war on a cane and an artificial leg. He married a girl he met at Roosevelt University, while he was attending night school on the GI Bill, and went to work as a broker with his father's insurance firm.

He hadn't been back to the Academy since he'd graduated, but on Memorial Day, 1947, Charlie brought his wife and baby girl to listen to the marching band and to watch a whole new generation of Morgan Park cadets parade across the meadow.

Changes had come to the Academy since he'd graduated. Lt. Col. Haydn Jones had died suddenly the year before, of a massive heart attack while making out a student's transcript. He'd been at the Academy for almost fifty years, and his memory was honored in the speeches following the parade.

The solemn Memorial Day ceremonies began with Cadet 1st Lt. Tom Prevost reciting Lt. Col. John MacCrae's famous poem:

"In Flanders Fields the poppies blow, Between the crosses row on row, That mark our place..."

The battalion was ordered to present arms. Cadet Capt. Wilbur Thornton then read the names of Morgan Park alumni who'd lost their lives in both World Wars. Those names from the Argonne and Belleau Wood were few, but those from the conflict just ended were familiar to many in the audience.

"Private First Class Albert Proudfoot."

"Private John M. Nelson."

"Major Robert C. Dempsey."

Holding his wife's hand, Charlie looked around him. Many of the people gathered there were in tears as the names were read.

"Lieutenant Robert Sullivan."

"Lieutenant Alfred Weinburg."

"Lieutenant Perry Gilson."

Charlie remembered Perry Gilson. He'd been a second-year man when Gilson was a senior.

"Private Arthur L. Howarth."

"Lieutenant Wilmer Esler."

The somber roll went on as distant thunder sounded and the afternoon began to threaten rain. Suddenly another string of names Charlie Forrest recalled as if it were only yesterday, seeing their boyish faces once again in mind and memory. Bob Shipplock, Phil Falk, Dick Engleman, Bob Parchman. At the conclusion of the roll, the drawn-out, mournful notes of taps drifted over the cadets and faculty, alumni and guests.

Briefly glancing to his right, Charlie thought he saw a face he recognized—a young woman holding her right hand over her heart and gently resting her left on the shoulder of a small boy who was saluting. As the final quavering note of taps faded, Charlie turned to his wife. "Honey, excuse me for a second. I think I see someone I knew once."

He approached her slowly, leaning on his cane and limping slightly. When she looked up and saw him, her face brightened and tears welled in her eyes. "Charlie Forrest—oh my gosh, Charlie, is it really you?"

"What's left of me, anyway," he laughed, hugging her tightly. "How are you Erna Mae?"

"We're okay, I guess. What's the matter with your leg?"

"Lost it," he told her. "On New Guinea."

"Oh, that's just awful," she said. "I'm so sorry."

"Where's Fred?" Charlie asked, looking around. "Is he here?"

Erna Mae stared at him and he could see the heartbreak in her eyes. "Oh, Charlie—you didn't know."

He shook his head.

"Fred was killed," she told him. "On Okinawa. And I lost my brother on Tarawa."

At first, Charlie wasn't certain he understood. Fred Stapp was married and about to be a father. He could have avoided going to war. When he asked her about it, Erna Mae nodded.

"When we heard about my brother," she said. "Fred didn't feel right about staying home where it was safe. We quarreled about it, but he wanted to do his part, too." She shook her head sadly. "I had to sign a paper saying it was okay for him to join up."

"I'm awfully sorry to hear that, Erna Mae," Charlie said.

She nodded and leaned down to pick up the little boy. "This is Parker Frederick Stapp," she told Charlie proudly. "Fred's son. He and Fred never got to meet each other. He's a good boy, though."

Charlie lightly brushed back the little fellow's hair and then he leaned forward to kiss Erna Mae on the forehead. He pressed his business card into her hand. "I want you to promise you'll call me if you and the boy need anything."

"I will, Charlie," she said. "But we'll be okay."

Walking back to where the car was parked, Charlie's wife was curious. "Who was that woman, honey?"

"Oh, just somebody I knew when I was here at school."

"Did you date her?"

He shook his head. "No, I never did."

"She's not very attractive," his wife observed.

"I guess she's not," Charlie said. "But I knew a guy once who thought she was the prettiest girl in the world."

CHAPTER 11

▼

HALFTIME AT CULVER

Fall Term, 1944

"Culver's no big deal," Les Crowley muttered, only half believing it himself. Morgan Park's first-string varsity halfback was tired of seeing the whole damned football team sweat bullets over playing Culver Military Academy in Indiana the following weekend. "Hell, they wipe their butts just like anybody else."

Pete Dooley peeled off his jockstrap and tossed it into the dark corner of his locker. Scrimmage that afternoon had been tough, and Dooley was looking forward to a hot shower and supper. "Maybe so, Crow," he pointed out. "But they wiped *ours* pretty good the last four years running."

"Yeah, I know," Crowley admitted. "But we *kicked* their asses in '39 and we can do it again if we want to win bad enough."

Les Crowley was talking about perhaps the most important MPMA/Culver game ever played—on Armistice Day and Morgan Park's Homecoming Weekend in November of 1939. Both Culver and Morgan Park came to the contest undefeated. Abells Field had been packed with over five thousand spectators, the largest crowd ever to witness an MPMA football game. Always doing things in a big way, Culver sent six hundred cadets to the game on a special train, and on arrival decked out in full dress uniform, they formed into units and, accompanied by the Culver marching band playing the school's fight song, marched crisply up the hill from Morgan Park Station to Abells Field.

MPMA kept its undefeated year intact, beating Culver's team with a 19-0 victory, and then going on to win their last game of the season against St. Bede's

Academy, to become the Mid-West Prep School Champions of 1939. They'd talked about that '39 season every year since.

Dooley was in the backfield, too—a big, burly fullback and a senior who'd already decided to enlist in the army air corps after graduation. He nodded in response to his friend's firm conviction that they'd beaten Culver four years before and could do it again. "Maybe, but Captain Mahon was coach back then, and Bugbee's no George Mahon."

"Bugbee's okay," Les Crowley argued halfheartedly. "He does the best he can with what he's got to work with."

Coach Maurice Bugbee, who taught social studies when he wasn't coaching football, had been driving them hard in practice. Lieutenant Bugbee was new to the Academy—a conscientious and competent instructor, but a coach of limited abilities. He'd pushed hard for the coaching position just because he loved the game. But he too, was feeling the frustration of a poor season—one miserly win out of five games so far—and the looming challenge of Culver only a week away.

He'd been serving his boys long afternoons of tough practice. Doubling and tripling the normal number of laps the team had to run around the field. The same with calisthenics and wind sprints—pushing the boys till their breath came in wheezing, rasping gulps. Scrimmage was the fun part of afternoon practice, but drills came first. Before he divided them into teams to run plays, he devoted an hour to backfield drills, offensive and defensive line drills, and finally the dreaded hamburger drills—running his backs straight into two rotating tacklers at a time, over and over again.

Both Coach Bugbee and Pete Dooley had reason to be uneasy. More than any other school the Academy played, Culver always stood as the team to beat, and to make matters worse next week's game was scheduled to be played *at* Culver, almost eighty miles away and too far for most parents to travel with wartime gas rationing in effect, and aging family autos keeping most folks close to home.

Culver—just the name often stirred feelings of being second-best among Morgan Park cadets. Located in a pretty Indiana resort town on the shores of idyllic Lake Maxinkuckee, the school shared the town with some of the most expensive residential real estate in Indiana. Even compared to Morgan Park, Culver was an exclusive institution. Considered one of the country's premier college-prep boarding schools, it attracted top students from around the world.

Pete Dooley's Hansen Hall roommate was a cadet from South Carolina named Trent Secord. The Secords were descended from old southern money and raised Tennessee Walking Horses as a hobby. Trent, of course, was a skilled rider, at home in the saddle, and captain of the *Cavaliers*—Morgan Park's mounted drill team. But as proud as he was of that captainship, he constantly talked about rival Culver's famous Black Horse Troop.

"Trent says those guys have been escorts to presidents, kings, and emperors," Pete told Les Crowley. "And that they marched in Washington, D.C. at both of Woodrow Wilson's inaugurations."

"No kidding?" Crowley said, as they walked naked across the locker room toward the showers. "Listen my large friend, do you know how to get one of those Culver Black Horse nags to buck?"

Pete shrugged. "Hell, how would I know?"

"Just shove a football up its big black hairy ass," Crowley laughed, snapping Dooley with his towel.

Captain Gray had gone to see Lieutenant Bugbee about getting a seat on the team bus to Culver. Frank Gray didn't own a car, but he liked to travel and he enjoyed watching football.

"Lieutenant Bugbee," Gray said, as the coach was busy fixing a broken cleat on one of his shoes. "Might you have a seat for me on one of the buses next weekend?"

"Sure, Captain Gray—we'll find room for you."

"Splendid, splendid," the old man said. "Are you confident of the outcome?"

Bugbee lit a cigarette and shook his head. "I wish I could say that I was."

"How is the team—up to the task?" Captain Gray asked, as he settled into a chair in the coach's small office.

Bugbee sighed. He didn't know the old man that well, but Cap Gray had always seemed pleasant enough. "I've been pushing the boys hard after last week's loss to Elgin—we should've never lost that game. But the team is down. Some of them look at Culver and think they're unbeatable."

Frank Gray grunted and stood up to leave. "Well, Culver is a first-rate school and they always field a strong bunch of boys. We can only do our best."

That last Sunday in October was cloudy and cold, with a sharp wind blowing off the lake. Coach Bugbee, his two assistants, and the thirty-one members of the varsity were aboard their chartered bus by seven that morning. Lined up, one behind the other in front of the gym, were five more yellow buses that would make the trip—one loaded with uniforms and equipment, and the others carrying faculty and cadets who'd signed up to cheer the Warriors on.

On the team bus, the drive southeast into Indiana was quiet. In one of the front seats, across from the driver, Coach Bugbee sat by himself—pouring over plays and studying his starting roster.

Les Crowley was slouched in a window seat toward the back of the bus. He looked away from the harvested fields of corn and soybeans they were passing, glancing at the coach from time to time. Bugbee looked nervous.

Not good, Crowley told himself. If the coach doesn't think we can win—we probably won't.

After two hours of travel, MPMA's buses turned off Indiana State Road 17 and arrived at the sprawling, forested campus of Culver Military Academy, where they were swiftly directed to the main entrance at Logansport Gate.

Situated on eighteen hundred heavily wooded acres along the shore of Indiana's second-largest lake, Culver began as a military institution in 1894. Some of the Morgan Park cadets on the buses had been to Culver for past sports events while many others hadn't, but the school's military heritage was apparent in the fortress-like turrets and parapets of the imposing campus buildings.

"Jeez, look at this place," Pete Dooley whistled. "It's huge."

"Get a load of that lake," another player said. He'd never seen the Culver campus before.

Coach Bugbee stood up and holding on to a grab bar, turned to face his team. "Yes, gentlemen, it's a big school all right—but they only put eleven men on the field, the same as us."

A Culver welcome party was awaiting the buses at Logansport Gate, with a band playing fight songs, and Culver cadets holding up signs that said *Culver Welcomes MPMA*.

As the chartered buses began to unload, a Culver cadet officer wearing full dress uniform came forward from the gate, snapped to attention, and offered a crisp salute to Captain Mahon, Captain Gray, and Coach Bugbee, all of whom were attempting to organize five busloads of excited Morgan Park cadets.

"Welcome to Culver," the officer of the guard said. "We've assigned a plebe detail to transfer your gear and show your team to the visitor's locker room—and we also have two upperclassmen to guide the rest of your group on a brief tour of the campus."

"Very good, young man," Captain Mahon replied, returning the Culver cadet's salute. "Lieutenant Bugbee will see to his team—while Captain Gray and myself will have the rest of our cadets follow your lead."

"Yes sir."

Before being allowed to enter, the MPMA cadets were given a brief history of the Logansport Gate—two massive brick columns, each topped by a large brass lamp, with the Culver emblem on one column and a large brass plaque on the other.

In the spring of 1914, the officer of the guard explained, the officers and cadets of Culver took a major part in the rescue efforts during the great flood of Logansport, a nearby Indiana community.

In mid-May of that year, the citizens of Logansport gave their thanks to both the Academy and the town of Culver by erecting the Logansport Gate.

"It has stood at the Academy's main entrance ever since," said the cadet OD, as he lowered the heavy chain to let the throng of Morgan Park visitors onto the immaculate grounds of Culver.

The day had brightened considerably. A slight westerly breeze rippled the blue waters of the big lake and the ripples sparkled in the early afternoon sun. A gentle slope of hills east of the football field was covered with the vivid red of dying sumacs, and beyond them the surrounding woods were a thick, leafy dapple of green, gold, and orange.

"Say, what's the name of that pond?" Asked an MPMA cadet named Stan Stebley. A small fleet of Academy cutters was docked along a pier that jutted far out into the water.

"Lake Maxinkuckee," the Culver cadet said proudly.

"Maxi—*what?*"

"Maxinkuckee, mister," the cadet said patiently. "They say it's an old Potawatomi Indian name that means *moccasin*—because the lake is shaped like one. But most people just call it Lake Max."

"Jeez," Stebley whistled, staring at the bobbing cutters. "Look at that, they even got themselves a navy."

"Yessir, Mr. Stebley," Captain Mahon pointed out. "Should a hostile naval force assault Culver Military Academy from the lake, I expect the school would give a good account of itself."

If a tour of Culver's grounds was meant to daunt visitors from rival schools, it worked well. The MPMA cadets who were there for the first time looked about them in awe. Culver had more than twice the number of buildings as Morgan Park. It had a fine herd of cavalry mounts, riding stables and grazing meadows, a large lake on which to sail, and eighteen hundred acres of woods and fields on which to drill and stage maneuvers.

It was the same in the visiting team's locker room. As Les and the others looked around they could see that everything was up-to-date and top-notch. Each locker was spotless, and the shower room was huge, with at least a dozen chrome showerheads projecting out from the tiled walls. There was a special taping room and even a small private office for an opposing coach to use. From everything Coach Bugbee could see, it was as if no expense had been spared to make Culver Military Academy the finest preparatory school in the country.

Once the team was taped and suited up, the normal hubbub of the locker room grew quiet and subdued as each of the boys turned inward to deal with their approaching pre-game jitters.

When Bugbee was satisfied with his game plan, he stepped out of the visiting coach's office to talk to the boys and to lay out the starting roster. The stillness of the locker room told him they were tense.

"Listen, fellas," Coach Bugbee told them. He lacked the gift of oratory many coaches possessed for rousing pep talks and halftime speeches. "I know you're nervous about this game. That's normal. But believe it or not, these Culver boys are jumpy, too.

"Having courage doesn't mean you won't experience fear, just that you won't let fear control you. Fear is a natural emotion. How you deal with it makes the difference.

"Think of it this way," the coach went on, making sure to meet the eyes of every player in the room. "This afternoon's game is no different than any other game we've played this season. Yeah sure, they're Culver, and they've got the best that money can buy—but over the years they've buffaloed MPMA into thinking that they're better than we are, and that's not necessarily true.

"Captain Mahon beat these guys four years ago, fellas—and we can do it again today. Let's go out and bring back a win!"

The grandstands edging the rolled green of Culver's football field were filled to overflowing and enlivened by the sun-splashed outfits of girlfriends and mothers, along with the blue and gray of excited cadets.

Culver lost the toss and kicked off to MPMA. Fielding the ball as it hopped and bounced, Pete Dooley made a good return and his runback was followed by two first downs. Then Les Crowley, on a sweep around right end, was smashed hard by Culver's defensive end and felt the ball squirt from his arms as he hit the ground.

Recovering the fumble, Culver made one first down and then met a determined defense that forced them to kick. The battle went back and forth for a while, with neither team threatening, until near the end of the first quarter, when Culver, by a series of off-tackle slices, combined with a wide, sweeping end run and two successful forward passes, saw the game's first touchdown. The kick for point after touchdown sailed between the bars and it was Culver—7, and MPMA—0.

Dark clouds gathered and the day grew overcast again, but the Culver fans were in high spirits—their applause and cheers echoed and re-echoed from the hillside and from the towering walls of the Riding Hall, to the west of Varsity Field.

"Okay—that's only one touchdown up on us," Coach Bugbee was shouting. "It's still anybody's game!"

Fired up, Bud Hall took the kickoff for MPMA, and the team methodically marched the ball to Culver's twenty-yard line before a short pass from Jack Parchman to Mel Bacon was intercepted—first down for Culver on their own ten-yard line.

"Goddamnit," Captain Gray grunted, shaking his head. He was sipping a cup of hot cocoa and sitting on the MPMA bench next to a second-string guard named Taylor Swope. Swope, a big boy with a mop of red hair and jug ears who was in his third year, had never had Captain Gray for math and didn't know him very well.

"Coach Bugbee tells us not to swear, sir."

Gray looked at the cadet with a raised eyebrow. "He does, eh? What's your name, son?"

"Taylor Swope, sir—I'm a junior. I play guard."

Captain Gray grunted again. "Well, Mr. Swope, you remind me of a critter with long ears. That could either be a jackrabbit or a jackass—you can take your pick."

"Yes sir."

Captain Gray nodded and patted the boy on his knee. "I'm just having a little bit of fun with you, son—why, when I was your age, my ears were so big they had to tie me to the well pump any time a wind came up. And your coach is right, you oughtn't curse if you can help it—rough language is a sure sign of low intellect."

"Yes sir," Swope repeated.

After intercepting Jack Parchman's pass, Culver battled their way downfield in a stunning display of accurate passes and skillful end runs that closed with a fourth down quarterback sneak over the goal line, giving Culver another six points.

The kick for the extra point was blocked by Bob Blew and the suddenly lop-sided score stood at 13—0, in favor of Culver.

After the kick-off, as time ticked away, Les Crowley was able to gain some hard-earned yardage as did Morgan Park's opposite first-string halfback, Bud Hall, and with just eight minutes left to play, Jim McHugh made a diving catch that brought the crowd to their feet, but what was left of the first half proved to be a standoff, with Morgan Park unable to move the ball far enough for even a last-minute field-goal attempt.

When the halftime whistle finally blew, a discouraged MPMA team made their way off the field and sat slumped on benches in the gloomy quiet of the locker room. The team's managers, John Kanelos and John Welsh busied them-selves dressing cuts and re-taping ankles.

"Jeez, thirteen to nothing," Bud Hall moaned, drinking water from a paper cup. "We're stinking up the damned field."

"Culver probably figures they're playing a girl's team," Wally Simak grumbled. Simak was the Academy's first-string center and he was holding a wet ice bag over a split and swollen upper lip. To make things worse, one of his front teeth felt loose when he poked at it with his tongue.

Finally, Coach Bugbee and Captain Mahon entered the room. "Fellas, I don't have to tell you this," the coach said with a sigh as he tapped his clipboard against the side of his leg. "You boys have played a total of maybe five or six minutes of first-class football today—but the rest of your game's been piss-poor lousy."

Les Crowley squirmed in his seat. His head hurt and his ribs were sore where he'd been hit earlier in the game. He knew they'd played lousy ball and it didn't help to hear it from Coach Bugbee. Culver was faster, bigger, and stronger, Les knew, and no inspiring halftime speech was going to do much to change that.

"I'm not much for speech-making," Bugbee went on. "The last team of War-riors that beat Culver was the 1939 team—they had an undefeated season that year, and went on to become the Midwest Prep School Champions.

"Captain Mahon was running the team then," Bugbee said, as he stepped aside. "And he'd like to say a few words to you today."

"Thanks, Coach," Mahon said as he looked out over the locker room. "Boys, speeches don't win ball games—players do. But I'd like to talk a little about why you're here today.

"That undefeated 1939 team that licked Culver and brought a championship home have all gone their separate ways. But those of you sitting in this locker room are an extension of them now—you men are a part of something special at

MPMA. You're the school's pride—its varsity football team. You care about the Academy and what it stands for. You care about your teammates and yourselves!

"Just as with the team of '39, this is one of those points in your young lives when you need to ask yourself: *How do I want to be remembered?*

"Few other people have what you have today. You've got the chance to affect the answer to that question.

"The moment is at hand. It's not about tomorrow, and it's not about yesterday. It isn't about what you did ten minutes ago. But part of your future and part of how you'll be remembered will be shaped by you over the next two quarters of this game."

George Mahon stopped for a minute to let what he'd said sink in. Even Les Crowley was surprised. Much of the team's fatigue and discouragement seemed gone as they sat straighter, looking to Captain Mahon for more of the same.

Mahon smiled and nodded. "Look around this room fellas, and look at the man next to you. How do you want him to remember you? How do you want him to remember the way you played in this game? How will you want your family and fellow cadets to remember your performance this afternoon?

"Twenty years from now," Mahon went on. "When you have your class reunion you'll see many of these faces again and you'll shake hands. You'll reminisce and you'll share that common bond that teammates have—a bond that can never be broken.

"Finally, men," Captain Mahon concluded. "You may win this game against Culver today—or you may lose it. But it's really not about that—as much as it's about *how* you win or *how* you lose.

"Play with heart. No matter what happens, don't let up—play with passion. For you seniors, there are just three more games as MPMA Warriors. Be remembered! Play every single down like it's the play that will win the game. Finish this contest like champions—with a champion's heart, mind, and spirit.

"Win or lose, go out there for this second half and show them what Warrior football is all about!"

"Thanks, Captain Mahon," Bugbee said as he stepped forward again. "Fellas, one thing the captain didn't tell you is that he'll be coaching this team again next season."

Every member of the squad looked at each other in surprise. It was the first anyone had heard of Mahon resuming his duties as the Academy's head varsity coach.

"What's going on, sir?" Mel Bacon asked.

Coach Bugbee looked at the floor for a moment and then back at the boys again. "I'm leaving the Academy, fellas," he told them. "I've enlisted in the navy, and when the semester's over, I'll be off to Great Lakes Naval Training Center in Glenview. Captain Mahon and Lieutenant Marberry will be in charge next year."

The war again, Les Crowley told himself. The goddamned war was changing everything. At the same time, he realized that in just eight more months, the war would change his life, too. .

Minutes later, the Warriors came out fired up. But the second half was to give them a lesson in life's realities that would serve all of them well in the tumultuous years ahead.

The kickoff was a low, bouncing ball that McHugh snatched up on MPMA's own forty-yard line, and ran back deep into Culver territory.

A first down lateral from Jack Parchman to Tom Blazina gave the Warriors another eight yards, and then a quick flat pass to Mel Bacon brought them to Culver's eight-yard line.

Captain Gray glanced to his right along the sidelines where the Culver pep squad was putting on a show: *Fight, Culver, down the field, Culver must win. Fight, Fight for victory! Culver knows no defeat!* These Culver fellows have another first-rate team this year, Frank Gray thought, but it's third and goal—and our boys are in a fine position to score.

The Warriors called time-out and huddled with Coach Bugbee on the sidelines. "Okay," Bugbee said excitedly. "Nothing fancy. Let's have Dooley punch it over. A handoff straight up the middle—everybody blocks—everybody knocks somebody down."

"Red forty-eight straight up," quarterback Jack Parchman told the team. It was going to be Pete Dooley carrying the ball.

They broke and took their positions on the line of scrimmage. Before he started the count, Parchman deliberately turned his head to glance back at Tom Blazina at the left halfback position.

"Hut one—" Parchman began.

"Watch him," a Culver linebacker yelled out, pointing toward Blazina. "Left back, left back—watch that guy, watch him!"

"Hut two, hut three—"

The ball was snapped, and as Pete Dooley held back for just a step, Parchman faked the handoff to Blazina who charged into the line and helped double-team Culver's right guard.

Hurtling toward a hole between guard and tackle, Dooley felt Parchman punch the ball into his stomach just a little too hard. Pete tried to cover it, to hold it close with his hands and forearms, but another Culver linebacker, a big, hulking fellow who'd managed to slip his blocker charged into the line fast and low—filling the hole and smashing hard into Pete's midsection.

"Oh shit," Dooley swore, feeling the ball slip from his grasp as he took the crunching hit. The football squirted from his grip and took a single, downward bounce off Wally Simak's helmet before hitting the ground and skittering crazily across the grass.

"Loose ball! Loose ball!" A Culver player shouted, scrambling to cover the fumble. Suddenly players from both teams descended upon the football. It soon disappeared beneath a pile of bodies and as the whistle blew and the officials worked to peel players away, a Culver lineman was found at the bottom of the pile, curled fetus-like on the four-yard line, stubbornly clutching the pigskin.

Culver had recovered and the MPMA drive was stopped.

The Morgan Park cadets and those along the sideline had risen to their feet in anticipation of a touchdown, but now sank back into their seats again, groaning, frustration in their faces.

"Damn it—goddamnit," Pete Dooley was muttering, with tears welling in his eyes.

"Hey, forget it," Crowley told him, giving his friend a slap on the rear. "Game's not over—we'll get the ball back."

But the remainder of the half held success just out of reach for the Warriors—becoming a stubborn battle between defenses, with neither team able to score.

Late in the third quarter, Les Crowley broke loose on a quick reverse and ran the ball fifty yards downfield, only to have the play called back by a holding penalty at the line of scrimmage.

The next time MPMA had possession, Bud Hall successfully took the ball around left end on a sweep but accidentally stepped offside before making much of a gain.

Finally, in the closing minutes of the fourth quarter, Parchman faded back and rifled a stunning thirty-yard pass between the heads of two Culver defenders covering Jim Nordby, a second-string end who Coach Bugbee had sent in to substitute for Mel Bacon, who'd pulled a hamstring. Nordby went for the ball but it bounced off his fingertips and rolled ineffectually offside.

As the Culver cadets cheered and shouted, the clock ran out on the Warriors for a thirteen to nothing loss.

That evening, on the team bus back to Chicago, a bleak shroud of silence hung over the players—each lost in his own thoughts of what had happened and what might have been—if only this or that had gone differently.

In the darkness, as the bus edged out of Valparaiso it began to rain. The large drops that splattered against the windows and rolled across the glass only added to the gloom.

Coach Bugbee sat alone in his regular seat, trying to study the playbook in the passing glare of headlights and the dim glow of the bus's dashboard. Only Les Crowley looked up when Pete Dooley left the back of the bus and made his way forward.

"S'cuse me Coach," Dooley asked hesitantly as he came to the front of the bus. "Can I talk to you for a minute?"

"Sure, sit down."

"Coach, I feel like crap. I'm sorry I lost the game for us."

Bugbee closed the playbook and laid it on the floor. He looked over at his first-string fullback. Even in the meager light of the bus he could see the boy's eyes were red.

"That's a helluva thing to say, Pete. You didn't lose it."

"I mean—that fumble I made."

"Hell, that fumble was only one play in the whole game," the coach told him. "It didn't make that much difference."

"Well, it made a difference to me."

"I can see that," Bugbee said. He stood up and faced the team, gripping the back of the seat as the bus swayed a little on the wet, slippery road.

"Fellows," he began. "I know you're all feeling pretty punk. But you need to know something. Maybe I should've told you this earlier, but I guess I'm already thinking ahead to the Pullman Tech game next Saturday.

"If you just look at the score," Coach Bugbee went on. "We lost a football game to Culver today—but I want you to look at it a little deeper than that.

"Those fellows outplayed us in the first half, no question about it. That might've been your fault, or it could've been mine—most likely some of both. But boys, the second half was another story."

"Coach—we didn't score a single point in the second half," somebody in the rear of the bus pointed out.

Bugbee shook his head. "The point is, *neither did they*. You guys played just as good football as Culver in the second half, and they're a school that's twice our size. But you played them to a standoff and didn't let them score. I'm proud of you for doing that, and you should be proud of yourselves as well."

In the dark, the team turned in their seats and began to look at each other. Many nodded, as a murmur of awareness made its way throughout the bus.

Coach Bugbee wasn't done yet. "Life's not all winning, fellas. It's about losing, too—and no locker room speech can change that fact. In years to come, each of you will see your share of loss. You might lose a promotion, even a job or two, and you'll certainly lose loved ones—your grandparents, your folks.

"Unfortunately, as long as this war is being fought, some of us may even lose our lives—that's just the way things are these days. What's really important is fighting hard and playing to win, which I think you've done—as well as facing up to losses and going on—which I truly hope that all of you will do."

After Coach Bugbee sat down again, Pete Dooley got up and made his way back toward his seat. Glancing over at his friend, he saw Les Crowley grinning at him.

"Hey fumblethumbs," Crowley said. "How about a few frames of bowling tomorrow afternoon?"

"Okay," Dooley said.

"Half a buck a game?"

"Sure, why not?"

Crowley grunted, slumping down in his seat. "Try not to drop the damned ball on your foot, okay?"

"Up yours," Dooley said.

"Up yours, too," Crowley chuckled, then added, "Good game today, Pete."

CHAPTER 12

▼

HOMECOMING

Fall Term, 1948

By the second week of November, still early into winter, Chicago had experienced only light, brief snow flurries. But the weather was welcoming both Veteran's Day and Homecoming Weekend at MPMA with a bleak, cheerless overcast sky and a brittle northeast wind blowing off the lake.

Paying his cab fare, Albert Strawn gave the taxi driver what he hoped was a generous tip. As the cabbie grunted and pulled away, Albert turned toward the Academy campus—in November, a gray, somber scene, unlike the pleasant green and leafy grounds of June he'd last looked upon more than twenty years before. He turned up his coat collar against the chill wind, lifted his suitcase, and made his measured, painful way toward Hansen Hall—limping as he walked.

From time to time, the permanent, debilitating pain in his right leg would remind him of how cruel the Japanese had been.

Albert Strawn had been a Marine captain in April of 1942—an ambitious career officer in the Fourth Marine Regiment, widely known throughout the Corps as the "China Marines."

Fifteen years earlier, on January 28, 1927, a year before Albert graduated from the Academy, the Fourth Regiment received orders to proceed to China. Less than a week later, they boarded the Naval transport *Chaumont* for duty to protect all Americans and United States interests in the international settlement in Shanghai.

Enamored of the military and still unsure about college, Albert enlisted in the Marines soon after graduation from MPMA and was assigned to the Fourth. He was sent to China and as time passed, rose through the ranks—a corporal in 1929, staff sergeant in 1932, sergeant major by 1935, chief warrant officer in 1937 and finally commissioned a second lieutenant in 1939. During those peacetime years, the word had spread throughout the Corps that for those on the fastest track to promotion, the choice duty was to be found with the "China Marines."

Albert found this to be true, but he also learned that duty in Shanghai was not without danger. In December of 1937, Japanese naval aircraft strafed and sank the U.S. Navy's Yangtze River patrol boat, *Panay*—and the following February, Japanese troops tried to provoke an incident by unsuccessfully attempting to enter the American sector with armed patrols.

Shortly after Albert was promoted to captain in the waning months of 1941, with world tensions rapidly growing, most other foreign governments ordered their troops out of the international settlement in Shanghai. The last bit of protection left for American interests in China was the small United States Seventh Fleet, the Fourth Marine Regiment and a scattering of Yangtze River patrol boats.

As the world skidded relentlessly toward a clash in the Pacific, the Fourth Marines were pulled out of China and transferred to the Philippines, arriving there just a week before Pearl Harbor and the outbreak of war. Their original orders were to defend the Olongapo Naval Station and the Mariveles Naval Section Base at the mouth of Manila Bay on the Bataan Peninsula. Albert still recalled the regiment's total strength as being just forty-four officers and less than eight hundred enlisted men.

The intended use of the Fourth Marines in the defense of the Philippines called for the transfer of the regiment to United States Army control, and General MacArthur eventually decided to use them for beach defense on Corregidor. Having command of this small, tadpole-shaped island was vital to the defense of Manila Harbor. Just two miles from Bataan, Corregidor was only three and a half miles long and a mile and a half across at its head. On this tiny spit of land was Malinta Tunnel, the location of MacArthur's headquarters as well as a makeshift field hospital.

Even though it was expected, Albert could still remember the sick feeling the regiment felt on learning of the fall of Bataan, and General Homma's seasoned Japanese Imperial 14th Army wasted no time focusing its attention on Corregidor, where Marine Capt. Albert Strawn and the rest of the regiment were hunkered down, many of them sick, and all of them desperately short of food and ammunition, nervously waiting for the Japanese onslaught.

Albert and the others were surprised at how quickly it came, and after attack and counterattack and attack again, they knew they could not hold for very long. Also realizing their defenses outside Malinta tunnel would fall and expecting more Japanese landings in the night, Corregidor's CO, Gen. Jonathan Wainwright, dreaded what might happen when Japanese troops overran Malinta Tunnel, housing over a thousand wounded, helpless men.

Sorrowfully, the general made the grim decision to trade one more day of freedom for thousands of American and Filipino lives, and at one o'clock in the afternoon, two members of Wainwright's staff approached the enemy carrying a white flag and the general's surrender message to General Homma.

Albert still remembered his first day as a prisoner of war.

After they'd been surrendered, curious Japanese foot soldiers crowded around them, inspecting the ranks of nervous Americans. One of the Japanese, an English-speaking lieutenant, approached Albert and began going through his pockets. The lieutenant had been a small man with round glasses and a pock-marked face. Finding a few coins, along with a wad of Filipino money, he threw it on the ground, scattered it around with his foot, and then slapped Albert across the face with his cap.

"Where you think you are going, now?" The Japanese officer had laughed. "To Filipino whorehouse?"

Farther down the line, two befuddled Americans were found with a few Japanese yen in their pockets. The enemy assumed such money could only have been taken from dead Japanese soldiers, and the two men were first slapped and kicked by their captors and then marched off into a grove of trees—forced to kneel, and shot in the backs of their heads.

A Japanese who looked to be a high-ranking officer stepped up and stood on a chair to address them. He was dressed all in green, with shiny black boots, and a small star on his cap. Hanging from his waistbelt was a holstered Nambu pistol and a fine samurai sword with a long, leather-wrapped hilt.

"American and Filipino prisoners," the officer barked, again in English. "I am Col. Genda Shinobu. You men have disgraced yourselves and your countries by your surrender. By this act, you are no longer considered honorable soldiers, but merely cowards and criminals."

Rubbing the dull, never-ending ache in his leg, Albert climbed the familiar concrete steps to the main double entrance doors of Hansen Hall, recalling those steps as having been poured the same year he graduated from the Academy, and remembering that he'd spent most of his senior year in one of the new second-floor rooms of Hansen Hall barracks. Opening one of the heavy wooden doors, he hesitantly stepped inside the building and noticed a sign with an arrow directing visiting alumni to report to the cadet OD's office.

Upon Albert's entrance, a cadet first lieutenant looked up from the desk and covered a copy of *Dime Detective Magazine* with a handy stack of papers. "Yes sir, may I help you?"

Once considered an accomplished debater in school, Albert's long wartime ordeal in captivity had left him with a peculiar, jerky manner of speech—his discourse now riddled with stuttering and odd, unexpected pauses—especially in the presence of authority. And to Albert, even an eighteen-year old cadet officer represented a figure of power.

"I'm...Albert Strawn," he said hesitantly. "They...told me to report to this office...when I got here."

"Are you an alumnus, sir?"

"Yes, I graduated in...1928."

The cadet officer of the day nodded and studied a typewritten roster. "Strawn," he mumbled to himself. "Albert A. Strawn. Yes sir, here it is—Class of '28. Why, you were a first lieutenant when you graduated—same as me."

"I...guess so," Albert said. "But then I was a captain," he went on, becoming nervous and confused. His left hand, as it often did, curled its fingers and began to slap lightly against his coat.

The cadet noticed. "Mr. Strawn, would you care to sit down?"

"No...I'd better stand."

Cadet 1st Lt. Rob Tischler had seen alumni like this before at every homecoming weekend—each of them back from a war in which he himself had been too young to fight. But his two uncles had come back from that war okay, and so had many others. Rob Tischler had occasionally wondered what it was that left most of them sound, while a few seemed broken and undone—like this fellow, Albert Strawn?

"1928. Boy, this must've been some place—back in the good old days," Cadet Tischler said with a grin, trying to make his guest feel comfortable. "Am I right, sir?"

"I...guess it was," Albert answered hesitantly. "I don't really remember..." He could feel his goddamned hand slapping against his coat. He tried to make it stop, but couldn't. His neck and face suddenly felt hot. This young man who was an officer was asking him things. Would something bad happen if he answered wrong? Albert briefly shut his eyes and tried not to think about answering questions.

After the fall of Corregidor, most of the Fourth Marines were grouped together at a location called the 92nd Garage. The 92nd Garage was an amphibian aircraft ramp that had been paved over and turned into a shantytown. The men used scraps of lumber and blankets to fashion crude shelters against the brutal Philippine sun and heat—heat that became more and more unbearable as they lived for days on top of sweltering asphalt.

Often the Japanese guards would taunt them with questions; "Hey Joe, you thirsty?"

One morning, a thirst-crazed Marine corporal had nodded.

"You okay, Joe," one of the guards laughed, pouring water from his canteen onto the asphalt. "You okay drink."

Already out of his head from thirst and dysentery, the corporal hurled himself at the little puddle of water. Albert and a few others watched helplessly as the corporal was executed with a sword as he was on his hands and knees, drinking with his head down, like a cat lapping milk from a saucer.

"Is there...anything else I need to do?" Albert asked.

"No sir," the cadet OD said amiably. "You're all set. You'll be bunking in Room 206 on the second floor. Unless we get any last-minute alums who want to stay in the barracks, you've got the room to yourself. I'll have a plebe bring up your valise."

"Oh no...please...I can carry it."

"Yes, sir—I hope you enjoy Homecoming."

Back in the lobby, his left hand finished with its embarrassing behavior, Albert carefully gripped the banister and slowly made his way up the wide staircase.

The second floor hallway looked familiar. Room 206 was no different than every other room in Hansen Hall barracks, and aside from new coats of paint on the walls every now and then, none of them had changed a bit over the past twenty years.

During Homecoming, a dozen upperclassmen on each floor were given weekend passes so those visiting alumni who wished to stay in a dorm room could use theirs—free of charge.

Like a number of others, Albert's assigned room had a hand-lettered sign taped on the door: *Visitor—Do Not Disturb.*

He knocked lightly, waited a moment, and then entered. The small, spartan room was neat and spotless, both beds were made, and it was all just as he remembered—a space fourteen feet in length and ten feet wide, with a large window centered on the exterior wall to bring in light. Beneath it, a hissing radiator running the width of the sill. Two metal-framed beds, their khaki blankets tightly drawn, stood against each wall, and both sides of the room had tall, matching cabinetry—a wardrobe, a study desk and chair, and a drawer-filled chiffonier.

This was a happy time for me, Albert thought, closing the door and sitting down on one of the beds with tears in his eyes. *A happy, carefree time—so many years ago.* For a long moment, closing his eyes again, he let mind and memory take him back on a journey of Sunday parades long past, casual hops and formal dances, football games, faces he hadn't seen or thought of in years, instructors, classes, and the warm, bittersweet joy of graduation day.

For the next fifteen years, the entirety of his life had been the Marine Corps. He lost both parents in an automobile accident on New Year's Eve of 1930. What was left of the family—two sisters and a younger brother married and moved to different parts of the country. In the Marines, his world had been made up of other men. There had been time for women of course, but those were hurried affairs with money changing hands when they ended. By chance and circumstance, the experience of a wife, a home, and children of his own had never been a part of Albert's life.

He slipped off his shoes and stretched out on the bed. From time to time, he could hear footsteps and horseplay in the hallway, the sound of young voices and laughter. The sound of cadets going about their business on a Friday afternoon after classes were over—no different than he recalled having heard twenty years before.

Staring at the ceiling, he felt weary. His leg had begun to ache badly—not just a simple ache in the muscles, but a nagging, deeper pain that seemed to dwell in the bones. Reaching into his pocket, he fished out a small bottle of pills—painkillers the disinterested doctor at the VA had prescribed soon after Albert came back from the war. He took two of the little white tablets from the bottle and quickly swallowed them without water.

Why did they have to hurt me like that? He wondered for what might have been the thousandth time in the last five years.

Assigned to head a burial detail in Cabanatuan Prison Camp, Albert had been like every other prisoner there—weak from lack of food, dehydrated from dysentery and fevered from who knew what? Death was as common as lice at Cabanatuan. Prisoners died every day, either from disease and neglect, starvation and suicide, or often at the hands of their Japanese guards. Albert quickly learned that grave digging at Cabanatuan was a busy profession.

The grave detail was split into two sections—those who dug the graves and those who carried the corpses. After the diggers had been out awhile, the second group gathered up the bodies that needed burying—usually taking those that had been dead for some time first. They were carried out in blankets strung from poles—the bodies straightened out as much as possible before burial.

The grave details tried to keep track of who was being buried. If the bodies still wore dog tags, Albert would collect them. If not, somebody would say who they thought the men to be and Albert would write it down.

One morning, they had fifteen holes to dig. Two days earlier, seven men on the water detail managed to overpower and kill their guard with a sharpened piece of steel, escaping into the tall cogon grass. Late that same afternoon the fugitives were turned over to a Japanese search party by a frightened Filipino farmer who'd come upon them hiding in his barn. All seven men were marched back to camp where Albert and his fellow prisoners were assembled to watch them executed by firing squad before the sun went down.

"That's seven holes to be dug in the morning," he'd mumbled to an army lieutenant as the two of them made their way back to their straw-filled sleeping mats.

"Yeah, well, the night isn't over yet, Captain," the lieutenant pointed out. "Lots of guys die between now and the sun comes up—you could have ten more deads by morning."

The lieutenant had called it right. In addition to the executed prisoners, eight others had died during the night and Albert's grim detail, carrying shovels over their shoulders, followed the guards out of the compound the next morning, after a miserable breakfast of weevil-infested rice and an inch-square piece of rancid fish.

They finished digging ten graves before one of the men in the detail, an army corporal named Walter Frye, was overcome with dysentery. As he stumbled off and dropped his ragged shorts, one of the guards rushed toward him.

"No time shit," the guard screamed. "Time work."

"I can't help it—I gotta go," Frye mumbled as he squatted.

The Japanese guard swore and unshouldered his Arisaka rifle with its attached bayonet. "No time shit," he screamed again, with the bayonet at ready.

Albert managed to get between them. "He's sick," Albert told the guard, pointing at his own stomach. "Let him crap—he'll get back to work."

"He dig—no time shit!" the Japanese screamed a third time, bringing up the butt of his rifle and smashing it into Albert's face. Albert's gums had been infected and bleeding for months and most of his teeth were loose. The vicious blow of the rifle butt bashed three of them out and knocked him to the ground.

Cpl. Walter Frye was bayoneted as he relieved himself. At the same time, a second guard picked up the dying prisoner's shovel and brought the sharp edge down on Albert's leg, smashing it again and again as Albert screamed in pain and struggled to get to his feet. When he did, his battered leg collapsed beneath him and he fell again, unconscious.

Now, relaxing on the dormitory bed three years later, Albert still wondered why the guards hadn't killed him that day as well. Instead, he was carried back to camp in one of the pole blankets and then examined by a doctor who'd been captured with the 57th Infantry—Philippine Scouts.

They'd put Albert on his bunk, semi-conscious and moaning in pain. His thigh, bruised and purplish, was split open in a number of places and he couldn't move his leg. The doctor who looked at him was suffering from malaria himself.

After a hurried examination, the doctor stood up, sighed, and motioned one of the men to follow him out of the huts. "I'm afraid the captain's luck has run out," he said, making sure they were out of Albert's hearing. "His leg's sure to infect. His femur's fractured in two or three places and he's bound to have a helluva lot of nerve damage. I'd need to open up his leg to see the fracture and all I've got is a dirty scalpel, some sutures, and a couple of aspirin. I've got no alcohol or sulfa, either. And even if I could get at those bones, I haven't any way to put them back together."

The doctor shook his head. "Keep him as comfortable as you can and hidden away. If the Japs find out he can't work, they'll cut off his rations or just shoot him. Either way, he's a dead man.

"But hell, the way things are going we might all be dead men anyway," the doctor added, shaking his head.

Through smuggled reports from sympathetic agents in Manila, the Cabanatuan captives knew that Japan was losing the war. Many prisoners had already bent taken from camp and then sent to Japan and Korea to work as slave labor. Those still in Cabanatuan feared they'd be killed if the Japanese were forced to surrender.

At American 6th Army headquarters, the fear was the same, and to avert this grim possibility plans had been put into effect to take the prison compound by surprise and hopefully evacuate the prisoners to friendly lines before the Japanese could react.

The doctor who'd examined Albert had been right. Just a week later, he was delirious and close to death when the U.S. Army's 6th Ranger Battalion staged a bold, successful raid on Cabanatuan in January 1945.

Albert and the others were first taken to a small jungle village called Talavera, then to the 92d Evacuation Hospital in Guimba, where his shattered leg had been treated and the bones set as well as possible.

Just two weeks later, Albert and more than two hundred other ex-prisoners left Leyte aboard the transport ship *USS General A.E. Anderson,* bound for San Francisco via Hollandia, New Guinea.

The *General Anderson* arrived in San Francisco Bay in early March 1945, and Marine Capt. Albert Strawn was finally home again. Taken captive less than five months after the war began, he was back in America, crippled and alone, just seven months before the Japanese surrendered.

Having nowhere else to go, Albert took the Greyhound bus to live with his sister and brother-in-law in St. Paul, Minnesota, and made weekly visits to the VA hospital in Minneapolis. He lived off a meager veteran's disability pension and earned extra money as an usher at the World Movie Theater in downtown St. Paul.

Now, three years after the war and at his sister's urging, Albert had traveled by bus from Minnesota to Chicago to attend Veteran's Day ceremonies and Homecoming Weekend at MPMA. "You need to get out more, Albert," she encouraged him. "You should take a trip or something and not just stay cooped up around here or at that movie theater."

So here he'd come, to Morgan Park Military Academy, a place where he remembered once being truly whole and happy.

Trying to relax, Albert lost track of how long he'd been laying in that room in his stocking feet, letting his mind and memory play among the years. He suddenly heard a bugle—the familiar mess call for supper in Alumni Hall.

Hearing muffled voices and hurried footsteps in the hallway, Albert stood up and made his way to the room's window. He could see cadets pushing out the doorway of Hansen Hall and beginning to form ranks on Post Walk in the early winter night.

Albert put on his shoes and overcoat, waiting patiently as the company commanders and platoon leaders voiced their commands. He watched the ranks execute a sharp left face and begin to march toward the dining room. It was only then that he slowly descended the stairway and went out the door to follow the column.

As the cadets stood at attention around each table, Capt. Frank Gray looked up toward the doorway and quickly took notice of the man with the pronounced limp. He spoke to the second-year cadet on his right. "Mr. Ellis, find another seat and escort that gentleman over here."

"Yes sir."

Albert recognized Captain Gray almost immediately. Standing at attention with the rest as grace was said, he remembered back to his math classes. Gray looked a great deal older and grayer now, but even more formidable than he did when Albert was in school.

"I remember your face, son," Cap Gray said as the assembly was given the order to rest. "But I can't quite recall your name."

"Strawn, sir," Albert said, shaking hands. "Class of…1928."

"Ah, yes, Strawn—Alfred Strawn."

"*Albert*, sir."

"Albert—yes, of course. You were in a few of my classes."

"Solid geometry and advanced algebra."

Gray grunted, helping himself to a serving of roast beef. "Did you get passing grades, Mr. Strawn?"

"Just…barely, sir. I think I got…mostly Cs." Albert felt his hand begin to shake and slap again. He slipped it underneath his leg to hold it still, but not before Cap Gray took notice.

"Are you all right, Albert?" Gray asked under his breath.

Albert nodded. "Yes sir…it'll…pass."

The hubbub of conversation and clink of glasses and tableware that dominated the sprawling dining hall sounded exactly the same as they had twenty years before. Albert couldn't help but marvel at how little some things changed. The school still felt astonishingly familiar, even though he, himself, was drastically different.

Cap Gray didn't say much during dinner, and Albert noticed how the man had aged over the years. His movements were slower and his face was creased and worn. His means of communication with the cadets at his table consisted mostly of gestures and grunts, as if the wide gap of years existing between them effectively ruled out pleasantries or sociable discourse. He was there to teach them mathematics, and they were there to learn. If there was anything more to it than that, the captain more or less ignored it.

While the boys at the table chattered among themselves during dinner, Albert and Captain Gray took their meal quietly, and when the cadets were again called to attention at the end of mess, the old man wiped his mouth with his cloth napkin and patted Albert on the arm. "Like to chat with you a bit, Mr. Strawn, after the boys are gone."

The white-coated cadet waiter brought them more coffee and a second helping of apple pie for Captain Gray. After he'd wolfed it down, the captain leaned back in his chair and lit a cigarette.

"How'd you come by your limp and that jumpy arm, son?" He enquired matter-of-factly. "Hurt in the war, were you?"

"Yes sir."

Gray nodded. "Lots of the boys were. Where'd you serve?"

"In the...Philippines, sir," Albert said slowly. "I was a captain in...the Marine Corps...when the Japs took Bataan."

Gray winced and drew deeply on his smoke. He knew about Bataan. "Seems to me you boys were left there way out on a limb," he said, then added, "goddamned politicians."

"Yes sir, I...guess so."

"Pretty rough, Albert?"

Albert nodded and swallowed hard, feeling his hand begin to shake and slap again. Now his left foot was tingling and beginning to twitch as well. "They...they busted me up...pretty bad, sir."

Captain Gray nodded again. "Well, it's all in the past now," he said. "Where do you live? How are you making your living?"

"I live with...my sister and...her husband in St. Paul." Albert said haltingly. "I work as an usher in a...movie house."

Gray looked at him quizzically. "An usher?"

"Yes sir."

"You were a captain in the Marines, and now you're a picture show usher?"

"Yes sir. I guess...I guess it's not...much of a job."

Captain Gray took another drag on his cigarette and snubbed it out in an ashtray the waiter had brought. "Doesn't seem like it," he said. "What did you study in college?"

"I never went, sir...I joined the Marines instead."

The old man stood and put on his cap and army overcoat. "It's a clear night—take a walk with me, Albert."

They walked off campus to 111th Street, and then turned west toward Academy Drugs on Western Avenue, where Captain Gray usually bought his cigarettes. As they passed Hansen Hall, Albert noticed the warm, yellow glow of lights from almost every room in the barracks.

"Study hour," Cap Gray grunted. "Half those young dimwits are probably tuned in to *Amos and Andy* on their radios.

"Most of our boys go on to college," the captain continued as they walked. "You're one of those who didn't—it seems there's a few in every class."

"Yes sir."

Captain Gray stopped. "It's not too late, Albert."

Albert shook his head and laughed nervously. "I'm thirty-eight years old, sir. I'm no...well, I'm not a kid, anymore."

Gray nodded. "Have you heard of the GI Bill, son?"

"Heard of it...don't know...much about it."

"Well, you ought to learn," Gray remarked sharply. "This isn't 1918, when discharged vets got only a sixty dollar allowance and a train ticket home. The government will pay to put you through school. You have a first-rate prep school education, and you were a commissioned officer in the United States Marine Corps. There's no telling how far you might go with a college degree—certainly a lot farther than just being a picture show usher."

"I don't...know, sir," Albert offered. "They hurt my leg pretty bad...nerve damage and all. Sometimes it hurts...so bad...I can hardly walk. My hand...gives me fits, too, and I...I don't talk very well anymore."

Cap Gray halted again. "Stop it, Albert. Stop making excuses and feeling sorry for yourself. You sound like a damned titty baby. Maybe you had a rough time, but goddamnit, you came home from the war—forty-nine of our boys didn't get that chance."

"I'm sorry, sir," Albert said. "I...didn't...know."

"Well now you do," Captain Gray said gruffly. "So consider yourself lucky."

Later that evening, Anna Gray sensed her husband's mood. He was even more quiet than usual, and once or twice she thought she saw the moist gleam of a tear in his eye.

"Is there something wrong, Frank?" She asked, waiting till the two of them had gone to bed.

He sighed. "Had a talk with one of our alums this evening and I had to speak harshly to him—but knowing what he went through in the war, he's probably ten times the better man that I am."

Stung from Captain Gray's unsympathetic words, Albert slept fitfully. He rose at reveille and went to breakfast with the boarding cadets. Hoping to avoid Captain Gray, he was able to find a seat at a table of twelve other alumni staying in the barracks.

After introductions and handshakes, the breakfast conversation revolved primarily around jobs and families. Albert told the others he was in the movie theater business and let it go at that.

Most of them were younger than Albert, and all were married and raising families, each of them on a fast track in various careers and enthusiastic about postwar opportunities in the country. A few had chosen to stay in the reserves, collecting drill pay and going to meetings once a month, but most had put their service behind them and were delighted to be just civilians again.

It was Veteran's Day and ceremonies were scheduled to begin at 11:00 o'clock that morning. The morning had turned windy and cloudy, threatening snow, as Albert, other alumni, faculty officers and cadets assembled in Jones Bowl for the annual observance. As he studied the gathering of people, Albert was disappointed to note that he was the only one there from the Class of '28.

After a short prayer, Army Chaplain Lt. Col. Raymond Strong gave a brief speech on Veteran's Day and its meaning. Then, Col. Sanford Sellers, the school's acting superintendent read the roster of former cadets who'd died in service.

Albert listened to the names of those killed and remembered what Cap Gray had told him the evening before; *you came home from the war—forty-nine of our boys didn't get that chance.*

After a wreath was placed, the ceremonies were ended with a rifle salute by the Academy's drill team, the Grenadiers, and the mournful notes of taps by cadet trumpeter Cpl. Billy Walsh.

The next day, Albert awoke feeling lost and alone. Others had come home from the war and gone on with their lives, but as much as he wished he could do the same, Albert felt too tired to try, too unsure to make the attempt, and too old to make anything more of himself. Suddenly, he wished he was back in St. Paul—where his sister made few demands and dutifully watched over him.

He sought out Captain Gray after breakfast. "I just wanted...to say goodbye, sir...and to thank you...for speaking so frankly the...other evening."

Cap Gray grunted, shaking Albert's hand. "I take it you won't be staying for the parade and football game, Mr. Strawn?"

"No sir, I think...I guess...I'd better be getting back."

Frank Gray looked into Albert's eyes and could see no light in them. The man had given up, he thought. Albert Strawn was a sad, broken product of the times the world had just gone through.

"Albert," the old man said, "Will you at least think about what I said about that GI Bill and going back to school?"

"Yes sir," Albert said dully. "I'll sure...think about it...sir."

No you won't, Cap Gray told himself sadly, watching Albert Strawn limp away, carrying his small, battered valise. I guess your life is what it is now, son. They didn't leave you what you need to change it. They took it all away and left you nothing.

Watching Albert standing alone, waiting for a taxi on 111th Street, Cap Gray finally turned, too, making his way slowly toward the school gymnasium, where the pep squad and cheerleaders were warming up, practicing their drills for the game against Argo High School later in the day.

Strolling along Post Walk, the captain glanced back once more and sadly shook his head. Not every story has a happy ending, the old man thought glumly, hoping the afternoon might offer a better result than the morning had.

1950–1957

CHAPTER 13

▼

BROTHERS

Spring and Fall Terms, 1952

Col. Clarence C. Jordan, MPMA's Superintendent, stood ramrod straight before the microphone. The Colonel was a retired Marine and every inch of him looked the part. Before beginning to speak, Colonel Jordan allowed his riveting gaze to fall upon the Corps of Cadets who'd assembled in the gymnasium, all braced at attention. Flanking him were Capt. A.J. Gumbrell, commandant of cadets, and Lt. Leland Dickenson, the school's assistant commandant.

Clearing his throat, the colonel began to speak. "Gentlemen, it has recently come to my attention that an advertisement appearing in last year's *Skirmisher* was ordered and purchased by a group of cadets calling themselves the Dracos. An inquiry into this matter has established that the wording of this advertisement was received anonymously in the mail, the envelope bearing no return address. Also enclosed was the required fee *in cash*. The yearbook staff ran it as a legitimate business ad.

"Well, gentlemen, *it was not.*

"I have made myself clear in the past how I feel on the subject of cadet fraternities and other such secret clubs. Organizations such as these are strictly prohibited.

"Gentlemen, MPMA is a military institution and a post of the Illinois National Guard. As such, it cannot tolerate gangs of cadets joining clandestine clubs or secret fraternities. There is no place for such activity on campus. Any club formed, must be recognized by the Academy and have a purpose for existence other than itself.

"You men may not realize it, but each and every cadet present is already a member of a club—a club called Morgan Park Military Academy. This large club has been divided into smaller units; your five companies, ten platoons, and finally thirty individual squads."

"Oh man, this is pretty lame," Cadet Ed Jerabek whispered out the side of his mouth.

"I would like to point out that we also have any number of fine clubs on campus, recognized clubs, legitimate clubs—the Camera Club, for example, and the Lettermen's Clubs. The Glee Club and the Drama Club, just to name a few."

"What about the Sophomore Crocheting Club?" Art Canfield suggested under his breath. He could barely keep from laughing.

"The Academy also has athletic teams, including intramural, for those boys not as athletically inclined. You may play varsity or intramural basketball, try out for wrestling and track, or join the touch football teams. You may join the rifle team, or become a member of the Grenadiers.

"I can mention more—there is the Music Club and the Chess Club, the Language Clubs, and the Debating Teams, and we even have a group interested in model airplanes."

Harry Klein, whose family had emigrated from Cuba back in the 1940s, could only listen and groan.

"Gentlemen," Colonel Jordan concluded. "I have undoubtedly overlooked many other organizations that are easily joined at the Academy. Needless to say, they are innumerable. But each, you will note, has a purpose. All of them exist for a specific reason. Therefore, it is the stated policy of Morgan Park Military Academy that no secret, unauthorized cadet clubs will be tolerated on this campus."

After Ed Jerabek, Art Canfield, Harry Klein, and Jim Bowden had graduated from MPMA's Lower School, the four friends went on to their freshman year at the Academy.

Confused and intimidated by the hazing of upperclassmen, and by their lower than dirt status as plebes, the four grew even closer, soon adding half a dozen others into their tight circle—hoping that in numbers might lay safety.

Over burgers and milkshakes one Saturday afternoon at a little grill on Western Avenue called Snackville Junction, Ed Jerabek and Harry Klein were bemoaning their standing as first year men and comparing levels of nastiness meted out to plebes by various members of the senior class.

The apron-clad fry cook and restaurant owner was a husky ex-GI named Pike Pecharski who held a passion for model railroads—so much so, that Snackville

Junction's gimmick was a stretch of O-gauge track and an electric train that ran from the kitchen through a tunnel and entirely around the horseshoe-shaped counter before it entered another tunnel back into Pike Pecharski's kitchen. Pike had fabricated wide flatbed cars on which he could put plates of food, running the orders out to customers by stopping the train wherever they happened to be sitting.

"You know Art Logan, right?" Ed Jerabek asked, watching the tooting and puffing Lionel locomotive deliver a steaming lunch of meatloaf and mashed potatoes to a customer down the line.

Klein nodded. "I try to keep clear of that guy."

"Yeah, he's a real prick," Ed said. "He likes to punch plebes in the arm until they break down and start bawling."

"He's a bastard, all right," Harry agreed.

"But you know what? The sonofabitch punched Bowden until he got tired of it, and Bowden never even flinched."

"Well, that's Jim," Harry laughed.

"Then Logan asked him if he'd ever heard of the Dukes."

"No kidding?"

Despite Academy regulations, four secret fraternities had been established on campus. They were Tri Decim, Alpha Draco, Phi Beta, and finally Sigma Triad—this latter group calling themselves the Dukes.

Ed nodded, taking a bite out of his burger. "They're lookin' all of us over, I guess."

Harry looked at him. "Think you'll pledge if you get asked?"

Jerabek shrugged. "I guess so, if everybody else does. But you know what's gonna happen, Harry? We won't all be able to pledge the same outfit. You and me, Jim, Artie, and the other guys—we'll all be split up for the next three years."

"That stinks," Klein mumbled.

Ed nodded as the Snackville train chugged past again, blowing its whistle and puffing steam as it delivered a slice of apple pie.

"Maybe we could just start our own," Jerabek suggested.

"Our own what?"

"Start our own fraternity—just us guys."

"That's a good idea," Harry said with a wide grin. "Let's have a meeting and we can kick it around."

Word was passed, and the group met in Art Canfield's living room on 114th and Oakley the following weekend—with all ten freshman boys wolfing down sausage, buttered pancakes and syrup as fast as Art's mother could manage to make them.

"So what's goin' on?" Jim Swank asked, chewing a piece of breakfast sausage. "What's this big meeting for?"

"Eddie's got an idea," Harry explained. "We're talking about maybe starting our own fraternity."

"Why?" Chuck Hart asked. "There's four on campus already. The Dracos already talked to me and Jack."

"That's right," Jack Peterson agreed. "They've got a few good guys."

"Sure," Ed Jerabek said. "All of them have some good guys, but if you pledge Dracos, you've got to hang out with Dracos for the next three years. It's the same with Tri, Phi Beta, or the Dukes. Once you join, that's it—and I hate to see us get busted up."

"I never thought of it that way," Art Canfield said. "We ought to try and stick together."

"Yeah," Bob French agreed. "Why *not* start our own?"

"The Dukes talked to me last week," Jim Bowden added, still rubbing his sore arm. "But I'm not joining any bunch that's got Art Logan as a member."

"I think Eddie's got a good idea," Corky Hendricks said. "We all get along real good—so let's stick together and start our own."

So far, the last member of the group had stayed silent. Finally, Bob Kiefer shook his head. "That's not gonna be easy," he warned. "If you turn those guys down, they'll take it as an insult. And if ten freshmen try to start something on our own—man, things could get awfully tough on us."

Ed Jerabek nodded. "It'll be the hardest on Harry and Jim," he said. "They're boarders. They'll have to take it twenty-four hours a day—every day."

"Just for one more semester," Jim Bowden pointed out. "And then they can't touch us—what do you think, Harry?"

"Sure," Klein said. "We'll stick together."

"Everybody agreed?" Jerabek asked. Those in agreement were unanimous, and once the decision was made, Jim Swank wondered out loud if there were any more pancakes to be had.

They called themselves the *Zetas*, the sixth letter of the Greek alphabet. In next to no time this caused a problem. They'd decided to limit the maximum yearly membership to fifteen—and someone mistakenly thought Zeta was the fifteenth letter.

"That's wrong," Jim Bowden insisted a few weeks later. "The fifteenth letter of the Greek alphabet is O*micron*—not Zeta."

"You got to be kidding," Ed Jerabek said.

"Nope, Zeta's the sixth letter, Eddie. I took the time to look it up—the fifteenth letter is Omicron."

"Crap—we gotta call ourselves the Omicrons? What the hell kind of name is that for a fraternity?"

Bowden shrugged. "I guess we can call ourselves anything we want—let's just stick to Zeta."

Less than a month after the upstart new fraternity was formed, cadets were whispering about it all over campus, and Captain Gray found himself summoned to the superintendent's office.

"Frank," Colonel Jordan asked. "We've heard rumors of a new secret club being started, but we know very little about it. Are any of the boys talking about a fraternity called the Zetas in your math classes? I've been asking all of our instructors the same thing."

"No sir," Captain Gray grunted. "I only allow the young fools to discourse on mathematics in my classroom."

Colonel Jordan nodded. "Yes, well, I spoke to the entire Corps of Cadets earlier in the year about the school's regulations against covert organizations on campus, and now there's word of a new one. This can't be allowed."

"Pardon me, Colonel, but I'm not sure the school can do much to stop the boys from starting clubs."

"Of course we can," Colonel Jordan huffed. "It's regulations—unauthorized, clandestine clubs are not permissible."

Frank Gray grunted again, recalling a long ago time when he'd been just a boy and joined a secret club called the Sangamon River Rabbits—their sole activities being to tease the girls and learn how to roll and smoke cigarettes.

"Boys like to start clubs," the old man said. "Especially secret ones—it's one of the things they do best."

"Not on this campus," Colonel Jordan insisted.

"Seventy-five percent of our boys are day students," Cap Gray pointed out. "They're back home by four in the afternoon. Who the boys see, where they go, and what they do on their own time away from school is something we can't control. This is a private school, Colonel Jordan, not the penitentiary in Joliet."

"Then I'll come down hard on any boarding cadets involved in this."

Captain Gray shook his head. "That wouldn't do either, I'm afraid. Singling out boarding students would hardly be fair."

The Superintendent snorted and slammed a fist upon his desk. "Damn it, Frank—then what would *you* do in my position?"

"Look the other way, sir. Let them have their clubs."

"You don't disapprove, then?"

"No Colonel, as long as it doesn't interfere with their efforts in their studies."

Colonel Jordan leaned back in his chair and nodded. "You've been a teacher here for a long time, Captain. I respect your opinion as highly as any instructor at this school."

Captain Gray nodded.

"So, as you suggest—I'll not interfere with their little clubs. If they become a problem on campus, however, I'll be forced to take measures against those boys involved."

Shaking his head, the superintendent turned in his leather chair and stared out the window just as classes were letting out for Mess II. "High school fraternities," Colonel Jordan sighed. "Good Lord, Frank, who ever heard of such a thing?"

The pressure wasn't long in coming.

"Bowden," the dreaded voice called out. "Stop right there and stand at attention."

Carrying his own briefcase as well as two others belonging to upperclassmen as all plebes were forced to do, Jim was on his way to Lieutenant Steinhardt's English class, walking toward West Hall with Jim Swank, Chuck Hart and Ed Jerabek—all of whom were lugging multiple briefcases, too.

The voice belonged to Cadet Cpl. Art Logan, a junior with one of the most vicious reputations in that year's junior class. Ignoring the other three, Art Logan stared at Jim, who was standing braced and stone still at attention, his back arched and his chin pulled in.

"Bowden," Logan said, delivering a short, hard punch to Jim's arm. "Didn't the Dukes ask you to pledge?"

"Yes sir," Jim answered.

"And you turned us down?" Another punch in the arm.

"Yes sir," Jim grimaced. "I did."

A third punch, this one a little harder. "You dumbass. Haven't you heard that Sigma Triad's the best on campus?"

"Yes sir, I've heard that, sir."

Punch. "Then why didn't you pledge?"

"Sir, I couldn't, sir."

Punch. "Why not?" Logan snarled.

"Sir, I'm a Zeta," Bowden answered, expecting another punch.

"A Zeta?" Logan laughed. "That deserves a few more." He hit Jim again, once, twice. "Who the hell are the Zetas, anyway?"

"There's three more of us right here," Jim Swank offered. Jim always treated their status as plebes with a mixture of amusement and contempt, and if he had anything to do with it, he wasn't going to watch Jim Bowden be hit much longer.

"Shut your mouth, plebe," Logan hissed, glancing at Swank. "I was talking to your four-eyed buddy here, not you."

Ed Jerabek took Swank's cue. "Well, we're all Zetas, sir, and if you talk to one of us, you talk to all of us."

"That is correct, sir," Charlie Hart grinned. Chuck was noted for a jovial temperament and his big ears—and his grin was almost wide enough to reach them both.

Suddenly, the boys were feeling their oats.

"Mister Logan," Jim Bowden said softly. "You've now hit me seven times. That constitutes physical abuse by an upperclassman to a plebe—which is against Academy regulations. If you strike me again, I'm going to bust your goddamned teeth out."

"Once he does," Jim Swank added. "The rest of us will gather up those teeth and shove them up your ass—*sir.*"

Art Logan was stunned. He'd never heard of plebes speaking in such a manner to upperclassmen. Logan was not a particularly big fellow, only mean—and like a few other juniors, he counted on tradition and his upperclassman status to intimidate and mistreat the younger boys. But now, right here on Post Walk, in plain sight of dozens of other passing cadets, he found himself outnumbered and faced down by four unruly plebes.

"Do you guys know who the hell you're talking to?" He asked them in an incredulous whisper, unable to grasp their disregard of his rank and position.

"Yes sir," Ed Jerabek answered smartly. "We're talking to the biggest dipshit in the junior class—*sir.*"

"You four have had it," Logan growled. Red-faced, he spun on his heel and stalked off, furious at having been made a fool.

Chuck Hart whistled through his teeth. "Oh man, I think we're in for it now—all of us."

"The shit is definitely gonna hit the fan," Jerabek agreed.

Jim Bowden rubbed his sore arm. "Maybe, but I sure wish that lousy bastard would've hit me one more time."

It took less than a day for the hammer to drop.

The next afternoon, Corky Hendricks found himself dragging six heavy book bags from Blake Hall across the campus to West Hall. Each briefcase belonged to a senior cadet—and they weren't all Dukes. The established fraternities had passed the word to crush these upstart freshmen who thought they could buck the status quo and simply start a frat of their own.

That evening, after study hour, Harry Klein had ten pairs of shoes to polish and ten brass belt buckles to shine. Four belonged to Dracos, two more to Phi Beta members, and four to Dukes—including Art Logan.

"Put spit shines on all those shoes, plebe," Logan said.

"Sir," Harry protested. "It's only an hour until taps."

"That's your problem," Logan snapped back.

Thirty minutes after taps was sounded and the floor chiefs had finished bed check, Harry was up and sitting in his chair, polishing shoes by moonlight. He'd finished two pairs when Art Logan burst into the room and snapped on the light.

"What the hell are you doing out of bed, Klein?"

"Shining shoes, sir," Harry answered.

"You're stuck, plebe," Logan growled. "Ten demerits—now get your ass back into bed, and say goodnight to your Zeta buddies from the Dukes."

Just as Ed Jerabek predicted, the increased hazing was tougher on Bowden and Klein than it was on himself and the others who had the luxury of being day students. But they paid for bucking the other frats by lugging five or six senior's briefcases wherever they went, or by getting stuck with unreasonable demerits in ranks.

"What kind of knot is that, Peterson?" Jack's platoon leader asked at morning formation.

"It's a Windsor knot, sir."

"That's no Windsor—it's a four-in-hand."

"No sir, it's a Windsor."

"You're stuck, plebe. Five demerits for improper uniform and five more for insubordination."

As far as the upperclassmen were concerned—those that were in fraternities, the Zeta's shoes were never shiny enough and their brass looked like crap, no matter how long they worked at it with Brasso or blitz cloth.

For months, the hazing pressure went on without respite, but it only toughened their resolve. After Christmas break, Art Canfield called another meeting at his house—to talk about increasing the membership up to fifteen.

Each of them had brought up names for consideration over the past month, but everyone they talked to wanted no part of what the Zetas were going through. "Naw, I don't think so," they would say. "The Dukes talked to me, too—I'll go with them." Or the Dracos, or Phi Beta, or Tri Decim.

"Hell, you can't blame 'em, I guess," Bob French said. "We're catchin' a lot of crap these days."

"How's it going in the barracks?" Bob Kiefer asked.

Klein and Bowden looked at each other and shrugged. "Not so bad as it was at first," Harry told him. "I think they're getting tired of kicking us around."

"Next year we're sophomores," Jack Peterson reminded them. "And then nobody kicks us around."

"Jack's right," Klein said. "We need five more good members, but if we can't bring in anybody else this year, why not just stay at ten and pick from next year's new guys?"

Before the following year's first semester was over, there were five new freshmen that pledged Zeta. Jim Bowden brought in his younger brother, Jerry, along with Jerry's roommate, Bob Clark, a serious and level-headed kid from a small town up in Michigan.

Ed Madsen and Rich Vitkus pledged, too. Eddie was a happy-go-lucky Swede whose folks had a swimming pool in the yard and a basement well suited for parties, while Rich possessed a sly sense of humor that always seemed to be in play. Each was a promising freshman both on and off the football field.

And finally, there was Andy Selva, a Southside street kid with a wide Burt Lancaster smile and a duck's ass haircut. Andy and Ed Jerabek were both from the same neighborhood and the two would go on to form a close friendship over the next three years.

The original ten were now sophomores and immune from any sort of hazing, but they were forced to stand by and watch the five newest members go through the fire—first as plebes and secondly as the next bunch of rebellious freshman bold enough to join the new fraternity.

One morning, when Jerry Bowden reported to wait tables for Mess I, he was met by cadet Headwaiter John Bacino, who handed him a huge mixing bowl of still steaming Cream of Wheat.

"You look kinda hungry, Bowden," Bacino stated. Known as Big John, Bacino was a tough senior—a heavy-set Italian kid from Calumet City. He'd been brought into Tri Decim two years before, when he was just a sophomore.

"No sir," Bowden said. "I'm not hungry."

"Well, you look hungry to me," Bacino insisted. "Real skinny, too. Have some of that mush—it'll make you feel better."

"I don't have a cereal bowl, sir."

"Drink it out of that one," Bacino told him.

Jerry lifted the six-quart bowl with both hands and took a sip.

"Drink it all, Bowden," Bacino said. "Curl a lip over that bowl and gulp it all down."

Bowden blinked. "Sir, this bowl holds a gallon and a half."

"All of it, plebe."

When he'd finished, Jerry was dizzy and sick to his stomach. He sat on a chair and held his head. His eyes blinked as he felt the room begin to spin. *Aaarrgghh*, he retched, promptly throwing up on the floor—six pallid quarts of warm cereal—scattering white-coated waiters in all directions.

Frank Sullivan, the Academy's cook, bolted out of the kitchen wiping his hands on his apron. Sully was famous among the Corps for two recipes—his barbecued pork, and a greasy, tasty platter of beef and rice meatballs in a spicy tomato gravy—a dish the cadets fondly dubbed porcupine balls.

"What in hell's goin' on out here?" Sully barked. "It sounds like a damn hog bein' slaughtered."

"Cadet Bowden got sick on your farina, Sully," Bacino said.

Sully shook his head. "Don' know why he would. That stuff's Cream of Wheat from the Nabisco Company—it's the real McCoy. Bacino, you better see this mess gets cleaned up before the whole damn bunch comes troopin' in for breakfast."

"Will do, Sully."

"Tell your Zeta pals Tri Decim says hello," Big John grinned, handing Jerry a mop and a pail.

In Hansen Hall barracks, Jerry and Bob Clark were suffering three times the normal workload of a plebe. They shined shoes and polished brass from after supper to study hour, and then after study hour through tattoo and taps. An agreement was made between the four established frats. Tri Decim and the Dukes would go after the two new freshmen Zetas who were boarders, while the Dracos and Phi Betas would put the screws to those who were day students.

On the Thursday or Friday before each Sunday parade, Rich Vitkus, Ed Madsen, and Andy Selva went home carrying at least a half dozen full-dress or semi-dress jackets, belts, shakos and caps—all of which had brass needing to be shined until it gleamed.

The unrelenting pressure went on for the entire first term, and the ten original founding members, all second year men now, were helpless to do anything but stand by and watch.

These five new guys want to be Zetas awfully bad, Ed Jerabek told himself one day, to put up with the kind of crap they'd been taking. It made him feel proud.

"I think we're the best, Charlie," he told Chuck Hart.

"Either that," Hart said. "Or our five plebes are the dumbest freshmen in the history of this school."

Ed shook his head. "No—I really think we're the best—but I wish we could do more to help them get through this."

Hart shook his head. "Well, we can't. If they weren't catching hell for being Zetas, they'd be catching it for being plebes. That's just the way things are."

Nothing would change until the spring term—and what caused the change was Art Logan's big mouth and bad temper getting him into some real trouble. Logan was a senior now, a first sergeant in C Company, and twice as obnoxious as he'd been the year before.

The problem started on a Saturday night at the popular Swank Roller Rink on 111th and Western. The Swank advertised itself as the *Only Knee Action Skating Floor in the Country* and it was a hangout for every high school kid in the Beverly and Morgan Park area. Frequented by MPMA cadets and their girlfriends, it also drew kids from Morgan Park and Blue Island High Schools—most of the boys affecting the James Dean look of cool—with turned up collars and DA haircuts carefully combed and held in place by Wildroot Creme Oil or some similar unguent.

On weekends, the Swank usually brought in an organist for its Wurlitzer, and featured couples-only numbers, along with trios, dance numbers, games and prizes. There was supposed to be a dress code. Girls had to wear skirts or skating dresses, and they could be no shorter than the middle of the knee. Accordingly, the boys weren't allowed to wear jeans or t-shirts, but nobody paid any attention to the rule and no one ever bothered to enforce it.

Art Logan had brought a date to the rink, and like any MPMA cadet with common sense, he was at the Swank out of uniform. It was a warm May evening and Logan had replaced his cadet grays with a white t-shirt, Levis, and loafers.

The sleeves of his t-shirt were rolled up to his shoulders. The roll of his right sleeve held an old Zippo lighter and a pack of Marlboro cigarettes.

Ed Jerabek, Andy Selva, Chuck Hart, and Jim Bowden were at the Swank together and each of them had a date that night, too—four girls from the nearby Loring School for Girls on Longwood Drive.

Earlier that evening, the rink's slickly polished floor had been crowded—with skaters gliding and weaving, stepping, kicking or spinning counter-clockwise around the rink at all speeds, solo and in groups, forward and backward, always to the beat of the music.

As the night wore on, the skating music of the Wurlitzer got to be a drag. Now the need was for Bill Haley's "Shake, Rattle and Roll" on somebody's juke-box, or Kitty Kallen's romantic "In The Chapel In The Moonlight" on the car radio.

The four Zetas and their dates had finished skating and were putting on their shoes as Art Logan and his girl skated past. "Hey, Jerabek," Logan shouted across the floor. "It's a relief to see some Zetas out with chicks. We thought you guys might all be fruits."

"What an asshole," Ed said, shaking his head and holding up a middle finger.

Sitting at tables just off the rink, the girls had to spend another fifteen minutes freshening their makeup and deciding where they'd like to eat—the usual choice was between Fox's Beverly Pizza or the old reliable A&W in Blue Island for burgers and fries.

But before they'd made up their minds, somebody was yelling *Fight!* The Wurlitzer stopped and dozens of skaters were suddenly flying across the wood floor toward the snackbar on the far side of the rink.

"What's going on?" Andy Selva asked, putting out a cigarette.

Bowden stood on a chair and craned his neck to see. "I don't know," he said. "Let's go have a look."

By the time they made it through the crowd, Art Logan had his back against a wall while four or five guys from Morgan Park High School were jabbing him in the arms and slapping him around. His date was sitting off to one side and crying.

"Aw Jeez," Bowden remarked, remembering when he'd been a plebe and all those times Logan had done the same to him. "This couldn't happen to a nicer guy."

Andy Selva shook his head. "Yeah, but five to one is piss poor odds for sure."

"It's Artie Logan," Bowden reminded him. "He's a prick."

"Maybe," Chuck Hart said. He didn't like the odds very much, either. "But he's still our prick."

Jerabek turned to a dark-haired girl standing next him, asking her what happened. She was wearing a pink angora sweater with *Angie* sewn onto it.

"Who knows?" The girl said with a shrug. "Somebody skated into somebody on the floor, I guess."

"Who's the guy doin' most of the pushing?" Jerabek asked. "I don't think I ever seen him before."

"That's Tommy Solana," the girl in the sweater said. "He goes to Morgan Park High and he's Puerto Rican. That's Sue Giannetti crying in the chair—the two of them used to go steady."

"Yeah, I've heard about Tommy Solana," Andy Selva put in. "They say he's a tough little punk—carries a blade, too."

Jerabek shook his head. "Man, she's gotta be awfully hard up to go out with a dipshit like Logan."

"Well, what do you guys think?" Hart asked.

"He's gonna get the crap kicked out of him," Andy said. "Five against one."

"Wanna even it out?" Ed asked.

"I guess," Andy said, shrugging.

Jim Bowden was still reluctant. "Hell, we all got dates with us. I didn't come here to get into a scrap—especially over Art Logan."

Hart shook his head. "Me neither, but Logan's an apple boy—just like us. A shithead, maybe, but he's still one of us."

Art Logan had covered his face with his arms, hunched over as Tommy Solana and four other boys slapped him around. One of them took away his cigarettes and Zippo lighter and dropped them in a nearby trashcan.

"Hey Solana," Jerabek called out over the noise of the crowd. "Five to one makes it pretty easy, don't it?"

Tommy Solana and his pals stopped and left Logan alone for a moment. "Who the hell are you, *pendejo?*" Solana called back.

"We're friends of his," Ed said, nodding toward Andy, Chuck, and Jim. "All four of us."

"What's that to me?" Solana asked nervously, suddenly aware that the odds had drastically changed. "Your asshole friend is here with my girl."

"I ain't your girlfriend anymore," Sue Giannetti cried out. "I broke up with you, Tommy—remember?"

"Shut up, *puta,*" he barked at her sharply, then looked back at Ed. "What do you want to do, *ese?* You wanna rumble or what?"

Ed shook his head, smiling. "*Nah*—we don't want trouble and you don't either—be a good guy and just let the kid go home."

Tommy Solana slipped his hand into his pants pocket, curling his fingers around the smooth plastic handle of the switchblade he carried. The kid they were slapping around was nothing, but these four facing him were confident—and yet, the one doing the talking was playing it cool, giving him a chance to save face.

"I could kick his *pendejo* ass," Tommy said, making sure that everyone in the crowd heard him.

"Sure," Jerabek agreed. "But for what? Let him go."

Solana thought about it for a moment, then grabbed Logan by the shoulders, spun him around to face Ed and the others, and gave him a hard shove in their direction. "Okay, take the little *maricón* home with you then, and tuck him into bed."

They hustled Art Logan out the door and into the spring night, with the girls just behind them. "You got a car?" Ed asked.

Logan nodded. "Yeah, I'm parked on Artesian."

"Well, you better get your ass home."

Blinking, Logan looked at each of them. "Listen guys, I really appreciate what you did in there. I won't forget it, either."

For Jim Bowden, the temptation was too great. He stepped up, balled his fist, and smashed Art Logan in the shoulder as hard as he could. "No problem, Artie—tell the Dukes that Zeta says hello."

By noon on Monday, the word had gotten around. Suddenly, there was no more hazing of Zeta pledges.

"I said we were the best, Charlie," Ed Jerabek told Chuck Hart that afternoon. "Now I guess the rest of them know it, too."

CHAPTER 14

▼

HOT TIMES ON BOURBON STREET

Spring Term, 1954

"Look around you, boys," Lt. Frank Newley said. Newley was the Academy's newest instructor of French and Latin and was reading from a small booklet titled: *Union Station—Chicago's Beaux Arts Masterpiece.* The young Lieutenant was stubbornly determined to make this an informative and highly educational trip for the young cadets in his charge.

"This booklet says the main waiting room where we're now standing," Lieutenant Newley told them, looking down at the description on the page, "with its skylight and connecting lobbies, staircases, and balconies, is called the 'Great Hall' and is regarded as one of the country's finest interior public spaces."

Jeez, how about that? Eddie Fallon thought.

Eddie was a senior this year. Along with thirty other cadets, he let his gaze wander around the vast, cavernous waiting room. The pink tinged Tennessee marble floors harmonized with the marble walls, the Corinthian columns, and bronze floor torches. The soft morning light filtering through the Great Hall's vaulted skylight seemed to put passengers at ease. The waiting room's colossal size had a tendency to hush people, and its long, smooth mahogany benches offered comfortable seats for travelers to relax, watch the crowds, admire the architecture, or just daydream as they patiently waited for their trains.

Lieutenant Newley, along with Major Chesebro and Lt. Fred Pardee who'd been teaching social studies at MPMA for the past five years, had volunteered to chaperone the school's annual spring trip for senior and junior cadets.

This year, casually dressed in civilian clothes and gathered in a restless group around Lieutenant Newley, they were impatiently waiting to board the early morning Illinois Central daytime coach to New Orleans, Louisiana.

It was a sixteen-hour run, and most of the journey took place during daylight hours so Pullman cars were unnecessary and fares were significantly cheaper—making it ideal for those cadets whose parents were of more limited means.

They were scheduled to board in fifteen minutes, but Major Chesebro and Lieutenant Pardee had gone off to buy cigars at one of the station's small tobacco stands.

"Seems kinda funny to see them out of uniform," Eddie Fallon pointed out to his best friend, Lou Bryson.

"Who?" Bryson asked, examining his ticket.

"You know, Chesebro and Pardee," Eddie said. "They look a lot different in civvies—Lieutenant Newley, too."

"Everybody looks different in civvies," Bryson offered. "Even you, I guess."

"Damned right I do," Eddie eagerly agreed. He lived near 63rd and Kedzie and his civilian clothes still leaned toward roll collars and pegged pants. "I bought some sharp new threads, too—I don't wanna look like a jerk on Bourbon Street."

"What's that?"

"What's what?"

"Bourbon Street."

"Jeez," Eddie sighed, annoyed by his friend's ignorance. "Just the heart of New Orleans—that's all Bourbon Street is."

"Well, what's so great about it?"

"Bars, jazz, and strip joints," Eddie explained. "More than you can count, man—and eighteen is legal."

A few minutes before the group was to board, Major Chesebro and Lieutenant Pardee returned and began a head count. "Hey sir," one of the boys called out. "Can we buy cigars, too?"

"Any cadet who has written permission to smoke is free to use tobacco on this trip," Chesebro told them, and then with a sarcastic note. "But I'd stick to cigarettes boys, cigars might make you little fellas sick."

"That's bull," Eddie said under his breath. "I've smoked cigars before—as long as you don't inhale, they're okay."

Lou Bryson didn't smoke, so it made no difference to him.

At exactly five minutes to eight, they heard the boarding call and hustled over to Track Four where two black baggage men were busy loading suitcases into a baggage car.

Lou took a minute to study the train they'd be riding on. It had what looked like a dozen passenger cars or more, each painted in the Illinois Central colors of brown, orange, and yellow.

At eight o'clock, the gray-haired, uniformed conductor looked at his watch and called out, *"Booaard*—all aboard!" He glanced at the milling crowd of young men gathered on the railroad platform and turned to Major Chesebro. "These the military school fellas?"

"Yessir," Chesebro said amiably. "They're ready to go."

"Well, they'll ride in coach number ten. Plenty of room."

Under the watchful eyes of Major Chesebro and the two other faculty chaperones, Eddie Fallon, Lou Bryson and the other cadets clambered aboard and found seats in their assigned coach.

On schedule, the train began its journey south, backing slowly out of Union Station and moving over a gritty crosshatch of tracks and railroad yards, crossing the South Branch of the Chicago River and then starting forward as it finally reached Illinois Central track. Southbound now, and staring out the windows, the cadets passed the storefronts of Chinatown, Soldier Field and the Field Museum of Natural History.

Twenty minutes later, having rumbled through the factory and faded tenement neighborhoods of Chicago's gritty southeast side, the train crossed the Little Calumet River and slowed as it went through the Illinois Central's Markham Yards.

Because the Illinois Central day coach was inexpensive, many cars carried colored folks traveling from Chicago to visit friends and family in Mississippi and Louisiana. Many had brought their own rations aboard and the mouth-watering aroma of home-cooked fried chicken filled their coaches.

Once the train had gained speed, a chair-car porter opened the door and stepped into the number ten coach. In his deep, baritone voice he welcomed the MPMA cadets aboard, making sure all of them were settled and relaxed.

"We call this train the *City of New Orleans,*" the porter stated proudly. Pinned on his starched white uniform jacket was a brass name badge that said *J. Holcomb.*

The boys didn't know it, but the chair-car porter had the worst job on the train. He was the low man on the pole and was never allowed to talk back to passengers, no matter what abuse he had to occasionally endure. Nevertheless, Mr.

Holcomb was an amiable, distinguished-looking black man who addressed every-one as Sir—with no suggestion of subservience.

"Mister, are we stuck in these seats for the whole trip?" One of the cadets asked—a junior named Andy Volk.

"Oh no, sir," Mr. Holcomb said. "We got a fine dinin' car and a smoker, too. An' way back in the rear we got a observation car. It real nice and comfortable—give you young gentlemens a first-rate view of the countryside we passin' through."

Little more than an hour later, they pulled out of the Kankakee station and as the boys stared out the coach's windows, they could see little of interest but farmhouses, barns, and cornfields passing by on either side of the tracks.

"I hope it gets better'n this," Wally Dunn grumbled. Wally was a senior from Loveland, Colorado, and held the opinion that snow-clad mountains trumped Illinois cornfields any day of the week.

"Not unless you like swamps," Eddie Fallon told him. A while later, Eddie and a few of the other boys made their way through the rumbling, pitching coaches and into the smoker, where they settled around a table to play some cards.

"Man—you smell the fried chicken in some of those cars?" A cadet named Harvey Maddox asked. "I could go for some of that."

Another boy, a senior named Ron Lippert, looked at his watch. "Major Chesebro said we get box lunches at noon. Just sandwiches and stuff like that, I guess."

"Box lunches sure aren't fried chicken," Harvey said.

"Maybe those colored people'll sell you some," Eddie said. "If you're so hungry for it. Who wants to deal?"

They played penny ante poker for a while, until Mr. Holcomb came into the smoker. "You boys be wantin' some refreshments?"

"Can we get beer?" Wally Dunn asked him.

The black man chuckled and shook his head. "Why, no sir, we can't be servin' you young fellas no spirits aboard this train. Root beer'll have to do—we got Seven-Up and Pepsi Cola, too."

"Where are we, Mr. Holcomb?" Ron Lippert asked, after they all ordered soft drinks.

"Comin' up on Effingham, Illinois," the porter told them. "We be servin' you some lunch real soon."

"Man, we're really haulin' ass," Wally Dunn said, glancing out the window. "What kinda mill does this thing have?"

"What kinda what?"

"Engine."

"We runnin' an EMD-E8 this trip," Mr. Holcomb said. "It got two separate twelve-cylinder diesels in that engine compartment—more'n two thousand horsepower. We highballin' for sure."

Back in their coach, the three faculty officers sat together near the rear of the car. Major Chesebro and Fred Pardee smoked their cigars, while Frank Newley was busy studying a tourist guidebook to New Orleans and methodically checking off anything he thought the cadets should see.

As instructors, Newley and Pardee held brevet commissions in the Illinois National Guard, valid only as long as they taught at the Academy. But Maj. John Chesebro was regular army. The school's professor of military science and tactics, Chesebro had enlisted in '36, been wounded on Guadalcanal and seen action in Korea.

"Where are we taking them, Frank?" Pardee asked. Lieutenant Pardee was single and looking forward to a few nights on the town after the chaperones made sure the boys were in bed.

"The St. Louis Cemetery, for sure," Newley said, pushing his glasses up on his nose, something he did constantly. "They can see the grave of the Voodoo Queen—Marie Laveau."

"How about a Mississippi riverboat?" Major Chesebro asked. "I've never been on a riverboat. Maybe they'd like that, too."

Nodding, Newley pointed his finger in the guidebook. "Here's one with a Dixieland Jazz band on board—the *Natchez*. It's got a steam calliope, too."

"The boys should go for that," Pardee said. "Provided none of them get seasick."

Lunch was ham and cheese sandwiches and Jay's potato chips. The boys grew restless. Watching the passing scenery, very little seemed to change. An hour or so after lunch, they crossed the river at Cairo, Illinois.

"Is that the Mississippi?" Somebody asked.

"No, that's the Ohio," Lieutenant Newley stated. "It joins up with the Mississippi just up ahead."

"Jeez, Newley knows everything," Eddie Fallon whispered to some of the others. "But Pardee and Major Chesebro just sit there smokin' their big cigars."

"Newley and Pardee are okay," Harvey Maddox offered. "But Chesebro's kind of a prick. We'll need to stay out of his way once we're down there."

"Could be worse," Wally Dunn said. "Cap Gray could've come along, too."

"Oh jeez," somebody groaned. Just the thought of old Captain Gray grumbling and mumbling, wandering around Bourbon Street was hard to get your mind around.

"Only thing good about that," Eddie observed. "It wouldn't be too hard to outrun the old bastard."

Dinner was in the dining car, and once, as the attendant carried a large tray of plates down the aisle, he suddenly stopped, put the tray down on Lou Bryson's table and said, "Here come de bullet."

At that moment, a freight train roared past their window on its way north, shaking the entire car as it passed.

"Hey, how'd you know that was coming?" Lou asked.

The Negro waiter laughed a low laugh and rocked back on his heels. "Gentlemens, when you been ridin' the trains long as I have, you can jus' feel it."

All the cadets knew each other, yet they were already breaking into smaller groups based on familiarity and friendship. Accepted was the fact that once they managed to evade the stern supervision of Chesebro, Newley and Pardee, it would be these smaller groups that would experience, each in their own way, the exhilaration of being nearly adults, on their own in a strange town notorious for its lack of restraint and famed for its bawdy delights.

Early evening found the *City of New Orleans* switching cars in the Memphis railyards. Then it was off again, for the long final run south through the night, thundering down through the Mississippi Delta as bluish-gray clouds drifted across the moon.

The train pulled into the New Orleans station at three-thirty in the morning. In the muggy Louisiana night, Eddie Fallon and the others, groggy from sleep, climbed aboard a chartered bus that was parked and waiting on Loyola Avenue. The driver sat on a wooden bench smoking a cigarette while the diesel engine ran and the bus's baggage compartment was already open.

"Welcome to Nawlins," the bus driver told Major Chesebro as he stubbed out his cigarette and began loading luggage.

"These boys are tired," Chesebro said. "How far to our hotel?"

"Have you there in twenty minutes," the driver promised.

Half the cadets fell back asleep once they were aboard, while those that stayed awake watched the driver snake his bus through the narrow streets of the French Quarter—dirty, littered streets that were already being swept and hosed down from earlier that night.

Finally the bus stopped in what seemed like the middle of the street, depositing the boys in front of the Andrew Jackson Hotel at 919 Royal Street.

"Two to a room, boys," Major Chesebro told them. "Pick your roommate and the desk clerk will tell you your room number. You can carry your luggage yourselves."

Far away, over Lake Pontchartrain, flashes of heat lightning lit the sky, and even at this odd hour Eddie Fallon thought he heard a few rippling riffs of a jazz trumpet somewhere down the street.

They were up early the next day. Lieutenant Newley had been amazed that even at four o'clock in the morning the hotel desk was able to arrange a group tour of one of the many cemeteries that had made New Orleans famous.

"Man, I'm glad it's daytime out," Lou Bryson said, as the tour made its way through the cemetery called St. Louis Number One. "This place is creepy—I'd hate to be here at night."

There were no graves to be seen, only large vaults and crypts and peculiar statuary, all built above the ground. The tour booklet described it as a City of the Dead.

"When I was your age, boys," the tour guide said. "I never gave too much thought to our New Orleans cemeteries." He was a short, pudgy little fellow who hobbled along with a limp. "I used to pass them all the time because they're located along major streets and easily seen. Why, there's *six* clustered right at the end of Canal Street, which is a main bus transfer."

"How come nobody's buried in the ground?" Asked one of the cadets. "Like they are up north, where we're from."

"A curiosity indeed, young man," the guide answered. "The remnant of a practical solution to the problem of burying wooden caskets, filled with air, in ground where the water table is often less than two feet from the surface.

"In the early days of New Orleans," the guide went on. "It was necessary to bore holes in the caskets and load them with rocks and sand bags to get them to stay down. Even so, a good New Orleans rain would often cause them to pop right up out of the graves."

"Jeez, that is *so* creepy," Lou repeated.

They followed the tour guide to a tall, old crypt, with a jumble of Xs and crosses chalked or scratched on its door. "This is where the Voodoo Queen is buried," he told them. "Her name was Marie Laveau and she died in 1881. Many believe that her ghost lives on in the minds of her faithful worshipers. Even today, they come to her grave asking for help and making marks on her tomb—these Xs and crosses." He grinned and chuckled, holding up a piece of yellow chalk. "Some say if you mark an X on her grave and knock three times, she will grant you a wish—do any of you boys want to try it?"

Lou Bryson stepped forward and took the chalk, marking a big yellow X on the Voodoo Queen's crypt and rapping on its door. "I wish we'd get the hell out of here," he said, as everyone else broke into laughter—all except Lieutenant Newley, who thought the tour of St. Louis Number One had been highly educational and a first-rate expedition.

That evening, the cadets hurried through dinner—it would be their first night in New Orleans unsupervised and on their own, and most had been approaching the prospect with both trepidation and unabridged enthusiasm.

Major Chesebro stood up before dismissing them. "Boys, the evening is free to spend as you wish. Lieutenant Newley and I will conduct bed check at 11:00 pm. Anyone not back in their room by then will be restricted tomorrow night, understood?"

"Yes sir!" The cadets responded in unison.

"Wherever you go and whatever you do," Chesebro went on. "The Academy expects you to conduct yourselves in a manner befitting MPMA cadets and gentlemen. Any errant, unsuitable behavior will be severely dealt with—is that understood?"

"Yes sir!"

"Very well, then—you're dismissed."

At that, the boys made for the hotel lobby and fanned out onto Royal Street, their eyes wide in nervous anticipation. Watching as they scattered, Lieutenant Newley couldn't help but compare them to bees in a garden—and that brought to mind the frenzied figures in Hieronymous Bosch's "Garden of Earthly Delights."

"These nights on their own could be a disaster," he pointed out to Major Chesebro. "Are you certain—"

"Free time's sort of a tradition on these spring trips," Chesebro shrugged. "I seriously doubt any cadet would go without it."

Bourbon Street was just a short block west, and Eddie Fallon, Lou Bryson, Andy Volk, Wally Dunn, and Harvey Maddox made for a place on Bourbon and Bienville that Lou had spotted from the tour bus earlier that day. The bright blue neon sign above the open door said "Hot Pockets" and painted on the window was a picture of a naked woman and the offer, *"Strippers nightly—No cover, No minimum."*

They took a table near the small stage and ordered beers.

"Are you boys old enough?" The waitress asked. She was tall and had a low, husky voice.

"How old you gotta be?" Eddie asked. He was wearing a pink roll collar shirt and a pair of charcoal gray slacks.

"Eighteen."

"Okay then, we're old enough—five Buds please."

As the waitress left, Eddie looked around the room, which was almost deserted except for them. He whistled long and low. "Jeez, you guys ever see a place like this? Eighteen to watch a strip show and drink beer. I think we died and went to Heaven."

Just as their beers were served, a spotlight opened on the stage and a blonde in a blue sequined dress came onstage. "Welcome to Hot Pockets, boys," she said, fluttering her long eyelashes down at them. "I hope you'll enjoy the show."

"Oh man, yeah," Wally Dunn said under his breath.

As the spotlight changed from blue to red to pink, and then to blue again, the girl brought a microphone to her red lips and began to sing a mediocre rendition of "Earth Angel."

"She doesn't sing worth a shit," Harvey Maddox whispered.

"She ain't supposed to sing good," Eddie pointed out. "She's a damned stripper."

"Well, why don't she take somethin' off, then?"

"Strippers gotta warm up sometimes," Eddie told him.

Not wanting to seem like complete fools, the boys kept quiet and patiently sat through the song, applauding when the girl was finished, then looking at each other stunned as she started into a version of Jerome Kern's "Smoke Gets in Your Eyes."

"You guys want another beer?" Asked the waitress. This time she'd come to their table smoking a cigarette.

"Hey, Miss," Andy Volk asked. "How come this girl's singing so much?"

Taking a drag, the waitress just looked at him and shrugged. "That's what she does, honey—Danielle's a vocalist."

"The sign in the window says Strippers," Eddie said, thinking it felt strange to say something like that to a woman—even though she was only a waitress.

"Oh, the strip show ain't here, boys. All that action's upstairs. Down here is only the vocalist."

That must be why nobody's down here but us, Eddie thought, feeling like a jerk. Then he asked "They serve beer up there?"

"Sure, liquor, too."

"How do we get upstairs?"

"Through that door, hon," the waitress said, pointing.

Illuminated by a single bare bulb, the stairway was shadowy and smelled of mildew and some sort of antiseptic. Standing at the top was a big man wearing a white undershirt. He was bald and the boys could see that his arms were covered with tattoos.

They heard music coming from an open doorway at the top of the stairs—it was a throbbing, urgent beat that held the promise of something prurient and illicit.

"You boys comin' up?" The big man asked.

"Yeah."

"Costs a sawbuck to get in."

"A sawbuck each?"

"Tha's right."

"That's pretty steep."

The man in the undershirt shrugged.

Eddie and the others fished into their pockets and each of them gave the bouncer a ten-dollar bill. "Y'all have a good time, boys," he said, motioning them inside.

The upstairs room was sweltering hot. It smelled of sweat and the air was heavy with cigarette smoke. Through the stagnant haze, Eddie could see a jazz trio set up and playing at the edge of another small stage on which a nearly nude dancer, wrapped in a lavender feather boa, had her back turned and was showing off her ass to the whistling, cheering crowd. This is more like it, he thought.

The dancer suddenly turned to face them, plucking off her tiny g-string to reveal something Eddie and the others found difficult to grasp. "Holy crap—it's a guy," Andy Volk whispered.

"Jeez, they're all guys," Wally Dunn said. "Look around."

He was right, Eddie saw. The upper room contained only men, not unusual for a strip joint, but many of them were in each other's arms, slow dancing, swaying to the trio's music. Others were off in corners, some in groups of threes and fours, doing things the cadets told dirty jokes about.

"Man, this place is full of fruits," Wally said, stunned by what he was seeing. "Let's beat it."

As they made for the door, the bouncer stood in their way. He looked at Eddie Fallon. "Leavin' so soon, sweetheart?"

"Yeah," Eddie gulped. "See, we didn't know—"

"It's ten bucks each to get back down," the bouncer told them. Over two hundred and fifty pounds, with a bull-neck and heavily muscled arms, he was blocking the stairway.

"Ten bucks—oh, sure," they dug into their pockets again.

Once back out on the street, Wally looked at Lou Bryson. "I'm out twenty bucks and the cost of a beer," he complained. "And I didn't get to see nothing but a bunch of damned fairies—you don't get to pick out where we go anymore."

"Suits me," Lou said, mortified by his ineptitude at choosing a suitable nightspot in a city filled with them.

They wandered around Bourbon Street for a while, edgy about any other nightclubs that advertised strippers. "They might be guys in those joints, too," Harvey pointed out. "Hell, you can't even tell the difference until it's too late."

After making certain that both men and women patronized the place, they stepped into a small, dimly lit establishment called The Dead Moselle Bar, on Bourbon and St. Ann.

The club featured a Negro blues singer who was just finishing "God Bless the Child" as the boys sat down.

"What's Dead Moselle mean?" Eddie asked when the waitress came for their order. She pointed to an old framed photograph that hung behind the bar. It showed three women standing side by side, wearing old-time Mid-Victorian gowns. In the faded brown photo, two of them smiled wanly, while the third— standing in the middle—wore no expression at all.

"That's Moselle in the middle," the waitress explained. "They say her people lived in New Orleans a long time ago. She got sick, and the doctors had to amputate her arm.

"But she died anyway," the waitress went on. "And the family wanted a portrait of the three girls together, so the two sisters had to prop the poor thing up between them while the one held that old cut off arm up to Moselle's stump. I suppose they wanted to make her look alive and whole again."

Sure enough, when the boys went up to study the photograph closely, they could easily see the appendage in question being held in front of the deceased.

"The sisters look about as cheerful as the corpse," Lou Bryson commented. This place was turning out to be strange, too, and Lou was thankful he hadn't picked it out.

"Anyway," the waitress sighed. "The owner bought the picture in a second-hand store and that's how this joint got its name—what can I get you fellas?"

They sat in the Dead Moselle until ten-forty five. As the black blues singer performed song after song, they drank their fill of beer along with a few Ten

High whiskey chasers, stumbling back to the hotel very, very drunk—but still in time for bed check.

The next morning, Lieutenant Newley had them assembled on the *Natchez*—a restored paddlewheeler—for a two-hour tour of the New Orleans harbor and the Mississippi River. The tour included an optional Creole lunch, prepared fresh on board, a live narration of historical facts and highlights of the port, a calliope concert, and a Dixieland jazz band called "Colonel Cotton and the Steamboat Stompers" that was performing in the dining room.

Almost half the MPMA cadets had been missing at breakfast, and now Eddie Fallon and at least a dozen others, all queasy and suffering hangovers from their first night on the town, were either being sick over the side or throwing up in the steamboat's heads.

"Lieutenant Newley," Major Chesebro observed. "I doubt that we need concern ourselves with the optional Creole lunch. Most of these boys just want to be back in their beds."

"A hell of a note," Lieutenant Pardee chuckled.

"This is a disgrace, Major," Newley huffed. "How are we to be expected to teach them anything worthwhile if we allow them to corrupt themselves into such a deplorable state? I'm afraid that this distasteful incident of drunkenness will require a detailed report to Colonel Jordan upon our return to the Academy—an example must be made."

"You'll report nothing," Chesebro said, lighting a cigar.

"I'm afraid I don't understand," Newley objected.

"These are boys, Frank," Chesebro stated coolly. "And they're soon to become young men. It may not be on *your* lesson plan, but this morning they're gaining practical knowledge of hangovers and the folly of overindulgence—lessons best learned when young."

Clutching a small educational booklet about Mark Twain and his adventures on the Mississippi, Lieutenant Newley looked over his glasses at Major Chesebro. "I certainly never needed to learn such base things, sir," he sniffed.

John Chesebro nodded and smiled, exhaling a thick cloud of cigar smoke, "No, Frank, I'm sure you never did."

Lieutenant Pardee chuckled again.

After the early-morning riverboat ordeal, Eddie and the others made their way back to the Andrew Jackson Hotel with dry mouths and pounding heads and slept the afternoon away.

Still stubbornly determined to offer the cadets an educational experience, Lieutenant Newley chartered a bus and arranged a tour of Fort Pike, a crumbling old fortress that had served as a prison for hundreds of captured Indians and their slaves in the Seminole Wars of the 1830s. The fort was little more than a twenty-mile bus ride from New Orleans, but to Newley's frustration, only a handful of cadets were up to the trip. He was further disheartened.

After dinner that evening, Eddie was still nursing the remnants of a headache. He groaned and rubbed his eyes. "From now on, no more shots and beers," he mumbled. "It just ain't worth it."

"I still wanna see a strip show," Wally Dunn said.

"We should ask a cab driver," Lou Bryson said. "I heard those guys can always tell you where to go."

"How many taxis you see on Bourbon Street?" Eddie asked.

"What about the desk clerk?" Harvey Maddox suggested. "I'll bet he knows a few places."

Since it was Harvey's suggestion, he was unanimously elected to approach the desk clerk.

"Uh, excuse me mister," Harvey said, looking around to make certain none of the chaperones were in sight. "Me and my friends were wondering if you could tell us where some good shows are."

"What kinda shows?" The desk clerk asked. He was a chubby little fellow who wheezed when he talked and who seemed to have trouble catching his breath.

"Uh, you know—like burlesque shows?"

"Oh, you boys are looking for strippers."

"Yes sir—but we wanna see real women, not guys dressed up like women."

The clerk nodded, rubbing his chin. "Well, I can tell you fellas where to go all right, but I usually get a gratuity for that kind of information."

"A gratuity?"

"A tip."

"Oh, sure," Harvey said, feeling stupid. He reached into his wallet and put a dollar bill on the desk.

"Lessee, you boys can see Lily Christine, the "Cat Girl," at the 500 Club," the clerk said, putting the dollar in his pocket. "Or how about Evangeline the Oyster Girl at the Casino Royale."

"Sure, cat girls or oyster girls—just as long as they're girls."

"Ooorrrrr…" the man wheezed, drawing it out just to heighten the suspense and convince the boys they were getting their dollar's worth. "There's always

Miss Cheyenne, at the Little Dakota Club on Chartres and Canal—it's a long walk, but Cheyenne puts on one helluva show."

Taking the clerk's advice and deciding on Miss Cheyenne, the resolute group marched toward Canal Street and soon came upon leafy Jackson Square, studded by ancient oaks and surrounded by a tall iron fence, the park was packed with artists, musicians, street performers, local people, and tourists.

From what the boys could see, the landscaped square seemed the French Quarter's center for eccentrics and human curiosities of all variety.

"Jeez, lookit that," Lou Bryson said, pointing to a woman who was roller-skating through the park while wearing a slightly soiled wedding gown and veil. In one hand she held a bottle of Budweiser and in the other a Kool cigarette. Behind her, hurriedly waddling to keep up, trooped half a dozen pet Pekin ducks.

"That's Ruthie the Duck Girl," offered a young performer who earned his small livelihood by juggling cups and saucers. "Ruthie's a regular around here."

For a few minutes, the boys watched the bizarre woman cadge money from puzzled tourists, and finally Eddie said, "Let's beat it—I'd rather see Miss Cheyenne."

The Little Dakota Club was dark and the air was heavy with a pall of smoke and the sour smell of tobacco and stale beer. It had a horseshoe-shaped bar surrounding three sides of an eight-foot wide stage, with a scattering of tables and chairs beyond the bar. In one corner was a small trio—piano, saxophone and drums.

The boys took a table and ordered beers. Minutes later, the trio took up a slow beat, with the drummer doing a riff of traditional Hollywood Indian tom-tom music.

As Eddie and the others sipped their beers, the room darkened and a single spot played on the stage. Then the curtains parted and a tall, graceful dancer appeared. She was barefoot and her costume was beads and fringed buckskin. In the spotlight, her long, straight hair shone raven-black, and around her head was a beaded band.

"Ladies and gentlemen," said an announcer. "Fresh from the reservation, the lovely Miss Cheyenne."

"Oh, hot damn," groaned a toothless oil rig roustabout in from his platform on the Gulf. He sat drinking at the next table with two dark Cajun fishermen. "Ain't this little gal somethin' to see?"

As the Indian tom-tom beat grew louder and faster in tempo, Miss Cheyenne moved with grace and control. Smiling, her teeth glistened in the spotlight. Her profile was darkly classic, and Eddie thought she was the most beautiful woman he'd ever seen. Her soft buckskin dress was snug at the knees and stretched tightly across her breasts. As she danced, the eyes of the men at the bar and the tables eagerly followed every erotic move, anticipating what was yet to come.

"Hell, this is more like it," Wally Dunn stated hoarsely, as he unconsciously peeled the Budweiser label off his beer bottle with a thumbnail.

Then Miss Cheyenne went into her routine. She loosened her buckskin dress zipper by zipper, strap by strap, finally letting it slip to the floor. As the men cheered and called out to her, she smiled, tossed her head and ran her fingers through her hair.

Now the trio picked up the tempo and the girl used all of the stage, swaying and grinding, flirting with the men at the bar. She looked as if she were enjoying herself. She faced one way, then the other, and slowly bent backwards until her head touched the stage, her black hair flowing downward as her sweating body formed a graceful arch. She rose, loosened her bra and let it fall to the floor. She was left wearing pasties, a tiny g-string and diamond-shaped patch. She picked up her bra, held it aloft and then cast it aside.

Flushed and nearly nude, she stood before her audience as the trio dropped all pretense of an Indian theme, launching instead into the old Burlesque standby "Night Train."

"Hot damn almighty," the oil rigger croaked, pounding his feet on the floor. "Did'ja ever seen anythin' like it?"

"She not no real Indian, her," one of the Cajuns remarked.

"Maybe she ain't," the old rigger hooted. "But she can damn well have my ratty old scalp anytime she wants."

The men at the bar and tables clapped and howled like wolves. Two small pasties and her g-string were all that Cheyenne was left wearing as she went into her dance, throwing neck, shoulders and head into the quickening beat of the music, faster and faster, with her body quivering, she came to the climax of her performance—plucking her pasties off and baring her breasts. Now, she threw her arms forward and her hips back, ending it convulsively as the g-string was cast off as well—finally standing naked, with her arms stretched above her head, smiling and breathing hard, pleased with the whistles and applause of the audience.

Stunned by what he'd just seen, Eddie Fallon realized he was a long way from 63rd and Kedzie and farther still from the stolid, structured campus of Morgan Park Military Academy. He stood up and left the table, heading for the men's room. On the way back, he felt a tug on his sleeve.

"Hello honey, you here all by yourself?"

The woman's face was sharp, but not unattractive. She had her blonde hair cut short and she'd managed to pack her hips into what Eddie figured had to be the tightest royal blue dress in Louisiana.

He shook his head. "Naw, I'm here with my buddies," he told her, motioning toward their table.

"What's your name?" The woman asked, without bothering to even look in that direction. She was smoking a Swisher Sweet.

"Eddie—Eddie Fallon."

"Like the show, Eddie?"

"Yeah, sure," Eddie said. "It was great."

"I can give you a better one, honey—just for you."

He felt his face flush. "Jeez, I don't know."

"You got twenty bucks, Eddie? That's all it takes."

Twenty bucks. Sure, Eddie thought. He had twenty bucks. For all his big talk and flashy clothes, he'd never quite managed to get past second base with any of the girls he knew back in Chicago. He suspected it was the same with his buddies, although none of them would admit it. Twenty bucks. And this was no high school chick—this was a real, grown-up woman. She even smoked a skinny little cigar, and he thought that was very cool. For twenty bucks, Eddie told himself, here was his big chance, his shot at finally finding out what *it* was like.

"Sure, I guess so," he agreed. "Where do we hafta go?"

"I gotta place close by," she assured him. "But you better get rid of your friends first."

"Yeah, sure. Okay." Eddie said, feeling his heart pounding. He made his way back to the table, looking behind him to make sure the woman was waiting. He hadn't even thought to ask her name.

"Listen," Eddie whispered. "I think I'm gonna get laid."

"Huh," Harvey Maddox said. "With who?"

"That broad over there—in the blue dress."

"The one smoking a cigar?" Lou Bryson asked.

"Hell—she's an old lady," Andy Volk said.

"She's not that old," Eddie told him. "You guys might as well go back without me."

Wally Dunn tapped his watch. "It's twenty minutes to eleven—you're gonna miss bed check."

"Who cares about bed check?" Eddie said. "Do I have to spell it out for you guys? I'm gonna get L-A-I-D. I'll see you later."

"Sure, see you later," they said, and even though the woman in the tight blue dress was no longer as cute or young as the girls they knew at Loring, Eddie heard the envy in their voices.

"**My** name's Florence," the blond woman told him. "But most people call me Flo. You look like you're a sport, how about buying me a drink first?"

"Sure," Eddie said. "You want a Budweiser?"

"No honey, I drink Dewar's scotch—straight up."

Eddie wanted to kick himself—he should have known that any woman who smoked thin cigars would most likely drink something classier than Budweiser beer. Now, he was embarrassed and afraid she'd think he was just a jerky young kid. "What kinda scotch?"

"Dewar's, honey—neat."

"Dewar's," he repeated. "Okay, I'll be right back."

She stopped him. "Just give me a few bucks and get us a table. I'll get the drinks—you drinking Dewar's, too?"

"Oh sure," Eddie said, thinking of the Ten High chasers they'd gotten sick on the night before. "Dewar's is fine."

Coming to their table a few minutes later, Flo put down two glasses of dark amber scotch along with a small amount of change. Then she drew out a chair and sat down, letting the tight blue dress creep up far past her knees. "Where you from, honey? Not around here, I'll bet."

"Naw, I'm from Chicago."

"Cheers," Flo said, clinking her glass against his. "Oh, that's a real nice town. I was in Chicago a few years ago. It was during a Lion's Club Convention, I think—that's a helluva nice town."

"Yeah, it's okay I guess."

Then he asked where she was from.

"Duluth, Minnesota," she said, sipping her drink. "The dullest, grayest, coldest town in the whole damned country."

Eddie shook his head. "Never been there."

"What d'ya do in Chicago?" She asked, lighting another cigar.

"Nuthin' much," he said, unsure of what to tell her.

"How's that work?"

"Well, I mean—I'm still in high school."

"Oh, Jesus."

Eddie saw her roll her eyes and quickly added, "But I graduate this year."

They were quiet for a while, listening to the trio play a mellow rendition of "Mood Indigo" and sipping their drinks. Eddie wasn't sure of the protocol here, should he suggest they drink up and get on with business or should she? He didn't know. And then another detail came to mind, threatening to further complicate matters.

"Uh—listen," he mumbled. "Am I gonna need something?"

"Like what?" Flo asked.

"Well, you know—like a rubber?"

She chuckled. "I'm a real clean lady, hon—but if it eases your mind to wear one, why you just go ahead."

"I got one in my wallet," Eddie said. "But it's been in there for a long time and I don't know if it's still any good."

He wasn't sure it had ever been good. When somebody gave it to him a few years ago, they'd said it was a novelty rubber and that it had a picture of President Eisenhower printed on the tip.

She smiled and patted him on the arm. "Then take that quarter out of your change and pop for a new one, baby—they got one of those vending machines in the men's room."

Eddie picked up the quarter and excused himself. In the men's room, someone had scratched *This GUM tastes like rubber* into the dirty white paint of the condom machine, and for a moment before inserting his coin, he wondered if Flo would find that as funny as he did.

After he came back to the table they finished their drinks and left the Little Dakota Club just as the trio began to warm up for Miss Cheyenne's last performance of the evening. The night was growing cool and Eddie wished he had his jacket. As if they were a proper couple, Flo held his arm as they made their way up Canal toward Dauphine Street. "I got a small place just a few blocks up," she said.

As they walked, Eddie suddenly thought the streetlamps were winking at him, and then each deep yellow light seemed to expand and grow huge as if it were a giant, slow-motion flashbulb.

His legs were feeling heavy, each step requiring great effort. His lips had gone numb and his tongue felt fuzzy. Shutting his eyes against the flaring streetlights, he stumbled and almost fell.

"Not feelin' so good," Eddie tried to say. "Dizzy."

"You're fine, honey," Flo said. "We're almost there."

Then the streetlights flared once more and winked out, and the rest of the world went dark.

Blinking and shaking his head, Eddie began to come awake in a narrow alley off Canal Street. His eyes wouldn't focus very well, his head felt fogged, and his mouth was as dry as cotton.

Eddie could make out a gray dawn just beginning to break. He was cold and stiff and had no idea where he was or how he'd come to be there. As his head gradually began to clear, he was puzzled to find Major Chesebro shaking him by the shoulders. "C'mon kid," the major was saying from somewhere far away. "Just take some deep breaths and shake it off—you'll be okay."

"What's goin' on?" Eddie slurred, still groggy.

"It's what's called a Mickey," Chesebro told him. "But you're damned lucky, son—it could've just as easy been a knife."

"I was with somebody," Eddie groaned, trying to sit up. "But I can't remember her name."

Major Chesebro nodded. "Well, whoever the lady was, she's long gone. If I had to guess, I'd say she left you a little poorer and maybe a lot smarter."

In the grayish, early morning light Eddie could see they were in a garbage-strewn alleyway. I must've been laying here all night, Eddie thought, and then wondered how Major Chesebro had even found him. Instinctively, he reached for his wallet but it was gone, and more than a hundred dollars with it.

"You missed bed check," Chesebro said. "Cadet Bryson told us you were okay—just that you'd be late. That was bad enough, but when it got to be three in the morning and you still hadn't showed up, your roommate got worried and knocked on my door. He told me where you fellas had been, so I got dressed and came looking for you—I had a hunch that something like this might've happened."

Eddie rubbed his eyes. "Jeez, sir—I'm awful sorry."

"So am I, son," Major Chesebro said, helping Eddie stand up. "You're going to be restricted to your room at night for what's left of this trip. No more nights on the town for the adventurous Mr. Fallon."

"Yes sir—sir, do you have to tell my folks?"

Major Chesebro looked at Eddie and shook his head. "No, I suppose not. Nobody told mine when it happened to me."

"It happened to you, sir?"

Major Chesebro nodded. "Yes, when I was just a young squirt like you." They were walking north on Bourbon Street, back in the direction of the Andrew Jackson Hotel. As early as it was, the only other people on the street were a few colored men hosing down the sidewalks. "It happened in a Hoboken bar," Chesebro said, "A few miles from Fort Dix, New Jersey. If I remember right, the girl was a redhead and I was eighteen. She made off with two months of my corporal's pay.

"That's where I learned *my* lesson, son," Chesebro went on. "I hope you learned yours here in New Orleans."

"Yes sir, I guess I did."

While Lou Bryson and the others explored the French Quarter each evening after supper, Eddie Fallon spent the next three nights restricted to his room, watching episodes of *Dragnet, I Love Lucy,* and *Sergeant Preston of the Yukon.*

For the entire trip home, Eddie's encounter with the prostitute was all the rest of the cadets could talk about, giving him a certain amount of worldly, devil-may-care élan, even though he'd been the unwilling victim in the matter.

A week after the group returned to Chicago, Eddie received a package stamped with a New Orleans postmark. Curious, he tore it open and found his wallet with driver's license, draft card, and social security card intact. His wallet photos and his small address book seemed untouched. Even the novelty condom printed with "I Like Ike" and the President's image was still in place, sealed in its plastic package and hidden away in a pocket where it had outlined itself as a worn leather circle on the wallet's outer hide.

As he carefully looked it over, Eddie saw that everything was there except for a hundred and thirty dollars in tens and twenties. Where the cash should have been he found a folded piece of paper on which was a hand-written message: *Kid, you really need to wise up. Don't never leave nobody alone with your drink in a bar. Have a nice graduation and a real nice life.*

The note was signed *F.*

CHAPTER 15

▼

A MEXI AND A SMALL BEER

Spring Term, 1956

The afternoon, Captain Gray thought, hadn't shown much promise. In class, nearly every one of his questions had been met by either a wrong answer or a blank, slack-jawed stare by his students.

"Jalopies, girls, and that damnable jungle music," Frank Gray grumbled to his wife as they ate dinner—his normal time to voice complaints. "That's all these young fools think about these days. Parents and teachers and school are minor inconveniences.

"If you want to hide something from those dolts," he quickly added, "Just put it in a damned mathematics book."

"It's doubtful you were any different, Frank," Anna Gray said with a patient smile. "Back around the time of Noah's flood, when you were still a young rake."

The old man grunted between forkfuls of meatloaf and mashed potatoes. *"Humphf*—I was a farm boy," Cap Gray grumbled, even as he ignored his wife's attempt at humor. "Not a rake. At their age I drove a broken-down Moline wagon pulled by a sway-backed old mare we called Button. Hell, the nearest girl anywhere close to my age lived in Illiopolis. Her name was Eloise Dinwittie and she was a Baptist—homely as sin and deaf as a stone, as I recall."

"Only time I heard music was at Sunday service," Frank Gray went on, lecturing his wife as if she, too, were a part of this latest generation of indolent louts that had his dander up. "Those church congregations favored hymns—not any of this Elvis Presley hound dog foolishness."

That warm and rainy April of 1956, President Eisenhower was six months into a second term in the White House. A young, gifted outfielder named Willy Mays had sportswriters convinced that he was about as close to baseball perfection as any player the country had ever seen. A sensitive and brooding young actor named James Dean was starring in *Rebel Without a Cause,* playing a double bill with *Blackboard Jungle* at the drive-in theater on 95th Street—and for teenage boys in Chicago and throughout the country, from Van Nuys Boulevard in Los Angeles, Jerome Avenue in Brooklyn, to Detroit's Woodward Avenue, and on Front Street in Philadelphia, Frank Gray was right—it was a time of hopped up cars, cute girls, and rock 'n' roll.

Eighteen year-old John Tuttle, a senior boarding student who wore the chevrons and rockers of B Company's first-sergeant, kept his maroon '49 Ford Convertible parked on 113th and Bell—close enough to be convenient, yet far enough away from the Academy to avoid suspicion—a strategy that was made necessary by MPMA regulations strictly prohibiting any boarding student from keeping an automobile parked anywhere on campus.

Not that anyone paid much attention. The leafy, tree-lined side streets of Morgan Park and Beverly were liberally dotted with cars that belonged to Hansen Hall cadets.

His first car, Johnny's used Ford had been a gift from his folks for his sixteenth birthday, as well as in recognition of a sophomore year with a straight B average. He'd found the Ford in a small used car lot on Harlem Avenue in Argo-Summit. The dealer was asking five hundred dollars for it, but Johnny's dad brought the man down to three-seventy five.

"It's a honey for the money," the dealer started out.

"It's a Ford, for chrissakes," Mr. Tuttle had said disparagingly, being a man who only drove Oldsmobiles. "This heap's six years old and the ragtop is rotten—c'mon pal, give us a break."

"Them tires is almost new," the dealer pointed out.

"Three hundred bucks," Mr. Tuttle offered.

"Four-fifty."

"Three-fifty."

The dealer grunted and shook his head. "Hell mister, I can't let that dreamboat off the lot for less than four hunnert."

"Three seventy-five—otherwise me'n the boy go home."

"Okay, okay—the kid's got himself a car."

Johnny didn't have the funds to do much to the Ford's flathead V8, but a summer job at a nearby plumbing warehouse earned him enough money to afford a few modification's to the car's looks—a salvaged convertible top from a junkyard, fender skirts and a set of dual baby spots from the J.C. Whitney Catalog.

On warm summer nights, Johnny worked on the Ford himself, shaving the hood and decking the rear before having it sprayed a rich burgundy red at the Earl Scheib shop on 79th Street.

Johnny knew that the kinds of cars cadets drove were usually dependent on the financial status of their parents, and that included Phil Schmidt, who was his roommate and financially more well off than most.

Marjorie Schmidt, Phil's mother, was middle-aged, divorced, and devoted most of her time to various social causes or political crusades. Sole heiress to her deceased father's considerable wealth, Mrs. Schmidt was spending that year in Washington D.C., fighting to root out Communists—traitors in the United States Government, and attempting to resurrect the disgraced reputation of Senator Joe McCarthy, who'd been dishonored two years earlier.

It was the reason Phil was a boarding student. Conservative in her beliefs, Mrs. Schmidt had been unwilling to let her teenage son spend a year alone in their large home on Longwood Drive.

Marjorie's Schmidt's father had died a widower, leaving her his sizeable estate, as well as a trust to his grandson, affording Phil a yearly stipend of eight thousand dollars—which the trust stated could be spent on any judicious purchase.

Phil had immediately set about to convince his mother that the acquisition of a new Chevrolet Corvette was as judicious as anyone could hope to be.

"I must say, it's cute," she'd commented, studying the sleek, low, Venetian red two-seater in the dealer's showroom. "But it's so tiny, dear—the car will only hold two people."

"That's why it makes sense, Mom," Phil argued. "Because it's small, you can't pile in a bunch of guys and go joyriding."

Mrs. Schmidt nodded. "Well, that's true, I suppose."

"Sure, and being small and made of fiberglass, it's real light," Phil pressed on. "Combine that with the fuel injection option, four-speed gearbox, and dual exhausts and what you've got is a sensible little car with great gas mileage."

"All right, son—get it if you like. Your grandfather was a very frugal man, so I'm sure he would have approved."

Jesus Christ, the cigar-smoking salesman thought, calculating his commission on four thousand dollars, this kid in the soldier suit ought to have my job.

Parking the Corvette on the street had never been an option for Phil Schmidt. Instead, he'd rented half of a garage from an elderly couple on 114th and Oakley Avenue. The old man kept his prized 1948 Buick Roadmaster parked on his side of the garage but every time he studied the bright red Corvette sitting next to it, he'd blink his eyes, grin, and shake his head.

Although happy with his Ford, Johnny Tuttle was caught up in the mystique of his roommate's Corvette, too. The car and its basic concept were still far too new and unprecedented to be taken for granted by Americans used to plain, utilitarian coupes and four-door sedans. The Corvette and its arch rival, the Ford Thunderbird, represented the first true sports cars produced in America since the sleek, elegant Stutz Bearcats and Mercer Raceabouts of an earlier era. To Johnny and the other cadets, Phil Schmidt's red fiberglass Corvette looked to be nothing less than the most visually stunning machine ever built by the hand of man.

Phil's girlfriend, Betty Hollings, was impressed with his car as well, and although disappointed Phil hadn't let her wear his senior ring, she was still delighted to display one of his sparkplugs around her neck. The Autolite plug hung from a thin, sterling silver chain and nestled in the cleavage of her ample bosom.

Johnny was going steady, too. He'd given his ring to Angelica Simmons, who was in her senior year at Loring School for Girls on Longwood. Angie's father, Fred Simmons, owned a profitable soft drink distributorship and held an opinion that his daughter's choice of Johnny Tuttle as a boyfriend was lacking in judgment.

"The boy hasn't even made officer at his military school," Mr. Simmons frequently pointed out to Angelica. "And I'm afraid that shows poor prospects for his success."

"Johnny's going to college next year, Daddy," Angie argued.

"Where does he plan to attend?"

"Blackburn College—downstate in Carlinville."

"I'm not familiar with it," Mr. Simmons grunted. "What good is it to go to some podunk school nobody's ever heard of?"

The day after Angie came home wearing Johnny's senior ring, her father and mother initiated a heart-to-heart discussion with her in the living room. Fred Simmons lit his pipe and stood behind his wife, who was sitting forward in their dark green Barcalounger.

"Dear, Johnny's a nice enough boy," Mildred Simmons said. "But your father and I feel you're much too young to go steady."

"Mom," Angie groaned. "All my friends at school are getting rings. Everybody's going steady."

Mrs. Simmons sighed. "Johnny's parents live near 55th Street, darling. His father works as an electrician. They're not—I'm afraid they don't—how can I say it? I'm afraid they don't share the same social position that we do."

"I don't care about that," Angie argued. "Johnny's cool, and I'm crazy about him."

"Nonsense," Mrs. Simmons sniffed. "There are plenty of more suitable boys from which to choose. What about Henry Prentice up in Saugatuck? We'll be spending two weeks with them in July."

"Oh *ick,*" Angie said, making a face. "Henry's my cousin."

"Henry's your *second* cousin, dear," Mrs. Simmons corrected. "Twice removed or something. And he's a very nice young man—he'll inherit his father's auto dealership someday."

"No thanks, Mother, I'll pick my own boyfriends."

Fred Simmons cleared his throat and spoke up. "Honey, your mother and I have talked it over. If you return the Tuttle boy's ring and end this going steady foolishness, we're prepared to buy you a brand new Chevrolet Bel Air as your graduation present. How does that sound?"

"I don't want to discuss it anymore," Angie huffed. "I'll be up in my room."

Along Western Avenue most weekend nights, from 87th Street south into Blue Island and back again, a cool, unhurried parade of boys showing off their wheels gave young girls excited giggles and kept police cruisers on edge.

Hopped-up cars crept back and forth on Western, a slow dance accompanied by the rumble of hot engines, teenage laughter, wolf whistles, and the soft burble of glass packs. As late afternoon gave way to evening, the nightly road show would begin.

For Johnny, Phil, and the others, cruising was more than just a way to pass the time—it was excitement for anyone old enough to drive. A dollar's worth of gas filled the tank for the night and their cars were like a gateway to the world.

The chopped and lowered Chevies, Fords, and Olds 88s shared the street with stodgy family sedans—parent's cars, crammed with girls. There were glances, smiles, winks, and constant flirting. The evenings were a time of play and flirtation. Carloads of young kids driving back and forth, cruising through parking lots of fast food joints and drive-ins, gathering in places where they could smoke, eat hamburgers, and show their stuff.

For everyone around Morgan Park and Beverly, the southern terminus of the strip was the Blue Island A&W Drive-in on 119th Street. Wearing their orange and brown outfits, hurried waitresses served ice-cold frosted mugs of root beer and brought out window trays of chili dogs, hamburgers and fries, along with the drive-in's specialty—a curious mixture of ground beef and spices piled high atop a hamburger bun and fondly known as the *Mexiburger.*

In one area of the parking lot were the home-built rods that belonged to the blue-collar kids, handy with a wrench, with after school jobs at local garages or tool and die shops. In another, the wealthier boys with their late model rides.

At MPMA, the Zetas drove some of both, and that summer some of the members caught up in the car craze decided to start a car club within the fraternity. Settling on the *Dashhounds* as the club's name, they displayed their membership with an aluminum plaque that portrayed a cartoon-like wiener dog with the name *Dashhounds* over it and *Chicago* beneath it. The plaques hung from chains attached to the rear deck of each member's car.

Eddie Madsen drove a white Thunderbird convertible—the only one at the Academy. Ed Jerabek tooled around in a new Studebaker Golden Hawk that had the convenience of a "hide-a-pint" armrest in the back seat, and Brian Donnelly, who was the club's "wrench," had an all black '48 Plymouth Business Coupe, shaved and decked, sporting zebra-skin seatcovers and as many horses as he could squeeze out of the willing little flathead six.

Although it was his father's car, Frank Bastis drove a white Buick Century with duals, tiny blue lights that glowed in the Buick's traditional portholes, and a Holley four-barrel carburetor perched atop its 322 cubic inch Fireball V8.

Art Canfield cruised the strip in his turquoise and white '56 Ford Fairlane, and Rich Vitkus was there in a new, powder blue Plymouth Fury ragtop.

And along with the cars, music was a big part of the mix.

That April, rockabilly singer Elvis Presley was leading the hit list with "All Shook Up" and "Jailhouse Rock, and following close behind, disc jockeys were spinning "Wake Up Little Susie" by the Everly Brothers, "Little Darlin'" by the Diamonds, and Buddy Holly's "Peggy Sue."

If cruising was cool, drag racing was hot. The racing started as social, but as time went on the kids were building quicker cars and the competition was ratcheted higher. Those confident in the performance of their rides and their skills behind the wheel soon began to run for money—usually ten or twenty dollars, but on occasion, when a challenge would turn really serious they'd head for lonely stretches of road out near DuPage County and race for "pink slips"—the titles to their cars.

When Johnny, Phil, or the others weren't cruising the burger joints or the streets, they were making out at the drive-in movies. Chicago and the suburbs didn't have that many passion pits, but one was in the neighborhood—the popular *Starlite* on 95th Street in west suburban Chicago Ridge.

It was at the Starlite, on a warm Saturday night in April that Johnny, Phil, Angie and Betty bought their tickets and found a slot ten rows back from the screen.

"That's one thing I don't like about Phil's Corvette," Betty complained, fingering the spark plug that adorned her neck. "We can't ever double in it."

"It's a sports car, honey," Phil said patiently. "It's not meant for double-dating."

"Well, Johnny and Angie are fun to be with," Betty argued.

Phil nodded. "Yeah sure, baby. That's why we're with them tonight. That's why I left the 'Vette in the garage."

Johnny and Phil had checked out with overnight passes. The Starlite was offering one of its special weekend triple features, beginning with "Hot Rod Girl," a potboiler in which actor Chuck Connors was a cop trying to stop "teenage terrorists on a speed crazy rampage." The film's lurid posters showed something for everyone—drag races, chicken runs and plenty of smash-ups.

The second feature was "The Devil on Wheels," about a teenager, influenced by his own father's poor driving habits, becoming a reckless hot rodder and finding himself involved in a fatal hit-and-run accident.

Finally, an old film from 1947 rounded out the triple bill. It was called "A Dangerous Age"—a black and white melodrama in which under-age lovers experience heartbreak when they run away together—the only film of the three that Angie and Betty really wanted to see.

All around them, cars were pulling in and attaching scratchy-sounding speakers to rolled down rear windows. As Johnny, Phil, and the girls watched, an old green Nash Ambassador pulled into a slot just ahead of them. After a few minutes passed, the teenaged driver stepped out, opened the trunk wide, and stood back as two couples clambered out laughing.

"Man, that's one ugly ride," Johnny offered.

"Yeah, but those old Nash Airflytes have beds in them," Phil offered with a sly grin, poking April in the ribs.

"You liar," she squealed. "They do not."

"Yes they do," Phil insisted. He knew his cars. "That's a 1950 Airflyte and it's got seats that fold down into a bed."

Angie laughed. "Maybe that's another thing Betty doesn't like about your Corvette, Phil," she teased.

"Oh heck, even if he *could* get a bed in that car it wouldn't do him much good," Betty retorted. "Phil knows how far he can go."

Sneaking into the drive-in by hiding in the trunk was a popular game, whether you had the money for a ticket or not. According to rumor, the drive-ins hired off-duty cops familiar with this scheme, keeping them busy recording license plates of those cars with only one or two teens in them. And later, if the car had more than the original number of patrons and they weren't able to produce ticket stubs, the guards would kick them out. But the challenge to sneak in always remained, and neither Johnny nor Phil had ever heard of this happening at the Starlite.

In the back seat of Johnny's Ford were four large Cokes and three bags of tiny hamburgers from the White Castle on 95th and Cicero. Printed in blue letters on each bag were the words, *Buy 'em by the sack.*

"Why *three* sacks?" Angie asked, wrinkling her nose. "That's thirty-six hamburgers for just four people, and I don't like them all that much anyway."

"Me'n Phil love 'em," Johnny told her. "Besides, they're only twelve cents each—we'll eat any that you and Betty don't."

"Angie," Phil said, as he leaned over the seat back. "You ever heard of White Castle farts? Oh man, those sliders smell the same goin' out as they do goin' in."

"Oh God," Betty groaned, whacking him on the arm. "That is disgusting— Phil, you are *sooo* crude. I'm surprised they even let you into that Academy."

As early evening turned to dusk, someone honked his or her horn, anxious for the movie to start. Soon other horns chimed in, and gradually a dissonance of tones filled the drive-in. From a car in the front row, a spotlight beam appeared and then the game began—with other spotlights turned on and playfully chasing each other across the empty screen. It was a Starlite ritual.

They ate the three sacks of White Castles and watched most of the first movie, and then made out through the second. Later, as the girls buttoned their blouses and put on lipstick while the old black and white third feature flickered on the screen, the boys decided to leave. "Let's cut out," Phil said. He wanted to get his Corvette out of the Oakley Avenue garage. "The A&W should be jumpin'."

"Hey, that's not fair," Betty complained loudly. "This next movie's got some love stuff in it."

"Who cares?" Phil said. "Let's see who's at the A&W."

Angie was angry, as well. "I suppose you want to leave, too?" She asked Johnny, her tone icy.

He shrugged. "Yeah sure, I guess so. Why not?"

Trying to be supportive and caring, Angie's mother once told her that there seemed to be a time in the lives of most young men when they were just callous boors—with all the sensitivities of a potato. Now, Angie remembered her mother's words and she was convinced that Johnny Tuttle and Phil Schmidt, senior cadets in their last year at the Academy, were prime examples of the breed.

As they left the Starlite and pulled out onto 95th, the Platters were singing "The Great Pretender" on the car's radio. The night had turned cool, too cool to put down the top. They drove to the rented garage on Oakley and waited as Phil and Betty climbed into the Corvette and pulled out into the alley. "See you there," Phil called out before they turned on 114th and headed toward Western Avenue.

"He thinks he's so big with that car," Angie grumped.

"What're you so sore about?" Johnny asked, sensing her anger as he followed the red Corvette.

"Nothing," she said sullenly, drawing into herself.

"C'mon, tell me."

"Cars," she blurted out. "Cars, drag racing, and hanging out at the A&W—that's all you guys think about. Are you ever going to grow up, Johnny?"

"What do you mean—grow up?"

"When are we going to get engaged, for instance? Don't you ever want to get married? Have a house and kids?

Hearing this, Johnny glanced over at Angie as she turned away and looked as if she was about to cry. We should've stayed for that last movie, he told himself. She wouldn't be in such a rotten mood if they had. Now she was talking about being engaged and getting married, for chrissakes.

"Hell Ang, I don't know," he said. "I still gotta graduate and then get through college before I can think about getting married."

"Well, you could be engaged in college, couldn't you?"

"I suppose, but I thought we were going to wait."

"Sure, sure," Angie said. "Why buy an engagement ring when you could spend that money on your car?"

"Ang, that's not what I meant."

"Oh forget it, Johnny," Angie said. "Just forget it."

The Blue Island A&W was as crowded as usual on a Saturday night. Carhops scurried from the pickup window to the cars, fitting trays of food to rolled down window edges.

Some of the cruisers drove slowly through with their windows down, eyeing whatever other hot rides were in the parking lot that night, while at least thirty car radios were playing rock and roll.

A few grew bored and decided to leave, pulling back out onto Western Avenue. The harsh crackle of glass packs and a squeal of rubber usually accompanied their exit.

When Phil Schmidt's Corvette eased in and backed into a slot, a pony-tailed carhop hustled out to take his order.

Angie was still quiet and sullen as Johnny pulled in next to the 'Vette. There was tension in the car, and nothing was said as they waited for the carhop to come over and wait on them, too.

"What'll it be?" She asked, a pencil poised over her order pad. Johnny thought she sounded tired.

"A mexi and a small beer," he said. "How about you, Ang?"

Shaking her head, Angie looked away. "I'm not hungry. How can you still eat after all those White Castles?"

"I'm a growing boy," Johnny laughed, lighting a cigarette and hoping to brighten her mood. He hated it when she was angry, and he didn't like it much when she started talking about engagement rings and weddings either. Unlike Betty, who seemed to be content wearing a spark plug necklace, Angie had his senior ring—so what was she sore about? He still had almost a full semester left at the Academy and then four years of college. After that, Johnny knew, the army would probably draft him for another two years. It was way too soon to be thinking about a wife and kids.

At Betty's urging, Phil dropped the top on the Corvette so they could talk between cars, and just as the carhop brought them their orders, Phil and Johnny suddenly stopped and stared, watching a local legend painted in gray primer slowly pull into the A&W lot.

"Oh man, it's the Skunk," Phil whispered.

The Jumping Skunk was a 1932 Ford five-window coupe with a chopped top and running oversized Goodyears in the rear, giving it a stubby, sinister rake.

Slouched behind the wheel was a fellow named Lester Hamm. Lester was nicknamed "Whitey" because he'd been born an albino. Both his skin and hair were a pale, ghostly white, while his pinkish eyes were ultra sensitive to daylight.

They blinked constantly and forced Whitey Hamm to wear sunglasses throughout the day and to prefer driving at night.

Largely ignored by girls at Blue Island High School, Whitey ignored them in return, and instead threw himself into laboring on his Ford "deuce" behind Lennart's Texaco Station on 123rd and Western, where he worked after school fixing flat tires and keeping the shop area swept and clean.

The look of Whitey's car suited its loud, blatty snarl. Most of it had been built with what were called "midnight auto parts"—or stolen parts. The coupe was running a nearly new three hundred sixty five cubic inch Cadillac engine that had been stolen from a south side salvage yard by Whitey and six of his friends.

They'd tossed a big soup bone to the foul-tempered German shepherd guarding the yard and while the astonished dog was busy with this unexpected windfall, Whitey and his pals pulled the Caddy engine and carried it away in the light of a full moon.

The potent little coupe boasted a Howard F-5 cam, mushroom tappets, tube pushrods, Mag rockers, Weiand dual quad manifold mounts and two four-barrel Stromberg pots supercharged by a bolt-on McCulloch blower. Whitey had also dropped in a LaSalle gearbox and a Hurst shifter, but where he'd stolen those, nobody knew for sure.

The gray deuce's front fenders and hood had been taken off to reduce weight. The Goodyears, also stolen, carried moon hubs all around and the interior featured a big, round Sun tach bolted to the dashboard and a full panel of Stewart-Warner gauges, with black and white pleated Naugahyde seats that had given the rod its name of the Jumping Skunk. Hanging from the Skunk's rearview mirror was a rubber shrunken head from a novelty catalogue. It had long strands of phony black hair, sewn lips, and green glass eyes.

The Jumping Skunk made one pass around the parking lot and then backed in next to Phil's Corvette. Whitey blipped the engine once and then switched off the ignition. In the seat next to him was a guy they called Stoop Sherman. Like Whitey Hamm, Stoop was a senior at Blue Island High School.

"Hey man, dig the apple boy," Stoop grinned, leaning out the window of the chopped deuce coupe. "Looks like his mommy and daddy bought him a plastic car."

"You're a funny guy," Phil shot back. "A real comedian—just like Milton Berle. Do they call you Stoop or *Stupid?*"

"Is that cute little thing all show or does it go?" Stoop asked, still grinning. His eyes had moved past Phil and settled on Betty, as Whitey Hamm just sat slouched behind the deuce's steering wheel, smoking a cigarette and saying nothing.

"It'll run," Phil said.

"Yeah? Will it run with the Skunk?" Stoop asked casually.

"How come you're the one asking?" Phil said. "I thought the Skunk was Whitey's ride?"

"He likes me to do the talking," Stoop answered with a shrug. "Whitey's kind of bashful."

"Yeah, I'll bet."

A different carhop approached Whitey and Stoop to take their order. She was blonde and somewhat chubby, and Phil noticed that even then Stoop Sherman was the one who told her what they were going to have. Whitey only sat quietly and smoked, not bothering to even look at the blonde girl outside his window.

Johnny heard what was going on and knew the beginning of a race was in process. Nevertheless, there was a certain protocol to be observed—certain tactics to be put into play. Stoop was feeling Phil out, testing his confidence, and a little more back and forth was needed before the challenge would be made plain.

"You can dig what Whitey's got," Stoop said, nodding toward the coupe's immaculate engine. "What's under your plastic hood?"

"That's my business," Phil told him.

"Fast?"

"Fast enough."

"You want to try us?"

There it was. Now Phil had little choice—either back down or accept the offer to race. He shrugged and turned to look over at his roommate. "Whadd'ya think, Johnny?"

Johnny shook his head. "The Skunk's quick. He's got a blown Caddy stuffed in there." He paused for a moment and then added, "Whitey doesn't usually run for kicks, Phil."

Phil nodded, glancing back at Stoop. "As long as you're doing all the talking, tell Harpo Marx over there I'll run him for a fifty."

"Fifty bucks?" Stoop laughed. "Shit—fifty bucks is chump money—Whitey don't run for nothing but pinks anymore."

"What's a pink?" Betty asked, curious.

"Pink slips—the titles to our cars," Phil told her. Things had suddenly got serious. It was one thing to lose fifty bucks—another to lose your car. Phil knew his Corvette was fast, faster than most of the wheels in the A&W lot. It couldn't help but be fast, with two hundred eighty three horses pulling only a little over twenty-eight hundred pounds.

But the Skunk was even lighter, and powered by a big, blown Cadillac engine. For a brief moment, Phil thought about his mother in Washington, D.C. and wondered what she might say if she came home and found out he didn't own the Corvette anymore.

"Are you going to race him?" Betty asked, fingering her spark plug necklace again.

"I dunno," Phil mumbled, looking past her at John Tuttle who was parked next to him. "What do you think, Johnny?"

Johnny shook his head. "Hell no, I wouldn't do it. You've got a cool set of wheels. Let Whitey be the dog with the big nuts. Why take the chance?"

Phil grunted, suspecting his roommate was probably right. He was thinking it over when Stoop Sherman leaned out the coupe's window again. "So, how about it, sport—you wanna run? Whitey's always wanted a little red 'Vette."

"Tell him to go buy one, then," Phil said.

Stoop giggled, flapping his arms. "Awww—the apple boy's a chicken. He don't wanna make his car go fast."

"Oh God," Betty groaned. "Are you afraid to race him?"

"No, I ain't afraid. But like Johnny says, why take the chance? That's all."

"Oh God," Betty groaned again. "I'm so embarrassed. You're backing down to a *spaz* like Whitey Hamm?"

Phil glared at her. "Who says I'm backing down?"

"Well, it sure looks like that to me," Betty said, sinking down into the Corvette's seat. "I thought you were so cool."

That was it. Phil couldn't take any more of that. He turned to Stoop in the deuce coupe. "Okay stooge—tell your boss we'll run for pinks. Where does he wanna go?"

Without even turning to talk to Whitey, Stoop said, "111th and Kean Avenue. Kean's nice and dark. It's got a little bitty curve to it but that don't matter. Once we shut down, everybody scatters and we meet back here—you got your title on you?"

"No," Phil admitted. "It's in a safe deposit box at the Beverly Bank. I can't get to it till next Saturday."

Stoop grinned. "Then we'll meet you here next Saturday night. Bring the pink and a ballpoint pen so you can sign the 'Vette over to Whitey."

"We ain't raced yet," Phil shot back. "What about Whitey? He know how to sign *his* name?"

Stoop shrugged and giggled. "I dunno. He's never had to do it yet."

As Whitey and Stoop casually finished their food, word went around the A&W lot that a serious race was on—the Skunk against the red Corvette—for titles!

"This isn't smart," Johnny told Phil as they sat waiting for the competition to finish eating. "I never heard of anybody who beat the Skunk. Whitey Hamm looks like a creep, but he makes a lot of dough doin' this. He'll beat you and then offer to let you buy your wheels back—if you can't, he'll sell them to somebody else."

"The 'Vette's quick," Phil argued. "You know that."

Johnny nodded. "Yeah, well—I hope you're right. Guess we'll see how quick it is."

Less than ten minutes later, a caravan of ten cars filled with teenagers snaked slowly out of the A&W lot, headed north toward 111th Street. Although every car in line was lowered or raked, had hot engines, dual exhaust and glass-pack mufflers, fender skirts and club plaques, everybody did their best to be cool—obeying all traffic laws and driving slowly and sensibly. On the way to a race was not the time to draw the attention of cops.

The caravan turned left on 111th, driving west past the Wilbert Burial Vault Company and the four sprawling cemeteries that had flourished on both sides of the street for as long as anyone could remember—Mount Olivet, Mount Greenwood, St. Casimir, and Holy Sepulchre.

As she stared out the window of Johnny's Ford, Angie shook her head. She still wasn't through being angry. "Burial vaults and graveyards on the way to a drag race," she said coldly. "That's real nice—just the thing to make a girl's evening memorable."

"Aw, nothin's gonna happen," Johnny told her.

"No, Phil's just going to lose his car. That is *so* dumb."

"It's his car," Johnny argued halfheartedly. "What do you care anyway? You're my girl, not his."

"Oh, you're just as bad," Angie retorted. "You'd take a chance on losing your car too, if some creep like Whitey Hamm called you a chicken."

Angie was on her high horse, Johnny told himself, and nothing he could say was going to make her feel better. It was beginning to get on his nerves and he wished she'd just be quiet.

"Betty doesn't get sore like you do," he said.

"Betty?" Angie laughed. "Oh my God, Betty Hollings wears a *sparkplug* around her neck, Johnny—she's not smart enough to get mad about anything."

When the caravan finally reached Kean Avenue it was already a little past midnight. Betty gave Phil a kiss for good luck and then got into the back seat of Johnny's Ford—excited about the race.

Stoop Sherman announced that he'd stand in the road to wave the deuce coupe and Corvette off. Still annoyed by Angie's mood, Johnny didn't say much as his car and the others maneuvered into position, seemingly just as smoothly as the Academy's battalion on Sunday parade.

Johnny took two more passengers in the Ford—two guys that were picked as judges if the race was close. They sat on either side of Betty, sneaking furtive looks at her breasts and grinning at each other like idiots.

North of 111th Street, lined up on a faded white quarter mile mark someone had painted on the road a few years earlier, Johnny backed onto the shoulder at a right angle to Kean Avenue.

He turned off the radio and rolled down his window, then let the judges out. Johnny tried to ignore the loud chirp of crickets and was listening hard for the first squeals of rubber on pavement.

"Eddie'll be on the other side of the road," one of the judges said, still staring at Betty. "I'll hunker down between your lights. Just don't forget about us and cut out—you might run over me or something."

"I won't leave you guys here," Johnny assured him. "Just get back in the car as quick as you can."

The chilly April night was dark this far out in the southwestern suburbs. With no streetlights, Kean Avenue was surrounded on all sides by woods and forest preserves. Phil and Whitey would race with their lights off, and it would be up to Johnny to illuminate the quarter mile marker and the end of the race by turning on his own headlights just as Phil and Whitey were halfway through their run.

The other seven cars were parked another hundred yards past that, on both sides of Kean Avenue with their motors running and their headlights off.

Throughout it all, Angie sat scowling. She was thinking of her parents, and their disapproval of Johnny as a steady boyfriend. She tried to defend him every chance she could, but now, sitting here on a dark road after midnight, bored to death and waiting to watch a stupid drag race with Betty Hollings and her huge tits in the back seat, jabbering about her boyfriend's fast Corvette—it all seemed a ridiculous waste of time.

Hunching forward in short, jerky fits and starts, the gray deuce coupe moved up alongside Phil's Corvette. He glanced over to see Whitey Hamm staring straight ahead, expressionless, his face and hair resembling a corpse.

"He's gonna blow you off, man," Stoop said with a grin. "It's all over but the shouting."

"Yeah, sure," Phil said. "I got something he can blow."

Sitting next to him, the Skunk sounded rough, with the hiss of its supercharger and the coupe's wild cam barely keeping the big Caddy engine at a ragged idle, but Phil knew all that would change when the little rod had its revs up.

Both cars inched closer to some invisible, imaginary line that Stoop Sherman was pointing at. When Stoop had the cars where he wanted them, he pointed to each driver, looking for a nod that they were ready. Then, wasting no more time, he quickly shot his arm up and twirled a finger in the air—the familiar signal to crank their engines and get set to go.

Suddenly the night stillness of the forest preserve was torn by the screech of burning rubber and the chirp of crickets eclipsed by the howl of two hot engines screaming off the line.

Parked and sitting in his radar-equipped cruiser on 95th and Mannheim, a state trooper heard the scream of tires and the sounds of engines at full bore. *Goddamned kids*, he thought, knowing that by the time he got there, there'd be nobody around to arrest.

Whitey Hamm mashed the throttle and worked the shifter like a craftsman. His left foot lightly punched at the clutch pedal as he redlined the engine and speedshifted in first, second, and third. The Hurst shifter changed gears as smooth as an automatic, with barely a whisper of protest from the big Goodyears in back.

Halfway through the quarter mile, Whitey was two car lengths ahead and Phil Schmidt was suddenly aware that the Corvette he was so proud of no longer belonged to him—that by not wanting to embarrass himself in front of his girlfriend, he'd thrown aside good judgment and gone up against a true artist at the game.

The coupe and Corvette flew past Johnny's lights with Whitey and the Skunk leading by nearly three car lengths, and as the pair of judges tumbled back into Johnny's car, the one named Eddie was laughing. "Whitey smoked him, man—not even close."

Everybody scattered like cockroaches, a few heading back to 111th, while most of the others drove east or west on 107th Street. After backing the Skunk down, Whitey turned left onto the forest preserve road that cut through Crooked

Creek Woods, then came out on Mannheim Road and circled back to pick up Stoop who was hiding in the trees.

Whitey Hamm was smiling. It had been a profitable evening.

When they pulled into the A&W the following Saturday night, Phil had the title to the Corvette neatly folded and tucked into his shirt pocket. He'd reluctantly gone to the bank when it opened that morning and took the car's title out of the safe deposit box.

"I just can't believe you're really going to give that creep your car," Betty was complaining.

Phil shook his head, sighing. "I don't have a choice. We bet."

"Well, it's just so stupid, that's all—and I'm embarrassed."

Johnny and Angie followed them into the parking lot. Saying nothing, Angie looked out the Ford's window and saw it was just another Saturday night at the A&W—the same hot cars, the same familiar faces. She was already bored.

But hopefully, Angie thought, things would get better later on. Once Phil signed over the Corvette's title to Whitey Hamm, they planned to hit a party that was being thrown by a friend of Angie's who lived in a large old Victorian home on Longwood Drive. The girl's parents were out of town for the weekend, and there was sure to be beer there, and maybe even some whiskey. Phil hoped so, He was planning to drown his sorrows even though he and Johnny were due back in barracks the next day for Sunday parade.

To Johnny, it seemed as if Angie had pretty much gotten over whatever had been bothering her last weekend, although she was still acting distant and a little cool.

Both cars backed in next to each other so they could easily see who was coming and going. Once the carhop finished taking their orders, Phil lit a smoke and glumly wondered where Whitey was. He wanted to get the whole thing over with.

"I'd have thought he'd be here waiting."

"Oh, he'll be here," Johnny said. "Whitey collects his bets."

Both cars were tuned to the same pop station, listening to Paul Anka sing "Diana," one of Johnny's favorites.

They ate their mexiburgers and sipped root beer, listening to the music and waiting for the time to come when Phil would have to sign away his red Corvette.

After an hour with no sign of Whitey Hamm, Johnny began to get the feeling that something was wrong. He turned to the car next to them, a lowered '49 Mercury that was owned by a Morgan Park kid named Bob Barker.

"Whitey been around tonight?" Johnny asked.

"Ain't you heard?" Bob Barker said. "Whitey and Stoop are in the can. They got stopped the other night with a six-pack and two open cans of Schlitz in the Skunk."

"You're kiddin' me."

"Naw, the cops checked everything out, including the serial number on that Caddy engine. It belonged to a mill that was lifted from some junkyard in South Holland."

Phil whistled. "Jeez—Whitey's in jail?"

"Hell, that ain't all," Bob Barker added. "The next day, a plain clothes cop checked where Whitey worked and found two Chevy engines wrapped up in oil-cloth and buried in that vacant lot behind Lennart's Texaco. Both of them came up hot, too."

Bob Barker shook his head. "They impounded the Skunk and they say Whitey and Stoop might be in the clink for a while."

Phil looked at Johnny and sighed with relief, figuring that by the time Whitey got out of jail, he'd probably have forgotten about the Corvette. And if he hadn't, it was odds on he'd be on probation of some kind and in no mood to cause any trouble.

"Looks like you dodged a bullet, buddy," Johnny said.

"Looks like," Phil laughed.

The party on Longwood drive turned into a celebration rather than an occasion to mourn the loss of Phil's car. Along with cases of beer, there'd been plenty of liquor there, too. The girl's parents had left without bothering to lock the liquor cabinet and five or six empty bottles of Chivas Regal and Cutty Sark, Jim Beam and Jack Daniels, rolled around on the hardwood floors.

The party chipped in for pizzas from Fox's Beverly Pizza and had them delivered—ten large pies with all the trimmings.

Phil drank beer and whiskey boilermakers until he passed out, and late in the evening, with the sweet sounds of Patti Page singing "Old Cape Cod" on the Zenith record player, Johnny got sick and managed to throw up all over Angie's new plaid skirt.

The next morning, she purposely awoke early, slipped into her robe and came downstairs to join her parents for breakfast.

"Daddy," she asked sweetly. "Remember that Chevrolet Bel Air you and mom talked about as a graduation present if I broke up with Johnny Tuttle?"

"Yes, honey," Mr. Simmons said, carefully buttering his raisin toast. "Of course I remember."

"Could it be a convertible?"

C H A P T E R   16

▼

POMP AND CIRCUMSTANCE

Graduation Day, 1957

No stunt like it had ever been attempted—and just a week before graduation, Brian Donnelly decided he was the cadet to try it.

"Get caught," Andy Selva pointed out when he got wind of the scheme. "And the school might just send you your diploma by mail—if they bother to send it at all."

Brian was undeterred. Under cover of night, his plan consisted of somehow climbing up onto Blake Hall's roof, crawling into its imposing Gothic tower and sounding the tower's bell fifteen times to both honor the Zetas and welcome the dawn of the eighty-fourth annual Commencement Exercises at the Academy.

"How you gonna get up there anyway?" Andy asked.

"I don't know yet," Brian shrugged. "I'll figure out a way."

He spent a few days studying on it and finally came up with a hundred foot length of heavy hawser that he knotted every two feet and attached to a steel grapnel anchor found in a marine salvage yard near the Cal Sag Canal.

At 5:00 am on Saturday morning, the 8th of June, Brian put on coveralls, quietly snuck out of his parents' house on Hale Avenue, and drove his Plymouth up the hill, parking it along the curb on 111th Street, directly in front of Blake Hall.

Just before dawn, the early June night was pleasantly cool and there was hardly any traffic to be seen. In four more hours, Brian knew, the streets surrounding the Academy would be so filled with cars that to find a parking space would take unusual luck.

At ten thirty that morning, sixty-three senior cadets of Morgan Park Military Academy would receive their diplomas and bid fond farewell to teachers and friends, to the green, leafy campus and the ivy-covered classrooms, to all the years of ritual and tradition that were part and parcel of the school.

Like most of his fellow graduating seniors, Brian had barely any sleep since Thursday night. Yesterday morning had been Class Day—imposing an ambitious schedule of activities that preceded today's graduation ceremonies.

First, there'd been an assembly in Blake Chapel in which next year's Guardians had been installed, along with the presentation of cadet honors and awards. Later that day was the final dress parade of the year, with the following year's officers, noncommissioned officers and Corps of Cadets reviewed by the Class of 1957.

And then it was Senior Prom night, by invitation only, with its receiving line of faculty and wives, stunning in formal attire, and the graduating seniors in dress gray and white ducks, with sashes and medals resplendent, shoes spit shined and gleaming like black glass, their brass buckles and buttons polished to a high shine, and lovely, orchid-adorned young ladies on their arms.

Each of the Academy's illegal fraternities had made their own plans for after the prom. For Brian and the other Zetas, it would be a change into civvies and a late evening dinner at Chicago's Chez Paree nightclub, and after that a long drive south through Gary and around the tip of Lake Michigan, for an all-night party under the star-filled sky of the Indiana Dunes.

It would be a bittersweet night of unspoken farewells, of close friends at a new, unfamiliar point in their young lives. They would reminisce about the past four years knowing they'd soon be forced to part, realizing that the coming weeks, months and years would scatter them in all directions.

With the campfire burning on the beach, the surrounding night offered a sense of all things familiar coming to an end and making way for something new. None of the boys would admit it, even to themselves, but for the first time in four years, they felt uncertain—as anxious and unsure as when they first were plebes.

It was a night of drinking beer and eating hot dogs, of laughter and celebration, of grand plans and solemn promises to meet again this summer, or perhaps the summer after that, all of it tinged with sad regret and a growing sense of anticipation.

The class of '57 was graduating and had come of age.

His hair full of sand and still feeling the effects of the Schlitz they'd been drinking, Brian Donnelly drove back from the dunes, dropped off his date and was home by four in the morning. He took off his shoes and stretched full length on his bed, closing his eyes, concentrating on the outrageous prank he was soon to attempt. The anchor and length of hawser were already in the Plymouth's trunk. Feeling sober again, Brian glanced at his watch and decided it was time to get started.

After quietly leaving the house, driving up the hill and parking the coupe on 111th Street in back of Blake Hall, he climbed over a thick hedge of bushes, moving stealthily toward the old building in the darkness, holding the anchor in one hand and the coiled rope in the other.

The roofline of Blake was less than forty feet from the ground. Measuring the distance by eye, Brian was confident he could make the toss, but whether he could hook up with one try was another matter entirely. He'd carefully wrapped and taped each anchor tine with shop rags, hoping to muffle any sound it might make as it landed and was dragged across the roof.

He misjudged in the darkness and his first throw was short of the mark, catching on nothing and forcing him to dodge the falling anchor as it hurtled to the ground with a thud.

Brian's second effort cleared the roofline and the tines hooked onto something solid. He hauled on the rope, putting all his weight on it to make sure it was secure.

Then he began to climb. Hand over hand, just as the dawn was beginning to break, using the knots for grip and leverage. Halfway up he stopped to rest and catch his breath. The muscles in his arms and shoulders ached and burned, and he could feel the morning sun warm on the back of his neck. Glancing upward, Brian saw he was only fifteen feet from the roof—almost there.

In a matter of minutes, he scrambled over the top and saw that the anchor had caught on the old building's masonry edge, as solid and secure as it could be. Satisfied, Brian scrambled up and across the pitched shingled roof until he reached Blake Hall's tower.

The cast iron bell hung just out of reach, and to make things worse, its clapper rope had rotted away. The words of Scottish poet Robert Burns came to mind— a quote that had always been one of his favorites: *The best laid plans of mice and men aft gang aglay.* Searching for a solution to the problem, he leaned over and peered down into the darkness of the belfry, making out what he thought was a heavy wooden ceiling joist of some sort. It was exposed, and if he could lower himself down onto it and keep his balance, he'd be within easy reach of the bell's rim and could ring it without the need of a clapper rope.

He crawled into the belfry and hung down, feeling for the joist with his shoes. Finding it, he steadied himself and then, sure of his balance, inched across the rafter toward the bell.

Suddenly there were soft sounds below him. First, a gentle *oh-oo-oor,* then an increasingly urgent *coo roo-c'too-coo*—and finally a babble of *oorrhh* and a thunder of frantically flapping wings and bodies brushing against him.

Oh Christ, pigeons, Brian thought, jerking his head back as he felt the beat of a wing against his face in the darkness. Instinctively raising a hand to slap the offending bird away, he lost his footing and fell a short distance to a planked floor, landing on his back and breaking through the thin crust of something knee-deep, putrid and disgusting.

Befouled and filthy, he struggled to hoist himself back up onto the rafter, climbing out of the belfry and swearing mightily as he quickly lowered himself down the rope. He was on the ground and stumbling toward the coupe, nauseous and almost gagging, when a familiar voice stopped him in his tracks.

"Hold on there, young fellow."

The voice belonged to Captain Gray, taking his early morning stroll to the corner drugstore to buy a package of cigarettes and the morning paper.

"Aren't you Donnelly?" The old man asked, squinting in the early morning light. He was a month away from his eighty-seventh birthday. His step was slow and his eyes were failing.

"Yes sir," Brian answered.

Cap Gray grunted. "Odd hour for you to be about, Donnelly. Don't you graduate today?"

"Yes sir, I do."

The captain raised his head, sniffing the air. "You smell badly, son—what's that malodorous odor?"

"Pigeon shit, sir."

"Pigeon shit?"

"I'm afraid so, sir."

The old man shook his head, an action that caused the wattles of his wrinkled neck to quiver. "Well, Mr. Donnelly, at this late stage in your Academy career, I'll not even attempt to ask how you find yourself in such deplorable circumstance. Carry on."

"Yes sir—thank you, sir." Brian saluted smartly and hastily made his way back through the bushes to the Plymouth, stumbling once more, as Captain Gray watched from the sidewalk.

"You're not drunk, are you Donnelly?"

"Oh no, sir," Brian called back.

"First rate," Captain Gray said, nodding. "I've heard stories of prom night monkeyshines and I'd not care to see one of this year's graduates accept his diploma as a drunkard."

"Absolutely not, sir," Brian said, his statement answered by another of Captain Gray's legendary grunts.

Brian slid into the driver's seat and started the car, hoping the old man wouldn't see the knotted rope still dangling from the roof of Blake Hall. A hot bath would do it for him, Brian thought, as he slipped the Plymouth into gear and drove off down the hill, but he suspected it would take a week or more of hard scrubbing to get the stink out of his little coupe.

By ten-thirty that morning, the early summer sun was already warm and Morgan Park Military Academy's battalion of over two-hundred cadets were assembled in Jones Bowl, with at least three times that number in family, friends, and faculty. The uniform of the day for graduating seniors was gray full dress jacket with white duck trousers and service cap, while the remainder of the Corps turned out in semi-dress blouse and ducks.

Promptly at ten-thirty, Colonel Jordan approached the podium and offered a warm welcome to the graduates, students, and all the others in attendance before introducing this year's commencement speaker—Mr. Edward H. Stulken, the principal of the Montefiore School in Chicago.

Mr. Stulken, a somewhat nondescript man in a gray summer suit, patted his forehead with a handkerchief and stood before the podium. He thanked the colonel and assured the crowd that he was deeply honored to speak to the MPMA Graduating Class of 1957, and then went on to present his topic—a long and tedious address that was titled "Learning in Mid-Century."

In the ranks of anxious cadets, parents, and faculty seated in white folding chairs, minds began to wander.

Lt. Richard Anderson, senior class advisor and director of the Academy's band and music program casually studied the faces of the graduating seniors. What secrets did the future hold for them? The lieutenant wondered briefly. The fighting in Korea was over and there seemed no other trouble spots brewing—but these days, the lieutenant knew, you could never be quite sure. Who among those boys seated in the first row would prosper in life, Anderson mused, and who among them would stumble along the way? Only time would tell.

There were eight Zetas graduating that day.

Listening to the speaker, Cadet Staff Sgt. Jim Vesely recalled hearing all about the Montefiore School when he was still a young boy in the Czech neighborhood of West Lawndale. Young Jimmy and the rest of his friends around 31st Street knew that Montefiore was a school for delinquents—a reform school, people said.

If you not behave like good boy, his immigrant grandmother often threatened as she pointed a finger at him, *we maybe have to send you there.* Turning to catch a glimpse of his mother, father, and grandparents seated in the gathering, Jim was thankful they'd chosen the Academy instead.

As Mr. Stulken spoke, Ed Madsen and Rich Vitkus glanced at each other and winked. Four years of competition had made them the best of friends, and their rivalry had ended in a draw. Both had earned the rank of 1st Lieutenant, both were well regarded by their classmates and popular with girls. They shared most of the same athletic honors and awards, and were elected class officers. Ed had been named captain of the football team and chosen most valuable player in his senior year, while Rich was a member of the Honor Society and the Guardians, and both had been awarded medals for being in the upper ten percent of their class.

The two other commissioned officers among the Zetas waiting to receive their diplomas were Jerry Bowden and Bob Clark, both 2nd Lieutenants and close friends. As a junior, Jerry had been in attendance at this same ceremony a year before, watching his older brother graduate. Thin as a straw, he'd nevertheless thrown himself into almost every sport the Academy offered, excelling in Varsity wrestling and baseball. Now, his brother Jim was in the audience watching Jerry collect his own diploma.

Bob Clark had always been quiet and reserved, a good student and the product of a strict Presbyterian upbringing. He was one of six grandchildren of the Reverend Dr. Richmond A. Montgomery, a man of solid faith and a follower of Jesus Christ and John Knox—in that order. It often fell on Bob to introduce a degree of discipline and common sense to the parties and sophomoric antics of his less inclined Zeta brothers. This June morning, listening to the address on education, Bob's thoughts were centered on Michigan, and the Manor Foundation in Jonesville, a home and school for mentally handicapped children his family had helped to establish and which someday, after his education was complete, he hoped to run.

Cadet Cpl. Frank Bastis was the only son of immigrant parents from Lithuania, and still uncertain about his future. Playing injured as capably as he played healthy; Coach Bloomer often said Frank was one of the best high school linebackers he'd ever seen. Frank and his parents lived in a modest home on 33rd and Halsted, but owned a profitable business in Wisconsin—the Lakeside Country Club in Pewaukee. The club bar had seen its share of Zeta party weekends, and Frank's father had always been unusually indulgent as his son's fraternity brothers drank the club's beer and liquor.

Andy Selva, C Company's First Sergeant for the past year, sat relaxed. Andy had always been smooth, sure of himself. He was anticipating a lazy, relaxed summer and then back to school in the fall—to Illinois College in Jacksonville, along with Donnelly and Vesely. Ed Jerabek and Jack Peterson had been freshmen there the past year and the five Zetas looked forward to being together once more.

Showered and shaved, with shoes polished to a high shine and brass shining, Cadet Staff Sgt. Brian Donnelly grinned to himself as he thought of his early morning adventure atop Blake Hall. Four long years at the Academy were ending, he told himself, and he'd leave it to someone else to someday ring that damned bell.

Once Mr. Stulken finished speaking, Lt. Col. Eugene Farmer, the Academy's assistant superintendent, stepped up to the podium to begin calling the names of this year's graduates. The graduating seniors stood and formed a line.

"John Vincent Ahern," Lt. Colonel Farmer announced, as each young man came forward, gave a final salute to Colonel Jordan as he handed them their diploma, then shook the colonel's hand. The audience responded with applause and the click of cameras.

"Ronald Vincent Aitchison…"

"Stephen Lewis Avard…"

Seated off to one side with his wife, and having watched this same ritual for the past forty years, Capt. Francis S. Gray studied each of the graduates as they proudly descended the steps, diploma in hand. He knew some better than others, and there were a few he barely knew at all—those who hadn't been in his classes.

But in the end, after all his grumble and bluster, he took pride in them all—in those boys who were naturally gifted and bright, as well as in those who studied as best they could and applied their particular talents to whatever was needed to bring them this day.

"William Henry Maitland…"

"Thomas Oliver Marzullo…"

Sitting in that warm June sun, Frank Gray realized his years of teaching at the Academy would soon be at an end—one more year perhaps, maybe two. Not many more commencement ceremonies for him, the old man mused, nor many more classes of new cadets to watch enter the school.

No, he'd had his time, Captain Gray thought, glancing briefly at his wife. For good or ill, the future would soon belong to these young louts and he could only hope he'd played his part in helping them prepare for it.

For a moment, the old man let his failing eyes wander past the podium and settle on the old, familiar sprawling campus, with its greening meadow that stretched south to the big gymnasium, with East and West Halls on either side.

The newly painted white frame house that was the Academy's infirmary was just at the edge of the meadow, and closer in were the ivy-covered brick walls of Alumni Hall—housing the first floor dining room, the basement armory, military classrooms and rifle range, and the recreation room and school library on its second floor.

Across the hollow of Jones Bowl, past the flagpole and the old French 75 howitzer, was Hansen Hall Barracks, whose three floors had been home to boarding cadets since 1928.

And then there was Blake Hall—venerable old Blake, with its rose window, creaky stairway, musty smells and hissing, banging radiators. It was within those walls that he'd taught the order and disciplines of algebra, quadratic equations, logarithmic functions, tetrahedrons, complex exponentials, and quadrilaterals to countless generations of boys. This green and pleasant place had comprised nearly his entire life, Frank Gray realized, and he cherished every moment of it.

He looked once more at the cadets. Their faces would change, he told himself, but the Corps would stay the same—and the spirit of the Academy would go on long after he was gone. Of this, Capt. Francis Gray, Instructor of Mathematics at Morgan Park Military Academy, was reasonably certain.

"Bruno Edwin Zubrick…"

"Richard Allen Zuspan."

The band played the Academy's alma mater. When they were finished, the cadet bugler stepped forward and sounded retreat. The colors were lowered for the final time that year and the flag was carefully folded by the color guard. Colonel Jordan approached the speaker's stand and for a brief moment gazed out upon his Corps of Cadets, wishing all of them good luck, Godspeed and farewell. "Ladies and Gentlemen, these Commencement Exercises for the Class of 1957 are now concluded."

The Academy band began "Auld Lang Syne." Cheers capped the morning as sixty-three service caps were launched high into the air. Parents and friends applauded, a hundred cameras clicked and cadets embraced each other, most with tears in their eyes, as they both honored an end and welcomed yet a new beginning.

Seasons of Harvest
The Awakening Land
Shadows on the Land
(The Corrales Valley Trilogy)

Journey
A Novel of America

Unlike Any Land You Know
The 490th Bomb Squadron in China-Burma-India

Coon Creek
A Novel of the Mississippi River Bottoms

Lonesome Whistle Blow
A Novel of Hard Times

Cadet Gray
Stories of Morgan Park Military Academy

All the author's books are available directly from the publisher—
iUniverse.com. They can also be ordered through Barnes & Noble and Borders Books, or online at: Amazon.com and bn.com.

978-0-595-41680-6
0-595-41680-2

19939178R00154

Made in the USA
Lexington, KY
13 January 2013